Colonial Legacy

Heather Garside

Colonial Legacy

Heather Garside

Yarraman Press, 2017

Yarraman Press,
PO Box 275,
Capella, QLD, 4723, Australia

www.heathergarside.com

Cover Art by For the Muse Design Copyright 2017

Chapter One

England, 1896

Matt glanced up at the big house as he turned his horse into the lane leading to the stables. A familiar nagging sense of resentment twisted his vitals and he spurred the mare with unwarranted vigour, making her toss her head and sidle nervously.

'Sorry, old girl,' he muttered, patting the mare's neck as he realized he'd taken out his frustrations on her. But the injustice of it rankled.

Here he was, out in the cold spring morning, working the gentry's high-strung, over-fed horses so they would be safe for his betters to ride, while them from the manor lay in their soft beds, waiting for servants to cook their breakfast and ready their clothes for the day.

'That's just the way it is,' his mother would say. But Matt had never been able to share his parents' stoic acceptance of the order of things.

A robust plume of smoke rose from the kitchen chimney, attesting to the activity below stairs despite the earliness of the hour. Matt imagined the cook preparing a breakfast of ham and eggs while the master and mistress still slumbered in the rooms above. For a moment he thought he could smell it and his stomach rumbled. He'd been out since dawn, and his own breakfast was but a memory.

Back at the stables, he unsaddled and led the horses past the open door of the feed barn. His father straightened from the task of measuring chaff, bran and oats into a row of buckets. The sweet smell of freshly-cut chaff, mingled with the familiar acrid stench of horse manure and stale urine, jostled his senses.

'How was the mare this morning, Matt? Any trace o' the lameness still?'

'No, but she was fresh from the spell, shying at shadows like a three-year-old.'

'You better keep working her, lad, in case the master wants to ride her. They want the brougham later, so check the harness over when you've rubbed the horses down.'

'So they're going visiting, are they?'

Matt's mocking tone provoked a disapproving frown from his father. 'No more o' this disrespect for your elders and betters, lad. You'd be out on your ear if they heard talk like that.'

Matt shrugged. 'Let 'em do their worst. If they think I owe 'em they're mistaken.'

Jones drew himself taller, his busy eyebrows bristling. 'You owe 'em your job and your life here with your mother and me! If they hadn't let us take you in, you'd have bin dumped at the orphanage.'

Matt turned away without answering and led the horses to their stables, his gut churning with a mix of emotions. The Joneses had provided him with a loving home when his unwed mother had died in childbirth, and he would never forget his debt to them. But he refused to feel grateful to the Ashfords for permitting something that hadn't cost them anything in effort, money or inconvenience.

Once he'd finished with the horses, Matt cleaned the leather harness that went with the brougham, oiling it until it was supple and soft, and polishing the bit and brass buckles until they gleamed. Next, he groomed Jasper, the Cleveland Bay gelding who always pulled it, picking out his shod hooves and brushing his mane and tail until the hairs separated into shimmering strands. He talked to the horse as he worked and Jasper nudged him trustingly with his head, his bright eyes and pricked ears betraying his eager anticipation of an outing from the stable. Then Matt backed the horse up to the carriage, sliding the collar over his neck, attaching the back pad and the breeching to the shafts, running the traces from the collar to the vehicle itself. Matt loved the horses and took pride in his work, but of late a growing restlessness had gripped him.

He knew his father was preparing him to take his place as coachman one day, but could he stand being at Squire's beck and call for the rest of his life? What choice did he have here in England but a life of servitude?

'Do you want to drive 'em today, Matt?' Jones was standing in the doorway of the tack room watching him. 'I think you're ready for it.'

Matt started wondering how long the old man had been there. He quickly gathered his errant thoughts and nodded, relishing this new challenge. 'I'll drive 'em carefully, never fear.'

His foster father came to hold the horse's head. 'Go and change, then, lad. They want you up there at ten o'clock. And you behave proper, like you bin taught.'

Jones watched after the boy's retreating back, noting with a tinge of pride that was always mingled with pain, how tall and strong he was. Dark-haired like his mother; his natural mother, that was. The one they had never spoken of to Matt, though Jones sometimes wondered if that had been a mistake. Perhaps the boy would have accepted the truth if he'd grown up with it, but if he found out now...

Jones led the horse and carriage into the yard, casting a cursory glance at the stableboy, Fred, who was supposed to be shovelling straw and manure from the pile in front of the stalls into a wheelbarrow. 'Get a move on there, Fred. We don't have all day. And no more smoking them cigarettes around the stable.'

Bloody Turkish cigarettes, Jones thought. Fred was no more than fourteen. The coachman suspected Matt joined him sometimes, for he'd caught the whiff of them on his son's breath. He wondered why they couldn't stick to chewing tobacco, which at least didn't pose a fire danger around the stables and the hay loft. But Matt was twenty, and old enough to be making his own mistakes.

And he was making enough of them, all right. He wasn't old enough to go to the pub yet, but Jones knew he'd been carousing with some of the village lads of a Saturday night. The sick look about him when he would finally surface on Sunday morning told its own story. He no longer accompanied his parents to church, which upset Martha no end.

And then there were the girls, who fell like ninepins for his handsome face and strong body. Jones knew from long service at Fenham Manor that the Ashford men were rakes, and Matt was showing disturbing signs of following in their footsteps. Was it just the desire to imitate, or it did it run deeper than that? It was all right for *them*, perhaps, with the money and the power to enable them to behave as they wished. But Matt was only the coachman's son when all was said and done, and he would never be acknowledged as anything else.

Matt waited in the sweeping driveway of the manor, sitting in the high perch driver's seat, having exchanged his working tweeds for white breeches, top boots, a buttoned coat and top hat. He stretched his legs and rested his long whip across his knees as one of the maids came out of the house, en route to the dairy. She saw him and was audacious enough to detour, her quick glance to the windows of the house betraying her guilt.

'Why, Matt!' She smiled at him, tilting her head coquettishly. 'And don't you look grand, sitting there like Lord Muck!'

He grinned at her, his eyes skimming casually over her trim figure and firm breasts under the starched white apron, remembering her wearing considerably less in the darkness of the lane last Saturday night. 'Will you be coming to the dance with me tonight, Eliza?'

'I'll think about it, Matt. Ask me again later.'

He grinned again as she continued to the dairy, eyeing the rounded backside which the sober gown tried hard to conceal. It amused him that she was pretending to consider his invitation. He knew she would no more refuse him than fly to the moon. She had already given him everything that she had to give, and now it was he, like the Pied Piper, who was calling the tune.

The master and mistress finally appeared at the doorway at half past ten, dressed to the nines to impress their friends from the other side of the village. Harry Ashford was no longer the imposing man he had once been. He was stooped and seemed to be shrinking as he aged. Mrs Ashford carried her years a little better, but her face had grown sterner over time. Matt privately thought her a stuck-up old biddy, although he would never have dared to voice such an opinion.

'Matt!' The master looked surprised and a bit displeased as Matt stepped down from the vehicle and opened the door for them. 'You driving us today?'

'By your leave, sir.' Though he spoke with a practised humility, a spark of defiance prompted him to meet the old man's eyes. 'Me father thought I was up to it.'

'Mind the ruts then, lad,' the squire snapped. 'These old bones don't appreciate being shaken about.'

Matt settled the aging couple in the hooded vehicle and closed the door before jumping up to his driver's perch and clicking Jasper to move off. He often wondered why the squire seemed to dislike him. Was it because he didn't bow and scrape enough to suit the old man? That was too bad, because he wasn't about to change his ways to please anyone.

He'd nearly finished feeding the horses that evening when he heard an urgent whisper from the stable doorway. 'Matt! I need to talk to you!'

He dumped an armful of hay in a nearby manger and crossed to the door. It was Eliza, hovering in the shadows. He drew her into an empty stall and closed the half door, tugging her to the back where it was unlikely his father or Fred would see them. His senses immediately responded to the intimate situation and he reached to pull her close, but she pushed him away.

'I said I wanted to talk, Matt!'

'What about?'

Her face was flushed, her eyes glittering with excitement. 'I overheard them talking in the stillroom. Mrs Evans and Miss Brown, that is. I was putting some jars away at the back and they didn't know I was there.'

Matt didn't bother to hide his impatience. What could the housekeeper and Mrs Ashford's maid have to say that would be of interest to him? 'I'm not concerned with old women's gossip.'

'Ha! But it's you they were talking about!' She turned away, as if she'd suddenly changed her mind. 'But if you don't want to hear it, I'll be out of your way.'

'Eliza!' He gripped her upper arm. 'Don't be a tease. You'd better tell me now.'

'Well, if you're sure you want to know...' The girl smiled her satisfaction, like a fisherman who'd just reeled in a juicy catch. 'They were talking about us, to begin with.' She coloured slightly. 'They were clucking like a pair of old hens about us walking out together. Then they said what a wild boy you were, just like your Uncle Charles.'

Matt stared at her, impatient in his confusion. 'I don't have an Uncle Charles.'

Eliza's smile widened. 'Apparently you do. I sneaked a bit closer then, so's not to miss any of it. Miss Brown said how Miss Louise was a wild one too, so it was no wonder you'd turned out the same.'

'Who's Miss Louise? That wasn't me mother's name.'

The girl shook her head. 'Just listen, will you? Mrs Evans said how Miss Louise had a heart, not like the rest of them. She wanted to keep that baby and it fair cut her up, leaving him behind when she went back to Australia.'

Matt's heart leapt and drummed unevenly in his chest. He put a hand on the corner post, suddenly needing to clutch something solid. 'What are you trying to tell me?'

'Can't you work it out?' Eliza's ample bosom swelled with importance. 'You remember Mr Charles, the master and mistress's son. And they had a daughter called Louise, too. There's a portrait of her in the hallway, along with the rest of the family.'

The blood drained from Matt's face. 'Are you hoaxing me, Eliza?' If so, it was a poor joke. 'I don't believe you.'

'Well, it's true. I went and asked Cook, and she told me so. Louise Ashford was your mother. She swore me to secrecy, but I didn't think that included you.' Eliza peered at him in the dim light, as if inspecting every detail of his face. 'I had a look at the portraits in the hall after that. You're so much like them, I'm surprised I didn't see it before.'

Matt had seen Charles Ashford many years ago, when he'd been visiting from Australia. He searched his boyhood memories for a mental picture of him, with little success. 'Christ!' He saw Eliza's reproachful look and apologized, shaking his head. 'Sorry. This is a bit hard to take in.'

He knew there were cases of so-called gentlemen from the big houses siring children on their servants, but this was a bit different. Questions whirled in his brain, colliding with each other like the colours of the kaleidoscope he'd once seen at the village fair. If this Miss Louise was his mother, who was his father? Why hadn't she married him? And surely the Ashfords wouldn't have let their own grandson be raised by their coachman? Suddenly he was hot and sweaty, the walls of the horse stall closing in on him.

'I thought you'd be excited about this, Matt. If I found out I was related to the nobs…'

He stared at her through a mist of disbelief. The squire acted as if he hated him. They didn't want him, never had.

And this meant the Joneses had lied to him, too. They'd told him his mother was Ma's niece, and that she'd died in childbirth.

Finally he managed to speak. 'If only I could see the paintings…'

'I could show you.' Eliza's voice dropped. 'There'd be no-one in the hall at this time of day.'

He looked uneasily towards the house. He'd never been further than the kitchens and would probably be dismissed if he was discovered in the hall without good reason, and Eliza too, if she was suspected of abetting him. But the need to verify her story was strong.

'All right. I'll have to finish feeding the horses. Where can I meet you?'

'At the back of the kitchens. Send one of the scullery maids to find me if I'm not around.'

Half an hour later he found himself in the big house, sneaking through the narrow servants' corridor in the wake of Eliza's long, swishing skirts. She stopped at a solid oaken door and turned to whisper in his ear. 'This opens into the hall. The recent paintings are nearest the front of the house, on the far wall.'

'Aye, thanks.' He bent to kiss her briefly. 'Wait here. If I get caught, there's no need for you to be involved in this.'

He opened the door a crack and peered around it, checking the hall was empty. With no-one in sight he stepped cautiously into the cavernous space, staring in amazement at the portrait-laden walls.

Were these all Ashford ancestors? Yet he barely registered the faces and styles of bygone eras as he made his way down the hall, slowing to scrutinise the paintings more carefully as he neared the front of the hall. There was a portrait he thought was the present squire in earlier days, wearing a frock coat and carrying a cane and a top hat. The lady next to him was probably his wife. Then there was a young man in a cutaway coat with dark hair and eyes and a thin, handsome face. Probably Charles. But it was the young woman beside him who drew Matt like a magnet.

She had long dark hair drawn back from a centre part, and a serious, unsmiling mouth. Her eyes appeared to be grey, like his, and the curve of her lips was somehow familiar. She was good-looking in a severe way, but it was the sadness in her eyes that struck him. He'd never seen her in his life, but the recognition was instantaneous. His heart missed a beat and then settled into a steady, heavy thudding in his chest. He knew, without being told, that this was Louise Ashford, and suddenly he no longer doubted that she was his mother. He'd only to look at his own face in the mirror to verify that.

He stared at her for a long moment, committing the portrait to memory. Then he moved back to Charles, admitting the truth of Eliza's observation. Charles Ashford as a young man bore an unmistakeable resemblance to himself. Even the devilish glint in the eyes struck a chord with him.

Someone cleared his throat behind him and he jumped, whirling around to find Mr Dawes, the aging butler, regarding him with a frosty stare.

'May I ask what *you* are doing here?'

Dawes managed to inject just the right amount of contempt into that 'you', as if Matt had no more right to look at the portraits--of his own family, indeed--than the lowest boot boy. Matt straightened and stared arrogantly back at the old man. 'And who are *you* to ask?'

The old fellow bristled, drawing up his stooped frame. 'You impertinent young whipper-snapper! You're just the groom here, Matt Jones, and don't you forget it!' He nodded his head towards the portraits. 'If you're getting any other ideas, squire will soon set you straight.'

He grasped Matt's elbow in his bony hand and propelled him down the passageway towards the servants' door with surprising strength. Matt pulled his arm free and glared at the old man, but he knew better than to resist. The butler opened the door and gestured for Matt to pass through. 'I'll speak to Squire about this. Think yourself lucky if you're not dismissed.'

Matt had little choice but to obey, knowing it wasn't an idle threat. Outdoor servants didn't wander at will about their employers' homes, and after the way he'd given lip to the butler he'd likely made an enemy. He had no doubt Dawes would report to Squire, and Squire would have his own reasons for reminding Matt of his place in life.

Eliza wasn't waiting where he'd left her. She'd probably heard the voices and decided it was prudent to be elsewhere. He found her when he emerged from the passageway at the back of the kitchens, eyes wide with fright.

'I heard Mr Dawes. We're in trouble, Matt!'

He shook his head and grasped her hand, squeezing it reassuringly. '*I'm* in trouble. They don't know you had anything to do with it.'

'They'll guess. Cook will tell them I was asking questions.'

'Well, I'll just say you weren't involved.' Matt spoke with a calmness he didn't feel. If the old man wanted to turn him out, so be it. He hadn't planned on staying forever, anyway. But if Eliza lost her job because of him, he'd feel responsible for her, and that was the last thing he wanted.

'I'd better go, before someone else sees me. Don't fret yourself. I'll meet you after supper and walk you to the dance.'

She clutched at his coat as he turned away. 'So what did you think? About the paintings?'

He shook his head. It was all so new and raw. 'Just leave it, will you, Eliza? I can't even think straight.'

Although it was approaching suppertime, he didn't immediately make his way to his foster parents' cottage. He couldn't face them at the moment. Instead he went to the stables and found an empty stall where he sank down on the clean hay, folding his arms on his bent knees and resting his forehead on them. He closed his eyes, his mind whirling with all the implications of today's discovery.

Having always believed his mother to be dead, he was surprised how much it hurt now to think she may have been alive all this time. She'd apparently given him away, discarding him like an unwanted puppy. She was like the rest of the Ashfords, no doubt, cold and uncaring, heedful of nothing but her good name. And yet, those sad eyes—there was something there that didn't seem cold or uncaring. Why had she gone to Australia—so she wouldn't be faced with the evidence of her shame? She didn't return for visits as her brother Charles occasionally did. Matt hadn't heard her name mentioned once in all his twenty years.

He swore under his breath. What was he supposed to do now?

Sunday morning saw him with a throbbing hangover. He struggled out of bed to attend to the horses, but since he had the rest of the day off, he returned to his bedroom to sleep. Late in the morning he was roused by his parents arriving back from church. He sat at the kitchen table with a pot of strong tea, listening to the joint sizzling in the oven of the coal-fired range. As its savoury aroma filled the room his empty stomach gnawed at him, reminding him he'd missed breakfast. Sipping his tea, he watched idly as his foster mother peeled potatoes over a bowl on the scarred table.

Martha Jones looked up at him, her mouth tightening as her work-reddened hands deftly plied the knife. 'How was the dance, Matt? I didn't hear you come in.'

'It was just fine. I was home pretty late, so I sneaked in quiet-like.'

Martha sniffed. 'You can sit there, as bold as brass, with the smell of drink about you, and—o' She broke off, flushing. 'I know what you're up to with that Eliza from the big house. Your Pa and I, we brought you up to be decent, Matt Jones, not to drink and run around with girls like that.'

Matt remembered the sermons he had used to listen to at the village church every Sunday, before he'd stopped going, how the vicar had thundered on about the evils of fornication and the fires of hell. Perhaps he would burn for it one day, but at least he would know he'd lived.

He looked up at the woman's flushed face, unrepentant. 'Perhaps it's me mother's blood coming out in me, Ma.'

Martha started, her red face changing to pale just as quickly. 'Your mother was a decent girl, Matt. She made one fatal mistake, like lots of others before and since.'

'Was she?' Matt knew his mother didn't approve of their employers' morals. 'Or was she like the rest of the Ashfords?'

Martha dropped the paring knife with a clatter. Her eyes widened. 'What are you saying? Who's been talking to you?'

'Is it true, then?' His heart thudded heavily in his chest, his foster mother's reaction dispelling any lingering doubt. Looking at the portraits, he'd been sure of it, but in the hours since uncertainty had returned to plague him. 'Me mother was Louise Ashford from the big house?'

Martha's voice was a strained whisper. 'Where did you hear that?'

Matt watched her carefully. 'Eliza heard Mrs Evans and Miss Brown talking the other day. How I was like me Uncle Charles. They said Miss Louise was a wild one, too.'

Martha looked angry. 'They should have been more careful.'

Matt's own temper began to stir. 'I was bound to find out some day. Why didn't you tell me who my mother was? Why the story about your niece?'

She shook her head, her mouth trembling. 'We just tried to do what was best. The Ashfords didn't want you to know, and they certainly didn't want the story to get about.'

'Aye, I can understand that.' Resentment curdled his stomach. 'They must've hated it, having that happen to *their* daughter. It's a wonder I wasn't drowned at birth.'

'Matt, don't talk like that!'

'Well, I don't suppose it changes anything. Whoever me mother was, I'm still a bastard.'

She flinched. 'Please don't use that word.'

'That's what they used to call me at school.'

Flushing, she picked up a half-peeled potato, staring at it as if she didn't quite know what to do with it. 'You should have told us.'

He shrugged. 'What could you have done? Besides, once I learned to fight they didn't dare anymore.'

'Oh, Matt!' She put down the potato, looking at him in obvious remorse. 'Is that why you behave like you do? Because you think you're only a—' she struggled with the word—'*bastard*'?

It was Matt's turn to colour and he turned away from her in embarrassment. 'I'm single and I'm not doing any harm.'

'As long as you don't get a baby! You won't be single for long if you get a girl into trouble, Matt Jones! And I don't care who it is, you'll be marrying her, you hear me? So if you don't want to be tied up before you're ready, you leave the girls alone.'

Matt pushed back his chair and got to his feet, leaving his cup of tea half-finished on the table. He walked outside and sat on the back step, raking his hand through his hair, remembering how he'd walked Eliza home the long way and how they'd stopped in the lane for an hour or more, curled up together on his coat on the cold grass in the dark shelter of the hedge. He'd taken her urgently and more than once, needing the momentary oblivion the act had brought him as much as the physical release.

At the memory his body quickened again, and he thought, no, I can't do without it, not anymore. If the vicar and people like him had their way, every pleasure on this earth would be considered a sin. He could take or leave the grog, but girls were something else again.

He stirred restlessly as his parents' strictures closed in on him, adding to the feeling of claustrophobia that came with his position in the stables. And now, knowing what he knew, he was even less inclined to spend his life in Ashford servitude. How could he bow and scrape to Squire and his kin for the rest of his days, knowing they were his blood relatives?

The next morning he and his father were working with the horses when Harris, the bailiff who ran the estate, came to the stables.

'Jones!' he demanded, looking at the old man. 'Squire wants to see you right away, in his study.'

Matt's nerves leapt. He'd been expecting a summons, but it seemed more ominous that they'd asked for his father. He went on with his work as Jones departed with the bailiff, but it was difficult to concentrate when his mind kept visualising the meeting inside the house.

It was nearly an hour before his father returned, looking grim. Matt stared at him anxiously. 'What was all that about?'

'I think you know.' Jones walked past him, hardly pausing as he added, 'We've got work to do—we can't talk about this now.'

All day his father hardly spoke, except to snap orders in an irritable tone that had Fred the stableboy staring. Much as Matt wanted to know what Squire had said, he began to dread the approaching interview with his father. It seemed his intrusion into the house was being taken seriously.

At last the horses were all fed and bedded down for the night and Fred had left. The old coachman motioned Matt to join him in the tack room, where he had a bit of a desk with a chair behind it. Jones sat at the desk and stared up at Matt, who remained standing.

'Your mother told me that Eliza's been blabbing, told you who your real mother was.'

Matt stiffened. 'Don't blame Eliza. You should have told me yourselves. Did you think I wouldn't find out someday?'

Jones sighed heavily. 'We were ordered not to tell. I wasn't about to risk losing me job over it. But I thought I'd lost it anyway, this morning.'

A quick rush of dismay coursed through Matt. He hadn't thought Squire would take it out on his father. 'What did Squire say?'

Jones stared up at him, his eyes angry. 'What do you think? What do you think you were doing, wandering about the house like you had a right to be there? It doesn't matter who your mother was, you're nothing but the coachman's son to them. Squire's not about to have you throwing things in his face he'd sooner forget. He didn't say you had to go, but you won't be getting another chance. I promised I'd take you in hand pretty hard, but he'll be watching you like a hawk from now on.'

Matt's resentment tasted sour in his mouth. 'The old bugger's me grandfather, whether he likes it or not! Doesn't he care that I'm his own flesh and blood?'

The old man's face flushed a deep red. 'Matt, you're overstepping the mark here! The gentry's got their own ways, and they won't be dictated to by the likes of us. Either you forget who you are, or they'll send you away before you can make trouble, mark me words!'

Matt swung away furiously, leaving his father there at the desk as he strode down the lane to their cottage. The old man could kowtow to the Ashfords if he wanted to, but Matt was blowed if he'd join him. Knowing the old people were his grandparents made the whole situation impossible.

By the time he joined his parents at the supper table, he'd cooled down slightly, but he'd also made a decision. It would upset them, but he couldn't sacrifice his dreams and his pride for their sakes. Once grace was spoken, he looked at his father over the stewed beef and bread and butter, taking a deep breath before plunging head first.

'Pa, I've been thinking about what you said before. I know you thought I'd have the coachman's job one day.' Matt fiddled with a teaspoon, drawing patterns on the tablecloth. 'But I don't think that's likely now, and I don't want it anyway.'

Jones laid his knife slowly on his plate and put his hands under the table, but not before Matt noticed the tremor in his father's fingers. He glanced quickly at his mother, seeing how white she had gone, and swallowed against the sick twist of guilt in his stomach.

Jones stared hard at him. 'What are you trying to say, Matt?'

'It's always riled me, being at their beck and call. Perhaps it's because I carry their blood, even though I didn't know it. I've decided I can't stay here.'

His father looked more resigned than surprised. 'So what are you planning to do?'

Matt hesitated. 'There's not much chance of me making a better life here in England. I'd like to go to another country--like Australia. I've heard there's opportunities in the Colonies for a man to make something of himself.'

The very notion of that vast, raw country excited him, made his nerves tingle. He'd heard reports of huge cattle stations, goldfields where anyone had a chance of striking it rich, and overlanders who took herds of cattle and sheep for hundreds of miles from the northern stations to the railheads in the south. Surely for excitement the untamed outback must surpass the routine of the stables any day.

'Australia!' Jones drew in a deep breath. 'That's where your mother is.'

'Eliza mentioned that. Do you know anything about her?'

'She was living there before you were born. She was expecting you when her brother Charles brought her here. When you were about a year old, she took off back to the Colonies. I haven't heard anything since. Is that why you want to go there—to find her?'

'I don't know. I don't know if I want to see her. She didn't want me when I was a baby, so she's not like to want me now.'

Martha made a protesting noise, her fingers fluttering against her throat. 'I've not told you this before, but she *did* want you, I know that much. They took you from her and she'd no say in the matter.'

Matt's belly squirmed again. 'How do you know that?'

'Because that was how she gave herself away, how the gossip started. She was riding with the man everyone thought she was going to marry, and she came on me out there at the gate one day. I had you in my arms.' Martha took a deep breath and shook her head. 'She slid off her horse and had hold of you before I could stop her, like. She could hardly bear to let you go, and that Mr Langley she was with guessed the truth of it all. He left her high and dry, and that was when she took off back to Australia.'

Matt stared at his mother, his heart drumming in his ears. He'd told himself it didn't matter, he didn't care that his natural mother hadn't wanted him. But suddenly he knew he'd been deluding himself. The pain was a tight band across his ribs, constricting his breathing, making his next words come out like a croak. 'Do you know who me father was, then?'

Martha shook her head. 'He was never spoke of. Maybe Miss Ashford told Mrs Evans and Miss Brown, for they were the ones that attended her. But they've not said a word and I'm sure they never will.'

Matt rested his head on his hands and stared down at the checked tablecloth, trying to steady himself, knowing how much he was hurting this loving couple who'd given him everything they had to give. But he knew also he would only resent them if he stayed for their sakes.

'This isn't just because of me mother, you know. I want something better than *this* for the rest of me life.'

Jones pushed back his chair, the sound grating as harshly as the unaccustomed rancour in his voice. 'I *hope* it's not because of your mother! No matter if she loved you once, just think what it will do to her now if you turn up out of the blue. She'll be married no doubt to some man who don't even know you exist. She won't want you coming back to haunt her and ruin her life.'

Matt flushed. 'I suppose not. I'd do better to stay away from her. But I still want to go to Australia. They say land's cheap and ready for the taking.'

The old man made a rasping sound in his throat. 'You'll be on your own if you do that. You won't know a soul.'

'What about young Mr Ashford?' His mother looked uncertainly at her husband. 'If I were to find out where he lives—he might give Matt some work.'

'Aye, he's got a big cattle run somewhere.' The old coachman nodded to himself. 'That might tide you over until you find your feet. As long as you mind your manners, lad. Don't throw the family secrets in his face.'

'Much good that would do me.' But there could be a chance to find out something about his mother. Perhaps his Uncle Charles would be more accommodating than his grandfather.

Once the wheels were set in motion things happened very quickly. Jones found an opportune moment to mention the matter to his master, hesitantly, for he was still smarting from the dressing-down he'd received a few days earlier.

'It's the boy, sir. Young Matt. He's got it in his head that he wants to leave us, to go to Australia.'

Harry Ashford stared at him, his face cold. 'When does he plan to go?'

'That I'm not sure. As soon as can be, I think. He hasn't booked his passage yet.'

'Does he have the money for it?'

'He has a little put by, and his ma and I were to give him the rest.' It would take the bulk of their life savings, but he hadn't told Matt that.

'I'll pay for Matt's passage. He's a troublemaker, that boy, and I'll be glad to see the back of him.'

Jones mumbled his thanks, turning away quickly before Squire read his inner disgust. It was guilt money, obviously. Anything rather than acknowledge his own flesh and blood.

He talked to Martha that night. Perhaps he was clutching at straws, but he'd feel better about the whole business if Matt had somewhere to go. Even if it was to another member of the Ashford family.

Martha talked to the housekeeper, who had assisted at Matt's birth and still had a sentimental interest in the lad. Mrs Evans was able to tell her Mr Charles lived near a town called Rockhampton, in the colony of Queensland. It was easy enough for the housekeeper to gain access to the library, where she made a rough sketch from an atlas which she asked Eliza to pass on to Matt. They had done as much as they could for the boy, and the rest was up to him.

Chapter Two

A month later Matt boarded the train in Exeter, bound for the seaport of Plymouth. It was the first time he'd travelled by rail, or indeed journeyed further than Exeter. The rocking carriage with its clacking wheels, and the huge engine with its blasts of steam and piercing whistle, were an exciting novelty, distracting him from the nagging memory of those left behind. Eliza's pleas to take her with him had driven him to distraction, but more poignant had been his parents' grief.

The Joneses had farewelled him at the station, his foster mother crying and clinging to him desperately, his foster father silent and withdrawn in the way he always was when he was upset. They'd made him feel guilty and selfish, and unaccustomed to such emotions, he focussed his thoughts on the future in a determined effort to put them from his mind. He would never forget how much he owed the Joneses, but it was time to make his own life.

Before he left his home village, Matt hadn't realized just how much times were changing in England. He'd listened to his parents speak disapprovingly of the Prince of Wales, who frequently shocked society by flouting the strict standards of his mother's early reign. But at Fenham Manor things had gone on much as they always had. It was only when he picked up a discarded newspaper in the train and read about the horseless carriages they were building in America and Germany, that he realized how much he had to learn about the outside world. He'd heard of these horseless vehicles before, of course, but had hardly pictured what such a thing would look like, let alone imagined why anyone would want to drive one. Yet here was a photograph of a strange-looking contraption, complete with its inventor in the driver's seat.

There was also a story about the female Suffragette movement, to which Matt, struggling with the unfamiliar words, paid less attention. Since only men of property were able to vote, it was not a subject that interested him particularly. A world where women defied their menfolk, escaping their drawing rooms to attend political rallies or play lively sports like tennis, had little to do with him. The women he knew lived their lives as they always had, working from dawn to dusk in their homes and on their farms.

Plymouth, where he viewed the ocean and its giant ships for the first time, was another new experience. After asking around, he was directed to the Australian-bound steamship, the SS Durham. But once on board, Matt found his confidence faltering. Worse was to come, and for the first few days after leaving port, he almost wished himself back at Fenham Manor.

Conditions in steerage were cramped and uncomfortable, the lack of hygiene appalling to one who'd been raised in a clean, respectable cottage. The accommodation housed two rows of bunks either side of a narrow aisle, where twenty men slept, dressed, and ate in close proximity. His meagre bed had only a straw mattress which wore thinner as the weeks went by, until he could feel the iron bars pressing through to his back.

He was not a good sailor, and he ate little for the first week. Eventually he found his sea legs and was able to do justice to the food, which seemed to be plentiful, if monotonous. Breakfast was porridge and coffee. The midday and evening meals consisted of soup, boiled mutton and beef, salt pork, potatoes and bread.

When the weather was rough the waves washed through the portholes, soaking their bunks and forcing the only form of ventilation to be closed. The stuffy air was soon fetid with unwashed bodies. Matt attempted to forget his surroundings by socialising with his fellow male passengers, a mixture of humanity from the British Isles and Europe. He found his horizons broadening as he mixed with men of many different backgrounds. Most of the Europeans were unable to speak English, but the few who did, entertained him with stories of their homelands. They played endless games of poker and euchre to relieve the boredom, but after losing some of his meagre savings to cards he decided gambling with real money was only for fools.

He was thankful to be a single male. The families with children suffered more in the cramped, squalid conditions, with some of the children becoming seriously ill. First one, and then another baby, died as the voyage progressed; the tiny bodies fed to the hungry sea while the grieving parents looked on in despair. Matt tried not to think of their distraught faces as he sought refuge with his friends, distracting himself with cards and conversation.

After a six-week journey, he was down to his last few shillings when they disembarked at Moreton Bay. Coming from the old English towns of Plymouth and Exeter, Brisbane looked like a raw backwater, a huddle of low buildings along the muddy Brisbane River. Queen Street was distinguished by several imposing buildings, including the Post Office, the Telegraph Newspaper Building and the National Bank, but other more lowly buildings still wore the silt-stains from the flood that the town had apparently suffered the previous year.

There was a frontier quality about this, the capital of Queensland, which excited him. Private homes, in contrast to the stone and brick cottages of Devon, were built of timber with corrugated-iron roofs. Matt was amazed by the flimsy appearance of the dwellings, some on high stilts with the space underneath apparently used for storage. The weather was as warm as midsummer in Devon, although it was May and supposed to be almost winter here. There was a bite to the sun that he hadn't felt before, but when night fell the air turned surprisingly cold, almost bitter enough for frost.

Matt earned a few shillings by loading a teamster's wagon and sought lodgings for the night. He bought a beer in a corner pub, hoping no-one would ask his age, and struck up a conversation with the barmaid, a dark-haired girl in a tight-fitting bodice. She was pretty and fresh-faced, and after closing time he invited her to take a walk outside with him.

Pressed up against the rear wall of the hotel, she responded readily to his kisses and he spent a pleasant half-hour getting acquainted with her. Yet he was almost relieved when she didn't invite him to her room. He had never valued what came too easily.

The girl found him temporary work with an acquaintance, presumably not realising this job would give him the means to leave her. He was grateful for her help, since the colony seemed to be in the grip of a downturn and work was hard to come by. Yet he didn't let his gratitude sway him into staying. A mere three nights after she surrendered her virtue he was gone, having accumulated enough money to take the steamer to Rockhampton.

The port on the Fitzroy River surprised him. After Brisbane, he hadn't expected much, but the town was bustling with a look of prosperity. He took the time to walk down East Street before leaving town. A grand new post office with stone columns and a tall clock tower graced the main street, while Quay Street fronting the river had several imposing buildings. He spent the last of his money on stockman's garb—moleskin trousers, Crimean shirts and a broad-brimmed hat—and asked questions of the shopkeeper while he was at it.

'It's the gold mine at Mount Morgan.' The dapper little man was quick to inform him. 'It's bringing a lot of money and business to the town, and people too, of course. Just as well, because times are tough elsewhere. Are you going mining?'

Matt shook his head. 'I'm hoping to get a job on one of the stations. You might know Mr Charles Ashford, of Banyandah.'

The storekeeper's eyes widened. 'Everyone knows Mr Ashford. He's one of the most important men in the district. What's your connection to him?'

Matt ignored the question. 'Can you tell me where he lives?'

'That I can. It's only about twenty miles from town.'

An hour later Matt was on the road, riding a horse he'd hired from a livery stable, his possessions strapped to the borrowed saddle. He wondered if it would all be as easy once he arrived at Banyandah. He was yet to discover if his uncle was prepared to offer him work. He could only hope Ashford felt some kind of family obligation and didn't order him off the property.

Blanche Ashford laid her embroidery on the table at her elbow and tugged at her high collar, wafting hot air about her face with a gauzy paper fan. It was supposed to be late autumn, but summer had decided to return with one final blast before stepping aside for the brief, blessed winter that always seemed to be over in a trice. After fifteen years in this godforsaken country, Blanche found the heat no easier to bear.

She rang a little bell and waited impatiently for one of the maids to appear. 'Oh, Molly, fetch me a glass of lemonade, will you? Where are the girls?'

'They went for a walk with Miss Potter, ma'am. Would you like a plate of biscuits to go with the lemonade?'

'One will do.' Blanche gained weight easily these days and tried to avoid sweet snacks, although she sometimes wondered why she bothered. If Charles appreciated that she had kept her figure and her complexion, even after four children and all these years in this wretched climate, it didn't prevent him straying. Charles was always one for challenge and adventure and she'd realized years before that other women represented an invitation he couldn't resist.

She stared disconsolately across the brown paddock, wishing it would rain. Most of the time they wished for rain, but just occasionally it poured down until they prayed for it to stop. Such were the extremes of the Australian climate.

A flowering creeper climbed the lattice that edged the veranda, providing shade and blocking the harsh glare. The garden was a green oasis, a tribute to the aging Chinaman who tended it. Blanche couldn't have survived out here without her gardener, without this little haven of greenery and the fresh vegetables he kept supplied to their table. Queensland had come as an unpleasant shock to her when she had arrived here as a young, innocent bride, so much in love with her dashing husband, and so enthralled by the physical world of marriage to which he'd introduced her. How naive she'd been, not even wondering how he'd come by so much expertise.

'Excuse me, Mrs Ashford.' The elderly man who worked around the homestead hesitated at the foot of the steps. A tall young fellow stood beside him, a stranger who politely removed his hat as Blanche's gaze fell on him. 'This young cove's just turned up, says he's from Fenham Manor in England. Since the boss isn't here, what would you like me to do with him?'

Blanche folded her fan with a snap. She rose and moved to the top of the steps. Her eyes swept over the lad, thinking how striking he was with that dark wavy hair and hawklike features. Then he spoke in a soft Devon accent that made her heart clench with homesickness.

'How do you do, Mrs Ashford? I'm Matt Jones.'

She nodded at him and turned to the other man. 'Thank you, Dodds. You may leave him with me.'

Dodds looked dubiously at Jones but left them to it. Blanche knew what he was thinking—the visitor was obviously not gentry. But Blanche was bored and anyone who could talk to her about her part of England was always welcome.

'Come up onto the veranda, Mr Jones. Tell me what brings you to Banyandah.'

He mounted the steps and stood there, looking at her uncertainly. 'I worked in the stables at Fenham Manor, like, and they gave me this address to come to. I don't know anyone else in Australia, ma'am.'

'Well, sit down and allow me to offer you some refreshment.'

The lad hesitated and she smiled. 'This is Australia, Mr Jones. We're not so formal here. You can tell me all the news of England. It was my home too, and I still miss it.'

Mostly she just wanted to listen to his voice. It brought back happy memories of her childhood, of a big house and servants who were more like faithful family retainers than employees. She had noticed the difference at Fenham Manor, where everyone firmly knew their place.

He left his hat at the step and waited courteously until she had resumed her seat in the wicker chair before pulling up another. She watched him covertly, thinking he looked somehow familiar. How tall he was, how lean and strong, and also, how young. Yet the muscular shoulders under the flannel shirt were those of a man, not a boy, and his jaw was shadowed with a dark beard. She wondered if her own son, who was attending school in Sydney, would grow as handsome.

She rang the bell for Molly. 'Are you looking for work, Mr Jones?'

He nodded. 'Please call me Matt, ma'am.'

'I will have to ask my husband, of course, but you've arrived at an opportune time. One of our men has just left for the goldfields. Oh Molly, bring Matt a glass of lemonade, will you? And some brownie. Now, you must tell me about the doings at Fenham Manor. How were Mr and Mrs Ashford when you left them?'

He was surprisingly confident, answering her directly but politely. They spoke of England, and Blanche asked him his impressions of Australia.

'I like it. It's so big and open and new—just like England is so small and closed-in and old.'

She smiled. That was it in a nutshell. Only she found comfort in the very confined, civilized antiquity of England, while the vast rawness of Australia frightened her.

She studied him surreptitiously as he drained his glass, puzzling over the dark grey eyes, the slightly aquiline nose. He reminded her of Charles as a young man; not that she had known Charles when he was this young. She wondered if Matt was like Charles with the women.

They had been joined by her three daughters and were still sitting there, chatting about England, when Charles arrived an hour later. He looked hot and dusty in his riding breeches and blue shirt with rolled-up sleeves. Blanche glanced up at him disapprovingly, wrinkling her nose at the odour of sweat and horses which clung to him. That had been another shock when she came to Australia; the transformation of the well-dressed gentleman to the grazier who worked in the paddocks with his men.

Ashford's face tightened as he regarded the visitor, his wife, and his daughters who were sprawled on the veranda steps, eagerly listening to the conversation. 'Well, this is a cosy scene.'

Blanche flinched at his sardonic tone. Matt was already on his feet and she performed the introductions with an outward show of calm, while recognizing the anger in her husband's eyes. She should have guessed he would be like this. 'This is Matt Jones, Charles. Matt has been telling me stories of England—' she broke off at her husband's start, wondering what was wrong. He was staring at Matt, his eyes wide and shocked. It was as if their visitor had suddenly grown horns.

Matt's reaction was even more surprising. He didn't appear to be offended or surprised by Charles's obvious repugnance. He stared levelly back at him, something almost defiant smouldering in those dark eyes.

'What are you doing here, Matt Jones?'

'I'm looking for work, sir. I'm fresh out from England and I don't know anyone.'

'I'm not sure that I can help you. You had best be on your way in the morning. But for tonight, you may stay in the men's quarters. The head stockman's over there now. Go to him; tell him you're to have a meal and a bed for the night.'

Matt nodded politely at Blanche. If he was disappointed, he was doing his best not to show it. 'Thank you for your hospitality, ma'am, and for the refreshments.'

'You are welcome, Matt.' She gave him a sympathetic smile, feeling uncomfortable at her husband's abrupt dismissal of him. 'I enjoyed our talk.'

By the time Blanche had persuaded the girls to return to their governess, Charles had infuriatingly disappeared. Even when they changed for dinner, he managed to avoid her. He looked grim at the dining table, but it wasn't until they retired to their room to undress for bed, that she finally had the chance to voice her indignation.

'What was all that about, Charles? You were positively rude to that young man.'

He subjected her to a flinty stare, no longer bothering to hide the anger that had obviously been simmering inside him all evening. 'What do you mean by inviting that cheeky young upstart onto the veranda and making him at home?' He shrugged out of his coat and dropped it onto a chair. 'Next thing you'll have him sitting to dinner with us.'

Blanche became defensive. 'There was no harm in it. I enjoyed his company, especially talking to him about England. You know how homesick I become.'

Charles scowled, lifting his chin to unbutton his high collar. 'Will talking about it cure that? After ten years it's high time you got over it.' He placed the collar in an ivory box on the top of his dressing table and slipped off his gold cufflinks. 'Isn't the home I've provided for you good enough?'

'Oh, Charles, you know it's not that!' Blanche moved restlessly to the duchess and sat before it, unpinning her hair with trembling fingers.

'What is it, then? Surely you're not so lonely you need the company of an uncouth stableboy.'

Blanche paled, her hands stilling. 'He was very polite and correct towards me.'

'That's a surprise, knowing where he's come from!' Charles shed his shirt and flung it furiously into the corner.

Blanche stared at him suspiciously. There was something not quite right here—a violence in Charles's reaction that had its roots in more than just his usual snobbery. He'd looked positively shocked when the lad had said his name. She studied her husband's stern, handsome face, and then, sickeningly, it dawned on her. Hadn't she been thinking Matt looked familiar?

'What aren't you telling me, Charles?' Her voice broke. Oh, please God, don't let the boy be one of his by-blows!

Charles looked up at her. Something in her expression must have reached him, for his face softened a fraction. 'It's not what you're thinking.'

'What am I thinking?'

He didn't reply directly. 'I know the lad. I remember him from the last time we were at the Manor. He must be about twenty-years-old, and he's the son of Jones the coachman.' He paused for emphasis. 'Foster son, I should say.'

'Are you trying to tell me he's really yours?' Blanche heard the cold note in her own voice while pleading silently. *No, don't let him do this to me!*

'No, but you are close.' He met her eyes, smiling mirthlessly. 'He is Louise's son.'

'Louise?' she gasped. 'But how... I never guessed...'

'Louise was pregnant when I took her to England, back in 1874.'

Blanche flinched at that indelicate word. Sometimes Charles could be too forthright by half.

'Of course,' Charles continued. 'I didn't know at first, or I should have left her here. It was an exercise in futility.'

Charles had already told her how Louise had run away from the relatives she had been visiting rather than accompany him to England. She had worked as a governess for six months or more before he found her, and had meanwhile become entangled with the man she was to eventually marry.

'So... Lloyd Kavanagh... is he the father?'

Charles smiled grimly. 'Who else? Perhaps you understand now why I loathe the man.'

'Why didn't you tell me this before?'

Charles shrugged. 'There was no need. The fewer people who knew the better.'

Blanche stared at him. 'Does the boy know?'

'I'm not sure. But I suspect he does.'

Blanche unpinned the brooch she wore at the throat of her blouse. 'So now you plan to send him away? We're short a man, I know we are. Why can't you offer him a job?'

'I don't want him blabbing to the men who his mother is.'

'Isn't he more likely to do that if you turn him away? If you hire him, he'll have good reason to keep his silence.'

Charles looked at her thoughtfully. 'Perhaps you're right. But if I employ him, he'll be treated like any other stockman. He's been raised as a servant, after all. There'll be no *tête-à-têtes* on the veranda, or anywhere else.'

'I'm not going to snub him, Charles.'

'You'll do as I ask, Blanche. If we encourage him, he'll make trouble. And don't remind me he's my nephew, because he's also half Kavanagh, and we all know Lloyd Kavanagh came from the gutter!'

Blanche turned in her chair to stare at him. 'I only met Mr Kavanagh the once. He seemed respectable enough to me.'

They'd encountered Louise and her husband in the streets of Rockhampton one day. She'd been surprised to find that Charles's sister, while rather sun-browned, hadn't resembled the impoverished drudge Charles seemed to consider her. In fact, she was a tall, handsome woman, dressed respectably if not richly. The husband who had been the cause of the family estrangement had seemed surprisingly unobjectionable to Blanche. Lloyd Kavanagh was a pleasant-mannered, good-looking man who was reported to be comfortably established as a grazier. His voice was uncultured, hinting at a background which would doubtless not stand up to scrutiny. But that wasn't unusual. Australia was full of rough types who had made good.

Louise had been polite, even friendly to Blanche, but quite cold to Charles, and the animosity between the two men had been palpable. They hadn't lingered beyond brief introductions and a meaningless exchange on the weather. If Charles regretted the brevity of the meeting he didn't admit to it.

'That's what all this stems from, isn't it?' Blanche continued now. 'Your hatred of Lloyd Kavanagh! Just what did he do to you?'

'It's not what he did to me. It's what he did to Louise. He ruined her.'

'From what I can gather, Louise was happy to be ruined. Perhaps she is content with her life.'

Charles sat on the bed to pull off his shoes and socks. 'She wasn't old enough to know her own mind when she got herself into trouble. After that it was too late. She did become engaged to a chap in England, a friend of mine, actually. But he found out about the baby, so that was the end of that.'

Blanche picked up her brush and dragged it through her long hair, taking a deep breath to calm herself. 'Oh, Charles, don't let us argue about this.' The tugging strokes of the brush soothed her agitated nerves and she managed to smile at him in the mirror. 'I don't imagine I'll see much of Matt in future, so stop worrying about him.'

Charles crossed to her, his chest and feet bare, looming over her in an intimidating manner that made her spine tingle. 'We won't discuss him again. Just stay away from him and make sure the girls do too.' He lifted her hair and bent to kiss her neck, watching her face in the mirror as he nuzzled the sensitive skin behind her ear. She tried to stifle her quick, indrawn breath, but the glint of satisfaction in his eyes told her he had noted it. What a fool she was to love him still, in spite of everything.

Matt was gathering his things in the morning when the head stockman approached him. 'The boss said you can have a job, if you want one.'

Matt stared at him in surprise, but he knew better than to comment. 'Aye, I'd appreciate that. When would you like me to start?'

'Right away, if you've had breakfast?'

Matt nodded. He'd eaten breakfast and the previous night's dinner at the workers' kitchen. The other men had seemed tolerable enough, although he was the only Englishman amongst a group of different nationalities, including Irish, Scottish and Australian-born. The Colonials called him a new-chum and treated him with a touch of disdain, but Matt did his best to ignore that. Time would prove his abilities, or otherwise.

Larry Brown, the head stockman, was a lanky, pipe-smoking individual who looked Matt up and down with a sceptical glint in his eye. 'Can you ride, lad?'

Matt smiled. 'Of course. I grew up with horses.'

The man cast him a measuring glance. 'We'll soon see.'

As they ran a big bay gelding into the round yard, Matt dumped the saddle and bridle they had allotted him onto the middle rail. He assessed the animal for a moment, noting the gelding's good condition and the way he cantered around the imprisoning yard, stopping to wheel on his hind legs, nose low to the ground as he sought an escape. The horse had obviously not been ridden for some time.

Matt swung over the top rail and approached the gelding quietly, murmuring soothing words. The animal halted and turned to face him, snorting and rolling white-ringed eyes. Best be careful here, Matt told himself. A horse that showed white in its eye was often a bad one.

After the third attempt he was able to catch the horse and coax him to accept the bridle. He talked quietly all the while, easing the gelding's nervous trembling as Matt placed the saddle on his back and studied the unfamiliar girth. The saddle itself was different from anything Matt had seen in England, with high knee-pads and small thigh-pads that seemed designed to hold the rider in. Once he solved the riddle of the girth and pulled it up, the gelding hunched his back, walking stiff-legged as Matt led him out.

This one could buck, he thought.

The other men were all leaning on the rails, watching him. Matt noticed a few derisive smiles but did his best to ignore them as he worked quietly and confidently, calming the skittish animal. He suspected the gelding had been handled harshly in the past, and if some were scornful of his gentler methods, that was too bad. He drew the split reins together at the top of the horse's neck, grasping a fistful of mane and swinging lithely into the saddle.

The gelding flinched and jumped, his back still hunched, the entire body tensed for action. Matt knew a sudden move on his part would have him ducking his head and plunging into a buck. One way to win the men's respect would be to provoke that, and then hope like hell his own skill and the saddle would be enough to keep him on board. But that would be the action of a brash show-off, not the serious horseman he considered himself to be. So he risked the ridicule of his audience by taking the horse slowly and gently, coaxing him into a walk and trot and finally loosening him into a canter.

He knew he had done the right thing when he dismounted and opened the gate of the round-yard, leading the now relaxed horse out of the yard. He looked up at Larry Brown and caught his nod of approval.

'Good job, Matt,' the head stockman said. 'Plenty of louts can ride a buck-jumper, but it takes a horseman to take him quiet like you did.'

'But could he have rode him any other way?' Blue, a red-haired stockman of about Matt's own age, scoffed. 'He's just a new-chum Pommy.'

Larry just looked at Blue and smiled without answering, while Matt did his best to stifle a prickle of annoyance. With the head stockman as an ally he could afford to ignore such jibes.

If horses were familiar territory to Matt, the day's mustering was definitely a challenge. He was yelled at more than once for being in the wrong place, for pushing the cattle too hard, for turning tail on a beast. Yet he found himself relishing this new challenge, loving the very ruggedness of the job, adapting to the heat, dust and flies as if it was in his blood. Which, after all, it was.

'Wait till summer comes, Pommy,' Blue sneered. 'You'll be whingeing then.'

Matt stared at Blue's flaking, sunburnt face, allowing himself a sense of smug superiority at his own unblemished skin which was tanning browner every day. 'How do *you* get on in the summer time, Blue? Does your skin peel right off, like?'

Blue glared at him and swung away without answering, but after that he left Matt alone.

It was Charles Ashford's attitude that Matt found puzzling. He wondered why his uncle had relented enough to give him a job when he seemed so hostile. Matt was well aware that Ashford had been angry that day he'd arrived home to find Matt on the veranda, talking to his wife and daughters. Charles had obviously realized very quickly who he was, and he'd received the message loud and clear that he was not to be treated as family. As if he'd expected anything else from an Ashford. He wondered if his mother was the same as the rest of them.

He didn't see Mrs Ashford again, except at a distance. Which was a pity as she'd seemed a nice lady, nothing like his uncle. He supposed she was keeping clear of him to please her husband.

Matt quickly settled to the work at Banyandah, his natural ability with horses extending to an affinity for working with cattle which he hadn't guessed he possessed. He made friends with a couple of the stockmen, leaving Blue, whose jealousy was palpable, the only irritant. He should have been happy, but at night in his narrow bed with the other men snoring and rustling in their bedclothes beside him, his thoughts would take flight to an imagined family and a mother who had perhaps not wanted to give him up after all.

It was Charles Ashford's coldness that kept him silent. He'd been at Banyandah for nearly two months before the opportunity presented itself to question his uncle.

Matt had been out on horseback, checking a fence-line, and he let his horse free in the paddock before carrying his tack back to the saddle room. Ashford was there, stowing his own saddle on a rack, and for once there was no-one else around. Ashford merely grunted his acknowledgment, but Matt was not deterred.

'Mr Ashford, could I have a word with you in private, like?'

Charles Ashford looked up quickly, his eyes coldly measuring. 'What about?'

Matt took a deep breath and plunged in headfirst. 'It's about me mother.'

'Ah.' Charles gave a little jeering smile. 'I wondered when we were coming to this.'

Matt met his uncle's eyes, determined not to be intimidated. 'I think I have a right to know what happened to her.'

'How much do you know?'

'Nothing, really, but that she was your sister.' He didn't bother to add what his foster mother had told him. Somehow he didn't think Charles Ashford would be interested in hearing about a young woman who had held her baby in her arms as if she cared.

'She's living not far from here.' Charles hung his bridle on a hook and glanced sideways at Matt. There was a gleam of something in his eyes that made Matt uneasy. 'She married a small time selector and lives on the Dawson River, near Banana. Why don't you visit her?'

Would she be glad to see me? Matt wanted to ask. Yet he kept silent, determined not to expose his uncertainty to this man. His stomach churned and his heart thudded against his ribcage, making him despise his own weakness. For years he'd told himself his mother didn't matter, and here he was feeling sick just at the thought of meeting her.

'What's her married name?'

'Kavanagh. She married Lloyd Kavanagh and they live on a place called Myvanwy on the other side of Banana.'

'What's this Kavanagh like?' Matt asked in a carefully casual tone.

Ashford snorted derisively. 'He's like a lot over here who try to forget where they came from, but don't succeed in fooling anyone. He's the grandson of convicts. Your mother always had a penchant for slumming it.'

Matt didn't know what 'penchant' meant, but it hardly mattered. 'Do you know who me father was?'

Charles Ashford looked at him and grinned. 'I'll leave that for you to find out. Are you planning to visit her?'

Suddenly the need to meet his mother and ask the questions that were burning inside him was intense. 'Aye, I guess I will.'

Charles shrugged. 'I won't hold your job for you. It's your decision.'

Bugger you, Matt thought. There were other jobs, and all he'd achieved so far was an exchange of one Ashford boss for another. True, the work was different and more exciting, but he could do it at places other than Banyandah. He wasn't a raw new-chum anymore and he could stand his ground with most of the stockmen.

'How soon can I leave?'

'I'll give you your wages at the end of the week.' Ashford looked at him and smirked. 'Give my regards to Louise, won't you?'

Chapter Three

It wasn't often that Isabella Jamieson visited Rockhampton. She was a born and bred country girl, but she enjoyed her rare holidays with her sister. Today she and Maggie had taken the children to the Botanic Gardens for an afternoon treat, while Horace, Maggie's husband, was busy at work. It was a pleasant, sunny day and the gardens were crowded with people. The sisters searched for a quiet seat where they could sit and talk while the children played. The three little boys ran to the swings and seesaws, while the girls contented themselves with feeding the ducks and the tame kangaroos which hopped about, cropping the short green grass.

'You'll be twenty this month, Bella,' Maggie observed, settling her plump frame more comfortably on the hard bench. She was twelve years older than Isabella, who had been an after-thought in the Jamieson family. 'It's time to think about getting married yourself.' She angled an archly curious look at her sister. 'You're pretty enough to have a few beaux dangling after you. Isn't there anyone you fancy?'

Isabella adjusted her shady hat and shook her head. 'All the young men around Banana are so tedious. They're mostly spotty and plain and none of them know how to talk to girls.'

Maggie smiled. 'When we're young we all long for someone dashing and handsome to sweep us off our feet, but it seldom works that way. The plain, spotty ones often make the best husbands. Perhaps you'll meet a nice lad at the races next week. I'll ask Horace if he has anyone in mind.'

'Don't put him to any trouble.' Maggie had married a bank teller who had risen to branch manager in a few short years. He was a stuffy, unexciting little man in Isabella's opinion. 'I'm not even sure if I want to get married.' She watched as two of her nephews squabbled over a swing. Much as she loved them, it was nice to know they were ultimately someone else's responsibility. 'I don't want to be tied down with babies and housework. Besides, who would look after Father?'

Maggie shook her head. 'Mercy was like you. She used to love the horses and the cattle work. But if you're not careful, Bella, you'll ruin your skin with all that sun and you really will end up an old maid.'

Isabella laughed carelessly, concealing her inner sorrow. Mercy was her eldest sister and had raised her from an infant after their mother died. She didn't deserve the hand life had dealt her. 'Mercy would have been better off an old maid. I know she has her children, but what possessed her to marry Alfred?'

Maggie's expression changed. 'What's Alfred been up to?'

Isabella shrugged. 'The same old thing. Drinking, wasting money. And he's never at home. Poor Mercy's worked half to death.'

Maggie sighed. 'It's such a shame. It just shows how falling in love with the wrong man can ruin your life.'

Isabella looked at her sharply. 'Do you think she ever really loved him?'

'No, not Alfred. But she couldn't have the one she wanted, so she married Alfred on the rebound.'

Isabella's pulse tripped. This was news to her. 'Who was it she wanted?'

'Don't tell anyone, will you?' Maggie looked about her as if to ensure there were no listening ears and lowered her voice. 'She used to be sweet on Lloyd Kavanagh.'

'Oh, no.' Isabella straightened, her heart twisting with compassion for her sister. 'Is that so? And he didn't feel the same way?'

'Apparently not. Poor Mercy fell for him when she was only sixteen. He was twenty-three, so she was a bit young for him.' Maggie sighed, a regretful expression in her eyes. 'But perhaps he would have married her one day if Louise Ashford hadn't come to work as our governess.'

Isabella blinked. 'Mrs Kavanagh, you mean? I didn't know she was your governess.' She stared at Maggie in confusion. 'Why would a silvertail like the Ashfords work for us?'

'That's a good question.' Maggie smiled. 'Louise was a bit of a rebel. She'd run away from home and none of us knew who she really was—including Lloyd.'

'Did she pretend to be someone else?' It was hard to believe of the genteel Louise Kavanagh. 'I always wondered how they came to marry.'

'Yes, she told us she was Lucy Forrest. It was obvious to everyone but Mercy that Lloyd was smitten by her. I thought they'd make a match of it, until her brother Charles arrived one day and carried her off to England.' Maggie paused as her youngest child, tiring of the seesaw, requested bread to feed the ducks. She waited until the boy had run off, clutching a brown paper bag in his grubby hands, before resuming her story. 'Lloyd was badly hurt, I think. While she was safely out of the picture it looked as though he might marry Mercy after all. But then he rode up one day with the news that Louise was back in his life. Poor Mercy was heartbroken.'

'Why did you never tell me this before?' Isabella's head was whirling. She'd known these people all her life and never guessed there was so much intrigue attached to them.

'It's not a story for a young girl.' Maggie brushed breadcrumbs from her skirt. 'But you're old enough now to be trusted with it. I know you won't gossip. I always liked Louise, even though she lied to us. She was a wonderful teacher and friend to us children.'

'She's always been kind to me. Mr Kavanagh, too. He must have been dashing when he was young.' Isabella sighed wistfully. Fancy having two girls in love with him.

Maggie smiled. 'He *was* charming and a lot of fun. Mercy wasn't the only one who adored him; we all did. For a man in his forties, he's still quite handsome.'

Well, compared to Horace, he probably was, Isabella thought. He was getting on a bit though.

Maggie's story had given her a new insight into her oldest sister. Poor Mercy. It was no wonder she seemed bitter. Fancy wanting Lloyd Kavanagh and having to make do with Alfred.

As she mulled it over, Isabella remembered details that suddenly made sense to her. She'd always wondered why Mercy disliked Louise Kavanagh, who was such a pleasant lady. She'd put it down to jealousy of Louise's happy marriage and comfortable lifestyle, and it seemed she'd been partly right, but there was more to it than she'd ever imagined.

At the end of the week, Matt borrowed a horse from Charles Ashford and rode to Rockhampton. From there, he caught the train to Westwood, where he purchased a fare on the weekly coach to Banana, due to leave the next morning. He spent the night in a rundown hotel. The room was freezing and the blankets threadbare, and he was glad to leave it at first light the next morning.

His breath steamed in the frosty air outside and the cold nipped at him through his heavy coat. He walked to the Post Office where the coach was already waiting. One horse was harnessed to the pole while the other three stamped restlessly in front of the swingle-bars. A boy of perhaps fourteen held a fifth, wild-eyed horse, wearing its collar and traces like the others but not yet hitched to the coach. A bearded man in a Crimean shirt and waistcoat heaved baskets of mail, casks of rum and other goods to the roof of the vehicle, while another stood on top to position them and lash them down. A large crowd had gathered to watch.

'You going on the coach?' A male bystander grinned at Matt. 'You're in for a lively ride. They're breaking in a new horse. Most of the passengers pulled out.'

Matt surveyed the remaining victims: a man in his forties and a petite girl with chestnut hair piled under a narrow hat trimmed with ribbons. He gave her a second look. She was pretty and well-dressed in a draped dark green skirt and matching jacket which fitted snugly to her trim figure. As she caught his glance Matt touched his hat to her. 'Good day, ma'am.'

She inclined her head in polite acknowledgment, holding his gaze for a moment before dropping her eyes, her cheeks tinged pink. The man in the waistcoat, whom Matt took to be the driver, turned from his task as if noticing her for the first time. 'Are you sure you want to come, Miss Jamieson? All the other women've pulled out.'

She nodded, lifting a determined little chin. 'Yes, Mr Baxter. I'm sure you wouldn't take passengers if it was that dangerous, and besides, I enjoy a bit of excitement.'

Matt smiled inwardly, his interest quickening. She was obviously a girl with mettle. The trip to Banana promised to be entertaining in more ways than one.

Baxter waited until all the luggage was stowed and the girl and the other male passenger settled inside, before beckoning to the horse-holder. 'Bring him up, Bob.' He glanced at Matt. 'You coming with us?'

Matt nodded. 'I'll sit up front with you if I can.'

'As long as you're prepared to hold on.'

The horse snorted and tossed its head uneasily as they backed it into place and quickly harnessed it to the pole. The boy was left holding its bridle as the driver climbed to his seat. Matt sprang up lithely beside him and the driver nodded. 'Stand back, everyone! Let'em go!'

Now Matt understood the large audience. The fidgeting horses sprang into a gallop, pulling the unsuspecting new recruit along with them. The unbroken animal jammed its tail against its rump and threw its blinkered head high as the coach thundered in its wake. It would have bolted had it not been already at full gallop with the other horses holding it on course.

Baxter looked at Matt and grinned, obviously relishing the excitement. 'This is one ride you won't forget in a hurry!' he bellowed over the thundering hooves and rumbling iron wheels.

Matt returned the grin as adrenalin pumped through his body. He threw back his head and let out a wild yell. This surely topped driving a carriage for the swells back in England.

Baxter's strategy was simple—to gallop the horses until they were exhausted. At last, when their coats were dark with sweat and foam lined the leather harness, he drew them back to a walk. Even the new addition to the team seemed content to travel quietly now, too spent to do anything but plod with head hanging and nostrils flaring.

Horses were changed at several stations en route, enabling them to keep a steady pace. Matt exchanged a few words with the girl when they stepped down from the coach, but she was reserved, keeping him at a distance. Which, since they hadn't been introduced, was proper behaviour in a well-brought-up girl. He asked Baxter who she was.

The man gave him a sidelong look. 'Fancy the look of her, d' you? She's a respectable girl, so mind your manners. Her name's Isabella Jamieson and her old man has a run on the Dawson River.'

The Kavanaghs were supposed to live on the Dawson River. If she was in the area, perhaps they'd meet again. Not that he knew how long he'd be staying. It depended on his reception at the Kavanagh household.

The seventy miles to Banana took them just over ten hours. At sunset, the coach topped a rise and the town was spread before them, straggling down the hill to a large, scrub-fringed lagoon. A line of trees with peculiar bloated trunks dotted the main street, along with a cluster of weatherboard buildings and slab shanties. The lagoon appeared to be a popular camping spot and on the outskirts of town, Matt spied a cluster of bark gunyahs and corrugated iron humpies. An Aboriginal camp, he guessed. Black children and white ran to greet them and accompanied the coach down the street, shouting their excitement as it drew up in a flurry of dust in front of the Post Office.

Matt climbed from his high seat beside the driver to help unload the baggage and mail-baskets from the top of the vehicle. It seemed as if the whole town had come to welcome them. Perhaps some were awaiting a parcel or important letter, but most seemed to be there merely out of curiosity. Matt watched the Jamieson girl from the corner of his eye and saw that she was met by a little, ageing man in a bowler hat. Probably her father. He was momentarily distracted as Baxter handed him a mail-basket and when he looked back, they were gone.

After retrieving his own luggage he sought a room at the Banana Hotel and ordered a drink in the bar. As he passed over the coins for his beer he eyed the barman, a burly, rough-looking individual with a heavy black beard and bulbous nose. 'You a local here?' Matt asked.

The man bared his yellow, broken teeth in a grin. 'About as local as anyone. Came here in '69 as a bit of a kid, working as a teamster's offsider.' He paused, wiping wet rings from the bar with a grimy rag. 'You're not, that's plain. Been out here long?'

'Only a couple of months. Do you know people called Kavanagh? Supposed to live near here, like.'

The man's dark eyes sharpened with sly curiosity. 'That'll be Lloyd Kavanagh from Myvanwy.'

'Aye, that's the one.' Matt's stomach tightened with anticipation.

'You got a job with him?'

It was none of this man's business. Matt shifted uneasily but decided evasiveness would only add suspicion. 'I worked for the Ashfords at Banyandah for a while. Mrs Kavanagh's Charles Ashford's sister.'

The man's eyes gleamed avidly. 'Ah, but there's a story. There's no love lost there. They reckon the Ashfords cut her off when she married Lloyd Kavanagh. A bit of a step down, you might say.'

'What's this Kavanagh like?'

'Lloyd Kavanagh? A decent cove, but not in the same class as the Ashfords, by a long shot. A bit wild when he were young.' The fellow chuckled, looking Matt up and down slyly. 'Weren't we all? I bet you have them fillies swishing their tails at you, too.'

Matt just grinned. 'The fillies are few and far between out here. Human ones, anyway.'

'Yeah. But there's a woman lives on the edge of town—'

'I'm not looking for that sort of company.' Matt changed the subject. 'How do I find the Kavanaghs?'

'Myvanwy's about twenty miles from here, on the other side of the Dawson. You take the western road and turn right once you've crossed the river. Can't miss it.'

'Any chance of me borrowing a horse?'

'Yeah, we hire horses out. As long as you can get it back in a day or two.' The fellow's lazy scrutiny suddenly sharpened. 'Are you some relation to the Kavanaghs? You look a bit like 'em.'

This was touchy ground. Matt stiffened. 'I'm no relation. I told you. Charles Ashford gave me an introduction to his sister.' He downed his beer and turned away before he could be interrogated further. 'Thanks for your help, mate.'

By the time Matt had reached the river crossing the next day, the so-called road had degenerated to a few wagon tracks in the soft sand. One track followed the river upstream to the left, another forged on ahead, and the third swung sharply right. Matt turned his borrowed horse to the right, the nerves that had been stirring his stomach all morning now buzzing like a swarm of bees. Dread pressed on him like a heavy cloud, What if they wanted nothing to do with him?

The homestead stood a mile downstream on a rise above the river. A large slab house with a corrugated-iron roof was surrounded by a greying picket fence, a riot of bougainvillea and a bed of red-blooming geraniums. A cabbage gum and another tree he didn't recognize cast welcoming shade against the heat. He reined his horse for a moment, taking in the scene.

Amongst a cluster of outbuildings he identified a small square meat-house with gauzed upper walls and overhanging eaves, a building that was probably workers' quarters, and an open-ended shed which housed a blacksmith's forge, an anvil and an array of saddles and harness. Scattered in the thin shade of some gum trees were four cut-off sections of a hollow log, the remnants of some giant dead tree which now seemed to serve as dog kennels. Most of the dogs were apparently absent, their chains and collars lying abandoned. Only an old blue bitch emerged from the shed, barking her agitation.

A flashy thoroughbred filly with gleaming chestnut coat neighed from an exercise yard adjoining a set of stables. Eyeing Matt's horse, she impatiently circled her yard as he approached, pausing to stare with head held over the top rail. No grass-fed animal this. Perhaps Lloyd Kavanagh participated in a small way in the racing game.

The premises were no match for the scale of Banyandah or Ashford Manor. Louise Kavanagh, nee Ashford, had certainly come down in the world.

Louise Kavanagh sewed with tiny, almost invisible stitches, hemming the frock she was making for her five-year-old daughter Hannah. She glanced at her daughter, allowing her tired eyes to rest fondly on the bent, brown head as Hannah read from her school reader. The girl was a bright, willing student, in pleasing contrast to the boys who had constantly fought against learning. Whatever was happening outside the window had always held more appeal to her sons' imaginations.

It was the barking that first attracted her attention. Lloyd and Ben were away for the day, mustering, and they had most of the dogs, leaving only the old blue heeler, Sally, who was past travelling more than a mile or so. But she was still a handy watchdog. Louise pushed back her chair, laid down her sewing and moved to the window. She noted the approaching horseman with surprise. Visitors were a rarity this far from town.

'There's someone here, Hannah. You can have a break for a few minutes.'

She stepped into her bedroom to smooth her upswept hair in front of the mirror. A few strands of grey streaked the dark and these days, fine lines fanned from her eyes and mouth. Too much sun and hard work had taken its toll on her skin, but that was the sacrifice she had willingly made. Straightening the waistband of her brown serge skirt, she glanced critically at her blouse. It was neat and clean, if a little crumpled.

A young man sat his horse at the front gate, while the dog Sally circled him threateningly, growling a warning. At Louise's sharp command Sally dropped her head, abashed. She retreated a few yards, her tail drooping but her eyes still wary.

The man dismounted and raised his hat, while keeping an eye on the dog. 'Good day to you, ma'am. Would you be Mrs Kavanagh?'

'Yes, I am.' She stared at him as the familiar accent tugged at her memory, evoking images of the Devonshire countryside and a grey stone manor teeming with servants. He was very young, little more than a lad in his stockman's moleskins and striped Crimean shirt, dark rumpled hair revealed by that momentary lifting of his stained hat. She stared at his brown face, feeling her skin prickle with something she couldn't define. He looked familiar, yet she was certain she had never seen him before.

'Are you from Devon?'

'Aye.' His dark eyes were intent on her face. 'Matt Jones, late of Fenham Manor.'

The air rushed out of her lungs and her stomach dropped. 'M-Matt J-Jones?' She stumbled over the words, staring at him. Had he really said that name, or was this a dream?

She clutched the gate to steady herself as the blood pounded in her ears, making her feel lightheaded. Her lips trembled as she faltered over the words she was too afraid to ask. At last she managed a compromise. 'Are-are you related to Jones, the coachman?'

He nodded, watching her with an unfathomable expression. 'Aye. He's me foster father.'

Disbelief and yearning rushed at her then, mingled with years of aching guilt. 'You're Matthew?' she whispered incredulously. 'You must know who I am, then?'

He nodded again, silently eyeing her in that unrelenting yet guarded way, as if he still expected her to deny him. It tore at her already ravaged emotions.

'Oh, Matthew.' She fumbled with the gate catch, her fingers trembling and useless. He came to her aid, pushing the gate wide, and then there was nothing between them but a foot of space she hardly knew how to bridge. She studied his face, seeing his father in his mouth and chin, the Ashfords in that arrogant nose. Her eyes swept over him, noting how tall and strong he was. He was beautiful, and he was her son.

A rush of possessive emotion prompted her to do what her mind was afraid to direct. With a sob she moved forward, grasping his hands in both of hers as tears filled her eyes.

'Oh, Matthew, forgive me for letting them take you away. I loved you so much, and I've never stopped thinking about you, even after all these years. Tell me what we did was best for you.'

He didn't answer her but she saw his Adam's apple move as he swallowed. Silently she acknowledged that particular assurance was more than she could realistically expect.

'The Joneses were good to me,' he finally said.

Hannah's gasp behind her made her realize that she was still holding his hands. She abruptly pulled away, swinging to face her daughter's uncomprehending eyes.

'Hannah.' Louise struggled for composure, taking her handkerchief from her sleeve to wipe her eyes. 'This is someone from my old home in England.' She drew her daughter forward with one arm. 'I'd like to introduce Matthew Jones. This is my daughter Hannah, Matthew.' Your sister, she wanted to say, but couldn't. How could she explain this other son to a five-year-old?

Hannah turned curious eyes on him. 'How do you do, Mr Jones? If you're from England, you must talk funny.'

Matt gave a forced-sounding laugh. 'How do you do, Hannah? You Colonials talk funny to me.'

'But Mother talks like a Pom. Father says so.'

He grinned, his face softening. 'I suppose she does, at that. Different to me though.'

There was an awkward silence. What to do and say now? Louise tried to gather her scattered thoughts. Food provided a convenient refuge. 'It's lunchtime. Hannah, please take Matthew and show him where he can leave his horse. Then he can come and eat with us.'

Matt paused before turning away, his horse's reins looped over his arm. 'I've always been called Matt.'

Louise uttered a choked little laugh. 'Give me time. I've thought of you as Matthew for all these years.'

Since her menfolk hadn't been expected home for lunch, she'd given Betsy, the maid, a couple of hours off. She was glad of the few minutes alone as she set the table and prepared food. Her hands were trembling, her mind whirling, her stomach queasy. And yet there was joy bubbling beneath the surface. After all this time, the child she had dared not claim had come to her. She tried to imagine Lloyd's reaction when he arrived home, remembering how he'd hated to think of his son growing up at Ashford Manor. Surely he would be as thrilled as she was?

Perhaps this was just a fleeting visit, and Matthew would be gone tomorrow. That thought brought another pang, making her feel physically sick with the mixture of emotions churning inside her. But if he stayed, there were her other two other sons to consider, sons who knew nothing of this elder brother. How would they react to Matthew?

Chapter Four

When Hannah led Matthew into the kitchen she was chatting easily with him as if she had known him all her life. Although she was usually a friendly child, Louise had never seen her display such rapport with a stranger before.

Louise wished she could feel the same ease. She asked questions about the boy's foster parents, but was not brave enough to ask after her own mother and father. When she sent Hannah to the dining-room with a plate of food for the table, Matt cut across her questions.

'I don't know if I should stay here. What are you going to tell your husband? Does he know about me?'

Louise stared at him, feeling a little tremor of shock run down her spine. 'Of course he does. Don't you know?'

'Know what?'

'Who your father is?'

'How could I? No-one at Fenham Manor seemed to know, or if they did they weren't talking, like. I asked Charles Ashford, but he wouldn't tell me.'

'You've seen Charles?'

'Aye, I worked there for two months when I came over from England.'

Louise didn't bother to hide her annoyance. 'Charles would prefer to stir the pot. He'd sooner leave you wondering than tell you that the man I married is your father.'

'Lloyd Kavanagh's me *father*?'

'That's correct.'

Matt took a deep breath. The surprise and relief on his face was palpable. 'So Hannah's me full sister?'

'Yes. You have two brothers, also. Ben is eighteen and works here with his father. Tom attends boarding school in Brisbane.'

Matt's expression was bemused and a little anxious. Louise could only guess how it must feel to suddenly have a readymade family, to wonder if he would be accepted by the male members of that family as readily as he had been received by her and Hannah. Of course, Hannah wasn't aware of the complexity of the situation yet.

Louise could see the questions forming, questions that would need to be asked. But then Hannah returned and the moment was lost.

Lunch was awkward. Louise filled the silences with queries about Fenham Manor and the people there, at last managing a carefully indifferent inquiry about her parents.

Matt looked at her curiously. 'The master and mistress are getting old. They're both looking frail, but they seem to have kept well enough.'

She hadn't been in contact with them in almost twenty years. It sounded strange to hear him refer to them as 'the master and mistress'. Louise wondered if that was how he thought of them, or if he dwelt much on the fact they were his grandparents. She wondered how long he'd known, but it was impossible to ask with Hannah present. Besides, it was all so new and fragile. She was afraid to dig too deep.

She watched him surreptitiously as he ate. He was so handsome, his natural self-assurance shining through even in these awkward circumstances. A lock of dark, wavy hair fell over his forehead from a centre parting. His grey eyes were dark like hers, his face tanned a deep brown from the weeks of Australian sun. He was only twenty, but the shadow of beard darkened his jaw and a straggle of chest hair was exposed by the open neck of his shirt. As he forked corned beef into his mouth she noted the sinewy strength of his forearms.

Favourably contrasting him to Ben, who was gangling, shy and awkwardly thin, she felt a pang of disloyalty to her second son.

She was almost afraid to ask Matt if he was staying. Could she bear to have him returned to her, only to lose him again? Perhaps he only wanted to satisfy his curiosity and move on, and she hardly had the right to expect any more than that.

After they had eaten, she shooed her daughter back to the schoolroom. 'I'll be there in a few minutes, Hannah. Carry on with your copybook in the meantime.'

After the girl had gone she drew a deep breath and turned to face her son. This was the moment that could not be avoided. 'Are you staying, Matt? For a little while, at least? I know it's a lot to ask, but it would mean so much to me if we could get to know each other. By blood you're as much a part of this family as anyone.'

His eyes faltered and he looked away briefly. 'What will the others think of that?'

She hesitated. 'The children don't need to know just yet. It's too... difficult. But Lloyd... your father... will want you to stay.'

He gave her a quick, penetrating glance that made her squirm inwardly. Perhaps she was being a coward, but how could she explain what had happened twenty-one years ago to her other sons, let alone Hannah? It was impossible to explain it to Hannah.

'I've no plans for a bit,' he muttered. 'I'd like to stay, so long as I'm welcome.'

Later, Matt unrolled his swag on a camp stretcher in the two-room slab hut that served as the men's quarters, and stowed his few possessions in a chest of drawers. Feeling a need for solitude, he was relieved to find the quarters unoccupied. Apparently the only non-family employee was an Aboriginal stockman who had his own makeshift camp near the river.

It was all a bit hard to believe. After the months of anxiety, his mother had turned out to be a beautiful, gracious lady who had accepted him with open arms. Well, not exactly beautiful, perhaps, but handsome in a purely Ashford way which should have made him uneasy. Yet the resemblance to her parents and brother seemed to stop with her looks. She was friendly, warm and approachable in a way that was typical of many of the Colonials he'd met—nothing like her stuck-up family. Even that plummy accent had flattened around the edges.

The most surprising thing, which he'd not managed to digest just yet, was that his mother's husband was actually his father. He'd certainly been born a bastard, but had their marriage made him legitimate?

Once unpacked, Matt wandered outside, strolling around the sheds and outbuildings, pausing for a closer look at the chestnut filly in the exercise yard. She was a beauty with a refined head, long slender legs, sloping shoulders and muscular hindquarters that hinted at speed. He wondered if he might be given a chance to ride her if he stayed.

A well-beaten path took him to a set of stockyards a mile or so from the house. Looking critically over the yards, he noted the careful craftsmanship, the rails mortised into each post and tied with a double strand of wire. The ends of the wire were twisted into a knot called a Cobb and Co. twitch. That much he had learned at Banyandah. Studying the design of the yards, he saw everything was well-maintained with no broken rails or gates, and even the pulley blocks in the branding pen were well-oiled. This was no broken-down enterprise, but obviously a business run with pride.

The sound of bellowing cattle prompted Matt to climb to the top rail of the branding pen. From his vantage point he spotted a cloud of dust, from which a mob of cattle gradually emerged. Three riders worked the mob, their shouts and whistles urging the cattle onwards and directing the dogs, which took off after a breakaway beast as he watched, two of them nipping at its heels and another lunging at its nose. The animal returned promptly, bawling, disappearing into the dust-cloud at the tail of the herd.

Sitting quietly, Matt looked on as the cattle were yarded, knowing the animals wouldn't notice him if he remained still. He waited until the herd had been secured in a second, smaller yard before he approached the riders.

A tall, skinny lad sat astride a sweaty bay horse and a half-caste Aborigine rode a mangy grey. But it was the man who'd dismounted to chain the gate whom Matt confronted.

He was tall and broad-shouldered, with that hard, sun-browned look Matt had come to associate with Australian bushmen. A broad-brimmed felt hat obscured most of his face as he bent to chain the gate, while sandy hair curled damply at the nape of his neck.

'Are you Mr Kavanagh?'

'That's me.' The man looked up from the gate with an inquiring glance. Matt guessed he would be in his mid-forties, though it was hard to tell with these bush types. Kavanagh held out his hand and firmly gripped Matt's. 'By the sounds of it, you're from England.'

'I'm Matt Jones.' Matt watched the older man's face closely, adding, 'From Devon.'

Lloyd Kavanagh's eyes flickered, grew intent, then wary with dawning suspicion. 'Whereabouts in Devon?'

'Fenham Manor. I worked as a groom in the stables there. Me father's the coachman.'

Kavanagh's eyes, red-rimmed from dust, were frozen on Matt's face. 'What'd you say your name was?'

'Matt Jones,' he repeated patiently.

Kavanagh drew in a deep breath and cast a quick, guarded glance at the skinny lad who'd just joined them. 'Ben, you and Banjo go and sort these cattle out a bit. Split the bulls up so they won't fight and knock the yard down.'

For a moment he watched Ben's retreating back before returning to Matt, letting that indrawn breath whistle out between his teeth. 'Are you who I think you are?'

Matt grinned sardonically. 'If you mean am I your bastard offspring, so I've been told.'

'Flaming hell, that's a blunt way of putting it!' Kavanagh stared at him grimly. 'Why couldn't you have written, given us a bit of warning? Have you seen your mother yet?'

Matt flinched at the sharp tone and Kavanagh put out a placating hand. 'It's not that I don't want you here, but I never expected to have you waltz in as casual as you please. How'd your mother take it? Is she all right?'

Matt held his ground defiantly. 'Strange enough, she seemed pleased to see me.'

'Oh, she would be, no doubt about that. But you must've given her an awful shock. She's been giving herself a hard time over you for the past nineteen or twenty years—how old are you now?'

'I'll be twenty-one in December.'

Kavanagh stood back and looked him up and down, shaking his head incredulously. 'Struth, this is hard to believe. You're different to the other boys; you look like the cursed Ashfords.' He took a pipe and tobacco pouch from the pocket of his shirt. For all his outward coolness, Matt noticed his fingers trembling. 'How'd they treat you?'

'The Ashfords?' Matt smiled thinly. 'Mostly as if I didn't exist. I didn't know I was related to them until a few months ago. But the Joneses gave me a good home.'

'I'm glad of that, then.' Kavanagh tamped tobacco in the bowl of his pipe and returned the pouch to his pocket. 'The Ashfords hated me, and I was always worried they might take it out on you. Charles especially.'

'I've just come from Banyandah. I think he still hates you.'

Kavanagh looked derisive. 'He always will. He was the one that split us up, you know, and when your mother went and married me after all, that was like rubbing his face in it.' He fumbled in his pocket for matches and lit the pipe with awkward fingers.

'Aye, that sounds like Charles Ashford.' Matt was surprised at the bitterness in his own voice. He could feel his heart thudding. In its way this encounter with Kavanagh was more challenging than the earlier one with his mother. It was hard to believe this good-looking, tough-faced man with the broad Australian accent was actually his father. He had been partly prepared for Louise, because she was an Ashford, but this man was different from what he'd imagined his father might be.

'I would've married her before you were born if he hadn't taken her away. We both gave ourselves a hard time over what happened to you, but you weren't as real to me. I never saw you, didn't know you existed until you were more than a year old. It was bloody tough on your mother though. ' Kavanagh paused, looking at him in mute appeal. 'Do you realize we have to keep this quiet? For the sake of the other kids and your mother? There'd be one heck of a scandal if we told everyone you were our son—born nearly two years before we were married.'

Matt hadn't thought that far. He stiffened. 'What about the rest of the family? Won't you tell them either?'

'Not just yet, anyway. Hannah's too young to understand.' Kavanagh's eyes and voice softened. 'Did you meet Hannah?'

His daughter was obviously a favourite. 'Yes, I met her. She's a pretty little girl.'

'There's Ben and Tom, too. Ben you just saw, and Tom's away at boarding school. I guess they'll need to know one day, but it'll be difficult.'

Kavanagh looked discomfited and resentment flared within Matt. 'So where does that leave me? Mrs Kavanagh said I could stay.' Hell, he didn't know what to call her. It was all too new and strange to call her Ma.

'Matt, of course you're welcome to stay. Would you like to work here for a while? For now we can say you're someone from the Ashford estate. It's the truth, anyway.' He looked up as a chain rattled and Ben stepped through the gate. 'We'll talk more later. Ben, this is Matt Jones, come here from Fenham Manor, your mother's family home in England. He wants some work for a while.'

Ben, a gangling boy with fair hair like his father, shook Matt's hand in his own bony, over-large one. He gave Matt a look that was shyly curious. 'How'd you find us here?'

Matt mentioned his job with Charles Ashford and Ben nodded silently, his eyes warily assessing. Matt wondered if Ben had ever met their uncle. It hardly seemed that the two families mixed.

From the veranda Louise watched the three of them walk up from the horse yards, Lloyd flanked by Matt on one side and Ben on the other. A lump formed in her throat as she studied them, her husband the mature, more solid figure, Ben with the awkward thinness of youth, and Matt somewhere in between. Matt resembled the Ashfords more than he did his father, but the likeness was there, nevertheless. Would people only have to look at him to guess their secret?

Opposite the men's quarters they parted ways, Matt turning to his room while Lloyd and Ben continued to the house. Ben was the first to join her, after stopping to wash at the rainwater tank outside the house. In a moment of confusion, Louise hardly knew what to say to her second son as years of guilty secrets crowded her mind. After exchanging a few words she hurried down to steps to her husband. He looked up at her, smiling quizzically as he rinsed off his soapy forearms and reached for a towel.

'So, he's found us after all this time.'

She gave a shaky little laugh and moved into his arms, feeling the moisture on his skin dampen her blouse as he abandoned the towel. 'I can hardly believe it.' Stifling a sob, she pressed her face into his shoulder.

Lloyd tipped up her chin and looked at her questioningly. 'Are you all right?'

She wiped her eyes. 'I don't know whether to laugh or cry. I've longed for this day, but I never thought it would happen.'

She saw him stiffen. 'Don't get too carried away. He might be gone again in a few weeks, or less. And remember, even though he's our son we know nothing about him. We don't know what sort of person he's grown into.'

'I keep telling myself that, but the Joneses are decent people. I'm sure they've raised him properly.'

'Yeah, but something about him reminds me of your brother...if he does stay, people are going to have to know who he is, eventually. That will make things very awkward.'

Louise moved out of his arms. 'I'm past caring what people say and think. My family's the most important thing to me.'

Lloyd followed her to the dining room and stood watching her as she set the table for supper. 'That's just the problem. Remember that the other children could be hurt, especially Ben.'

She didn't reply and he made an impatient noise. 'Louise, I know what this must mean to you, and especially after losing Rose...but after what we went through then, I don't want any more strife.'

She turned to face him, illogically angered by his cautionary words even though she knew his concern was justified. 'He's my son, Lloyd—*our* son! Perhaps he won't stay, but I've loved him and grieved for him for all these years. Now I want to enjoy him while I can.'

Lloyd was silent, just standing in the doorway with his shoulder propped against the frame. Louise took serviettes, each rolled in a silver ring, from the drawer of the dresser and placed one at each setting. His very restraint was an unwelcome reminder of how badly she'd taken that other loss, pushing Lloyd aside when he'd obviously been sorely in need of his own comfort. Perhaps it was not surprising he was concerned now.

She went to her husband and slipped her arms around his waist, reaching up to kiss his rough cheek. He smelt of sweat, horses, and the cattle-yards, but it was a familiar, comforting scent. 'Let's just take it one day at a time, Lloyd. There's nothing else we can do.'

He straightened and slid his arms around her, holding her tight. He spoke against her hair. 'It's not that I don't want him here, Louise. He's my son, I know, and I used to worry about him growing up over there in England—but I stopped feeling guilty about him years ago. Of course it's different for you.'

After that initial awkwardness, Matt found himself settling into both the work at Myvanwy and the family circle as if he had indeed been born to it. He would find his mother watching him with a fierce pride in her eyes that made him squirm. He wondered that Ben didn't notice, but his younger brother seemed ready to accept him at face value, not questioning his presence at the family meal-table, enjoying his company and showing him the property with pride. His father appeared pleasantly surprised by his ability with cattle and Hannah idolized him. Sometimes he wondered if it had all happened too easily.

He made a couple of trips to town on his days off, befriending a group of young fellows he met at one of the hotels. They introduced him to rum, which seemed to be the favoured drink in Queensland, played billiards together in the room next door, and invited him to join their two-up games. They called him a new chum, but with good humour, and Matt accepted their jibes in the same spirit. He demonstrated he could out-drink and out-gamble the best of them, and at a pinch he thought he could outfight them as well.

The highlight of those first weeks was meeting the girl from the coach. Isabella Jamieson turned out to be the neighbour's daughter. She stopped by with her father one day after a trip to Banana, with a bundle of mail for the Kavanaghs. Matt would have missed her if he hadn't been sent home with the dray to collect posts for a new fence, a lucky chance that made him think someone must be looking out for him.

He was throwing posts into the bed of the dray when they drove up in a hooded buggy. The grizzled, bearded little man in the 'going to town' suit and bowler hat introduced himself, in a broad Scottish accent, as Jock Jamieson.

'And this is my daughter, Isabella. Ye must be the young lad from England.'

'Matt Jones,' Matt offered, brushing dirt and pieces of bark from his hands before accepting the old man's handshake. He smiled at the girl at Jamieson's side. 'I met your daughter before, though we weren't properly introduced, like. We rode on the same coach from Rockhampton. How d' you do, Miss Jamieson?'

She looked even prettier on the second meeting. Surely she was too young to be the old man's daughter? She was definitely the most promising bit of petticoat he'd met so far, and she lived right next door.

As she responded to the introduction, she looked at him with unconcealed interest, obviously secure in the company of her father as she hadn't been that day alone on the coach. There was something fresh and natural about that frank, open regard which both appealed to Matt and presented a challenge. He watched after the buggy as they drove on up to the house, wishing he could find some excuse to follow them but not wanting to appear too obvious. Besides, in their eyes he was only the working man.

They were still at the house with his mother when the dray was loaded. There was no reason for him to linger. So he clicked up the three draught horses and set off to rejoin his father at the fenceline, wondering how he could arrange to meet Miss Jamieson again.

He quizzed Ben about her when his father was out of earshot. Matt was wielding the crowbar, thudding it into the hard clay at the bottom of a posthole, while Ben worked beside him with the shovel, scooping out the loosened dirt. 'I met Jock Jamieson and his daughter when I was back at the house. They live close by, don't they?'

Ben nodded without particular interest. 'They're on Kilbride, about five miles up the road.'

'How old's the girl? Isabella, isn't it?'

Ben looked up curiously, wiping his sweaty brow with his sleeve. 'Do you fancy her? She's a real tomboy. She's about three years older than I am.'

Ben spoke in a dismissive tone, and Matt guessed he had known Isabella all his life and that she held no mysteries for him. 'What do you mean, a tomboy?'

'She spends more time out on a horse than she does at home. She'll wheel a cleanskin micky quicker than a lot of men. Her mother died when she was born and her father lets her do what she likes. I just can't see her as any man's wife.'

Matt grinned. He relished the idea of a challenge, and he was beginning to think it might be fun to court this wild-sounding girl. If she was unconventional, so much the better. 'I'm not looking for a wife just yet.'

Ben glanced up quickly from his shovel, his eyes suspicious, his colour heightening. 'The Jamiesons are old friends. You better treat Isabella right.'

'What are you, her protector?' Matt mocked. 'Do you think I want me wicked way with her?'

Ben's colour deepened, along with Matt's grin. 'Hell, I bet you never even kissed a girl. I know they're in short supply around here, but surely you can do better than that.'

Ben scraped the last of the dirt from the hole and rammed his shovel in the mound beside it, before stomping off to drink from the canvas water-bag hanging on the dray. Matt continued with the crowbar. He knew he'd upset the lad but he didn't care. Who did the little upstart think he was, telling him what to do?

Ben seemed uneasy with Matt for a few days, as if he didn't quite trust him anymore. Matt, who liked to think of himself as a man of the world, told himself Ben was just a naive kid. He'll get over it, he thought.

But Ben didn't get over it. When he took the wagon into town to fetch supplies, he returned in a pensive mood. Matt caught his brother studying him whenever he wasn't looking, and watching his mother as if there was something he wanted to ask her. Ben was distant, withdrawn, throwing himself harder into work. If he was no ladies man, it seemed he was determined to outdo Matt in other ways. Instead of working companionably together, they began to compete against each other, to see who could work hardest and longest. By the time Matt realized he had lost a friend and gained a rival, he didn't know how to rectify it.

Chapter Five

Isabella Jamieson was tired of people nagging her. Her father was all right—secretly she had to admit he indulged her—but her married brothers were like old women and her oldest sister Mercy was even worse.

Mercy lived on a small, tin pot holding on the other side of the river, struggling to raise a handful of kids with little help from her ne'er-do-well husband, a shearer who was absent more than he was at home. Isabella often wondered if it was this constant struggle that made Mercy seem bitter and old beyond her years. There was never any money; the few cattle they ran kept them in meat and basic necessities, but Alfred Forbes spent most of his wages on beer and rum.

Mercy was always at Isabella, repeating the same words like a mantra. 'You'll ruin your skin. Look at your hands! And behave like a lady. You'll have the whole countryside talking about you if you're not careful.'

Isabella knew that it was actually Mercy they talked about, in pitying whispers—Mercy whose own hands were work-worn, whose skin was as dry and wrinkled as an old woman's. She couldn't understand what her sister had ever seen in Alfred, who was as bad-tempered as he was unattractive. Perhaps, as Maggie had suggested, she had married him on the rebound, but Isabella was determined she'd end her days an old maid in preference to tying herself to someone like Alfred.

Matt Jones, though...he was another story. Just thinking of him made her heart thud and her breathing quicken. That day they'd travelled on the same coach from Westwood, she'd thought him the most handsome young man she'd ever seen. She hadn't expected to encounter him again, and finding him living next door had seemed like fate was smiling on her. She guessed he was no older than she was, but he had the worldly air of someone who'd been around, and he'd smiled at her with a confidence that was both challenging and exciting. He was so unlike the local boys. That soft English accent was a link to a different world. Since the day she'd encountered Matt at Myvanwy, she'd thought of little else but him, and she knew she needed an excuse to see him again.

Little Hannah's birthday gave her the pretext she needed. She was fond of Hannah, with whom she shared a particular bond. They were both the youngest of their families, and Hannah's lonely childhood reminded Isabella of her own, when there'd been no siblings of a similar age to play with. No mother, either, in her case, though Mercy had filled that role admirably, with help from her younger sisters. Those other sisters were scattered now, all married with families of their own, and only her oldest brother, Andrew, lived in nearby with his family and helped her father run their property, Kilbride.

As a gift for Hannah, Isabella had crocheted an edge around a linen handkerchief and embroidered her young friend's initials in one corner, proving that female accomplishments were not beyond her. She wrapped it carefully in a sheet of brown paper and announced her errand to her father, who was busy in his study with a stack of bills.

'It's Hannah's sixth birthday today. I want to ride over and give her this.' She held the tiny parcel up.

Jock Jamieson nodded absently, fingering his grey beard. 'Whatever ye like, lassie.' As an afterthought he added, 'Oh, tell Lloyd I saw some steers of his in the River addock. We'll be mustering there in a couple o' weeks, if he wants to send someone over.'

The ride to Myvanwy was something Isabella had done countless times before, without a second thought. Today her stomach fluttered foolishly, and when the homestead came in sight, her fingers trembled on the reins. Would Matt even be at home on a Saturday afternoon? He could be out working, or perhaps he had gone to town.

Hannah and her mother seemed to be alone at the house. Isabella duly hugged the excited little girl and presented her parcel. Louise smiled approvingly.

'It's very good of you to remember Hannah, Isabella.' Louise was gracious as always. A familiar yearning, that this warm, elegant lady was her own mother, pierced Isabella. She remembered Maggie's gossip about the Kavanaghs and wondered why she had fallen for Mr Kavanagh despite the huge gap in their status.

She'd said as much to Mercy one day and received a short response. 'Louise Kavanagh isn't half as high and mighty as she likes to make out,' Mercy had snapped. At the time Isabella had wondered at Mercy's dislike, but after her Maggie's recent revelations she thought she understood.

'We're having a party.' Hannah tugged at Isabella's hand, bringing her back to the present. 'Mother's made me a cake and put candles on it, and Dad and Ben and even Matt are coming home for it.'

'It's just a little celebration at afternoon tea,' Louise explained. 'The men are working close to the house and they promised they'd be home at three o'clock. I'm so pleased you'll be able to join us. Come inside now. I was just setting the table.'

Isabella hardly noticed Ben and his father when the men arrived, with Matt occupying her full attention. It was difficult not to stare at him when just the sight of him sent little tingles up and down her spine. If anything he looked even better than at their other meetings, bare-headed now, his dark hair neatly brushed, his face and hands scrubbed clean. He treated her to a broad smile which made her heart trip and thud crazily.

Afterwards Isabella could remember little of the conversation, mostly Hannah's childish excitement as she blew out candles and cut her cake. She remembered to tell Mr Kavanagh about his stray steers, and that they would be mustering in a couple of weeks.

'Let me know when you're due to start,' he responded, smiling indulgently at her. He had pushed back his chair and was filling his pipe with tobacco-stained fingers. 'I'll send Ben over to help.'

Isabella sought to hide her disappointment. She had hoped Matt might come. Unable to resist a quick glance in his direction, she found him watching her. He smiled and she blushed, looking away. Oh no. He was probably used to girls swooning over him—if she wasn't careful he'd think she was just another conquest.

She didn't look at him again until it was time to leave, and then she was deliberately cool. He didn't bother with any such pretence, however, meeting her eyes with a frank, unconcealed interest which she found unsettling. When he was audacious enough to wink, her face heated again. She turned away and hastily made her escape.

After supper, Matt was surprised when his mother caught him at the kitchen door as he was about to return to his quarters. For a moment he thought she was going to say something about Isabella, but apparently her mind was on a different track. 'Matt, I've been wondering. Have you written to the Joneses?'

He looked down at her in the lamplight, noting the stray wisps of hair that had escaped the knot at the back of her head. She looked younger in that gentle light and quite fetching for a woman of her age. He wondered what had made her think of the Joneses. Perhaps it was the birthday party which had set her thoughts along family lines.

'Not since I got to Banyandah. I wrote then, let 'em know I'd arrived safely.' He still hadn't learned to call her 'Mother'. Sometimes in company he called her Mrs Kavanagh, for appearances sake, but when they were alone he avoided calling her anything.

'Oh, Matt. You must write again. Why didn't I think to remind you before? You owe them so much.'

'I will,' he mumbled. He hated writing letters. The blank page always intimidated him and the words wouldn't come. 'But they can't read, you know.'

'Oh, I hadn't thought of that. But they sent you to school, didn't they?'

'Aye, at the village.' He looked up as Ben entered the room, his brother's face twisting with something that could have been jealousy as he saw them together. Sometimes he wondered if Ben suspected there was more to this situation than he'd been told.

'Please be sure to write, Matt. They'll find someone to read it to them. They must be worried, and I'm sure they miss you terribly.'

As he went out the door he heard Ben say, 'But *can* he write, Mother? He's only the coachman's son, isn't he?'

Matt flushed angrily. His strides quickened, carrying him swiftly in the direction of his hut. The little upstart, smug with his education at some rich man's school in Brisbane. It hadn't done much for his manners or his charm.

He took tobacco and papers from his shirt pocket to roll a cigarette, then sat on his doorstep, smoking. As he drew smoke into his lungs it seemed to calm him. He remembered Isabella's visit that day and the way she'd smiled at him, along with her obvious disappointment when his father had said Ben could help with their muster. Her admiration was like balm to his wounded pride. Would she care that he hadn't had much education? He doubted it. He was determined that it would be he, not Ben, who assisted the Jamiesons to bring in their cattle.

As Matt strode away Louise glared at her younger son, dismayed by this streak of maliciousness that she'd never seen in him before. 'I didn't much care for that remark, Ben,' she said coldly.

'Why? What's so special about Matt Jones?' He stared at her, his face flushing. 'When I was in town last time, I ran into Bert Smith, the barman at the Banana Hotel. He mentioned how Matt had asked him for directions out here. He asked if he was some relation of ours. Why would he say that?'

Louise's stomach churned. So people were noticing the family likeness. She knew the man in question, an unsavoury type. No doubt he would be the first to make coarse observations.

What should she say to Ben? She knew she eventually must tell him the truth, but the part of her that wanted his love and respect shrank from it, and now hardly seemed the appropriate time for confessions.

She hesitated, but Ben made it easy for her. 'Forget it, Mother,' he muttered, swinging away from her and heading for his bedroom.

Troubled, Louise watched him go. It was almost as if he wasn't ready to hear what she might have to say. Guilt knifed through her. Much as she wanted to love her sons equally, he had full reason to be jealous. But Matt was the son she'd lost, and his presence now was new and precious to her. She sometimes found herself comparing the two boys and hated herself for it. Ben was at an awkward age and it was up to her to make amends, to suppress this favouritism she knew she was showing to her firstborn, before the situation spun out of control.

As for Lloyd—he didn't speak of his feelings, but she sensed his quiet pleasure in having both his sons working by his side. She wondered if he was aware of the rivalry that had sprung up between the boys.

She joined her husband in the sitting room, taking up her embroidery and setting the lamp so it would throw light on her work. Lloyd looked up from his newspaper and smiled at her. 'Has Ben gone to bed? D' you fancy an early night too?'

She made an effort to cast off her worries. She would talk to Lloyd about their sons, but not right now when he had that gleam in his eye. 'I've only just picked up my fancywork,' she countered lightly, teasing him a little.

'Well, I'm going to bed.' He passed by her chair, running his hand caressingly over her shoulder. 'Are you coming soon?'

She smiled up at him, setting the needle into the fabric and folding it carefully. 'I'll be there in a moment.'

Her husband's easy invitation and her own response were things she'd never take for granted again. After Rose's death she'd wallowed in a melancholy so deep she could hardly bear to have Lloyd touch her. At the time it was as if she'd been struggling through quicksand, with all the pressures and anxieties of everyday life distorted until they threatened to suck her under. She suspected he'd strayed at one stage, but at the time she hadn't felt strong enough to confront him with it. Now she preferred not to dwell on that or let it spoil their renewed closeness.

She picked up the lamp and used it to light her way to the outside lavatory. Once in their bedroom she undressed in the flickering shadows, conscious of Lloyd lying against the pillows, watching her. As she was about to slip into her nightgown his voice came softly out of the darkness. 'You don't need that.'

She turned and smiled, feeling a little thrill of anticipation. Draping the garment over a chair, she joined him in bed wearing nothing but her camisole and drawers. 'I thought you wanted an early night.'

He pulled her close, murmuring against her ear, 'I meant early to bed. Not early to sleep.'

His body was firm and muscular under her hands and his mouth on her lips and breast still had the power to rouse her. Louise's ready response didn't shame her. She knew how empty a marriage could be if the physical side of it was lacking, how divisive it was when a man had needs his wife could not fulfil. Lloyd was forty-five years old, and if he was not the impatient and lusty twenty-three year-old who'd first bedded her, he was still gratifyingly passionate.

Afterwards Louise lay awake with her back curled into her sleeping husband, his arm heavy across her breasts. And as always once the pleasure was over she worried there might be another child, in spite of Lloyd's precautions. She was forty-years old, and she could never forget how Mrs Jamieson had died in childbirth after that last, presumably unplanned pregnancy when she was about Louise's age. She had left poor Isabella and her siblings without a mother and her husband Jock a widower for twenty lonely years. Although Louise had only four living children—three, in the eyes of the world—she'd given birth to five, and she had no desire to put her life and health at risk again.

Matt went to work on his father the next day. He'd taken the thoroughbred filly for a ride before breakfast, trotting and cantering her along the dirt track that led to the river crossing. As he set her down the bank the sun stole above the trees, sending fingers of light to define the deep ruts crisscrossing the sandy bed. Duchess snorted and shied, hesitating momentarily before the strong pressure of his legs forced her on down the bank. This early morning ride had become another kind of competition between him and Ben; whoever was first out of bed enjoyed the privilege of exercising her.

Back at the house, he unsaddled the sweating filly, rubbed her down and mixed her feed before carrying his tack to the saddle room. Spotting his father at the cow-yard, milking the two house cows, he seized the chance to catch him alone.

After a brief greeting, Lloyd turned back to his milking. Matt leant on the rails and watched his father who sat on a wooden block, head bent, hat brim brushing the bailed cow's red and white flank. Lloyd's calloused brown fingers squeezed the full teats, squirting twin streams of milk into the frothy contents of a metal bucket, the sweet scent of warm milk mingling with the earthy smells of cattle and fresh dung. A calf bleated plaintively for its mother and a butcherbird warbled from a nearby tree. With the warm sun beating upon his back, a sense of peace seeped into Matt, edging aside his impatience, his need for action. Memories of his childhood, when he'd sometimes helped the cowman at Fenham Manor with the milking, flooded back.

He brushed aside these whimsical thoughts and came straight to the point. 'Guv'nor, you mentioned sending Ben over to help the Jamiesons with their mustering.'

'Yeah, that's right.' Lloyd looked up at him curiously. 'What about it?'

'I wondered if I could go instead. I haven't been over there yet and I like seeing how other people do things.'

Lloyd studied him silently while his hands moved up and down on the teats. Suddenly he grinned. 'This hasn't got anything to do with young Isabella, eh?'

Matt grinned back, unabashed. 'She's a pretty girl.'

'And she was looking pretty hard at you, too.' He began stripping the teats, cupping the udder with one hand while he coaxed the last, creamy milk into the bucket. 'I guess it doesn't mean much to Ben. You'd better let him ride Duchess for a few mornings, though.'

He obviously knew what was going on. Matt hesitated. 'Ben seemed to like having me here at first, but he's not so keen now. He still don't know who I am, does he?'

Lloyd shook his head. 'I haven't told him yet. He's not going to like it. Can't you try an' get along?'

'Perhaps I should move on.'

Lloyd paused in his task, staring hard at Matt. 'Your mother will be heartbroken if you do. It means so much to her to have you here.' He turned back to the cow, his voice roughening. 'We lost a little girl a few years ago and I think it was all the tougher for her because she'd lost you as well.'

'What happened to your little girl?'

Lloyd rose and hung the bucket from a hook on the rail before slipping the leg rope off the cow. Releasing the tethered calf, he allowed it to push against its mother's side and bunt lustily at the empty teats. He pulled the pin from the head bail before answering, low-voiced. 'She drowned in the river. She was only missing for a few minutes before we started looking, but that was long enough. It's pretty hard to forgive yourself over something like that.'

Matt swallowed uneasily. 'I'm sorry.' Seeing that his father had finished, he vaulted over the top rail and opened the cow-yard gate to free the cows, so avoiding the need for further response. What was he supposed to say?

'I'll tell Ben you're going to Kilbride.' Lloyd slid through the rails and grabbed a milk bucket in each hand. 'I'd better tell him the rest of it, too. It's time he knew the truth.'

Hardening his resolve, Lloyd called his second son into the office that night, after Matt had gone to his quarters. 'I need to talk to you, Ben.'

Ben stood in the doorway, his face reflecting his uncertainty. 'What's going on?'

Lloyd angled his chair sideways to the desk, looking up at the lad. He decided to tackle the easier stuff first. 'Matt asked if he could do the mustering at Kilbride and I said he could. He hasn't been over there yet.'

Ben made a harsh sound in his throat. 'He's got his eye on Isabella. That's why he wants to go there.'

Lloyd raised an eyebrow. 'Have you got something against that?'

Ben coloured. 'He was skiting about the girls he's had. I wouldn't trust him with Isabella.'

Lloyd was silent, remembering his own experiences with the fairer sex. He'd been no angel, but he hadn't been in the same league as Charles Ashford. He hoped to God Matt wasn't following in his uncle's footsteps. He'd heard tales about Matt after his visits to town. Not about any women, thankfully, but it seemed he knew how to kick over the traces. The stories went that he was a wild one, drinking and gambling with some of the rougher element in town.

Ben shifted uncomfortably. 'Matt's supposed to be the working man around here. Why does he get treated like he's someone special?'

Lloyd sighed heavily. 'I think it's time you knew. This isn't easy for me to tell you, because it doesn't reflect well on either your mother or me.'

Ben's face whitened. 'What are you saying? That barman from the hotel said something; reckoned there was a family resemblance. He was lying, wasn't he? I can't see it.'

Lloyd managed a cynical smile. 'So they're talking already. I should have told you when Matt first arrived.' He paused and took a deep breath. 'He's your brother, Ben. He takes after the Ashfords in looks.'

Ben seemed to freeze, his mouth hanging open. 'But how...?'

'Your mother was working at Kilbride when I met her.' Not strictly true, but that would do for now. 'She was their governess; I think you know that. We fell in love, but your mother knew her family wouldn't approve of me. She'd run away when her brother Charles was supposed to take her to England. But bloody Charles Ashford found her and dragged her over there anyway.'

He shifted restlessly in his chair, fiddling with the papers on his desk. 'Neither of us knew there was a baby on the way. He was born over there in England and her parents took him from her.' He hesitated, clearing his suddenly husky throat. 'They gave him to the coachman and his wife to raise.'

Ben was staring at him, shame, anger and disbelief warring on his face. For a long, heartrending moment he held his father's gaze. 'This baby—it was Matt?'

Lloyd nodded.

'And—you weren't married?'

Lloyd shook his head.

'Do you mean, all this time I've had an older brother and you never thought to tell me?' With every word Ben's voice rose higher, his face pinched with fury. He slammed his fist on the desk, making the ink well rattle in its stand. 'I thought I had a family I could be proud of, and you tell me this.' He swung on his heel and flung out the door, leaving his father looking helplessly after him.

Sick with the conviction that he'd just made a mistake, Lloyd turned and propped his elbows on the desk, pressing his face into his hands. Though what else he could have done he didn't know. In trying to do right by one son it seemed they were wronging the other.

He looked up when Louise came in and gently touched his arm. 'What's the matter, Lloyd? I could hear Ben from the other end of the house. What did you say to him?'

Lloyd grasped her hand in his, squeezing it briefly. 'I just told him about Matt. He didn't like it.' He rubbed his face tiredly. 'Our sins are coming back to haunt us, Louise.'

'Oh dear.' She frowned. 'Of course he had to be told, but I knew he wouldn't like it. He and Matt don't seem to be getting along.'

'He's jealous of Matt, that's the cold hard truth. Matt's older and game for anything. And we've treated him like a son—Ben was upset about that.' He looked up at her. 'He heard some gossip in town. Someone was wondering at the family likeness.'

'Yes, he mentioned that yesterday.' Louise pulled up a second chair and sat heavily, sighing. 'Imagine the talk if the truth comes out.'

'Tom won't need to be told until he comes home from school. I wouldn't put this in a letter.'

'No, you're right.'

'Matt asked me if he could do the mustering at Kilbride. It seems he's a bit sweet on Isabella.' Lloyd decided he wouldn't repeat Ben's opinion of his brother's womanising tendencies.

Louise smiled. 'I noticed them eyeing each other at Hannah's party. Perhaps she will entice him to stay here.'

Lloyd frowned. 'You know I warned you not to get your hopes up.'

'I know you did.' Louise laid a placating hand on his arm. 'If he leaves, so be it. That doesn't prevent me from hoping he'll stay. But for now, I had better try to talk to Ben.'

Ben's bedroom door was closed.

Louise knocked tentatively. 'Ben? May I speak with you, please?'

When there was no reply she opened the door to find him sitting on a chair by the window, staring out into the darkness. 'Ben.' She crossed to him and put her hand on his shoulder. He felt tense, unyielding, and he didn't look up or acknowledge her in any way. She was conscious of hard, sinewy muscle under her palm and, with a sudden sharp pang, she remembered the little boy who used to seek comfort in her arms. The years had flown by and now he was growing into a man.

'Ben.' She tried again. 'I know this has been a shock to you, but please don't feel you're being pushed aside. Having Matt returned to us means the world to your father and me to, but that doesn't make us love you any less.'

He turned and looked up at her, his eyes bleak in the dim light cast by the lamp on his dresser. 'I thought you and Dad were respectable and decent. How do you think this makes me feel? If people find out they won't stop talking.'

'I'm sorry. I wanted to spare you this. Your father and I loved each other. We were planning to marry, but your Uncle Charles found me and carried me off to England. I didn't know there was going to be a child until after we'd sailed. Not that there was any reasoning with Charles.'

'It makes me look like a fool. All this time the three of you knew, and I had no idea.' He moved away from her touch, his voice angry. 'You should have told me when Matt turned up.'

Louise drew a deep breath. 'I can see that now, but it's easy to know in hindsight. It's difficult to admit your past mistakes to your children. We wanted to set a good example, not flaunt our sins in your face.'

'It's a bit late for that, Mother. Perhaps this accounts for Matt's free and easy morals. He's only following in your footsteps.'

Dismay tugged at her. 'What do you mean, free and easy morals?'

Ben shrugged. 'He has an eye for the ladies, I know that much.'

Louise digested that in silence, wondering how much of Ben's rancour was prompted by jealousy. It was inevitable that Matt with his good looks should be successful with the opposite sex. She ached for Ben, who was overshadowed in so many ways by his older brother. What was a mother to do in a situation like this?

'Please, Ben, try to forgive us. I know it's been a shock to you and you must feel Matt is usurping your position as the elder son. But we won't forget that this has always been your home and your birthright.' Louise touched his shoulder again. 'We don't want to tell Tom until he comes home for Christmas, so in the meantime we'll keep this to ourselves. Hannah will need to know eventually, but not yet.'

'Whatever you reckon, Mother.' Ben shrugged off her hand, his voice sulky. 'I sure won't be spreading it around.'

Louise watched him for a moment, her heart twisting with love and compassion. She desperately wanted to pull him into her arms and reassure him with hugs and kisses, but suddenly that was impossible. He was no longer a child and for the moment he was beyond her reach.

Sighing, she turned away. She found Lloyd still sitting at the desk, a pile of bills in front of him, and stood in the doorway for a moment as he dipped a pen in the inkwell and laboriously filled out a blank cheque. With his limited education, writing didn't come easily to him, but she loved him for his dogged persistence. Crossing to his side, she slid her arms around his neck. He looked up enquiringly, pen poised in midair.

'How's Ben?'

'Not happy. It'll take him some time to adjust to this.'

'It was a shock, but he'll get over it. He had to know sometime.'

'Yes, I know.' Typical man, trying to make light of things. 'But I'm worried he'll resent Matt even more, now.'

Chapter Six

Isabella had always looked forward to the mustering. She wondered what was wrong with her this time. In readiness to start first thing the next morning, Andrew was fitting new shoes to her horse while she held the mare's head. But for some reason, she was unable to summon her usual anticipation.

She watched her brother's bent brown head as he hammered a nail through the wall of Fortune's hind hoof. Andrew propped the hoof against his aproned knee to twist off the sharp protruding end, his plain, serious face beaded with sweat, his lips pursed in concentration. This was the critical momen—should the mare suddenly jerk her leg free, that sharp end of nail was likely to tear Andrew's clothing or skin, or cut the animal's own legs.

Luckily Fortune behaved this time and did nothing to provoke Andrew's uncertain temper. Isabella often wondered if her brother was happy. If he had ever possessed a sense of humour, it hadn't survived the responsibilities of adulthood. He worked hard, and between disciplining his five children and placating his querulous wife, Clara, his home life was nothing to be envied.

'There's someone coming.' Andrew set down the hammer and reached for the clenching tool. He brushed back his hat and wiped his sleeve over his sweaty forehead. 'Wasn't Ben Kavanagh supposed to be coming over to help us?'

'Yes, he was.' Isabella squinted against the glare, studying the approaching horseman. 'But it's not Ben.' She struggled to keep her voice even. 'It's Matt Jones.'

'That's the Pom they've got working there? I wonder why Lloyd sent him? I hope he knows what he's doing.'

'I'm sure he does. He's been there a few months now.' She couldn't quite keep the excited tremble from her voice and Andrew glanced up at her, his expression sceptical. He set down the horse's hoof and straightened as Matt drew rein beside them and swung out of the saddle.

'Good day, Miss Jamieson.'

'Good afternoon, Mr Jones.' Isabella treated him to her best welcoming smile, thinking how splendid he looked in his striped Crimean shirt and slim-fitting moleskins. 'This is my brother, Andrew.'

'How do you do, Mr Jamieson?' Matt was suitably polite. 'I was told to be ready for an early start in the morning.'

Andrew nodded. 'Pleased to meet you, Matt. We start at daylight. You can put your horse in the yard with a bit of hay and throw your swag in the men's quarters over there.'

As he began to turn away, Isabella added, 'And you may join Father and me for supper tonight, Mr Jones.'

'Aye, thank you, Miss Jamieson.' He touched his hat to her in a courteous gesture. 'What time might that be?'

'Seven o'clock.' She watched him lead his horse to the yards, spurs jingling on his booted heels. Suddenly the immediate future was fraught with promise.

Matt arrived for supper looking scrubbed, his hair slicked wetly back, his clothes clean. Isabella was glad she had found the time to bathe and put on a fresh gown after helping Elsie, their aboriginal cook and housekeeper, to prepare the evening meal.

After saying grace, her father carved the roast leg of mutton while she served vegetables from covered dishes onto their plates. As they ate she set about satisfying her curiosity.

'Whereabouts in England are you from, Mr Jones?'

'Devon.' He took his plate from her, picked up the sauce boat, and poured gravy over his mutton. 'I grew up at Fenham Manor, the Ashford estate. Have you heard of it?'

He looked at both of them and Jock Jamieson nodded, his eyes suddenly wary. 'Mrs Kavanagh was an Ashford. I know that much.'

Isabella turned to Matt, surprised. 'I didn't realize you had a connection with Mrs Kavanagh, Mr Jones.'

He cleared his throat. 'Me father was the coachman at Fenham Manor, and when I decided to come to Australia they found me the address for Squire's son. That's Mr Charles Ashford, of Banyandah, near Rockhampton. I worked there for a couple of months. When I wanted to leave Mr Ashford sent me on here.'

'What did you do at Fenham Manor?'

'I was a groom in the stables.' He smiled at Isabella, his dark eyes holding hers a second longer than necessary, his fork poised in midair. 'It was different from this, a lot different. Exercising the Ashfords' fancy horses, mixing the feeds, mucking out stables, like. I love working with horses but mustering cattle's a lot more fun. I've been learning how to throw a micky and cut out a beast.'

'Ye have a good teacher, lad,' Jock commented, sipping at a cup of black tea. 'Lloyd Kavanagh's one o' the best when it comes to horses and cattle. He taught my boys everything they know. I grew up on a wee farm in Scotland and we rounded up our cattle on foot.'

Matt grinned. 'Aye, it's the same in Devon. The cows are so quiet they'll hardly get out of your way.' He turned to Isabella. 'I hear you're a good hand in the mustering camp yourself.'

Isabella's face heated. 'I've grown up with it, as my brothers did. I love the mustering. My sister, Mercy, keeps telling me to act like a lady.'

Jock shook his head. 'Mercy forgets she was just like ye when she was a lass.'

'Do you have many brothers and sisters, Miss Jamieson?'

The gleam of interest in his dark eyes was enough to make her head spin. 'Three brothers and four sisters,' she managed. She pushed back her chair and began to collect their plates, using the activity to collect herself. 'I'm the youngest by seven years and they all say I'm spoilt.'

He grinned up at her. 'I was an only child, so I was probably spoilt, too.'

She took the crockery to the kitchen for Elsie to wash and brought bowls of creamed rice and stewed prunes back to the table. Matt ate the dessert with obvious appreciation, leaning back in his chair with a replete sigh when he was finished. 'That was delicious, Miss Jamieson. Thank you for the meal.'

A thrill of pleasure tingled her spine. 'I can't claim all the credit. Elsie's a wonderful help in the kitchen.'

The next morning they ate an early breakfast. Isabella and Elsie packed lunches while the men brought horses to the yards and saddled their mounts for the day. When she joined the men at the yards, Isabella noticed Matt eyeing her divided skirt. He looked surprised when she swung into a conventional stock saddle, unassisted and with as much ease as a man, and she wondered if he had seen a woman riding astride before.

She supposed it wasn't the done thing in England, where, she imagined, only upper-class women would have the opportunity to ride. Even here in the bush, older women rode side-saddle and riding astride was still frowned on by many. For the sake of her reputation she preferred to use a side-saddle in town, but here on the property riding astride was far more practical.

The sun was not long up when they rode away from the homestead. The paddock they were to muster was at the farthest end of the property and it would take a couple of hours to reach it. Andrew and her father took the lead, leaving Isabella in Matt's company.

She felt his gaze on her and lifted her chin defiantly. 'Haven't you seen a woman riding astride before, Mr Jones?'

He shrugged, his eyes twinkling. 'Not a respectable lady, at any rate. It must be more the thing for mustering, though.'

'It certainly is. I'm sure side-saddles were invented by men to keep women at a disadvantage.'

He raised his eyebrows. 'You sound like one of them female suffragettes, Miss Jamieson.'

She tossed her head. 'I believe in equal rights for women. Don't you?'

'Can't say I've thought much about it.'

'They're talking about giving women the vote in South Australia.' She gave him a challenging look. 'Letting them stand for Parliament, too. I'm sure it won't be long before we have the vote here in Queensland.'

His mouth curved in an expression of good-humoured tolerance. 'I suppose we'll all be governed by a pack of women soon. Perhaps they'll do a better job of it, too.'

Isabella smiled, encouraged by his seeming acceptance of the idea. 'What about England?' she asked. 'Have women been granted the vote there?'

Matt shook his head. 'I think they're trying hard to get it. But there must be more important things, like better wages for workers. There's too many rich people living off our sweat and paying us a pittance for it.'

A note of bitterness crept into his voice, making Isabella glance sharply at him. 'What was it like, working at an English mansion?'

He shrugged. 'I was just a servant over there. That's what I like about Australia; someone like me has a chance to do better. I want a run of me own someday.'

'Are the Ashfords anything like Mrs Kavanagh? She's very much a lady, but I can't imagine her living in a manor house with a lot of servants.'

He shook his head. 'She's nothing' like her mother or her father. In looks, I suppose, but not otherwise. We servants were nothing to them. Charles Ashford is more like his parents than Mrs Kavanagh is.'

'It's hard to believe that she worked here, as a governess. That was before her brother Charles found her and took her to England.'

He didn't respond and Isabella suddenly remembered her promise to Maggie not to gossip about Mrs Kavanagh. She cringed inwardly. The Kavanagh's station hand was the last person she should be discussing her with.

After that, their conversation seemed to lose its spark and she was almost relieved when her father and Andrew drew up at a set of sliprails. 'This is the paddock we're going to muster, Matt.' Andrew said. 'You and I can check the other side of the creek. You go with Father, Bella.'

Of course they wouldn't send her off with Matt. She tried to tell herself it was a good thing. At least she'd have time to regain her composure, to get past the awkward silence which had risen between them.

By lunch time they had about two hundred cattle in a mob— cows and calves, with the occasional big cleanskin which had been missed in the last muster. Isabella noticed one of these, a micky bull approaching two years old, which had obviously not been yarded before. The micky stared wildly at the horsemen, and Isabella knew it was only a matter of time before fear overtook its herding instinct.

When they tried to yard the mob into a small holding paddock, the pressure proved too much for the young bull. As it left the mob with head held high, Matt spurred his horse in pursuit. He galloped straight onto the shoulder of the beast, attempting to turn it back to the herd while keeping clear of its sharp horns. When it refused to yield, he leapt from his horse mid-stride and grasped the micky's tail, flipping it neatly off its feet as it swung around to confront him. Matt whipped a leather strap from his waist and immobilized the beast by tying the two back legs together. The Jamiesons brought the mob up close, allowing him to release the subdued animal, which now seemed only too willing to rejoin its own kind.

Isabella watched Matt swing back into the saddle, glowing with admiration. She had seen her brothers do similar things in the past, but these days Andrew seemed to avoid such dangerous stunts, complaining that he didn't bounce the way he used to.

Her father, sitting his horse close by, chuckled. 'For a new chum, he does all right. I was a wee disappointed Kavanagh hadn't sent Ben over, but this lad's just as good.'

Isabella didn't reply. She thought it safer not to tell her father how pleased she was with the current arrangement.

Once the cattle were confined in the holding paddock, they took a break beside a nearby waterhole to eat their lunch. After filling their quart pots, the three men gathered wood for a fire while Isabella borrowed Matt's matches and set alight a pile of twigs and dry grass. Sitting under a shady ironbark, her back against its rough trunk, she listened to the men talk horses and cattle while they waited for the quart pots to boil. Once the water was bubbling, tea leaves and sugar were added to make a hot, sweet brew which helped to wash down their dry corned beef sandwiches. The two cattle dogs, Bonnie and Blucher, crept close to beg for crusts, their tails thumping the dusty ground in mute appeal.

It was nearly dusk when they set off for home, turning their weary horses down the same track they had followed that morning. The cattle were safely penned in the holding paddock, ready for driving to the stockyards the next day.

Andrew returned to his own home and family but Elsie had the evening meal ready for the three of them when they finally stepped inside the house. It was too late to bathe and change before dinner and Isabella felt acutely conscious of her dusty, sweaty clothes as she sat across from Matt. It was fortunate that he was just as dirty. Although she doubted he was as tired as she, he excused himself as soon as the meal was over.

The next morning, they saddled fresh horses and retraced their steps of the day before. After collecting a few missed cattle which had come to the waterhole to drink, they released the main mob from the holding paddock and turned them towards home. Dust rose in billowing, choking clouds and cows and calves, separated in the confusion, bellowed frantically to each other .

Andrew rode in the lead to steady the flightier animals. Left as always to bring up the tail, Isabella muttered uncomplimentary things about men. It was tedious work, particularly as the day grew hotter and the calves tired. The dogs sneaked up to nip the heels of anything that lagged, but even this encouragement wasn't enough to keep the smallest calves going, and several had to be left behind with their mothers. Isabella grew hot, thirsty and cross, as she dealt with angry cows which, in their zeal to protect their calves from the dogs, made the job not only difficult but sometimes dangerous. When Matt left his position on the wing to help, she could have kissed him with gratitude.

As they neared the homestead, one small calf slunk off under a tree, its flanks heaving and tongue lolling. Isabella decided to carry it on her horse for the remainder of the trip. She dismounted and tried to lift it onto the pommel of her saddle but her mount was uneasy about the whole business, flicking his ears back and moving away at the crucial moment.

Next thing, Matt was beside her, swinging out of the saddle and dropping his reins. Isabella, struggling with the weight of the inert calf as she held it chest high, gratefully relinquished it to him. His arms brushed her as he wrapped them around the calf and she was conscious of the closeness of his body as he effortlessly lifted the animal. He steadied her gelding with soothing words and a gentle hand on his neck. The horse stood obediently as he draped the calf over his withers with its legs dangling either side. He held it in place, one hand on the gelding's rein, as Isabella mounted.

'Thank you.' She smiled down at him, slightly piqued that the horse had behaved for him, but privately acknowledging he had a way with them. 'It's a bother being so short.'

His teeth glinted white in his dusty face as he grinned. 'Don't they say good things come in small parcels?'

She smiled back. 'I've been told that before.'

It was lunchtime when they reached the homestead and herded the cattle into the stockyards. After eating, they set about drafting—separating the calves, weaners and culls from the main herd. Andrew took the job of drafting the cattle through the pound, while Isabella, her father and Matt each operated a gate. Matt also assisted Andrew to drive a fresh mob of cattle into the forcing yard whenever it was empty. Jock Jamieson, at almost sixty, had long since handed over the strenuous tasks to his son.

The micky Matt had thrown the day before hadn't dared to leave the mob again, entering the yard with the press of other bodies surrounding him. Now he stayed at the back of the forcing yard until it was almost empty, at last rushing into the pound in the company of some older calves which were big enough to wean. The close confines of the small yard and the proximity of people seemed to panic him as he raced about the pound, crashing into the rails and snorting his fear. In order to separate him from the weaners, Andrew was forced to let him back into the larger yard.

Once alone, he became aggressive, threatening to charge when Andrew tried to bring him up. Isabella watched nervously as Matt came to her brother's assistance, taunting the young bull into charging him and then running at full speed into the pound with the animal close behind him. Matt seemed to fly up the rails with the micky's raking horns missing his boots by inches. The animal snorted and moved back, staring wild-eyed and tossing his head at the lad on the rails above him while Andrew slammed the gate to enclose him.

'I think we'll leave him there until we're ready to brand him,' Andrew said. 'I know we can get him into the crush from here.'

Isabella turned to Matt as he swung over the rails and dropped to the ground. 'That was close. He didn't get you, did he?'

Matt shook his head. 'He snorted all over me boots, that's all'

Isabella glanced involuntarily at his dusty, spattered boots and back up the length of his long trousered legs. Suddenly she realized what she was doing and looked quickly up at his face, hoping he hadn't noticed. But his eyes, dark and watchful, met hers and hot colour flooded her cheeks. She turned away in confusion, hoping she'd only imagined that speculative look in his eye.

The next morning was another early start to do the branding before the worst of the heat. Isabella didn't participate, staying at the house and busying herself with some cleaning. Her father indulged her in most things, but he put his foot down about this. Ladies were not supposed to witness the branding, even though she knew how it was done.

A fire was lit in an upright length of hollow log to heat the brands. The calves were caught with ropes on one front and one hind leg and pulled over onto their side with the aid of pulleys to hold them tight. Then an earmark was punched in one ear, the hot brands applied, and the bull calves castrated. She knew it was the castrating that her father objected to her seeing, and in this instance she was content to oblige him. She was determined to show Matt she was a lady in spite of the often rough work she did.

After lunch the cattle had to be returned to their paddock, another four-hour drive that included the same battles with cows and calves as the previous morning, followed by the long ride home. Although it was tiring work, Isabella found it satisfying. It made her appreciate simple pleasures, like a long cool drink of water when her throat was parched with thirst and a nourishing meal when she was ravenously hungry. Even sinking onto her cool sheets at night was a simple, exquisite pleasure, a welcome rest for aching muscles. Her only regret was being too busy to spend much time with Matt, who always disappeared promptly after supper in the evenings.

The next paddock to be mustered was the one adjoining Myvanwy where her father had noticed some of the Kavanagh's stray cattle. It was smaller than the first paddock and closer to home, which meant they had cattle in the stockyards and were back at the homestead by six o'clock. When supper was over that night she decided to take matters with Matt into her own hands.

He had lingered at the table, talking to her father as she and Elsie cleared the dishes. Guessing he was about to leave, she gathered up the tablecloth and walked outside onto the veranda to shake it over the railing. She stood there for a moment, looking up at the clear night sky, pinpricked with a profusion of stars. The bellows of cattle drifted from the stockyards, accompanied by wafting dust. Then her patience was rewarded by something closer to hand--a step on the wooden boards behind her. She turned, her heart thumping.

'Isabella,' he murmured, looking down at her. It was the first time he'd used her Christian name and it sounded different with those soft English vowels. She could just make out his smile in the darkness. 'I was wondering when I could catch you alone.'

She stared up at him, clutching the tablecloth to her like a shield. Suddenly she was bereft of words.

'Will you come for a walk with me?'

'I have to wash up first.' She hesitated. 'Can you wait for me in the garden?' Her father knew they were out here together; much better to slip away when he thought she was in bed. 'The emu apple tree's a good spot.'

He nodded. 'I'll be there.'

Isabella raced through the dishes, wiping as Elsie washed, little caring if they were properly dry. Once the job was done she went to her bedroom and slipped onto the verandah through the French doors. As she walked through the back garden to the emu apple tree at the front, there was just enough moon to light her way, and for once she forgot to be cautious about snakes. Matt was waiting patiently, leaning against the fence, his cigarette a bright tip in the darkness. He turned quickly, throwing down the cigarette and grinding it under his heel.

'You were quick.' His teeth gleamed in his dark face as he clasped her hands and drew her towards him. 'I just wanted to tell you, today was me birthday.'

Her fingers tingled at his touch. 'Oh, I'm sorry. You should have told us. Happy birthday.' Her voice shook and her breath seemed to catch in her throat. 'How old were you today?'

'Twenty-one. And how old are you, Isabella?'

'I'm twenty-one, too.' She was four months older than him, but she didn't tell him that. It didn't matter, surely.

He pulled her closer until she could smell the tobacco on his breath. His hands released hers to slip about her waist. 'Can I kiss you?'

She nodded, too excited to think of resisting. This was most improper, being alone with him in the dark without her father's knowledge, but she didn't care. Tipping her face up, she met him halfway as he bent his head to hers. His lips moved over hers, nudging them apart, and in spite of the fact that her head only came to his shoulder, it was as if they magically fitted together. She had kissed a boy once before, and it had been an awkward, disappointing affair of clashing teeth and bumping noses. There was nothing awkward about this, and she settled closer into his arms with a blissful sigh, winding her own around his neck.

At last he drew back, smiling down into her eyes. 'I've been wanting to do that since the first time I saw you.'

'You mean on the coach?' Isabella thrilled, remembering how she'd watched him that day when he wasn't looking, and how handsome she had thought him. But then she hadn't really expected to see him again, and much less had she anticipated being in his arms like this.

He took the next kiss deeper, so their saliva mingled and his tongue touched hers, but instead of being repelled Isabella was strangely excited. When he let her go she wanted to cling to him, to stay with him and see where this would lead them. But some instinct for self-preservation made her draw back.

'It's late, 'she murmured. 'I must go in.'

'Aye.' His breathing sounded unnaturally loud in the still night air. 'You'd better go. Will you meet me here tomorrow night?'

'Yes, Matt, of course.' Wild horses wouldn't keep her away. She smiled up at him. 'I'll see you in the morning.'

Her last waking thought, and the first the next morning, was the memory of his mouth on hers and the press of his body against hers. As she helped Elsie prepare breakfast, she found herself listening for him. She was putting out their bowls of steaming porridge when he came through the door. Her heart jolted, their eyes meeting for a moment before he turned to greet her father, and it was as if they'd exchanged some secret message. With their kisses last night, an invisible barrier had been crossed.

As they ate breakfast, Isabella glanced at her father, wondering if he had noticed anything. But he applied himself to his porridge in apparent unconcern. He had withdrawn into himself over the years, seeking solace in his bible and the outdated newspapers the mailman brought once a week. It was obvious he liked Matt, and perhaps he would not disapprove if he realized Matt was courting her; but she honestly doubted if he suspected anything more than friendship between them.

By lunchtime, they had drafted the second mob of cattle through the yards and branded the calves. Back at the homestead, Matt caught her alone in the dining room and put his hand on her arm, his face intense. 'Can you still meet me tonight?'

Isabella nodded, her breath catching. 'The same place, after I've washed up.'

He squeezed her arm briefly and turned away as her father walked in. Isabella scuttled back to the kitchen lest her flushed cheeks betray her.

The branding was finished, the cattle returned to their paddock. Three Myvanwy strays remained in the yard, waiting for Matt to drive them home the next day. Tonight would be his last night and Isabella was acutely conscious of this as she joined him under the emu apple tree.

He didn't even speak, just pulled her up close against him and took her mouth with his. Anticipation had fuelled the fire until now it blazed fiercely, taking Isabella past her natural caution. As the kiss went on she was acutely aware of Matt's slim hard body against hers, the press of his thighs and the caressing movements of his fingers on her spine. His hand travelled over her rib cage, stroking her skin until her nerve endings tingled. He trailed his mouth across her cheek, nibbling at her ear, moving down her neck before going back to her mouth. His hand moved under her breast, cupping it, and Isabella pulled away, shaking her head.

'No, Matt!' She was startled. This wasn't supposed to happen. Surely he knew she wasn't some light skirt with whom he could have his way. Perhaps she shouldn't be meeting him out here and letting him kiss her like this.

'I'm sorry.' His voice was husky, his breathing uneven. 'You make me lose me head, Isabella.'

At his words, a flood of response coursed through her. She couldn't imagine one of the boys who'd partnered her at dances saying anything like that. She had the feeling they'd be just as scared of further intimacy as she was. Matt was so worldly, in spite of his youth.

She let him kiss her once more and then drew back. 'I must go inside now.'

'Aye.' He grasped her fingers to delay her. 'When can I see you again?'

'It'll be Christmas in a few weeks. We usually get together with the Kavanaghs over the Christmas season. I'm sure we'll see each other then.'

Matt stood there under the tree, watching her retreating back, fighting the need that had him in its grip. He hadn't been with a girl for months, but Isabella wasn't the type to tumble under a hedge with him as Eliza had. Unconventional she might be, and her father was lenient to the point of neglect, but she was still a lady. There lay his problem. It was too soon to think of marriage—he was only just twenty-one, for God's sake, too young to be tied down. There were lots of things he wanted to do, adventures to be had. But the sort of female who would happily provide the satisfaction he needed was generally unappealing to him.

He had known girls as pretty as Isabella, but none he liked or admired as much, and that untried yet eager way she'd responded to his kisses had stirred him deeply. If he wasn't ready to commit himself, he probably shouldn't be hanging around, but he knew he wasn't sufficiently noble or selfless to walk away. He was enjoying this little interlude, and he planned to see where it led him.

Chapter Seven

Christmas arrived with hot, dry winds that sucked what little moisture remained from the parched soil. There had been no rain for months and drought had seized the land in its unrelenting grip. Although Matt had never particularly liked the cold weather, he found himself thinking wistfully of Yuletide in England, of roasting chestnuts over a glowing fire and enjoying the hot rich food that seemed totally inappropriate now in the hundred degree heat. For the first time he felt homesick and was glad he had written to his foster family.

The Joneses had sent him a Christmas card with a picture of a horse-drawn sleigh travelling over the snow, and had included a letter dictated to Mrs Evans, the aging housekeeper from the Manor. They were missing him, Mrs Evans had written in her bold scrawl, and hoped he was happy with the Kavanaghs and not causing trouble for them.

Matt's mouth twisted wryly. He knew his parents—he was used to thinking of the Kavanaghs as such now—were happy to have him, and if Ben couldn't get used to it that was his bad luck.

Christmas Day was spent at Myvanwy, with just the immediate family. Tom, an easy-going fifteen-year-old, was home from boarding school. His father had told him the truth about Matt soon after his return, and the boy seemed to have accepted it without animosity, though sometimes Matt noticed him studying them all with a look of bafflement.

The Christmas tree was an oak from the river, a poor imitation of the fir trees to which Matt was accustomed. They waited to cut it on Christmas Eve, since it would wilt rapidly in the heat. Hannah was young enough to be excited about the festive season and the imminent arrival of Father Christmas, accompanying Matt and Tom as they hitched one of the draught horses to the sled to bring home the tree. Ben declined to accompany them, preferring to spend time with the young horse he was handling.

Tom shook his head. 'What's wrong with Ben these days? He's as cranky as an old scrub bull.'

Matt didn't comment. He guessed Tom would work out what the problem was eventually.

For Boxing Day, they had been invited to the Jamiesons. It was apparently tradition for the two families to spend Boxing Day together, and last year it had been the Kavanaghs' turn to play host, so this year they were meeting at Kilbride. Everyone brought their leftovers from Christmas dinner to share. Louise Kavanagh told Matt that Isabella had included him in the invitation, thinking he had no family of his own to visit.

Matt smiled crookedly at his mother. 'If only she knew.'

Louise flushed. 'You know I'd like to acknowledge you as our son, Matt, but it would cause such a scandal. Ben's upset and ashamed enough, without us setting the whole countryside afire with gossip.'

Matt could have said more, could have pointed out the advantages Ben had already enjoyed as the son of a middle-class grazier—advantages he'd been denied, growing up as the coachman's son at Fenham Manor. But he kept his silence. He consoled himself with the knowledge that Isabella had wanted him to come to Kilbride and had managed to find an excuse to invite him.

For the first time, Matt met Isabella's two oldest sisters, Mercy and Maggie, and their husbands. Mercy's husband, Alfred Forbes, was a harsh-featured man, red, spidery veins feathering the coarse skin of his cheeks and nose. He had the look of a man who drank hard and lived hard, and he seemed incongruously out of place amongst the sober Jamiesons, hardly mixing with the other men. Mercy was thin and work-worn, her face tired and strained. Once Matt noticed her watching Louise Kavanagh with a strange, almost hostile expression, and wondered why.

Maggie was very different from her sisters; soft and plump, with white lady's hands that contrasted strongly to Mercy's freckled, wrinkled claws and Isabella's strong, capable ones. Maggie lived in Rockhampton, Matt remembered Isabella telling him, and Horace, her bank manager husband, had hands just as soft and pale, to go with his pallid, pudgy face.

Absent were two other sisters and two brothers who lived further afield, Matt understood. He was relieved they weren't all present. The house seemed to be bulging at the seams as it was.

Maggie's children mixed rowdily with Hannah and Andrew's five offspring, while Andrew's wife Clara watched with sharp eyes, annoying the other women with her fond tolerance for her own children's bad behaviour and her criticism of everyone else's. Mercy's brood of four were older; gawky adolescents, along with Tom caught halfway between the careless play of their younger cousins and the buzz of chatter issuing from the adults. Matt was the outsider as he observed them all, feeling suddenly conscious of his own lonely childhood.

A couple of times he noticed Mercy watching Lloyd Kavanagh when she thought no-one was looking, her face wearing a hungry, yearning expression that made him wonder. Perhaps there was some past history there.

After the huge dinner of ham and cold roast meats left over from the day before, along with reheated Christmas pudding and custard, the more mature members of the party seemed inclined to do little else but sit and doze in the heat. Bored and restless, Matt asked Isabella to go walking with him to the river. Hannah overheard and pleaded to accompany them, but Matt was firm.

'Not this time, Hannah. You play with the other kids.'

'But we could all come...'

Inwardly he shuddered, envisaging not only having his and Isabella's privacy interrupted but trying to keep this lively mob of children from falling in the river. 'No, Hannah,' he told her sternly. Her little face fell, for he usually indulged her, but he hardened his heart. She'd get over it.

Down at the river, he led Isabella to a shady tree by the water. As they sat on a patch of short, couch grass, grey, yellow-headed quarrions flew with fluttering wings from the muddy edge where they had gathered to drink. A flock of black ducks scudded to the far end of the waterhole, followed by a clutch of tiny ducklings.

Isabella pulled off her hat and fanned herself. 'Oh, it's hot,' she complained. 'This must be a very different Christmas for you, Matt.'

'Aye, it is that. In Devon we'd be sitting around a roaring fire, roasting chestnuts. We always hoped for a white Christmas, but often we didn't get the first snow until later.'

She searched his face. 'Do you miss it?'

He plucked a stalk of grass and popped it into the corner of his mouth, chewing thoughtfully. 'A bit. This is the first time I've been homesick. But I like Australia and I mean to stay here.'

Pleasure and relief lit her face. Had she been worried he might return to England?

Desire coursed through him. She was looking particularly pretty today in a soft white blouse with a high neck and deep ruffles at the shoulders. He caught her chin in his fingers. 'Besides, I don't want to leave you.'

'I'm glad,' she whispered.

Hearing the little catch of breath in her throat, his body responded to her obvious emotion. He gathered her close and kissed her, caressing the points of her shoulders with his hands, then sliding one of them down her spine to the small of her back while he fondled the nape of her neck with the other. He dragged her hard against him, squashing her breasts against his chest, moving his lips to her ear and neck before returning to her mouth with increased passion. He kissed her endlessly, oblivious to the bright afternoon and the Christmas gathering up at the house, aware only of his hot desire and the pliant girl in his arms.

'Auntie Isabella!'

Matt jerked his head up, looking up the bank. Hannah and Maggie's oldest daughter Emily stood there, staring at them, the vanguard of a troop of children, while Maggie and Mercy scrambled down the steep path behind them. Hoping the two women hadn't seen them, he set Isabella away from him. He scrambled to his feet, drawing her with him.

Maggie smiled at them a little uncertainly, obviously taking in their flushed, rumpled state. Mercy was stony-faced and silent while her sister gabbled. 'The girls wanted to come down. Sorry to interrupt. It's so hot in the house.'

Isabella looked flustered. 'That's all right. Sit here with us while the children play.'

'Aye,' Matt murmured, doing his best to be gracious. 'It's cool here in the shade.'

That was the end of their time alone, of course. They sat and chatted with Isabella's sisters for an hour or so, while the children splashed and paddled at the edge of the water and skipped stones across the still green surface. By four o'clock Maggie insisted they all return to the house, as she had planned a singsong around the piano.

She and Louise took turns to play, while the adults—with the exception of Alfred, who seemed to have disappeared—and the older children gathered around to sing Christmas carols. As the voices joined in singing *Silent Night, Away in a Manger* and *Hark, The Herald Angels Sing,* Matt was reminded of the carollers who trooped from house to house back in England, rugged up in coats and woollen scarves against the cold. He started feeling homesick again and distracted himself by watching Isabella, remembering how that pert, pretty mouth, now opened in song, had responded to his kisses.

Then, with dusk approaching, Lloyd sent Matt out to harness the horses to the buggy. As he stepped out into the warm evening, a flock of cockatoos screeched overhead, on their way to roost for the night; and any fleeting comparison to England evaporated in the dry air.

Isabella expected her sisters to say something about the little interlude they'd interrupted, but it wasn't until they were washing the dishes after supper that night that they were finally alone. Elsie had been given the afternoon off and Alfred Forbes had caught his horse and taken himself home, leaving his family to follow the next day. No-one was sorry to see him go.

It was Maggie who introduced the subject, commenting in her gentle way, 'Matt's a handsome boy.' She smiled teasingly at her youngest sister as she took a tea towel from the rack near the stove. 'So you've finally found someone who takes your fancy.'

'Do you blame me?' Isabella decided to go along with the banter. 'As you say, he's so handsome, and charming into the bargain.'

'Handsome is as handsome does,' Mercy interjected sourly from the dishpan. 'You be careful of that boy, Bella. He looks like a ladies' man to me, and I've heard reports of him.'

Isabella's heart skipped a beat as she wiped a handful of cutlery. 'What sort of reports?'

'Alfred's seen him at the hotel, reckons he was as drunk as a lord. He was gambling as well, throwing his money around as if it grew on trees.'

'Alfred's a fine one to talk!' Isabella bristled indignantly, but inside her stomach was sick and seething with nerves. She'd guessed Matt was a bit wild, but that was different from having his failings coldly described to her.

'How old is he?' Maggie was always anxious to soothe troubled waters.

'He's just twenty-one.' Isabella took a stack of plates and put them in the dresser. 'He had his birthday at the beginning of December.'

'Well, he's got plenty of time to settle down, then. He's still sowing his wild oats.'

'Humph!' Mercy scrubbed furiously at a dirty saucepan. 'There's more than one way to sow wild oats, and I wouldn't be a bit surprised if he was hoping to sow a few with you, Bella.'

Isabella flushed, suspecting her sister spoke the truth. But nothing would make her admit that to her sisters. Instead she found herself defending him. 'He's done nothing to upset me.'

'I think we interrupted something this afternoon, by the look of you both.' Mercy's mouth twisted. 'Men are always after the one thing.'

'Mercy!' Maggie didn't look up from the pan she was wiping, her cheeks pink. 'That's not true of all men—Horace for one is a gentleman. Still, Bella, you shouldn't be allowing Matt to take liberties. It's easy to give a man the wrong impression.'

Of course, Isabella thought. She couldn't imagine Maggie's milksop Horace kissing Maggie the way Matt kissed her. Perhaps Matt was a bit wild, and perhaps he shouldn't be wanting what she knew he wanted from her, but he was exciting and wonderful and she didn't want to change him. At the same time, she couldn't help wondering how much experience he'd had. Surely he wasn't the sort to go with loose women; yet a suspicion that he knew exactly what he was doing disturbed her.

'I wish Father would take a bit more notice of what's going on.' Mercy had seemed to ignore Maggie's interjection. 'He's just doesn't keep an eye on you, Bella.' She was quiet for a moment, her face settling into grim lines. 'He was a bit like that with me, too, after Mother died. Seemed to bury himself in his bible.'

Thank goodness her father wasn't the anxious sort. 'It hasn't been easy for him. I think he still misses Mother after all these years.'

'Well, I wish he'd taken a bit more interest in me when I was your age,' retorted Mercy testily.

'You were already married when you were my age!'

'Yes, I know.' Mercy wiped the wooden table with her dishcloth and lifted the pan of dirty water in both hands. She began to carry it outside, pausing to say over her shoulder, 'I wish he'd stopped me.'

Isabella and Maggie exchanged speaking glances, feeling pity for Mercy. But what could they say?

Louise was relieved Boxing Day was over. She could never go to Kilbride without reliving those days when she had worked as governess to the Jamieson children, before Isabella was even born. Most of her memories of that time were good ones, but that ignominious day when Charles arrived and carried her away, after revealing that she was not Lucy Forrest as they had all believed her to be, remained a blot on her past. And when Mercy was present it always seemed as if her sins hadn't been forgotten.

Mercy would never forgive her lies, and nor would she ever forgive her for stealing Lloyd away from her. The woman never visited Myvanwy, and when the traditional Boxing Day gathering was held there, she was always absent. Her animosity on this occasion had marred the day for Louise. Disconcerting also was the way Mercy still watched Lloyd, after all these years.

Not that she could blame Mercy for being dissatisfied with her own circumstances. Her husband Alfred was a scoundrel, and her life was hard and lonely. Louise pitied her and wondered guiltily if Lloyd's marriage to her had influenced Mercy into consoling herself with an unsuitable man. Life in the bush was hard enough with droughts, floods and isolation to contend with, and Louise could not imagine surviving it without Lloyd, who had done his best through most of the difficult times.

And now they were facing another drought, along with the economic depression of which the papers seemed to be full. Fortunately they weren't in debt to the banks, and although far from wealthy, their property was large and fertile enough to provide a comfortable income. She pitied the smaller settlers, trying to wrest a living from a tiny patch of ground which would barely run enough stock to support them in the best of times.

She knew Lloyd was disappointed that the race meeting, usually held after Christmas, had been postponed until the weather conditions were more favourable. With the help of his sons he'd been training the filly, Duchess, for some months, and she thought it was important to keep enjoying these social functions, rather than becoming totally immersed in the drudgery that came with drought. Of course hay and grain was becoming more expensive and harder to obtain. Louise could only hope it rained soon, so all his preparation would not be wasted.

But the race meeting was a minor consideration in the overall scheme of things. Waterholes were drying daily and feed was becoming scarce. The cattle were losing condition, and already some of the weaker cows had died, leaving pitiful orphaned calves which battled to survive by stealing milk from other cows. Most of the stock had been forced to concentrate on the permanent water in the river, which increased grazing pressure on these areas. Almost every day Lloyd and his sons rode around the cattle, shifting animals from waterholes which were nearly dry, pulling some from the bog.

The Aborigine, Banjo, and his wife were now camped permanently on a creek at the far end of the property, pumping water. The men had dug a hole in the sandy creek bed, lining it with an old ship's tank which had the bottom cut out. Water from the sand seeped into the hole and Banjo used a whip--a lever set in a forked stick, with a weight on one end and a bucket attached to the other--to bail the water from this soak into a trough. One of Matt and Ben's regular tasks was to carry fresh supplies on a packhorse to the aboriginal couple.

Louise was relieved that the older boys appeared to have put aside their differences, at least temporarily. Tom seemed to act as intermediary between the two with his easy-going good humour. They obviously weren't yet friends, but at least there had been no open quarrels. Tom would soon be back at school, so she hoped things wouldn't degenerate again once he was gone.

As always, she dreaded Tom's return to school. He only came home twice a year, in June and at Christmas. It was always harder after the long Christmas holiday, when she was forced to adjust to his absence all over again. Fortunately he seemed happy at boarding school, settling better than Ben ever had. Ben had always had his heart in the bush, and she knew Myvanwy meant everything to him. She could understand his fear of Matt usurping his position here, and decided she must talk to Lloyd about that.

If Matt was ready to settle down, perhaps they should look at purchasing more land in the district. He was obviously sweet on Isabella and if they wanted to marry he would need a home of his own. Besides, this would be Tom's last year at school, and Myvanwy wasn't large enough to support the three boys.

When it was time for Tom to return to school, Lloyd took him to Banana to catch the coach to Westwood, from where he would take the train to Rockhampton and then the steamer to Brisbane.

Louise started Hannah back at lessons the same day, while Matt took a load of provisions to Banjo and his wife. Ben was off checking cattle at the other end of the property.

A hot wind was blowing, settling a layer of grit over the furniture which Louise had dusted and polished before Christmas. The air was brittle-dry, with no hint of rain, and Louise's hair was like straw, her skin drawn and tight. The view from the schoolroom window was depressing; a nearly-bare paddock with grey grass tussocks and straggling gums which had already shed most of their leaves in response to the drought. Much as she loved her home, at times like these she thought longingly of a holiday at the seaside with cool moist breezes blowing off the water. Perhaps she should suggest it to Lloyd, once it had rained. They hadn't been away for over a year, and now Matt was here, he and Ben would be able to take care of things in their absence.

She settled Hannah with her copybook and took out the handkerchief she was edging. As she looped her crotchet hook through the fine cotton she heard a dog bark and glanced out of the window, wondering if something was amiss. As usual Sally was the only dog left at home. The barking came again, more insistent, and she thought she heard a male voice. She could see nothing from the window, so she put down her work and went to the front veranda.

A man stood at the foot of the steps. He had evidently let himself through the house yard gate and shut it behind him, leaving Sally, her hackles raised, barking indignantly on the other side of the paling fence. Louise's heart sank.

The man was an unsavoury specimen with long, unkempt hair under a tattered hat, greying beard to mid-chest and threadbare, much-patched clothing. Even from this distance she could smell the rank odour of his body and clothes and was forced to suppress an urge to hold her handkerchief to her nose. The swag across his back confirmed his itinerant status. Why was it that such individuals never seemed to arrive when the menfolk were present?

Since the financial crisis and the failure of the banks in 1893, swagmen like this had become common, tramping the roads of the outback looking for work. Some of them were decent men fallen on hard times, but something about this fellow made the hairs prickle at the back of her neck.

'Good day, Missus.' He grinned up at her from the bottom of the steps, exposing broken, yellow stubs which must have once passed for teeth. 'Any chance o' a bit o' work?'

She would have preferred to send him on his way, but charity demanded she give him a chance. It was usually Banjo's job to chop the firewood, and with him away she always seemed to be nagging one of her sons to do it.

'There's wood to be chopped, if that suits you,' she said stiffly. 'The pile's out behind the kitchen, and the axe is beside it.' She pointed him in the general direction and stood watching while he sauntered off. He had a sly look to his eye which she didn't trust.

She went into the kitchen where Betsy was kneading bread dough, her plump brown arms dusted with flour. Betsy's mother was an Aboriginal woman, her father a white man who had never acknowledged her. She was caught between two worlds, neither at home with Banjo and his wife nor belonging in the white world that employed her. Though Betsy worked cheerfully and never complained, Louise often reflected how lonely she must be. No wonder girls like her were easy pickings for unscrupulous men.

'A swaggie has just arrived,' she told the girl. 'I've asked him to cut some wood. Keep out of sight if you can—I don't like the look of him.' Crossing to the window, she watched him set down his swag and pick up the axe. Shrugging, she turned back to the school room. She could only hope he wasn't as bad as first impressions suggested.

At lunchtime Louise checked the thermometer in the hallway. One hundred degrees. Easing her high collar around her sticky neck, she spared a moment's thought for the swaggie. It was too hot for chopping wood. She'd give him a few shillings and some meat for his tucker bag and send him on his way.

She stepped out of the kitchen to find him sitting in the shade of the building, drinking from his canvas waterbag. To his credit the pile of chopped wood looked healthier than it had since Banjo left, and what little could be seen of his face beneath the beard and dirt was red and sweaty. He got slowly to his feet, fixing her with that insolent grin she disliked so much.

'This should keep you in firewood for a week or so, Missus. I had t' knock off. It was getting too hot.'

'Yes, it's definitely too hot now. Thank you.' With an effort she managed a warmer tone. 'I'll ask Betsy to fix you a plate of food for lunch, and meanwhile I'll fetch your pay and a bit of meat to see you on your way.'

His face fell. 'I was hoping you might have some more jobs for me.'

'Not just now, I'm sorry.' She turned away and re-entered the kitchen, instructing Betsy to prepare a meal for him and to fetch a piece of salt meat from the cask in the meat house. Then she walked down the passageway which separated the kitchen from the rest of the house and entered the office, rummaging in a desk drawer for money.

The rank smell alerted her, making her swing around with her heart pounding. The man stood in the doorway, leering at her.

She gasped. 'What are you doing here?'

'Just collecting me pay, Missus.'

'There was no need.' Her voice sounded cold and level to her own ears despite the fear that bubbled inside her. She took two shillings from the drawer and handed it to him. 'As I said before, Betsy is preparing your lunch.'

He fingered the two silver coins and looked up at her again, baring those hideous teeth in another grin. He slipped the money in his pocket and reached inside his shirt. As his hand reappeared,

Louise started in disbelief. The short blade of a knife glinted wickedly in his grimy fingers.

'Two measly bob, Missus? D' you think that's fair pay for a morning slaving in the hot sun?' He advanced towards her, licking his lips. 'On the other hand, you could pay me another way. I could've had the gin, but I prefer women with a bit o' class. I like your style, Missus.'

'No!' She backed away from him until her elbow touched the rear wall. 'I'll give you more money!'

'Ah, but I'd sooner—' He broke off with a start as she grabbed a rifle from the rack behind her, pointing it at him with shaking hands.

'If you come one step further, I'll shoot you.'

He licked his lips, eyes wavering. 'That gun's not loaded. People don't keep loaded guns in they office.'

'Well, we do. We have to, with people like you around.' She heard the note of hysteria in her voice as she thought of Hannah, who had gone to her bedroom to play with her dolls. Hannah, she pleaded silently, please don't come out here now!

'You're bluffing.' The swaggie smirked. 'I got a good mind to jus' take that thing out o' your hands.'

'If you try, you'll be a dead man,' she assured him through clenched teeth. Holding the rifle on him with one hand, she scrabbled for money in the drawer and thrust a couple of pound notes at him. 'Here, take this and go.'

He grabbed the money and stared at her for a moment, then slowly backed out of the room. When he had gone Louise reached behind her for a box of cartridges and, pulling back the bolt with trembling fingers, thumbed a shell into the empty chamber. Dropping a handful of spare ammunition into the pocket of her apron, she forced herself to follow him out of the room. There was no sign of him. Carefully she retraced her steps down the covered walkway to the kitchen, pausing in the doorway to check that it was empty. Moving to the back door, she spotted the vagrant picking up his swag beside the woodheap. She waved the gun at him in a sudden surge of anger.

'Get away from here, and don't you ever come back!'

Something in her face must have told him she meant business, for he quickly hoisted the swag over his shoulder and hurried away. Louise sank down on the top step, shaking all over, though she kept the rifle trained on the man's retreating back until he was out of sight.

'Ma!' The voice had her jumping up, nerves jangling, until she saw it was Matt with Betsy beside him, hurrying towards her from the direction of the horse yards. 'Are you all right?' He leapt up the three steps and took the rifle from her trembling hands, passing it to Betsy while he pulled her into his arms. 'Did he hurt you?'

She shook her head, clinging to him. 'No, Matt, I'm all right.' Suddenly she jerked back, staring up at him. 'Where's Hannah? Find Hannah.'

He took the rifle again and left her with Betsy while he went to do just that. Betsy made a pot of tea, talking all the while.

'Goodness, Missus, that was a bad man! He came into the kitchen, looking mighty queer, and when he followed you into the house I ran outside, looking to see if any of the men had come home. And Matt was down at the yards, unsaddling his horse, so I ran down and got him.' Betsy dumped the pot of tea on the table, her hands shaking visibly.

'Good thinking, Betsy.' Louise sank into a chair at the kitchen table, shuddering with revulsion as she remembered the man's lewd, suggestive manner. Just the thought of him touching her made her skin crawl.

She looked up as Matt returned, Hannah in tow, the girl's face white with alarm. 'Mother! What happened?' Hannah ran to her and Louise pulled her onto her lap, hugging her tight and kissing her cheek.

'It was that swaggie, darling. He tried to make me give him money.' She stroked Hannah's silky hair, comforting herself as much as the child with the contact. 'But he's gone now.'

Matt loomed over them, watching her closely. 'Did you have to give him any?'

Louise swallowed, nodding. 'I gave him a couple of pounds. It was worth it to be rid of him.'

'The rotten bugger!'

Louise frowned at Matt's language and he looked quickly at Hannah. 'Forget I said that, Hannah. He won't be gone far.' He picked up the rifle and pulled back the bolt, dropping the cartridge into his palm. 'I'll soon catch him on a horse.'

A sudden memory flashed into Louise's mind. As clearly as if it was yesterday, she pictured Lloyd grabbing a rifle and announcing his intention to set off in pursuit of the Aborigines who had speared Jock Jamieson. Jock and Lloyd had caught the natives killing a steer and, in their fear, one of them had thrown his weapon, badly wounding Jock. It was during the anxious time that followed, that she and Lloyd had first become lovers.

For a moment Matt could have almost have been his father as a young man. She grasped his hand, detaining him. 'Matt, the money's not worth it. It's only two pounds. You could be hurt.'

Matt shook his head. 'A knife's no match for a gun. He needs to be taught a lesson.'

Heedless of her protests he strode out the door, rifle in hand, and Louise sank her head into her hands. Betsy poured a cup of tea and put it in front of her.

'Here, Missus, drink this. Matt'll be all right.' The dark girl stared hard at her again and Louise suddenly realized what was on her mind. With a little jolt of surprise and pleasure she remembered that Matt had called her 'Ma' and had held her in his arms. Hardly the behaviour of a station hand to his employer. No wonder the maid looked bemused. No doubt she would guess the truth, but did that matter? Who would Betsy tell?

It was an anxious wait for Matt's return. The three of them sat together in the kitchen, school lessons forgotten, a second rifle loaded close by. Just in case.

It was Ben, all hot and sweaty from the heat, who poked his head around the door to find them there.

'What's going on? Why are you sitting in here, Mother?' He glanced at the rifle. 'Is there a snake about?'

Without waiting for her reply he grabbed a cup and sat opposite her at the table, pouring himself tea from the pot.

'We had a visitor,' Louise said slowly. 'A swaggie.' She told Ben the events of the morning, editing her story for Hannah's benefit. 'Matt went after him to get the money back.' She sighed anxiously. 'I hope he's all right.'

Ben's eyes narrowed. 'Well, he's got a gun, hasn't he? Pity he didn't get home a bit sooner. Must have been awful for you, Mother.'

'I'm all right now. I'll just be thankful when Matt gets home.'

Ben thrust back his chair and stood up. 'Can you get me some lunch, Betsy?'

Louise looked at him anxiously, sensing his anger. Mentioning her concern for Matt was obviously a mistake. 'None of us have eaten yet. We'll all have some lunch.'

They were eating in the dining room when they heard a step on the veranda. Ben went to investigate, rifle in hand, and returned with Matt following. Louise looked up at her eldest son, searching for signs of battle. His face and clothes were unmarked, but the knuckles of his right hand were red and raw.

'What happened, Matt?'

He gave a triumphant grin. 'I put the fear of God into him, like.' He pulled a roll of notes from his pocket. 'Got your money back, Ma.' He crossed to her chair and gave her the money, gripping her shoulder reassuringly with his other hand. Suddenly he stopped short as if realising what he had called her and glanced at Ben. His brother looked thunderous.

Hannah was staring at Matt, her little face alive with curiosity. 'Why did you call Mother 'Ma', Matt?'

He shrugged, tossing a defiant look in Ben's direction. 'It's what I used to call me mother back in England. Your mother's special to me, too.'

'Matt.' Louise smiled warmly up at him, covering his bruised hand with hers. 'I didn't mind about the money, but thank you, anyway.' She was uncomfortably aware of Ben's stony stare, but Matt didn't deserve to be rebuffed. 'Now you'd better have a wash and Betsy will get you some lunch.'

Once night came, it was less easy for Louise to dismiss the unpleasant ordeal, despite her husband's comforting presence. The experience had left her sick and shaken, and she knew sleep would be a long time in coming.

But she feared more lasting repercussions from the incident than the loss of a few nights' sleep. Whatever progress had been made in the relationship between her two sons seemed to have been destroyed in the space of a couple of hours. Ben's old hostility was back in full force, and Matt was defiantly churlish in return. Louise, caught between the two, was at a loss. It wasn't fair to Matt to exclude him from the family just to please Ben, yet she understood Ben's insecurity.

She voiced her anxieties to Lloyd after they had gone to bed, but he only shrugged. 'They'll have to sort 'emselves out. Not much we can do.'

'I think it's time we did do something.' It was a moonlit night, and Louise could just make out his strong profile in the darkness as he lay on his back staring at the ceiling. 'We should be looking to the future, perhaps buying more land so we've room to set Matt up.'

Lloyd snorted. 'Matt hasn't proved himself yet. We don't even know if he wants to settle down.'

'Perhaps you should ask him.'

'Humph.' Lloyd rolled towards her, pulling her into his arms. 'I'm more worried about you right now. Sounds like it was a close call with that rotten swaggie.' He gently brushed her hair with his hand. 'I wish you women hadn't been alone. Next time you'd better get the gun out first.'

She let him kiss her, knowing the subject of Matt was closed for now. But if Matt stayed, Lloyd would be forced to face it sometime.

Chapter Eight

At Kilbride, the drought was cutting just as deeply as at Myvanwy. Jock and Andrew decided to send cattle to agistment on a station south of Banana which had been lucky enough to receive some scattered storms. Another muster was begun; this time collecting the two and three- year-old steers to send away. Young dry cattle were much easier to drove than breeders with calves.

With four hundred head of cattle confined in the holding paddock near the homestead, they began preparing for the droving trip. The men shod their horses and Isabella packed the packsaddles with corned beef, flour, tea, sugar and treacle. A stockman had been hired to help Jock and Andrew with the mob, and Clara was taking the opportunity to take her children to visit her mother in Banana, leaving Isabella and Elsie alone on Kilbride.

'We'll only be gone six days,' Jock told his daughter. 'If ye have any trouble, ask the Kavanaghs for help. Lloyd said they'd keep an eye on ye—one of them will come over to make sure o' things.'

'I'll be all right,' Isabella assured him. 'I'll check on the cattle and ask them for help if I need it.'

The droving party set out at daylight next morning, accompanied by tinkling horse bells and jangling hobble chains. Each man had a spare horse, which together with the two packhorses had to be driven along with the cattle. Isabella watched them depart in a cloud of dust, half-wishing she could accompany them, but at the same time enjoying the responsibility that came with being in charge at home. Perhaps Matt would be the one to come from Myvanwy. She longed to see him again.

Of course, with her father and brother away, the situation was potentially compromising. She remembered Mercy's dour warning with a tinge of defiance. No-one would know if she was alone with Matt, and she wasn't about to let him take liberties.

The first day she spent at home, catching up with household tasks after a week of mustering and drafting cattle. She helped Elsie with the washing, boiling the dirty clothes in the copper behind the kitchen and lifting them, dripping and steaming, onto a wooden drainer before wringing by hand and rinsing in cold water. All the used water was saved and thrown onto the vegetable garden in the back yard. The clean clothes were hung on a simple clothesline made from a length of wire, propped up with a forked stick. As Elsie brought the dry garments in, Isabella began the task of folding and ironing with a flat-iron heated on the stove.

It was hot work, not helped by the muggy, oppressive heat that hinted of building storms. Although Isabella longed for rain, she kept thinking of her father and brother on the road with cattle, unprotected from the elements. The chance of a cattle rush during a storm was a frightening hazard of droving.

The next day she decided to saddle a horse and ride out to check cattle, setting off early with a cut lunch in her saddle bag. She couldn't remember when it had last been so dry. Heat waves shimmered off the bare red soil, the grey grass reduced to isolated clumps. Dust rose from her horse's hooves in little puffs, while the trees drooped dispiritedly, shedding leaves which curled up and scattered in the wind. Cattle hung around muddy waterholes or grazed dispiritedly on the meagre feed. Some of them were so poor they looked like a bundle of bones with a hide stretched over it, their coats dull and matted with dust.

By late morning she found herself following a cattle pad which deepened as it neared a creek, dividing as it tackled the treacherous bank and converging again on the shrunken waterhole below. Reining in her horse, she made an involuntary exclamation of dismay. A cow was bogged in the waterhole, standing belly-deep in the pungent, greenish slime. At Isabella's approach the poor beast struggled to free itself, floundering helplessly for a few moments before giving way to exhaustion. A sickening odour of decay drifted from the waterhole, embracing the cow in a presentiment of death.

Sickened with pity, Isabella watched as crows hopped about on the stinking mud, monitoring their intended victim with evil, cunning eyes. A surge of anger propelled her from the saddle. Shuddering, she picked up a stick and shouted as she hurled it into their midst. The crows cawed in protest and, flapping their coal-black wings, flew to a nearby tree, where they perched to watch her warily. These cruel scavengers didn't wait for death. In previous droughts she had witnessed the horror of animals still alive with their eyes pecked out.

There was little else she could do. Without a rope, her own strength would not be enough to move the cow. Her sense of pride and independence warred with the need to save the animal. That and a sneaking hope of seeing Matt made her decide to ride to Myvanwy for help.

Her neighbours' house was five or six miles away. She trotted and cantered her horse as much as she dared, careful not to exhaust it in the enervating heat. Her spirits lifted when she spied Ben and Matt at the stockyards, replacing some broken rails and posts. As she rode up they lifted a heavy yard post on its end, heaving in unison as they slid the bottom third into a freshly dug hole. Ben held the post straight while Matt shovelled dirt around it.

He paused to look up at her with a welcoming grin, his brown face streaked with dirt and perspiration as he rested on the handle of the shovel. Isabella's heart missed a beat as he touched his hat.

'G' day, Isabella.' His eyes swept her sweating horse. 'You look like you rode here in a hurry.'

Ben's smile was more perfunctory. 'Everything all right, Bella?'

She told them her story. 'Can you give me a hand, Matt? I didn't fancy trying to pull her out myself, and besides, I don't have a rope.'

'It's no job for a woman.' Matt's mouth quirked. 'Sounds better than yard building in this heat.' He slanted a quick look at his companion. 'Can you manage here for a while, Ben?'

Ben merely nodded, turning away with a stony expression on his face as he began to ram the base of the post with a crowbar.

'I'll get a horse and a rope.' Matt appeared to ignore the younger lad's obvious resentment. He glanced up at the horizon. 'Looks like a storm might be coming.'

Isabella had been watching the menacing clouds. Rain would definitely be welcome, but it would be ironic if it fell now, preventing the rescue of the cow.

'I'll ask Mrs Kavanagh to pack you some lunch.' She wondered at the calmness of her own words as anticipation bubbled within her. Distressing as the animal's plight was, she couldn't help but relish the prospect of a few hours in Matt's company.

Up at the house, Louise Kavanagh was immediately concerned. 'You shouldn't be on your own like this, Isabella. It's not safe. I had a swaggie turn up here the other day, and he was threatened me. Hopefully he's far gone by now.' She grimaced a little as if the memory disturbed her. 'Come inside and we'll make some sandwiches for Matt.'

They bundled the bread and meat together, wrapping it in a serviette and newspaper for Matt to carry in his saddlebag. It was almost lunch time, but with the storm threatening there was no time to eat now. As they worked Isabella asked what had happened with the swagman, and Louise's expression darkened.

'I gave him a job cutting wood, and when I was about to pay him he followed me into the office and menaced me with a knife. Luckily the rifle was on the wall behind me and I was able to frighten him off with that.' She changed the subject, then, and Isabella didn't ask any more. It was obvious Louise was reluctant to talk about it.

Matt was at the yards saddling a thickset bay horse when she joined him. 'Old Drummer's broke to harness, so he'll pull the cow out with no trouble.' He grinned at her as he gathered up the reins and swung into the saddle. 'He's as rough as guts to ride, though—excuse the language. I'll be cursing him before the day's over.'

Isabella smiled at his use of the Australian vernacular. 'We'll have to hurry to beat this storm. I hope he can gallop.'

When they reached the waterhole, the cow was still there, struggling half-heartedly at their approach. The crows continued to watch her with beady, calculating eyes. Matt dismounted and removed his boots and socks, rolling up his trousers to his knees. The animal lurched in fear as he ploughed through the mud to her side, thrashing her head about as he looped the greenhide rope around her horns and drew the noose tight. Back on firm ground, he tied the rope to a makeshift collar he'd fitted to Drummer's thick neck and led the horse forwards. Feeling the tug of the rope, the cow renewed her struggle, moving a few inches through the mud. Matt allowed Drummer to rest for a moment before urging the horse on again.

The wind was blowing now, gusting dust and dead leaves and bringing with it the sharp smell of rain, while black clouds rolled over their heads. Thunder growled and lightning flickered on the horizon. Isabella watched anxiously, knowing the storm would soon be upon them.

At last they had the cow on dry ground and Matt dodged her swinging horns to slip off the rope. He moved to a safe distance as she struggled to regain her feet. The first few attempts were fruitless, but after resting, the cow finally managed to stand, swaying on mud-encrusted legs.

Matt gestured to her sagging, slime-covered udder. 'She has a calf somewhere.'

'Poor old thing.' Isabella had witnessed scenes like this many times before, but she was too soft hearted to ever become inured to it. The cow was so thin her ribs and hips threatened to poke right through her harsh, filth-matted coat. 'She'll probably get bogged again next time she has a drink.'

Matt glanced up at the clouds. 'With luck there'll be enough rain to fill the waterhole and her troubles will be over.'

Isabella followed his look. 'There's a shepherd's hut further up the creek. Let's try and make it before the rain.'

Matt wiped the worst of the mud from his feet and legs with a clump of dry grass before replacing his boots. They set off at a hand gallop, the restless horses reinvigorated by the approaching storm. The first drops of rain stung Isabella's cheek and spattered her dusty hat. She glanced at Matt riding beside her, his own hat pulled low over his eyes and the wind billowing his shirt. He met her look with a grin that told her he was enjoying this, and Isabella forgot her concern for the cow.

By the time they reached the hut, rain was teeming down and their clothes were soaked. They pulled off their saddles and turned the horses loose into a small yard before carrying their gear inside. The shack was a single windowless room built of split slabs, and when Matt pulled the door to behind them, the only source of light came from a few chinks in the walls. As Isabella's eyes adjusted to the gloom she could just make out the empty fireplace, the rough table and the homemade wooden stretcher in the corner with its covering of dusty blankets.

Matt seemed to sum up the situation in a glance. 'I'll get some wood,' he muttered, opening the door again and disappearing outside.

He returned shortly bearing an armload of damp firewood from the stack beside the wall. Isabella took the lunches from their saddlebags and tore off a piece of the newspaper wrapping. She knelt beside Matt, who was arranging chips of wood and bark in the fireplace. 'This might make it easier.'

He accepted the newspaper and fumbled in his pocket for matches. The paper flared readily but the damp bark smouldered, and Matt fanned it gently with his hat until it caught alight. The tiny flames licked at the larger pieces of kindling, turning the moisture in it to steam, but the wood was bone-dry underneath and was soon burning brightly.

Matt rose to his feet, pulling Isabella with him. Her heart thudded unevenly as his strong calloused palm enclosed her own. Rain still pelted the roof above them and wind crept through the cracks in the slabs, bringing a tinge of moisture with it. She shivered in her wet clothes, surprised at the sudden drop in temperature.

'Cold?' He wrapped his arms around her and held her close to his warm body, shielding her from the wind. As the fire began to blaze he set her away from him, lightly patting her waist. 'Stay close to the fire while I bring the chair over.'

There was only one, a primitive affair of greenhide stretched over a wooden frame. Isabella perched on the edge of it, her senses alive and tingling as she watched Matt fetch their food and squat beside her on the dirt floor. Fleetingly she wondered what her father and Andrew would say if they knew she was here alone with him. But she pushed the thought aside, determined to enjoy the moment.

Matt passed her sandwiches to her before unwrapping his own, biting hungrily into the bread and meat. Isabella observed him as he ate, the firelight flickering over his strong features and sending searching fingers into the gloom. Without his hat, his dark hair stuck to his head, damp from sweat and rain. His sodden shirt clung to his broad shoulders and his wet trousers hugged his thighs. As her eyes lingered on him, a shaft of raw desire coursed through her and she shifted uncomfortably, startled by her response.

Matt wolfed down the food with little regard for manners. When it was gone, he stood up and grabbed the blackened billy that hung beside the fireplace. 'There should be enough water outside to fill this.'

A gust of wind blew the rain in when he opened the door and Isabella shivered again. She moved to his side and looked out, fascinated by the downpour. The hard-baked ground was already a sea of water, while the slope towards the creek was a rushing torrent. Matt held the billy under the edge of the overhanging eaves, allowing it to fill with water from the shingle roof.

A loud crack of thunder, startlingly close, made them both jump. Matt quickly closed the door and hung the billy on a blackened wire over the fire. He squatted on his heels to add more wood.

'Isn't this wonderful?' She crouched beside him, watching his strong brown hands as he stoked the hissing, crackling flames. 'I love storms. Especially after a drought.'

'Mmm.' As he rose he drew her to her feet with him and slid his arms around her waist, holding her loosely as he looked down at her. 'That's because you didn't grow up in England. I used to hate the rain over there.'

'But here it's different.'

'A lot of things are different here.'

She smiled, knowing she was flirting but unable to help herself. It was as if something bold and wanton had overtaken her natural modesty. 'What sort of things?'

'You, for a start.' He grinned down at her. 'I've never met a girl like you before. You're not bound by rules, like.' He pulled her closer. 'I like that.'

He moved his mouth over hers, gentle and light as the brush of a feather. Yet when that kiss was over he returned for another and another, each one deeper and more lengthy than the last. Isabella was breathless, her head spinning. Even that last time down at the river he hadn't been so passionate. His hands stroked her back, waist and hips, moulding her against him, letting her feel his aroused body. She knew where this was leading and she knew she must end it, though all her instincts screamed at her to stay in his arms, to let him do with her as he would.

Abruptly, she pushed him away, pressing her hands against his chest where his heart thudded. It was cold away from his warmth. The rain hadn't eased and evening was approaching. She fought for good sense, remembering something Mercy had told her. If you give a man what he wants, he'll never marry you.

'We have to get back,' she said firmly.

He watched her steadily, his breathing uneven. 'It's still raining and I can hear the creek roaring.'

Sure enough, over the drumming on the roof there was another, rushing sound. She had heard it often enough to recognize it. Was propriety sufficient reason to swim the horses over a treacherous flooded creek and ride home wet and cold through the dark rain? Perhaps it was.

'We should at least have a look.' She met his gaze resolutely. 'Perhaps it's not running deep.'

'I'll look, then.'

'No, I'll go with you.' She followed him to the door, folding her arms tightly across her chest to ward off the cold outside.

It took determination to brave the storm again. The light was fading quickly and the wind gusted. In moments their clothing was drenched once more as they splashed through mud and running water to the bank of the creek. Isabella was almost relieved at the sight that greeted them; she could return to the warmth and dry of the hut with a clear conscience.

Already the creek was half full, a dirty brown flood that swirled angrily around the ti-trees which grew in its bed. Only the trees' uppermost branches protruded, straining against the force of the water. It was difficult to equate this torrent with the dry watercourse they'd crossed less than two hours earlier. Attempting to swim the horses over it would be foolhardy.

Matt put her thoughts into words as he slid his arm about her waist. 'You're shivering now, and we could be drowned crossing that. I dunno about you, but I can't swim. Come on, let's get back to the hut.'

With the door pushed shut behind them, he dragged a blanket from the bed in the corner, shaking it until the dust rose to tickle her nose and make her sneeze. 'Here. You'd better take those wet things off, like, an' wrap this around you.'

Isabella was too cold to protest. In time the fire would dry the outer layers of her clothes, but her undergarments would still be sodden. 'If you turn your back.'

He smiled. 'I'll sit here at the fire and I promise I won't look.'

She moved to the bed and managed to remove her clothing while keeping the blanket more or less around her; glancing furtively at Matt to be sure he was keeping his word. Discarding her blouse, corset and heavy divided skirt, she hung them on a peg on the wall. Modesty prevented her from removing her wet chemise and drawers. If she sat close enough to the fire, perhaps they would eventually dry. Wrapping the musty blanket firmly around her, she nervously joined Matt at the fire. He had shed his shirt in the interval and she tried not to stare at his broad, muscular back.

He turned to look at her with a quizzical smile, one eyebrow raised. 'You're still shivering. Come here and warm up, like. The billy's boiling.'

He left her momentarily to fetch tea and sugar from his saddlebag. Once the tea was brewed he shared it between their two quart pots and she sipped slowly, sitting close to the flames. The hot, sweet tea tasted delicious, warming her entire body. Matt had draped the second blanket about his shoulders. Isabella felt more comfortable with him covered, and tried to forget that under her own blanket she was wearing nothing but her underwear. Her sisters would be scandalised if they could see her now.

'We could do a lot worse than be stuck here,' he commented.

'That's all very well for a man to say,' Isabella retorted impatiently. 'I'm sure you're not concerned about *your* reputation.'

'Who's to know? I thought there was no-one at home at your place?'

'Only Elsie, the black maid.'

Matt shrugged dismissively. 'She'll keep quiet if you tell her.'

'That's not the point.'

'You can have the bed. I'll sleep on the floor.'

Isabella could not admit her real concern, which was her lack of trust in herself. Their earlier kisses had proved just how vulnerable she was, and an entire night alone with this man could easily be her undoing. He'd already let her know what he wanted.

Perhaps conversation, something to divert their minds, was the answer. 'Mrs Kavanagh said she'd had some trouble with a swaggie.'

'Aye, that was a bad show.' He looked at her over the rim of his quart pot. 'She ended up chasing him off with a rifle, but only after he'd got two quid out of her. She was pretty shook up, like. I got home just after he'd gone, so I followed him and got the money back.' He finished off the tea and set the quart pot on the floor, giving a humourless grin. 'I doubt he'll be back in a hurry. Ben was pretty riled that I was the one to see him off, though.'

She asked a question that had been niggling at her all day. 'What's wrong with Ben? He didn't look too happy about you coming with me this morning.'

He shrugged, staring down at the fire. 'He's just jealous.'

She shook her head. 'But why? He's like a brother to me, and he's too young for me, anyway.'

'I didn't mean it that way. He just resents me.' He looked up at her. 'It's not surprising, really.'

'Why's that?'

'You probably won't want anything to do with me if I tell you.'

'Matt!' A trickle of alarm seeped through her. 'What have you done?'

A tight smile flickered over his face and he took a deep breath. 'It's not what I've done. This isn't common knowledge, but you probably should know. I wasn't just the Ashford family's groom.' He paused, searching her face as if wondering how to proceed. 'Ben don't like it, but he's me brother. We have the same mother and father.'

Isabella gaped at him. 'How can that be? You were born in England! Weren't you?'

He nodded, staring sombrely into the flames, his brown face lit with a ruddy glow. 'Aye. Me mother was brought to England by her brother, Charles Ashford, a few months before I was born.'

'You mean Mrs Kavanagh? She's really your mother?'

'Aye, she is that.'

Her words seemed to stick in her throat. 'And Mr Kavanagh's your father?'

'Aye. Ben, Tom and Hannah are me full brothers and sister.' A note of bitterness entered his voice. 'But they weren't born bastards like me.'

She flinched at his language, staring at him soundlessly as she tried to make sense of it. In the space of a few words he'd turned her neat, circumspect world upside-down. Illegitimate babies happened to other people, immoral people, not to her respectable friends and neighbours.

Then she remembered what Maggie had told her about the romance between Lloyd and Louise Kavanagh, when Louise was the Jamiesons' governess. She studied Matt's profile, realising for the first time how much he looked like Louise. And she could see Lloyd there too, now that she looked for it.

'Who knows about this?' Her voice sounded thin, uncertain, even to herself.

'At Fenham Manor, a few of the servants did. But here, only me mother and father, Tom and Ben. And Ben hates me for it.'

'So your parents back in England—they adopted you?'

'Aye. The Joneses must've been in their forties when they took me in, but they'd never had children of their own. They gave me a good home.'

'And your employers, the Ashfords—they were your grandparents?'

He nodded, his face twisting. 'Aye, not that they ever acknowledged me. I didn't know the truth until just before I came out here.'

Her hands shook as she sipped at her tea, her mind whirling. 'Why did your mother give you up?'

'She wasn't given a choice.' He told her how his mother had been hidden away, her baby taken from her soon after the birth.

Isabella shook her head. She could only imagine how Louise must have felt. How could people put their reputations above the emotions of those involved, callously separating a mother from her child? 'Your Uncle Charles must be a cruel, heartless man. And your grandparents as well. You worked for your Uncle Charles when you first came to Australia, didn't you?'

He nodded. 'Aye. I didn't know then exactly what he done. But I can believe it.' He paused. 'This is all pretty private. I'd prefer you didn't say anything to anyone.'

'Of course not.' A glow of pleasure that he had entrusted her with this secret, warmed her. 'Thank you for telling me.' She was still shocked but able to look at him with new eyes. He had always seemed so confident, so careless of his emotions, but this confession had given her a glimpse of vulnerability, of inner pain.

He obviously resented his illegitimacy and having to work as a servant for his own relatives. She couldn't blame him for that. In comparison his younger siblings had enjoyed a respectable, privileged upbringing.

She asked him questions about England, about the time he'd spent working with his Uncle Charles. Then, fearing he'd think her too inquisitive, she spoke of her own childhood when the house at Kilbride had been full of children and young adults. As they sat before the fire the drumming rain eased, beating one final tattoo across the tin roof before stopping completely, and the flow of conversation seemed to die away with it.

Isabella yawned and stretched. 'I think I'll go to bed.'

Matt glanced up at her. 'I'll sleep here beside the fire.'

She nodded and rose, clutching the blanket to her. Wrapping it around her, she lay on the dusty mattress, but once away from the warmth of the flames, her still-damp underclothing soon had her shivering. Sitting up in bed, she removed her drawers and camisole under cover of darkness, hanging them on the wall to dry. Hopefully she'd wake early enough to rescue them before daylight revealed them to curious male eyes.

She lay awake, listening to the rustling movements made by her companion, his dark shape outlined against the fire. She was conscious of her nakedness beneath the blanket as she remembered his kisses of earlier, the hot press of his body, and then the confidences he'd shared with her. A rush of compassion and longing swept through her and she wanted to call him to her, to have him lie beside her and hold her in his arms. But no, for that would be truly her undoing.

Eventually she slept, only to dream that he was there with her, kissing her, stroking her hair, her arms, and her breasts with his calloused palms. She woke with a moan, her body throbbing with need, and saw him moving in front of the fire, adding more wood to the burnt down embers. A chill wind crept through the cracks between the slabs and she shivered in her thin blanket.

'Matt,' she called, not giving herself time to think, to change her mind. 'I'm cold.'

He turned and walked slowly towards her, his own blanket draped over his bare shoulders. At the side of the bed he paused, looking down at her. She reached up to him, touching his hand, edging across to give him room. 'Warm me up, please.'

The bed creaked as he sank full length beside her, pulling her into his arms. As in her dreams he came above her, taking her mouth in his kiss. As her blanket parted the dampness of his trouser-clad legs pressed against hers.

It didn't take him long to discover she was naked. When his exploring fingers parted the blanket to find her bare breast he muttered some guttural sound as he deepened the kiss, his tongue tangling hotly with hers. He was breathing heavily, his hips moving hungrily against her, and under her hand, caught to his chest, his heart thudded madly. Her own heart was racing and as he touched bare flesh, ripples of pleasure travelled through her body, seducing her from any thought of resistance. He kissed the flesh he'd uncovered, caressing and stroking until she was moaning with need.

He shifted away only long enough to remove his own clothing. She hadn't expected the pain when he took her, nor the pleasure that built in spite of it as he thrust deep within her, hinting at some unknown conclusion; nor that he would suddenly pull out of her, shuddering against her stomach. Even less had she anticipated that he would use his fingers to replace his body, making the pleasure build again until she cried out, with everything spinning out of control.

She lay against him, breathing rapidly. Her body that had earlier been cold was all throbbing heat, while he was equally warm and damp with sweat. He kissed her and gently stroked her hair.

'Oh, Isabella,' he murmured at last. 'Don't be mad at me.'

She shook her head, feeling at once overwhelmed and confused by the things he'd done and her own surprising response. Mercy's stern warnings certainly hadn't prepared her for any of the intimate, pleasurable details. But how could she be mad at him for something she'd invited?

'I'm warm now,' she murmured, fingering his bare chest.

'Aye.' He kissed her again. 'So am I.'

He pulled up the tumbled blankets, covering them both. The coarse wool was rough and scratchy against her sensitised skin.

'Thank God for the storm,' he murmured. 'I can't think of anything better than spending the night right here.'

A part of her agreed; the part of her that luxuriated in the touch of his hands on her skin and the feel of his strong body in her arms. As he kissed her again, it seemed sleep was still a long way from his mind. But now that her initial urgency was sated, guilt was creeping in. There was still the morning to be faced.

Next day the rain was gone, leaving a few fluffy clouds drifting loose in a sky of cobalt blue. The muddy coats of the horses and the pools of water on the rain-washed ground remained as tangible evidence of the storm, with the roaring creek reduced to a benign gurgle.

Quickly they saddled the hollow-flanked horses, their own stomachs empty and rumbling. Matt returned to the hut to check that the fire was out before joining Isabella, who waited with her mount beside the yard. He drew her close for one last kiss and she rested against him, reluctant to let him go, unwilling to step away from that magic little world they'd created last night. She hadn't known that giving herself to a man would make her feel so vulnerable. Now she must face reality.

Finally he stepped back. 'I hope Elsie's got a good breakfast cooked when we get to your place.'

'She'll be worried sick.' She patted her tangled hair which hadn't responded well to a finger-comb, conscious of her damp crumpled clothes and unwashed body. Elsie would see through her lies, she was sure. 'She's got no idea where I am.'

She winced as Matt helped her into the saddle and he looked up at her anxiously. 'Are you all right?'

She blushed. 'It's nothing.'

Understanding dawned in his eyes. 'I asked too much of you last night.'

She smiled in spite of her embarrassment. She wanted to tell him she loved him, that last night had meant everything to her, but how could she when he remained silent? Was he going to ask her to marry him? More fool her for forgetting the cardinal rule by giving him what he wanted first.

Back at the Kilbride homestead, they unsaddled, turned her horse into the paddock and shut Matt's in the yard with some hay. Isabella's hunger gnawed at her stomach as painfully as the guilt that gnawed at her conscience. She glanced at Matt covertly as he walked beside her into the house, her eyes lingering on his body as she remembered him naked and aroused. The sharp pang of desire reminded her that instead of freeing her, last night's joining had bound her to him, strengthening a need that would not be easily quenched.

Elsie came out of the kitchen to meet them, her plump black face twisted with concern. 'Oh, Missy Bella, are you orright? I bin proper worried.' She glanced at Matt and her expression changed. 'What you bin doing?'

'I'm sorry, Elsie.' Isabella ran a hand through her hair. 'I found a cow in the bog and I had to get Matt to help me pull her out. Then we got caught in the storm and sheltered in the shepherd's hut.'

Elsie looked again at Matt, her eyes anxious, but then she turned away. 'I get you breakfast. You proper hungry, might be?'

'We're starving,' Isabella responded. 'Can you cook us some chops?' She touched Matt's hand. 'I'll put the kettle on and cut some bread to keep us going.'

They sat together at the kitchen table, eating hunks of bread spread with fresh butter and honey while Elsie heated the frypan on the wood stove. Soon the smell and sizzle of frying chops made their mouths water, while the bubbling kettle prompted Isabella to brew a pot of strong tea.

'How much rain do you think we had, Elsie?' she asked around a mouthful of bread.

The Aboriginal woman turned from the stove. 'Two inches, might be? It bin proper heavy, wind proper bad.'

Isabella nodded. 'There was more up at the hut. The creek came down half a banker and we couldn't get across.' She turned to Matt. 'There must have been at least four inches, don't you think?'

He shrugged. 'I'm just a new chum. I've never seen rain as heavy as that before.'

'Doesn't it rain like that in England?'

He shook his head, smiling. 'It's nearly always raining, but generally soft and gentle like a whisper on your face.' He touched her cheek as he spoke, his fingers moving lightly on her skin. Isabella glanced up at Elsie who was carrying two plates of steaming chops to the table and brushed his hand away, her face flaming.

When he had finished eating he drained his cup of tea and pushed back his chair. 'I'd better be off home. They'll be worried, too.'

Isabella looked up at him, resisting the urge to accompany him outside, to have a moment alone with him and delay the parting. She was about to thank him for his help with the cow when she stopped herself. Hadn't she already thanked him in the most thorough way possible?

He looked down at her lingeringly when she made no move to rise. 'Goodbye, Isabella. I hope to see you soon.'

She managed a smile. 'Goodbye, Matt.'

When he had gone she sat there at the table, staring into space, telling herself she should go and have a bath. Heaven knew she needed it.

Elsie came and stacked their dirty plates, pausing at her side. 'Missy, what you bin up to with tha' boy? You spend the night with him, he give you bubby. Mister Jam'son be proper mad.'

Isabella looked up quickly, feeling herself flush again. She'd known Elsie would guess the truth. 'Elsie, don't tell Father, will you? He'll only worry. Matt's not going to hurt me.' He'd assured her he was taking care that there'd be no baby. As for the rest, she couldn't say.

Chapter Nine

Matt was deep in thought as he rode home, on the one hand savouring his full belly and that wonderful feeling of satiated lust, and on the other conscious of the little pinpricks of guilt that wouldn't quite leave him be. It was the first time he'd taken a virgin and he recalled with an unfamiliar glow of tenderness what a willing pupil Isabella had turned out to be. But she was no cheap slut to enjoy and discard. He'd never known a girl whose company and conversation he enjoyed as much, even when the presence of others made it impossible to touch her. Nor was she excessively feminine and delicate. She was down to earth, tough and sensible, and should he decide to settle down, he could imagine doing it with Isabella.

He knew that now he'd taken her, it would be hard to stay away. Yet arranging a repeat performance would be less than easy. Her father might be lax, but Bella had scruples of her own. He suspected his guilt was nothing to the remorse with which she must be flaying herself.

Back at Myvanwy he let his horse go and joined his father and Ben, who were finishing the yard repairs he'd left so hastily the day before. Lloyd, trimming the end of a rail with the adze, straightened up and looked at him curiously.

'What happened to you? Did you get caught by the storm?'

'Aye.' He didn't like lying, but what else could he do? 'By the time Isabella and I got back to the house it was pouring rain, so she said I might as well stay in the quarters overnight.'

Lloyd nodded, resting on the handle of the adze for a moment and wiping the sweat from his eyes. 'It was wonderful rain. We measured two hundred and eighty points. What'd they have over there?'

Matt shrugged, pretending nonchalance as he bent to help Ben lift a rail and fix it against the post. 'Isabella hadn't measured it when I left, but I think it was about the same as here.' He wasn't about to tell them about being caught in the hut, and the extra rain up there which had flooded the creek. He held the rail while Ben tied it in place with a double strand of plain wire, using the handle of his pliers to draw the wire tight in a Cobb and Co twitch.

Ben gave him a surly smile. 'A bit convenient, wasn't it, getting caught over there with Isabella?'

'Shut your mouth, Ben,' he muttered. 'It's none of your business.'

Lloyd glanced at him sharply. 'I've got no problem with you courting Isabella, but you make sure you treat her right, eh?'

Matt flashed him an ironic look. 'Aye, just like me old man would've done.'

Ben glowered while Lloyd's mouth tightened. 'Just because I made mistakes don't mean I can't warn you against doing the same.'

Matt didn't reply and they continued to work in an uneasy silence. Damn Ben. If it wasn't for Isabella he'd be gone like a shot. Just when he'd found somewhere he felt like he belonged, someone had to spoil it.

The following Sunday, he rode over to Kilbride to see her again. He sensed she was more pleased to see him than her quietly controlled manner suggested, as she took him to make polite conversation with her father. As always Jock Jamieson was friendly to Matt, and was agreeable to his request to take his daughter riding.

'I hear ye helped Bella while I was away.' The old man folded the newspaper he'd been reading and placed it on the arm of his squatter's chair. 'Thank ye for that. The rain was a blessing. Of course it had to come the minute we took cattle away. But we need a lot more yet before the drought's properly broken.'

'It's greened up nicely,' Matt commented, inwardly cringing at the man's gratitude. 'Perhaps the storms will keep coming, like.'

'A week of monsoon rain is what we really need. But ye and Bella go for your ride now.'

They didn't ride far—just down to the river where the waterhole was stained a muddy brown from the recent inflow of storm water. They tied their horses under a shady tree, and then they were in each other's arms, bodies pressing close.

After a moment Isabella broke off their kiss. 'Oh, Matt,' she whispered breathlessly. 'We mustn't...'

'I know.' Matt had hoped to tumble her there under the trees, but he couldn't stop thinking of her father back at the homestead, trustingly sending him off with his daughter. 'We'll just sit here in the shade for a while.'

But it was impossible to sit together and not kiss; and kisses were a temptation to other things. When his control began to slip, Matt moved away and stood up. 'Unless you've changed your mind, I think we'd better go back.'

Isabella flushed, but took his outstretched hand and let him help her up. She gathered her discarded hat and fussed with her hair before replacing it. At last she looked up at him. 'One of our mares has foaled. Do you want to see it before we ride back?'

'Aye, that's a good idea.' He grinned at her. 'If we stay on the horses we can't get up to mischief.'

Her colour deepened and she shook her head at him. 'You're shameless, Matt Jones! Whatever am I going to do with you?'

Now that the first rains had come, the season seemed to have taken a reversal. The clouds built again, venting their contents in a week of solid rain. The river came down in flood and the grass grew lush and green. Much as Isabella loved the wet, especially lying in bed at night listening to the steady drumming on the iron roof while frogs set up a noisy croaking chorus, she found herself bored, restless and lonely after a few days. Housebound, she did some sewing which she hated, made a batch of soap from fat and caustic soda, and cooked until there was more food prepared than she and her father could possibly eat. Reading had always been a favourite pastime, but after a few days she ran out of fresh material and resorted to re-reading her copy of *Pride and Prejudice*. The unaccustomed inactivity had already begun to pall.

When the rain stopped the mosquitoes came in hungry swarms, followed by the sandflies which bred in the floodwaters, adding to the misery of man and beast. Isabella and her father lit smoke fires for the stock horses and the two house cows, burning dung and green leaves. The animals soon learned to stand in the smoke to keep the biting insects at bay.

In lonely desperation she walked over to see Andrew and Clara, who lived a mile or so away. She was instantly sorry she'd bothered. She'd never been comfortable with Clara, who always seemed to make Isabella feel at fault in some way. A town-bred girl herself, Clara took no interest in the running of Kilbride and was disparaging of Isabella's work with the men. Her children were naughty and unresponsive to Isabella's attempts to make friends. Even Andrew seemed distant these days.

Returning angry and frustrated, the arrival of Matt with his horse all muddy and sweating from the ride on boggy roads immediately lifted her desolate mood. Isabella could have cried with joy, though she had no intention of letting him see just how excited she was. The visit turned out to be a circumspect one, with her father present. Isabella dug up a tattered pack of playing cards and she and Matt indulged in a competitive, high-spirited game of euchre while her father watched indulgently from his armchair, puffing at his pipe.

She was gratified that Matt seemed content to spend time with her, without seeking to see her alone. He left her in a rosy glow, hugging to herself the hope that he truly cared for her.

Once the river had finally gone down, Isabella and her father took the wagon to Banana to replenish supplies.

'We'll stay for the weekend, lassie,' Jock said. 'I know ye have a lonely time of it, living with an old man like me. Ye can have a bit o' fun in town for a change.'

Her father harnessed two of the draught horses to the thorough-brace wagon, which was large and sturdy enough to carry a big load of supplies. A high seat at the front allowed them to travel in reasonable comfort.

They broke the journey with an overnight stay at Mercy's place. Alfred was at home for once, since it was out of shearing season and most properties hadn't started their musters yet. Sometimes he supplemented his income with fencing work, but perhaps there was nothing offering right now. More was the pity, as he always made Isabella feel uncomfortable.

Amelia, Mercy's oldest daughter, accepted eagerly when Isabella invited her to go to town with them. At sixteen, the girl was old enough to yearn for the pleasures of town life and Isabella enjoyed her company.

'Thank you so much for asking me, Bella.' Amelia said for what must have been the tenth time as they started their journey the next morning, the three of them crowded together on the wagon seat. She heaved a heartfelt sigh. 'When Father's at home I'd sooner be elsewhere. He's such a beast to poor Mother and he flogs into us if we look sideways at him.'

Isabella exchanged glances with her father. She knew all the children were scared of Alfred, but she hadn't realized it was that bad. Surely Amelia was too old for beatings.

She put her arm consolingly around her niece. 'I'm glad he let you come with us. Just enjoy the few days and try not to think of him. I suppose he'll be off working again soon.'

'I hope so,' Amelia muttered.

At least the girls would be able to escape him eventually, Isabella reflected. Poor Mercy didn't have that option, unless she did the unthinkable and left him. Yet she didn't think her sister would ever do that. Sadly, Mercy seemed cowed by her husband, suffering his abuse without complaint.

When they arrived the town was busy with Friday afternoon traffic—men on horseback and families in buggies, sulkies and wagonettes. A horse team with a big tabletop wagon was pulled in at the rear of Martins' General Store, unloading goods while the horses stood patiently, swishing tails and jingling harness as they shook their shaggy heads at the flies. Jock drew up at the front and went inside to order goods to be packed ready for their departure on Monday morning.

It was an all-purpose store, carrying everything from hosiery to food to fencing wire. While Jock was busy, the girls amused themselves by shopping for dress fabrics, underwear and other feminine necessities, before Jock drove them on to the Banana Hotel. Here they stabled the horses and obtained rooms, the girls sharing one while Jock occupied another.

On Saturday Isabella took her young niece visiting, catching up with some friends of her own age. As they were returning to their hotel in the late afternoon, they walked past the Criterion, also known as the Bottom Hotel for its position at the bottom of the hill. Several young men spilled out of the bar amidst much talk and laughter, and Isabella stopped dead. One of them was Matt, and he was standing right in front of her.

He started and for a moment looked almost guilty. But then he seemed to recover, doffing his broad bush hat. 'Why, look who's here! Didn't expect to see you in town, Bella!' He lurched closer and slid his arm around her waist, supporting himself against her. 'Come and meet me girl, chaps. This is Miss Jamieson.'

He was dressed in working clothes and the strong smell of alcohol, together with his slurred speech, sent a clear, disturbing message. Isabella thrust him off, embarrassed and angry. 'You're drunk, Matt!' she muttered. 'Behave yourself!' She glanced up at his friends who were watching avidly, sniggering.

Matt staggered. 'Bella!' He looked wounded. 'Aren't you pleased t' see me?'

'Not in this state.' She grabbed Amelia's arm and pulled her away. 'Come on, Amelia. This is no place for ladies.'

Back at the hotel, she went blindly to her room, followed by a bemused Amelia. Throwing herself onto a chair, she pressed her hands to her eyes, nauseous with the shame and disbelief coiling in her belly. Matt, her beautiful, charming, funny Matt, so confident and competent. Drink diminished him, physically and mentally. To say nothing of the fact that he had outright embarrassed her. Surely their one night of passion hadn't given him the right to proclaim her as his property and handle her in such a public fashion.

'Are you all right, Isabella?' She opened her eyes to find Amelia watching her, her face confused and anxious. 'I can't believe Mr Jones behaving like that. I thought he was so nice at Christmas, and so handsome. I didn't blame you for being sweet on him.'

Oh dear! Was it that obvious? Aloud she said, 'Mr Jones was very drunk,' and then realized what an unnecessary statement that was. With Alfred for a father, Amelia probably knew far more about drink than Isabella did.

'Don't tell your grandfather about this,' she added. She wondered how her father would react if he saw Matt in that state. With one daughter already married to an abusive drunk, he surely wouldn't encourage *her* friendship with someone who over-indulged; for all that he seemed to like Matt.

What was she to do? The terrible truth of it was, she was so much in love with Matt that seeing him as something less than she'd imagined, wounded her to the core. She couldn't just walk away and forget him, and since she'd compromised herself with him that hardly seemed an option any more.

'It's not the end of the world.' Amelia took her hands, trying to offer comfort. 'Most men drink sometimes. Mother says so.'

Most men, perhaps, but not her father or her brothers. She knew Mr Kavanagh enjoyed the occasional beer or rum, and he was Matt's father, after all. Perhaps when he'd been younger, he'd been less discreet. She wished there was someone to whom could she turn for advice. Mrs Kavanagh was easy to talk to, but she was Matt's mother, and Isabella wasn't supposed to even know that.

Not for the first time she felt the lack of a mother. If only Maggie lived closer. Amelia was too young to advise her, while Mercy was bitter about men in general and already prejudiced against Matt. Perhaps his behaviour today was merely a symptom of youthful wildness, which he would outgrow in time.

But not all men did. Alfred was a prime example.

'Why don't you have a rest before supper?' Amelia eyed her uncertainly. 'I'll see if Grandpa's in his room.'

'Yes, I think I will.' To tell the truth, she wasn't ready to face the world right now. Isabella slipped off her shoes and removed her skirt, blouse and corset, lying on one of the two narrow beds in her petticoats and chemise. The horsehair mattress was hard and lumpy and she tossed restlessly, knowing sleep was a world away. She reached for a book which lay on the duchess, but the words skipped crazily across the page, eluding her. She was a fool, she thought, surrendering herself to a man who hadn't even proposed to her. If people found out what she'd done her reputation would be in shreds. Remembering the familiar way Matt had touched and spoken to her earlier, in front of his grinning friends, she found herself wondering if they already knew.

By the time Amelia returned and it was time to rise and dress for supper, her head was thumping. Amelia chattered with forced brightness and Isabella did her best to respond. Poor girl, she deserved better company, but this much-anticipated visit to town had turned sour.

Seated in the dining room with her father and Amelia, they deliberated over a menu that offered either roast beef and Yorkshire pudding, or corned beef and cabbage with white sauce. She noticed the couple at the next table turning towards the door and followed their glances.

It was Matt. Her heart thudded uneasily. Gone was the rumpled, stockmen's clothing of earlier. He wore a coat and waistcoat and his face was freshly shaved, his hair slickly combed. He approached their table with a steady, easy stride, and if Isabella hadn't known he couldn't be fully sober, she wouldn't have guessed differently.

'Good evening, Mr Jamieson.' He nodded at the two girls. 'Isabella. Amelia. Is it all right if I join you?'

'Why, Matt.' Jock rose from his chair and shook Matt's hand. 'I didn't know ye were in town. Aye, come and have supper with us.' He gestured to the chair beside Isabella's. 'Sit down.'

As he took his chair Isabella caught a whiff of the brilliantine he'd used in his hair, along with the clean smell of soap. She thrust the menu at him, trying to crush the wayward leap of her senses. 'What will you have, Matt? As you can see, there isn't much choice.'

Matt took the menu and peered at it, even as she remembered him telling her he didn't read very well. Something else guaranteed at the time to evoke her foolish feminine sympathies.

'I'll have the roast,' he told her, giving her a wary smile. Obviously he could read enough to get by. 'I've had enough corned beef to last me a lifetime.'

'That'll be four roasts,' Jock told the hovering waitress. 'Where are ye staying, Matt?'

He shrugged. 'I've been camping down at the lagoon, but I took a room at the Bottom pub tonight so I could clean up a bit, like.'

And to sleep off the grog, Isabella thought angrily. Now he's talking to Father like butter wouldn't melt in his mouth.

She hardly spoke throughout the meal. Her father and Matt dominated the conversation, with the occasional contribution from Amelia. She noticed her father glancing at her strangely, but she didn't respond. If only he knew.

When the meal was over Matt was the first to rise, moving to pull out Isabella's chair. 'Will you come walking with me, Bella? If that's all right with you, Mr Jamieson?'

Jock looked at his daughter, plainly puzzled by her withdrawn manner. 'Aye, as long as ye have her back here in half an hour. Come on, Amelia. It's time we went to bed.'

Isabella accompanied Matt outside in silence. Taking her elbow he steered her away from the noise and activity of the hotel, guiding her to the bench in front of the darkened Post Office where it was quiet and private. He waited until she was seated, standing there looking at her.

'I'm sorry about this afternoon,' he said quietly. 'I can tell you're mad at me.'

'Yes, I certainly am.' She scowled up at him. 'How did you manage to sober up so quickly? I can still smell the beer, though. It's a wonder Father didn't notice.'

'I was drinking rum, actually.'

'Oh, you!' She turned away huffily. 'That makes it worse! What a silly fool I was, getting caught up with a drunk.'

'I'm not a drunk!' he protested. 'I was just having a bit of fun, like, and I didn't know you were in town.'

'That's another thing. How dare you handle me like that in front of your... *friends*?' She managed to inject enough contempt into her voice to make them sound like the scum of the earth. 'For all I know, you've been boasting about...well, about us.'

'No, Bella! I wouldn't do that.' He grabbed her chin in his fingers and made her look at him, his face earnest in the moonlight. 'I've never talked about girls with me mates, and I certainly wouldn't do anything so rotten to you.' He perched on the edge of the seat beside her, angling his body towards her. 'You're special, Isabella.'

And, God help her, she found herself believing him, succumbing to his charm. It was as if she had no will to resist him. He put his hand to her face, brushing her hair back, and then, obviously sensing her capitulation, pulling her into his arms. He kissed her and the blood rushed through her body, making her weak and dizzy with longing.

After a few minutes he set her away from him. 'I'd better take you back. Your father will be waiting for you.'

He's probably gone to bed, Isabella thought, angry with herself *and* her father. Fools that they were. Matt had both Jamiesons in his pocket and he knew it.

She was right. Her father was in bed, as was Amelia, but the girl was wide awake and full of curiosity as Isabella undressed and slid into the other bed.

'What did Matt have to say? Have you forgiven him?'

Isabella sighed. 'He was full of apologies, and yes, I suppose I have.'

'He was so nice tonight. I wouldn't have guessed he'd been drinking.'

Isabella sighed again. 'No, and I'm sure Father didn't.' She rolled over, kicking the sheet to the foot of the bed. It was too hot for any sort of covering. 'Goodnight, Amelia.'

And yet, she couldn't sleep. Her thoughts were full of Matt as she relived the time she'd spent with him tonight, and those other times when they'd been less discreet. His kisses just now had reawakened her desire, making her body pulse with love and longing. It disturbed her to realize that it would take far more than today's indiscretions to crush her ardour for him. She hadn't guessed being in love could be so painful and so fraught with uncertainty, and wished she could return to that easy, uncomplicated existence she'd enjoyed prior to his arrival in her life.

Matt called to see her the next morning, asking if she would accompany him on a picnic lunch. Isabella reminded him that she had her niece with her, and Matt smiled his easy smile.

'She can come with us.' He winked at her. 'You know I'd sooner we were alone, but at least this way no-one can talk, like. Ask your father too, if he wants to come.'

Isabella shook her head, feeling unaccountably breathless. 'Father won't want to be bothered. He's told me many times, he's had enough of eating meals outdoors.'

'Aye, I suppose you've had an awful lot of that, too. The picnic was a daft idea.'

That moment of uncertainty, brief as it was, tugged at Isabella's heartstrings. 'No, I'd like to go.' She smiled at him. 'It's the company that makes all the difference.'

They enjoyed a pleasant interlude beside the lagoon, finding a quiet spot away from the camping teamsters. Matt teased Amelia, charming her as effortlessly as he did the rest of her family—with the exception of Mercy, of course.

After the recent rain the lagoon was brimming full and covered in blue-flowering water lilies, the grass at its verges a bright green. It made a pleasant scene that was very different from the dry, dusty town of Christmas time. A group of children were catching crayfish nearby and heat shimmered off the fire they'd lit, a billy of water heating over it to cook their catch. Isabella sighed contentedly, pushing aside her earlier concerns. Life could hardly be better.

Matt rode home with them the next day. They made an early start with the loaded wagon so they could drop Amelia off on the way and be back at Kilbride by nightfall. The slow, normally tedious trip passed pleasantly with Matt riding beside them as they sat on the front of the wagon, keeping up a lively conversation for most of the way. When they reached Myvanwy it was late afternoon. The families hadn't been together since Christmas, and Lloyd Kavanagh hurried out to meet them, shaking Jock's hand enthusiastically while glancing sideways at Matt who was unsaddling his horse at the shed.

'Come in and have a cup of tea, Jock.' He smiled up at Isabella. 'You must want a break, Bella.'

'I'd appreciate that.' Isabella returned his smile, surveying him covertly. It was the first time she'd seen him since Matt had revealed that Lloyd and Louise Kavanagh were his parents, and now that she knew, the likeness was plain enough. She looked at him with fresh eyes. Once he'd been young and in love, and as imprudent as she and Matt. Perhaps less so, for he'd fathered a child out of wedlock. She wondered how it had felt to have his long-lost son arrive unexpectedly, casting the entire family into turmoil.

They climbed down from the wagon, her father moving stiffly, groaning. 'Och, me aching joints! I'm getting too old for this traipsing over the countryside. The sooner ye are married the better, lassie, so I can retire in peace.'

'Oh, Father! You need to get out once in a while, or you'll become an old hermit.'

'Too right,' Lloyd chuckled. 'The young ones keep us lively.' He looked up at Matt who had just joined them, his horse released and enjoying a roll nearby, grunting as its body thudded in the soft sand. 'What've you been up to, lad? I thought you were supposed to be coming home last night.'

'I'm sorry, Guv'nor.' Matt looked rueful. 'I met Mr Jamieson and Isabella in town, like, and it seemed a good idea to ride home with 'em today.'

Armed with her own particular knowledge, to Isabella the exchange was clearly one between father and son, not employer and employee. She looked at Jock, wondering if he had noticed anything out of the ordinary.

'Lucky we didn't have something special planned,' Lloyd growled, but to Isabella his annoyance seemed more assumed than genuine, and she was sure Matt knew it. Perhaps it was no wonder that Ben was jealous of his older brother.

Hannah came running out to meet them, hugging Isabella enthusiastically before turning to Matt, who picked her up and tossed her over his shoulder, carrying her squealing towards the house. Hannah kicked her legs in mock protest, displaying white ruffled pantaloons beneath her pinafore. The others, smiling at their antics, followed them to the dining room where Louise was setting a late afternoon tea.

Louise greeted Jock and Isabella warmly before turning to Matt, giving him a look that was part reproachful, part amused. 'Matt...need I ask what kept you in town?'

Isabella glanced at Ben, who had appeared from somewhere and was hovering in the background. She stiffened. Ben's face was harsh with raw hostility and anger. It seemed the situation was worse than she'd realized.

'Good afternoon, Ben.' She forced a wide smile, trying to hide the dismayed turmoil of her thoughts. She wouldn't have believed the gentle, quietly spoken boy was capable of such antagonism.

Ben started and seemed to gather himself enough to return her greeting. 'Good day, Bella. You been living it up in town?'

'We were very sedate this time. Just some shopping and visiting.'

Louise settled them around the table and continued the conversation in a cheerful vein, but Isabella, aware of the undercurrents as she hadn't been before, was unsettled and on edge. Matt and Ben sat at opposite ends of the table and each ignored the other. Isabella pitied Louise, who was obviously doing her diplomatic best to deal with a difficult situation. And yet, the worst could still be in front of her. She shuddered to imagine the talk in town should Matt's parentage become common knowledge.

Once the Jamiesons had resumed their journey and were well away from listening ears, Jock proceeded to drop a bombshell.

'Lassie, has Matt told ye who he really is?'

Isabella stared at her father, open-mouthed. 'What do you mean?'

'I think ye know. He's a Kavanagh, isn't he?'

It seems she'd underestimated him. 'How did you guess?'

'I heard a rumour in town, and looking at them all together today, it's as plain as day.'

'Oh, Father, I feel so sorry for Mrs Kavanagh. It's such an awkward situation, and there's bad feeling between Matt and Ben.'

'*I* don't feel sorry for her.' Jock's face had tightened. 'She was our governess, looking after our bairns, and as we found out later, pretending to be someone she wasn't. And all the while she was playing around with Lloyd Kavanagh. If Matt's hers, he must've been started right under our noses.'

Isabella blushed. Her father wasn't usually given to such plain speaking. 'I'm sure Mr Kavanagh was equally responsible.' A twinge of guilt nearly made her wince. Just as well her father didn't know she'd been 'playing around' with Matt.

Jock let out a little growl. 'It's different for a man. The woman's supposed to be chaste, to look after her reputation.'

Isabella squirmed inwardly. 'Whatever she did, I'm sure she paid for her mistakes. Imagine what she went through, separated from the man she loved and then having her baby taken away.'

'Was he taken away, or did she give him up to save face?'

Isabella bristled indignantly. 'He was taken against her will, by Mrs Kavanagh's own family. Matt told me so. Besides, it's obvious she loves him.'

Jock shook his head. 'It would be the devil of a thing, having your child turn up like that. After twenty years.'

'Perhaps, but I'm sure she wouldn't wish it otherwise. It's Ben who hasn't accepted it.'

Jock grunted. 'It's tough on Ben, that's for sure.' He turned to face her, pushing his hat back to scratch his balding head. 'At least this means he's got prospects. Matt, I mean. If he looks like marrying ye. He's not just a station hand.'

Isabella couldn't admit he hadn't mentioned marriage. 'Don't push us, Father. I wish you hadn't said that today—about marrying me off.'

Jock chuckled. 'Just teasing, lass, just teasing.'

It had given her a bad moment, nevertheless. She was too proud to think Matt might feel pressured into marrying her against his will. More than that, she was concerned that talk of marriage might frighten him away.

Chapter Ten

Matt could see Ben was in a particularly resentful mood. Overstaying his visit to town hadn't improved his standing in the eyes of his wowser younger brother. Ben was such an innocent. He suspected the boy had hardly tasted alcohol, and as they'd already established, had never kissed a girl. He seemed to begrudge Matt's ventures into a territory that was outside his own experience.

Of course, Matt was nearly three years older, and it was beside the point that he had patronized the hotels ever since he'd first arrived in Banana, before he became of age. Fortunately no-one had questioned him.

So far, Ben hadn't said a word, but Matt sensed the boy's anger simmering inside him, waiting for some incident set it off. But Matt was damned if he was going to tiptoe around him—instead, a perverse streak prompted him to carry on as usual, doing all the things he knew Ben hated. If there had to be a confrontation, they may as well get it over with.

On Tuesday morning Matt was out of bed early to exercise Duchess, the thoroughbred filly. The Christmas races had been cancelled due to the drought but the filly's training programme had been maintained, since there was another race meeting scheduled for July. Ben had ridden Duchess over the weekend and again on Monday morning, so Matt thought it only fair he should have his turn this morning.

It was obvious Ben did not agree with his reasoning. He was waiting at the horse yards when Matt returned, barely giving him a chance to dismount from the sweating filly.

'Who do you think you are, Matt *Jones*?' The emphasis on the *Jones* was a blatant reminder that Matt was not legally a Kavanagh. 'You slink off to town and don't come home until it suits you, and then you just waltz in and take over the choice jobs. Bugger off!'

'Listen, you little fool!' Matt let the split rains fall around the filly's neck, grabbing them just below the bit to steady her as she sidled away. He thrust his face close to Ben's, overpowering him with his superior stature. 'You've been trying to spoil things for me for months now, and I've about had enough! I belong in this family whether you like it or not. It's not my fault I was farmed out, so put that in your pipe and smoke it!'

Ben lifted his chin, scowling. 'I've worked here since I was old enough to sit on a horse, and you're not taking away what's mine!'

'Oh, piss off!' Matt swung away, unhitching the girth and dragging the saddle from the filly's back. She shifted restlessly, agitated by the angry atmosphere. He hung the saddle over a rail and walked off with the skittish filly, deliberately turning his back on his younger brother. He could feel Ben's eyes boring into his back as he rubbed the filly down, and as he turned her loose in the yard he noticed him stomping off towards the house. Muttering something rude, Matt stowed away his tack and fed the horse before following Ben to the house for breakfast.

At the meal table, Lloyd issued his instructions for the day. 'I want you two lads to get a killer this morning. There's some fat heifers over on Roundstone Creek. I've got a load of water to cart.'

Both boys accepted their orders without protest, though privately Matt wondered how they were going to work together after this morning's quarrel. As soon as he'd eaten breakfast, he caught the night horse and rode off to round up the work horses. In less than an hour he and Ben were riding off in the direction of Roundstone Creek, travelling together, yet apart, in surly silence.

The paddock in question was an hour's ride away. Once they'd reached it, they spotted a likely mob of heifers grazing on an open flat near a tree-lined gully. The cattle, fit and frisky with bellies full of green grass, flung their heads in the air and set off at a brisk trot which quickened to a canter as the horsemen set off in pursuit.

Matt was in the lead with Ben close behind him as they galloped to overtake the mob. The animals turned towards the gully, and spying a patch of brigalow scrub on the other side, Matt spurred his horse on. Once the cattle gained the sanctuary of the timber it would be difficult to hold them.

The gully loomed ahead, and dodging a low-hanging tree branch, Matt set his horse down the sharp bank. At the last minute he noticed a log wedged across the bed of the gully and reefed his horse sideways to avoid it. Ben's mount, coming up beside him, crashed into him and both horses fell together in a tangle of bodies and legs.

As his horse fell from under him Matt was thrown clear, narrowly missing the log. He hit the ground hard and lay winded, gasping for breath, until fear had him looking to the horses and struggling to his feet. Both mounts were scrambling to rise, Ben crawling out from under them. Sheer alarm had Matt forgetting his own pain as he rushed to drag Ben clear.

The lad was white-faced and smudged with dirt. He laid for a moment, moaning, as Matt crouched beside him, heart thudding. 'Are you all right?' Blood seeped from a graze on Ben's right forearm, but that was the only obvious injury.

Ben gasped. 'The horse fell on me leg.' He moved it tentatively and then slowly sat up, groaning. 'Don't think anything's broken.'

Matt assisted him to rise and Ben stood for a moment, breathing deeply. Then he shook off his brother's grip and hobbled painfully to his fallen hat, dusting it against his thigh before cramming it on his head. They both looked to the horses which were standing together, nuzzling each other nervously.

Ben swore. His mare's eyes were glazed with pain and her right foreleg dangled uselessly.

'Bloody hell!' Dismay and guilt settled on Matt like a lead weight as he realized the horse's leg was broken. The accident hadn't really been his fault—how could he have known the log was there —but he knew Ben would blame him, just the same.

As expected, the boy swung on him, his white face turning red with fury. 'You bastard! You tripped us up and now her bloody leg's broken! My best mare!'

'Bastard' was not a complimentary term at the best of times, and Matt had his reasons for being particularly sensitive about it. 'Don't blame me, you little bugger! *You* ran into *me*, not the other way round.'

In reply Ben lunged at him with clenched fists. Matt grunted as the punch landed on his cheek and retaliated swiftly, driving his own fist into Ben's belly.

It was an unequal fight, with Ben already hobbling and still partly winded from his fall, and Matt of superior size and experience. Ben only got in the one punch before Matt knocked him to the ground, where he lay gasping.

Matt turned away and caught the two horses. He knew Ben carried a Colt revolver in a holster strapped to his saddle, and now Matt retrieved that, along with cartridges from Ben's saddle bag. He turned back to his brother who was struggling to rise, breathing noisily.

'Do you want me to shoot her?' Matt asked grimly.

Ben shook his head and pushed himself to his feet, wiping blood from his cut lip. 'No, damn you! She's my mare. I'll do it.'

He limped over to take the reins. The horse stumbling on three legs, followed him away from the other animal. Matt watched as Ben removed his saddle before holding the gun to the mare's head. Matt flinched as the shot rang out, the horse crumpling slowly. He knew she was Ben's favourite, a well-bred mare and pretty handy on the cut-out camp. He couldn't blame his brother for being upset.

Compassion had him walking to Ben's side. The boy was staring down at his horse, the smoking revolver dangling from his hand. Matt took it from him and spun the cylinder, checking for bullets.

'Here, Ben.' He handed him the reins of his own horse. 'You ride home. I'll walk—we can pick up your saddle later.'

Ben turned to stare at him. Matt thought he saw tears glistening in the boy's eyes, before anger returned in full force. 'This is your fault, you bastard!' he hissed.

Heat rose in Matt like a red tide, threatening to overwhelm him. 'If you call me bastard one more time I'll flatten you again! Now get on that horse and clear off home.'

With one last, venomous look Ben did as he was bid, cursing his pain as he struggled into the saddle. Then he rode off and Matt followed on foot, quickly falling behind as Ben spurred the horse into a trot. Before long they disappeared amongst the trees, leaving Matt alone.

There was plenty of time for reflection on the long walk home, before his father found him. Lloyd was on horseback, leading a spare horse, which he handed silently to Matt. As he mounted Lloyd said quietly, 'Now, lad, you'd better tell me what happened.'

Matt described the events of the morning, without embellishment. Lloyd nodded. 'Like I thought. Just an accident, and no-one's fault.' He scratched his head. 'It's a bit late to get that killer now. The cattle will be scattered everywhere. We'll come back tomorrow.'

'Ben's blaming me.'

'Yeah, I know. He'll get over it, eventually.'

Matt stared at his father. He couldn't help but respect Lloyd's patience—a lot of men would be furious at both of them. A new, unfamiliar feeling of affection surged in him, making his throat heavy. 'I've decided to leave,' he said dully. 'This isn't working out.'

Lloyd drew a deep breath. 'No, it isn't.' He nudged his horse closer and put a reassuring hand on Matt's shoulder. 'We'll look around for a place for you, set you up on your own.'

Matt knew he should feel appreciative of his father's offer of help, but the feeling that his future was being decided for him provoked a spark of defiance. He wanted to achieve something for himself, instead of relying on his family's charity. Besides, the thought of being responsible for his own property was like a weight around his neck, anchoring him down. He wanted money and the freedom that came with it, not further ties. They'd have him all settled and married off, and he was only just twenty-one, for God's sake.

'No, I'm not ready for that yet. I want to go off and see a bit more before I settle down, like.'

Disappointment flickered in Lloyd's eyes. 'Where are you thinking of going?'

Matt shrugged. 'Probably the goldfields. There's blokes making their fortune up Clermont way, or so a bloke was telling me in the pub the other day.'

'Some find gold, some don't. And what about Isabella?'

He shook his head. 'She's a wonderful girl, but I'm not ready to get married just yet.'

Lloyd looked at him quickly, his face tightening. 'Does Isabella know that?'

Matt dropped his eyes, fiddling uncomfortably with his horse's reins. 'I haven't made any promises, like.'

Lloyd sighed heavily. 'You shouldn't court a girl like Bella if you don't plan to marry her.'

Matt looked away, resentment rising up in him. For Christ's sake, he wouldn't be leaving if it wasn't for Ben. He hadn't planned this. 'I'll pack when I get home, then I'll go an' see Bella.

If Ben's too sore to ride I'll help you get that killer tomorrow, but I'll head off after that.'

'Your mother's going to be upset.'

'Aye, I know.' Matt looked squarely at his father. 'But it's not like I'm never coming back.'

He explained his plans to his mother as he ate a late lunch. Ben was nowhere to be seen, probably skulking in his room. Louise sat opposite him, watching him eat, her face pale and her hands on the table top clasped so tightly together that her knuckles were white.

'I wish you'd stay, Matt. Having you here has made our family complete.'

He shook his head. 'If Ben and me are fighting we'll make everyone miserable. Besides, I'm not going for ever, Ma.'

'I hope not.'

He reached across the table and patted her clenched hands. 'I'll write, and I'll make sure I'm back for Christmas.'

She managed a wan smile. 'I know what you're like at writing letters. How many times have your written to your foster family in England?'

He gave a shame-faced grin. 'Twice, I think.'

She nodded. 'I thought so.' She rose to her feet and began gathering the used plates. 'Just be sure you don't forget us.'

Packing was a sad business. The quarters, sparse and functional though they were, had come to feel like home to him. He rolled his swag and gathered together his few clothes, stuffing them in a valise. Later in the afternoon he saddled his horse again and rode to Kilbride to see Isabella.

Isabella was busy in the vegetable garden, tending her beans and tomatoes, along with the pumpkin and watermelon vines that sprawled over half the backyard, invading the space between the orange trees. She'd planted the vegetables after the first rains and hoped they'd produce well before the frosts came. In the late autumn she would plant carrots and cabbages, so there'd be fresh vegetables for the table for most of the year.

She was tugging at a clump of weeds when a familiar voice called her name. Straightening abruptly, she stripped off her grubby gardening gloves and brushed the dirt from her skirt. Matt *would* arrive when she was looking her worst; although of course he'd seen her hot and dirty before.

Skirting the side of the house, she found him standing on the front veranda, hat in hand. 'Why Matt, I didn't expect to see you again so soon.'

He hung his hat on the veranda post and strode down the steps to her, taking her hands in his. He looked unusually serious, his mouth unsmiling. 'Where's your father, Bella?'

'He and Andrew are out on the run somewhere. Shifting cattle to another paddock.'

'Will you come for a walk with me?'

'Of course.' She was breathless, her heart thumping. She knew this was not going to be another circumspect meeting; there was an intensity in Matt's manner today that excited her. She ran her gaze over his long frame, letting her eyes linger just a moment too long. Looking up, she found him watching her with heat in his eyes.

'Come on.' Retrieving his hat and cramming it on his head, he grabbed her arm and propelled her through the garden gate, down the track towards the river. His fingers pressed urgently into her flesh making her pulse beat wildly, her entire body humming with anticipation. The spot where they'd stopped once before was under water now, but they found another just below the top of the bank, sheltered by a low-hanging tree.

Falling into each other's arms, they kissed wildly, bodies straining together. Even as Matt loosened her garments she was boldly unbuttoning his shirt, touching his bare skin with an abandon she hadn't dared show before. He moaned in pleasure and encouragement, and as their clothes were shed they sank together on the grass.

It was much later before she was able to think. She lay with her head pillowed on his chest, listening to the gradual slowing of his heartbeat. Her fingers traced idle circles on his bare chest. 'Why did you come, Matt?'

He turned his head to grin at her. 'That's a silly question. You know why.'

'So you came over just for this?'

He rolled his eyes. 'Not entirely. But it was driving me mad, spending' all that time with you and not being able to touch you.'

Arousal flooded her anew. So all that time they'd spent together in the company of her father and Amelia, he'd been thinking of this. It should have made her angry, but instead it excited her. 'I didn't know you felt that way.'

He grinned, that beautiful charming grin that made her heart turn over. 'Of course I felt that way, Bella. As a matter of fact'—he stroked her breast, bending to kiss it— 'I want you again right now.'

She laughed breathlessly and pushed his face away. 'Later. I want to know why else you came over.'

'Oh, aye.' He sat up and pulled her to face him, drawing her blouse together over her breasts. He took a deep breath. 'I'm leaving, Bella. Ben and I had a fight, and it's just not working out.'

'Leaving?' Her head spun as blood rushed to her brain. 'When? Where are you going?'

'I'm going tomorrow. I'd like to try the goldfields at Clermont, see if I can make a bit of money.'

She pulled away from him and drew up the string of her chemise, then tugged clumsily at the hooks of her corset. Looking up, she saw Matt watched her guardedly. If he dared to suggest they do it once more, now...

But no. He bent towards her, pulling the edges of her corset together. 'Here, let me.'

She sat motionlessly while he hooked her corset, and then she buttoned her blouse and retrieved her drawers, a hastily discarded bundle of cotton that lay nearby in the leaves and grass. Nausea churned her stomach, her euphoria of moments ago dissolving as rapidly as laundry starch when she added hot water.

Behind her, she sensed Matt buttoning his trousers, hearing the clink of his belt buckle. She made to rise, but he was already on his feet, putting out a hand to help her up. With downcast eyes she shrugged it off, gathering up her skirt as she stood.

At last she looked up at him. He just stood there, watching her, his shirt still open exposing that expanse of brown chest, his dark hair rumpled. He looked so blessedly attractive that even now, in the midst of her anger, her throat went dry.

'Bella, what's wrong?'

She stared at him, incredulous. 'You ask me that? You bring me down here and tumble me like some strumpet, and then up and tell me you're leaving?' What made it worse, she'd responded to him like a strumpet, too.

He had the grace to look ashamed. 'Bella, I'm sorry. I should've told you first. But I wanted you so much, and you wanted me. Would you have let me if I had?'

She cleared her throat. In other circumstances his honesty would have disarmed her, but she couldn't let herself be touched by it now. 'No, I wouldn't, and that's why I'm so angry.' She cast about for words to express her distress. 'Matt, what we've done together—if you leave me, that means I'm ruined.'

'No, Bella.' He took her arm, his expression pleading. 'I'll come back for you. I told you—you're special to me, and I want to marry you one day. I just can't stay at Myvanwy anymore and I need money to get a place of me own. Besides, I'm not ready to settle down yet. Give me a bit of time.'

Isabella turned and walked away without answering, her mind in a turmoil. Would he come back, or were they just words? As for marrying her—if that was a proposal, it was a very offhand one. It seemed like her worst nightmares were coming true.

She could hear him following her as she left the river, but she didn't look back. It was only when she reached the house-yard gate that she finally paused and turned to face him. He had buttoned his shirt during the walk from the river and had tucked it into his trousers. His hat covered his rumpled hair, and no-one would guess to look at him that he had been fornicating with her just a short time before.

Fornicating. What a bald, ugly word. And yet wasn't that what they had just done? She could hardly call it loving, in the circumstances. Surely loving was something that people did in bed in the hours of darkness, after they'd been properly married in the church. Or at least, after making some commitment. Not merely as a means of physical gratification before parting.

Before one of them left.

'Isabella.' He put out his hand to her. 'I don't want to leave like this.'

'Why not?' She looked up at him coldly. 'You got what you came for. Now you'd better go.'

His face twisted, and for a moment she wondered if there was real pain there, or just hurt pride. 'Bella...' There was mute appeal in that single word. His hand fell to his side and for a moment he stayed there, looking at her. But when she only stared woodenly back he turned and walked over to his horse, which he'd tied under a nearby tree. He mounted and rode away, and if he looked back Isabella never knew, for she refused to watch.

She got as far as the front steps before she collapsed nervelessly, sitting on the top step and burying her face in her hands. Grief flooded her and for a wild reckless moment she wanted to run after him, to call him back and beg him to stay. But no, for he wouldn't stay, she was sure of it. And then she would have lost everything; even her pride.

Sobs convulsed her. She sat there with her shoulders heaving, crying as if she would never stop. Elsie found her there and sank down beside her, drawing her into her plump motherly arms.

'Now now, dearie. It not that bad.'

'He's gone,' Isabella sobbed. 'He's going away.'

Elsie didn't seem to need to ask who. No doubt she knew Matt had been here. And no doubt she guessed why they'd gone to the river. She made sympathetic noises but did not comment.

Isabella turned her tear-blotched face to look into the kindly black one. 'You were right, Elsie. You warned me against him.'

'He coming back, might be?'

'Oh, he said he would, but I'm not sure that I believe him anymore.'

Elsie stroked her back soothingly. 'P'raps he will. He not bad, that boy. Just proper wild.' After a moment's silence she asked tentatively, 'Missy, you having a bubby?'

'No!' Isabella shook her head vigorously. 'He was careful.'

'But you go with him today, p'raps there might be bubby. You tell Elsie?'

'Yes, Elsie,' agreed Isabella wearily. Oh, how ghastly if she were to find herself with child after he'd gone. But if it hadn't happened before, surely it wouldn't now.

Matt had always taken his pleasure with little regard for morality, but Isabella's distress had reached him today and now guilt had him deep within its grip. Despite the excuses he'd made to himself, he knew he'd done wrong in seducing an innocent girl, and then compounding that by taking advantage of her today on the eve of his departure. The feeling of well-being that usually came with physical release had turned sour.

He was in no mood for conversation at the tea table that night. Thankfully no-one asked him about Isabella. Ben was hobbling around, his injured leg bruised and swollen. His hostility seemed to have faded now that Matt was leaving, but Matt was in no mood to meet him halfway.

Overall the atmosphere was strained and his mother was clearly upset. For the first time Matt wondered if he'd done right in coming to Myvanwy. What had his foster father said? His mother wouldn't want him coming back to haunt her? But she *had* wanted him, and she'd been married to his father, so he hadn't exposed any secrets there. It was just his brother who couldn't accept it.

The next morning he helped his father muster the killer, as promised, before setting off for Banana where he would wait for the coach. It wouldn't be in for a few days, but he could while away the time in Banana as well as anywhere. After the events of the past few days, the hotel sounded like a good place to forget his troubles.

His mother clung to him when it was time to say goodbye. He hugged her hard, wondering if it was the blood tie that made him feel more for her than he ever had for his foster mother, in spite of everything Martha Jones had done for him. Martha had raised him from a baby, showering him with love, while this woman had abandoned him, however unwillingly. Yet there was a bond, a sense of belonging with this couple which he'd never felt with the Joneses.

When it was his father's turn he gripped Lloyd's hand, realising as he looked into that strong, pleasant face how much he still wanted to learn from this man. They said Kavanagh was descended from convicts, but that didn't detract from Matt's opinion of him. He wanted to style himself on Lloyd Kavanagh as he'd never been inspired to emulate Jones the coachman. Perhaps the difference was that Lloyd was still comparatively young, not an arthritic greybeard like Jones. That one weak spot in Lloyd's character—having fathered a child out of wedlock—only made it easier for Matt to identify with him.

Hannah was demonstrative in her parting, hugging his legs and squealing when he grasped her up and threw her in the air. Then he set her down and knelt to her level, allowing her to enthusiastically kiss his cheek. It was as if she'd accepted him as a brother while remaining ignorant of the fact. Their parents looked on indulgently. Ben was conspicuous by his absence.

As he rode away, Matt was torn between two opposing forces, one pushing him onwards, the other pulling him back. He'd been ready to make his home here, and he didn't want to leave. Isabella's white, distressed face kept floating into his consciousness, no matter how firmly he put her away. And there were his parents, whose disappointment had only added to his guilt. But whenever he thought of Ben anger boiled to the surface and he knew he was taking the only possible course.

Besides, there were adventures to be had, and if he stayed he'd end up hobbled and tied, all those experiences forfeited in lieu of domestic entanglement.

Chapter Eleven

Clermont came as a surprise to Matt. Arriving on the train he'd boarded at Westwood, he stepped down to a railway station thronged with drays and wagons, already loading goods for stores and businesses in town. Passenger vehicles also waited for travellers to alight, horses standing patiently with heads hanging and tails swishing languidly at the pestering flies.

Matt stretched his cramped limbs with a sigh of relief and brushed the coal dust from his clothes. His valise in one hand and his swag thrown over his shoulder, he wandered down the hill to explore the town

Like Banana, Clermont was built on the banks of a lagoon which was presently blooming with waterlilies, but there the similarity ended. The town was obviously much larger than Banana, which he guessed was due to the booming gold and copper mines.

Continuing down Capella Street, he crossed the lagoon on the footbridge and turned left up Drummond Street. The main thoroughfare hummed with activity. Rough-looking miners in stained clothing spilled from the various businesses and he found himself feeling for the revolver in his belt, reassuring himself that it was still there. He'd purchased it in Banana on the advice of the publican at the Bottom Hotel, who'd warned him he might have need of self-protection on the goldfields.

Matt entered the foyer of the Commercial Hotel, an imposing double-storey building, and asked for a room. When the clerk handed him a key he paused, still carrying his valise and his swag. 'How do I go about prospecting for gold 'round here?'

The clerk smiled from behind his desk. 'Another fool hoping to get rich? You need a Miner's Right, which you get from the Gold Warden's office. Just down the street. Are you on your own?'

Matt nodded.

'I'd try to get a partner, if I were you. You need two people by rights, one to operate the windlass while the other one's down the shaft digging. Then there's claim jumpers, if you happen to find gold. If others get wind of a find, you'd be hard pressed to leave your claim.'

'Thanks for the advice. I'll keep it in mind.' Matt turned away and climbed the stairs, finding his room at the end of a narrow hallway. Light spilled through a dusty, cobwebbed window onto the narrow bunk against the wall, exposing the stains on the threadbare bedspread. A chipped enamel jug and basin stood on the washstand, and the floor was covered in cracked, worn linoleum. But he supposed this was luxury compared to living conditions on the diggings. He'd have to buy a tent and prospecting equipment, but first he planned to explore the town and wait for the bars to open. In his experience a hotel bar was a good place to make contacts and learn what he could of the area.

That afternoon, he paused in the doorway to the bar, eyeing the men in work-stained moleskins and Crimean shirts, most of them wearing full beards. They were a hard, rough-looking lot, and he felt conspicuous with his shaven face and neatly trimmed hair. Even his rumpled clothes were clean in comparison. Yet no-one seemed to give him more than a cursory glance. He supposed strangers were no novelty here. If a partner was what he needed, he should try to find another new arrival in town.

He shouldered his way to the bar and bought a beer. The barman was a big, hard-eyed man who looked as if life had battered and bruised him, wearing away all the soft edges to leave only the rugged sinew and muscle. The flinty eyes sharpened further when Matt asked if he knew of anyone who might be looking for a partner in a goldmining venture.

'There's new men in here ev'ry day,' he growled. 'Rogues, most of 'em. If ye want an honest partner ye'll need to look long an' hard.' He gestured to a man who was sitting at a table in the corner, sipping quietly at a tankard of beer. 'Try him. He seems quiet enough.'

Matt picked up his change and turned to appraise the solitary figure, a man probably in his early thirties with unkempt hair and a drooping moustache which made his long thin face look even thinner. The stranger was staring into his drink as if the contents fascinated him, and compared to most of his companions, he appeared harmless enough. He only looked up when Matt stopped at his table.

Matt held out an introductory hand. 'I'm Matt Jones. How do you do?'

The fellow looked him over for a moment before rising languidly and shaking Matt's hand. 'Seth Burrows. What can I do for you?'

'Mind if I sit with you, like?'

'Pull up a stump.' The fellow surveyed him idly. 'You a Pom?'

'Aye, from Devon.'

'You don't look like a new chum, though. Been here a while?'

'It'd be nine months. Long enough to get broken in.'

Burrows smiled briefly. 'So what brings you to Clermont? The gold, like everyone else?'

'Aye. Thought I'd try me luck for a while.' Matt sipped his beer and eyed the other man curiously. 'You been in town long?'

'A few days.' Seth pulled a pipe and tobacco pouch from his pocket. 'I'm taking me time, seeing which way the wind blows.'

He paused as he filled the bowl of his pipe. 'McDonald's Flat's been booming, but they reckon water's scarce there. Already miners are leaving their claims and going elsewhere. Black Ridge seems like the place to start. I've got me permit and I was planning to head out there pretty soon.'

Without stopping to think it over, Matt spoke. 'Would you be interested in taking on a partner?'

The other man's eyes glinted as he struck a match on the heel of his heavy lace-up boots. 'You know anything about gold?'

Matt shook his head. 'Not a thing. But I've got a strong back and I don't mind hard work. They was telling me I'll need a partner.'

The man shrugged. 'There's partners and there's partners. Many a man's been killed for his gold.' He looked Matt up and down. 'You don't look the murdering sort, though. You got yourself a licence yet?'

'Aye, I did that this morning.'

'There's nothing to stop us setting out tomorrow, then. They reckon there's a thriving town out there, so we can buy our mining equipment when we get there.'

Matt grinned and stood up, leaning over the table to shake Seth's hand. 'That sounds fair to me. We got ourselves a deal.'

They set off at first light the next morning. They had been told it was twelve miles to Black Ridge, and accustomed to riding as he was, Matt hadn't fancied walking that distance. But Seth had persuaded him not to buy a horse.

'If you've got a horse you've got to feed it, and you won't have no paddock to run it in. Horse feed's expensive on the diggings.'

'I suppose you're right,' Matt conceded, thinking he'd wait and see what the conditions were like. He wouldn't be coming back to Clermont very often if he was reduced to Shanks' pony.

He rolled a few clothes inside his swag and strapped it over his shoulders, adjusting the load across his back. He'd bought a pair of heavy lace-up boots the previous day, leaving his elastic-side riding boots in his valise with his surplus clothes. For a few shillings, the publican had allowed him to stow the lot in a dusty store room.

The road was rough and rutted, making walking difficult. It led over hard stony ridges timbered with rosewood and other spindly-looking trees, their meagre canopy of leaves hardly throwing a shade. The traffic was incessant; would-be miners like themselves, hurrying on horseback or on foot, some pushing wheelbarrows containing their worldly possessions. There was a nearly equal stream of travellers coming the other way; dirty, dishevelled-looking men, a few with a spring in their step that suggested they'd struck it rich, others defeated and hungry looking. There were also wagons, drawn by teams of labouring horses, loaded high with supplies of every kind for the goldfields, and empty ones returning to Clermont to meet the next incoming train.

There was time to talk on the long hike, and Matt learnt that Seth had come from the Mount Morgan Mine, where he'd worked as a labourer, shovelling ore into the little rail wagons which transported it to the battery for crushing. Mount Morgan was supposed to be the richest mine in the world, but Seth could see he wasn't about to get wealthy there doing someone else's dirty work.

'I'd sooner take a chance on either starving or getting rich, than knowing I was always going to be poor while the Halls and Knox D'Arcy got fat on my sweat.'

Matt nodded. He'd heard the prospectors who'd discovered gold at Mount Morgan had ended up with almost nothing, while the present owners, the Messers Hall and Knox D'Arcy, had made a fortune. 'I know what you mean. I left the Old Country because I knew I'd never be anything but Squire's coachman over there.' He didn't bother to mention his relationship to that particular Squire.

Black Ridge was a sprawling hodge-podge of tents and shanties, clustered around a central street. A couple of timber stores with galvanized iron roofs stood amongst lesser buildings, nothing more than timber frames swathed in calico. The area was as desolate as its name suggested, the ridge topped by a belt of brigalow with sombre grey leaves that added nothing to the beauty of the surroundings.

'They reckon the rush started here last year,' Seth remarked. 'It don't look much, but then we didn't come here to admire the scenery. There's no water for washing the gold, so dry blowers are all the go.'

Shafts and mullock heaps dotted the slope of the ridge and the canvas of miner's tents fluttered in the breeze. Hot, tired and thirsty, they walked past a hotel which invited them with a sign proclaiming the sale of beer, spirits and victuals. Instead they stopped at a soft-drink stall, indulging their thirst with a cool lemonade. The slab building next door had a sign that read, 'Mrs Kelly's Boarding House', and next to that a blacksmith laboured over a blazing forge in a rudimentary bark lean-to.

With their thirst quenched, Seth led the way into the prosperous-looking general store, ordering a tent, a wheelbarrow, an axe, picks and shovels, and a panning dish for the initial prospecting. They added basic groceries such as flour, tea, sugar, treacle, potatoes and onions, along with a camp oven for cooking the food.

'There's a butcher just down the street,' the storekeeper told them. 'He kills every day, so you can always get fresh meat.'

As they left the store, Matt pushing the wheelbarrow loaded with their purchases and their swags, Seth counted what was left of their small supply of cash. 'Two pound, twelve shillings and sixpence,' he muttered. 'This won't keep us in meat for long. Let's hope we find gold.'

Painfully conscious of his raw inexperience, Matt was glad to have Seth at his side as they wound their way past numerous claims. Miners worked busily, digging shafts, winching up bucket-loads of soil and rock and operating dry-blowers in a cloud of dust. Some of them looked up and acknowledged the newcomers with a nod, but others merely kept working, intent in their frenetic search.

Seth led the way past the shafts and mullock heaps until they came upon unpegged ground at the edge of the diggings. At the head of a shallow gully, he traversed the area with head bent, now and then picking up a piece of stone and inspecting it with narrowed eyes. He dug a shovelful of dirt and stone and swished it about in the panning dish, tipping it onto a sheet of newspaper from waist height. The wind took the loose dirt and blew it away. He repeated the process until there was nothing left but loose stone. The first attempt yielded nothing, but on the second he picked out a piece of whitish quartz, peering at it closely and handing it to Matt with a grin.

'See the gold, mate? Not enough to get too excited, but it looks promising.' He gestured towards the axe. 'You cut a sapling for pegs, and I'll start measuring off our claim.'

Since there were two of them, legally they were able to peg a double-sized claim. By nightfall they had it marked out, their tent pitched and a fire blazing. Matt made a damper and prepared in a hole in the ground for the camp oven, shovelling burnt-down coals from the fire into the bottom of the hole and scattering more over the lid. Seth boiled a billy of water over the flames and made a brew of tea to accompany the hot damper and treacle.

After their meal they sat beside the campfire, discussing the work that needed to be done in the morning.

'First thing we need to do is register the claim.' Seth stirred the dying embers of the fire with a stick. 'One of us better hike it back to Clermont tomorrow, while the other one gets digging on a shaft. P'raps I better stay here an' do that, since you don't know nothing about gold.' His eyes twinkled as he took in Matt's expression at the prospect of another long walk back to Clermont. 'For a shilling or two you should be able to catch a ride on an empty wagon.'

Matt stifled his disappointment. Realistically, walking would be easier than digging a shaft, but now that he was here he was anxious to get to work. But Seth was right. He knew nothing about digging for gold. 'How deep are we likely to have to sink this shaft?'

'Some of 'em are going down twenty feet or more. And we'll need a dry blower to work the wash. I reckon we can make one out of kerosene cases if we buy a set of bellows and get the smithy to solder up a hopper and a screen.'

Matt had noticed men operating the dry blowers beside their claims earlier that afternoon. It looked hot, dusty work as they manually pumped the lever up and down to work the bellows, which blew the loose dirt away as it travelled over a metal screen. What was left tumbled onto a riffled board which allowed the larger stones to roll off, trapping any nuggets of gold.

'It amazes me what this gold fever does to a bloke,' Matt commented. 'They looked like a mob of hungry ants this afternoon.' He shifted restlessly, imagining what it would be like to unearth a nugget rich enough to set him up for life. 'I think I'm starting to get a touch of it meself.'

Seth laughed. 'I thought you already had it. Why else did you come here?'

Matt wasn't about to share his life story. 'I just wanted to try something different.' It was partly true; he would sooner ride horses and chase cattle than shovel dirt, but there was something about the excitement of the goldfields that lured him, quite apart from the prospect of striking it rich. There was the opportunity for new experiences and the complete freedom of a single man with no ties and no family looking over his shoulder.

Yet, reluctant as he was to commit to any woman at this early stage of his life, as he lay in his swag that night he found his thoughts winging back to Isabella. He pictured her pert, pretty face, her long chestnut hair and the petite body he'd enjoyed so thoroughly. He missed the talk and laughter they'd shared and already the need for her was plaguing him. He'd been less than a week without her.

In a few days they'd settled into a routine. They'd started sinking a shaft, setting up a windlass to hoist the earth and stones from the hole as they dug in pursuit of a gold-bearing lead. They took turn about digging in the shaft and working the windlass, the man on top constantly prospecting with the dish to check for the presence of gold. Barren ground was discarded on the mullock heap, and when they found auriferous wash it was carefully segregated for later processing through the dry blower.

During the worst heat of the day they worked under a shady tree building the frame for the dry blower. Once the smithy had finished the metal screen and the funnel-shaped hopper which would receive the wash, they were able to put it all together, with the bellows positioned to blow air through the screen. Then their routine changed. All morning they would haul ground out of the shaft, and in the afternoon they would put the wash through the dry blower, one man pumping the lever while the other shovelled from the heap beside their shaft. Although so far they had found little gold, there was enough to fuel their anticipation of stumbling onto a rich lead. They'd named their mine 'Wishful Thinking' in an ironic comment on the continued absence of any major find.

Matt's eye was caught by a larger, prosperous-looking mine close by, where a whim was worked by a patient, plodding draught horse to haul ground out of the shaft. When Matt questioned a man from a neighbouring claim, the fellow snorted.

'Humph! That's the El Dorado. It's owned by some rich bugger, the same one that owns th' battery. Not that you see him 'ere much. He's got someone else in charge o' it all.' The man scratched his bearded chin with grubby fingers. 'He came riding in 'ere one day on his fancy horse to run 'is aristocratic eye over us.'

Matt smiled at the fellow's sarcastic tone. 'Not too fond of them 'rich buggers', are you?'

'Na, I'm not. But I guess we should be thankful to 'im, for it's a blessing to have the battery on our doorstep.'

The battery was available to any miner who had gold-bearing ore to crush, providing an essential service to the field. Matt and Seth were stockpiling rock that bore traces of gold, hoping they would eventually have enough to warrant putting through the stamper, but so far the pile was pitifully small. They had found specks of gold with the dry blower, but only enough so far to buy their food and water, with a little left over for recreation. Matt concluded that the miners lucky enough to unearth a fortune were few and far between. Or so it seemed at Black Ridge.

Those miners who'd struck it lucky had plenty of enticements to separate them from their gold. The hotels did a roaring trade, luring men from their lonely camps to drink, gamble and womanise.

Matt found the proximity of all this nightlife alluring at first, but whenever he drank too much he'd see Isabella's shocked, accusing eyes staring at him, as she had when she'd seen him drunk that time in Banana. He'd defiantly push the image away, but after one too many days spent down the shaft with a thumping headache and burning thirst, he found himself wondering if it was worth it. Besides, he had little money for booze or gambling. He began limiting himself, as Seth, did to visiting the hotels once a week on a Saturday night.

'Don't get caught up with them gambling coves, lad,' Seth advised. 'Handing out IOUs is all very well, but they got to be paid some day.'

The women might have been more tempting if Matt hadn't been witness to the varied and unsavoury parade of partners they entertained. One night he was drinking with Seth in one of the bars when he noticed a new girl with dark, tumbling curls, young and fresh-faced even in the harsh carbide lights. Her low-cut gown exposed a white, swelling bosom which drew his gaze like a magnet, and he found himself swallowing to clear a throat gone suddenly dry. She looked up at him, catching his eye, and sauntered over, swaying her rounded hips.

'What's your name, dearie?' She pressed close as he sat on a stool at the bar, laying her hand on his bare forearm to caress his sun-hardened skin.

Matt looked at her pouting lips and smooth rounded breasts, conveniently displayed for him as she leaned closer. His blood surged hotly and for a moment he wanted nothing more than to accept her obvious invitation.

She smiled with hard, perceptive eyes. 'I like a man who knows what he wants. So what's your name, handsome?'

'It's Matt.' He slid his arm around her waist and bent to kiss her, experimenting with the texture of those full lips under his. She smelt of sweat and cheap perfume and her mouth tasted of beer and some lingering essence of the men who'd been before him. Immediately he thought of Isabella's fresh, wholesome scent and comparative innocence and found himself pushing her away.

'What's the matter?'

He shook his head. 'Sorry love, not tonight.'

She stared at him, her dark eyes flashing anger and disappointment. 'D' you think you're too good for the likes of me?'

What could he say to that? He silently watched her with a mixture of relief and regret as she flounced away. Seth beside him cleared his throat, and he turned to find the older man regarding him with an amused smile.

'A wise decision, lad. She might look young, but she's been around since before you started to shave.' He sipped his beer before asking casually, 'Have you got a girl back home?'

Earlier Matt might have denied it, but now he found himself picturing Isabella's freckled, comely face and ready smile with a stab of longing. 'Aye, I do,' he said. 'Though she was pretty mad with me when I left. I don't know if she'll have me back.'

'Is she a good sort?'

'Aye, and she's a fine girl with it. She can ride and work cattle like a man.'

'You make it up with her and stick to her, then. These flashy sort are nuthing but trouble.'

Not for the first time Matt wondered about Seth, if he'd ever been married, but he thought it prudent not to ask. He obviously wasn't in the habit of consorting with whores, to Matt's relief. It was hard enough to deal with his own frustrations, without having a partner who flaunted women in his face.

But Seth was right about Isabella. She deserved better than the way he'd treated her. The next time he went to Clermont, he would write to her and apologize.

As the night went on, the drinkers grew rowdier. A couple of minor scuffles were quickly resolved, but when a full-scale fight broke out, the barman enlisted a few helpers to throw the brawlers outside. Here the fight continued unabated in the brisk night air, men spilling from the bar to shout encouragement and advice. One of the participants, a burly miner with an angry scar running from his eye and disappearing into his beard, eventually felled his opponent with a savage uppercut to the jaw. Matt moved forward in instinctive protest when the man ploughed in boots and all to finish the job. As he kicked the inert, lifeless body, even the hardened miners on the sideline began to complain.

One of them growled, 'Hell, he's going to kill him! Help me stop him.' It was all the encouragement Matt needed as he moved forward, Seth at his side, to help grab the frenzied man. Others soon joined them, and by force of numbers they eventually restrained the kicking, defiant miner.

'Let's chain him to the log!' someone cried, and before Matt knew what was happening he was elbowed aside by a surging group of men. They dragged their captive to a huge log which lay beside the blacksmith's shop. Someone held up a lantern, illuminating the iron rings which had been bolted into the timber.

'The closest Black Ridge has to a jail,' Burrows commented as the crowd shackled the cursing, struggling figure to the log.

'He'll have cooled down by morning,' one of them declared. 'If not, we'll take him to the traps in Clermont.'

Another man laughed. 'Cooled down? Half-frozen, more like. It's bloody cold out here. Anyone got a spare coat or a blanket?'

Someone threw a coat which was draped over the prisoner. The unfortunate man was left sitting there with his back against the log, cursing them all to damnation as the crowd gradually dispersed.

Fortunately one of the hotel women had thought to take care of his fallen adversary, who was now sitting up, moaning, while she sponged his bloodied face. Matt turned to a fellow onlooker with a wry grin. 'Does this happen very often?'

He caught the flash of teeth as the man leered at him in the darkness. 'You new here, lad? We have our own way of dealing with trouble on the goldfields.'

A week or so later the boss of the El Dorado Mine rode in on one of his tours of inspection. It was Matt's turn to operate the windlass with Seth below in the shaft, breaking rock with his pick. Matt first noticed the flashy chestnut blood horse the man was riding, and then his attention was drawn by the silvertail's tailored breeches and top boots. He stopped in mid-turn of the windlass as the newcomer reined in his horse and turned his head to speak to the mine foreman.

The man was tall and lean, and under his hat his hair looked dark. Even at a distance of a hundred yards, there was something disturbingly familiar about him and the way he sat his mount.

Then Matt realized he'd seen that same figure astride a horse on many occasions when he first came to Central Queensland. It was Charles Ashford.

From the shaft beneath him, Seth let out a yell. 'Hey mate, what're you doing? That bucket won't empty itself!'

Hastily Matt tipped out the bucket and lowered it back down the shaft, his mind whirling. Charles Ashford was the last person he'd expected to see on the goldfields. As if the bugger wasn't rich enough, he had to have a finger in this pie as well.

Later that day he and Seth found a small nugget lying in a riffle of the dry blower, and when work was over they decided to celebrate. As they were about to enter one of the bars, a wagonette drew up sharply in front of the building and a man in stockman's dress jumped down, grabbing a large case from the bed of the vehicle and hurrying with it into the lobby. The man's urgency piqued Matt's curiosity and he paused in the doorway to watch as the man approached the front desk.

'I've brought Mr Ashford's luggage,' Matt heard him say. 'Can someone send it up to his room?'

The clerk stood up quickly and bustled out from behind his desk, tugging at his high collar. It was cool outside, but the man's face shone with perspiration. 'Mr Ashford's been waiting for that!' he snapped impatiently. 'He's been wanting to change for dinner.'

'Sorry,' the other man muttered. 'I got held up.'

The clerk grabbed the bag without ceremony and scuttled off up the stairs, puffing vigorously under its weight. Matt grinned wryly. Obviously Charles Ashford had them all running to his beck and call. He glanced down at his own dusty moleskins and grimy shirt, wishing he could afford the luxury of a daily bath and a change of clothes. Water was too scarce on the goldfields to permit that—unless you were as rich as Charles Ashford.

'I wonder if that's the big boss from the El Dorado?' Seth said, mirroring Matt's grin.

Some devil inside Matt made him divulge what he'd had no intention of sharing. 'Aye, that's him. Charles Ashford, Esquire. He's me uncle and all.'

Seth turned to stare at him. 'You're pulling me leg.'

'No, I'm not. He's me mother's brother.'

In the faint light that spilled from the hotel, Matt saw Seth's mouth fall open. 'I didn't know you was well-connected. You don't talk like no silvertail.'

'No, I'm just the coachman's son. But Squire Ashford was me grandfather, all the same.' Matt could almost see the questions written on Seth's face, but he had no intention of providing all the details. Let him come to his own conclusions.

'Did the old man spread himself around, so to speak? Does this Charles Ashford know you?'

'Aye, he knows me right enough. Would probably prefer not to, but I don't let that bother me.' Suddenly an idea occurred to Matt and he grabbed his companion's arm, stopping him from entering the bar. 'Why don't we join me uncle in the dining room for supper?'

Seth shook his head, a slow grin spreading over his face as he watched his friend. 'You're trying to stir up trouble. You think he'll let *us* sit at his table?'

'Probably not. But I've got a mind to eat a decent meal, now that we can afford it. Why shouldn't we eat in the dining room with the nabobs?'

'Ah, Matt, you're a devil,' Seth chuckled. 'I'm going to enjoy this.' He looked down at his clothes. 'Pity we don't have any flasher duds.'

Matt had left his best suit of clothes back in Clermont, and for all he knew Seth didn't possess one. After a skimpy wash in their tent they'd dressed as best they could in clean shirts and moleskins. Luckily the local hotels were too accustomed to catering for rough miners who'd struck it rich, to demand a strict dress code in their dining rooms.

Charles Ashford was seated at a table when they entered, sipping at a glass of wine. He looked up curiously before dismissing them with a quick frown of distaste. Matt smiled to himself and moved to a table close by, knowing Charles could not fail to eventually recognise him if he positioned himself in his uncle's line of sight. He watched the other man surreptitiously as the waiter came to take their order and saw Ashford watching them, saw his eyes narrowing. Ashford turned back to his drink with a studied air of indifference, and Matt knew his uncle had no intention of acknowledging him. A perverse streak stirred within him. *I'll make you talk to me, you bastard.*

'Your uncle don't seem to know you, mate,' Seth observed ironically when the waiter had gone.

'Like hell, he don't!' Matt picked up his tankard of beer, downing half of it in one gulp in defiance of the man at the other table with his cultured manners. 'Bloody stuck-up snob!'

The roast beef, potatoes, pumpkin and onions tasted good, at least to the two men who'd been existing on camp-fire cooking of corn beef, bacon and damper for the last few weeks. Matt wondered if Ashford was relishing it to the same extent. He pictured that luxurious house at Banyandah and Charles's plump but pretty wife, who'd always seemed so friendly and warm— nothing at all like her cold-hearted swine of a husband.

They finished with plum duff and custard for dessert. Matt patted his full stomach in appreciation. 'To hell with Ashford. This was a bloody good idea.'

Seth looked up and gestured in the direction of the other occupant of the dining room. 'If you want to talk to Ashford, you'd better be quick. Looks like he's leaving.'

Matt turned slowly and pushed out his chair. He watched as the waiter fussed obsequiously around their important guest, taking his serviette and pulling out his chair as Ashford rose to his feet. Simultaneously Matt left his table and moved to accost his uncle before he reached the doorway.

'Why, Mr Ashford!' He inclined his head in a mock-fawning manner. 'You must remember me, sir. Matt Jones. I worked at Banyandah for a few months.'

Ashford stared hard at him, his face cold. 'Yes, I remember you. What brings you to the goldfields?'

'Trying to make me fortune, sir, the same as everyone else.'

Ashford smiled thinly, running a derisive eye over Matt's rough clothing. 'Need I bother to ask if you've succeeded?' He brushed a crumb from his own fine coat, as if to emphasise the difference. 'So, when you left us at Banyandah, did you meet up with your parents?'

'Oh, aye. I worked there up until a few weeks ago. It was nice to get to know 'em, like—me Pa as well.' This with a meaning glance, remembering how Ashford had neglected to tell him Lloyd Kavanagh was his father.

'Pleased to see you, were they?'

Ashford's smirk made Matt want to punch him. With an effort he controlled the impulse, abandoning any pretence of subservience as he met his uncle's gaze insolently. 'You might find this hard to believe, but they were real glad to see me.' That little flicker of something—was it shock or regret —in Ashford's eyes was satisfaction enough. 'Well, I won't hold you up. Just thought I'd renew our acquaintance, like, you being me *uncle* and all.' He raised his voice as he uttered the last words, and the waiter, moving past them with a tray of dirty dishes, cast him a startled glance.

Ashford whitened but did not reply, merely turning arrogantly away and striding out of the room as if its occupants were beneath his notice. Matt chuckled and turned back to Seth, who was watching the proceedings warily.

'Strewth, mate, I thought you were going to get us thrown out of here!'

Matt merely grinned. 'Not likely. He's afraid I'll spill me guts. Somehow I don't think he wants to claim me as his nephew.'

'You already knew that.'

'Aye, I did.' He grinned. 'And you know what? I don't really care.'

Chapter Twelve

Isabella knew her father was wondering what was wrong with her. She was not usually prone to melancholy. He kept casting her concerned looks, and once he even said, 'Are you all right, lassie?'

But she brushed him away, afraid he'd question her about Matt. And she couldn't bear to talk about Matt right now. Her grief was like an open wound, festering with her mortification at the way she'd allowed herself to be used. She'd compromised her reputation for a man who hadn't once professed to love her, nor made any real promises regarding their future. Now he was gone and she was a fallen woman, anxiously counting the days since her last monthly bleed.

She was late. Strangely, she'd never really worried about the possibility of a baby before. Matt had assured her there was no danger, and she'd believed him, but that blind trust in him seemed foolish now.

Elsie had taken to watching her with anxious eyes. One day she cornered her in the hallway, saying, 'Missy, somethink wrong, might be. You tell Elsie.'

Isabella looked at the black woman with a quiet desperation. Suddenly the need to confide in another female was overwhelming.

'Oh, Elsie, I'm so ashamed! I loved Matt so much, but we did wrong and now he's gone. What would Father think if he knew?'

Elsie gave her a searching look. 'You having bubby?'

'I don't know.' Isabella hung her head, hot colour flooding her cheeks. 'I just don't know!'

'You see Mrs Forbes,' Elsie advised. 'She help you now.'

Elsie was right. Mercy was definitely the one she should be talking to, much as she dreaded the prospect. She would ride over there tomorrow.

When she arrived Mercy was hard at work as usual, ironing clothes with the flat-iron she'd heated on the stove. Newly-pressed garments hung over chair backs, while pillowcases, bed sheets and tea-towels sat in neatly folded piles on the kitchen table. The pile still waiting in the basket looked equally daunting, and Mercy appeared hot and cross, her hair sticking to her forehead with perspiration.

'This *is* a surprise, Bella,' she observed tartly. 'I haven't seen you much lately.'

Isabella glanced despairingly at the children who hovered around their mother. 'Mercy, can I talk to you in private, please?'

Mercy's gaze sharpened. 'What's the matter?' She turned towards the stove where her eldest daughter was stirring a big pot of something that smelled like pie-melon jam. 'Amelia, pull the jam to one side and take over the ironing for me.'

Mercy led her youngest sister into the tiny office and firmly closed the door. 'Let's hope they don't listen at the keyhole. Is this something to do with that boy?'

Isabella nodded miserably. 'Did you know he's left?'

'No, I didn't.' Mercy's eyes flared with something that could have been satisfaction. 'I warned you about him, didn't I? When did this happen?'

'Nearly a month ago.' Isabella gritted her teeth and plunged on. 'Mercy, how do you know if you're having a baby?'

Mercy let the breath hiss out between her teeth. 'Oh, Bella! Have you let him have his way with you?'

'Yes, more than once.' Isabella faced her sister defiantly. 'He said he was careful, but now I'm running late, and I'm so scared!'

'Oh, you silly, silly girl! How late are you?'

'Just a week or so.'

Mercy sank onto the only chair with a sigh. 'It's too soon to say. Is your bosom...tender? Do you find yourself going out the back all the time?'

Isabella shook her head. 'I haven't noticed.

'Well, perhaps you're not, after all. It might be all the upset that's making you late.'

Isabella clutched at the desk edge, feeling her legs trembling. 'Oh Mercy, I'm ruined. What am I going to do?'

'There's only one thing we can do.' Mercy sat up straighter, all grim determination. 'We get him back here and make him marry you. How dare he seduce you and then just up and leave?'

'No!' She cringed with humiliation. 'He said he's not ready to settle down. If he doesn't want to marry me I'm not going to force him!'

Mercy stared at her grimly. 'If he didn't want to marry you, he shouldn't have done what he did. How dare he take advantage of an innocent, motherless girl! If there's to be a baby, he has no choice. I wonder if the Kavanaghs know where he is.'

Isabella looked blankly at her sister. 'They probably do.' Then she realized that Mercy thought Matt was just the Kavanaghs' employee. 'But of course, you don't know, do you?'

'Know what?' Mercy stood up, twitching her skirts impatiently.

'He's their son.'

Mercy stared at her, her face turning white. She sank back into the chair. 'Do you mean... Lloyd and Louise's son?'

'Yes.' Belatedly Isabella remembered her promise to Matt not to tell a soul. But her father had guessed for himself, and it was unlikely to remain a secret. 'He was born after Mrs Kavanagh was taken to England. Her parents took him away from her—gave him to the coachman to raise.'

Mercy's lips pinched. 'I should have guessed it.' She clasped her hands tightly together in her lap, her knuckles turning white. 'He looks a bit like Charles Ashford, and now I think about it, the likeness to Lloyd is there too. I knew Lloyd and Louise were...intimate.' She jumped to her feet and paced the tiny space, giving a short, mirthless laugh. 'Well, the high-and-mighty Louise Ashford wouldn't have felt so grand when she found herself an unwed mother. It must have been a come-down to her.' She swung abruptly as if coming to a sudden decision. 'We'll go and see the Kavanaghs. If Lloyd's his father, let it be his responsibility to bring him back here.'

Isabella shrank with mortification. She could think of nothing worse than baring her folly to her neighbours. Mrs Kavanagh, perhaps, but another man! Yet, they must surely be sympathetic to her plight, considering their own history. 'What about Father?' she asked aloud.

Mercy shook her head. 'Poor Father! I don't know how he'd handle this. We'll talk to the Kavanaghs first. Perhaps we can get Matt to come back and agree to marry you without involving Father in the sordid details.'

Isabella was about to remind her sister of her aversion to forcing a reluctant bridegroom. But then she remembered the awful possibility that she could be in the family way and swallowed her pride.

Trembling with shame and dread at the approaching interview, Isabella thought the Myvanwy homestead had never looked less inviting. Mercy had decided there was no time to be wasted and had left Amelia in charge of the ironing and her younger siblings while she accompanied Isabella to see the Kavanaghs. They tied their horses under a shady tree near the front gate and walked up the path to a chorus of barking from the dogs at their kennels.

Louise met them on the veranda, Hannah at her side beaming in welcome. Louise smiled warmly at Isabella but cast a doubtful glance in Mercy's direction. 'What a surprise! How are you, Mercy? It's lovely to see you both. It's been quiet since Matt left.'

'That's what we came about,' Mercy stated abruptly, dispensing with small talk. 'Is Lloyd here?' She glanced around as if expecting him to suddenly appear.

'No, not at the moment. He should be home within an hour or so.' Louise frowned and put her hand on Hannah's shoulder. 'Run inside, dear. We grown-ups have to talk.' She turned back to Mercy once the obviously reluctant Hannah had gone. 'What's the problem?'

'It's Matt.' Mercy spoke in an undertone, her face hardening. 'He's done the wrong thing by this poor girl and then up and left her.'

Louise paled. 'Do you mean...' She glanced apologetically at Isabella. 'Has he seduced you?'

Mercy nodded grimly, not waiting for Isabella to respond. 'Yes, he has, the scoundrel! And now he's left her in the lurch! Do you know where he is? He has to come home and marry her.'

Louise faltered and Isabella hung her head, wishing the floor would open and swallow her. She glanced up gratefully as Louise put a reassuring hand on her arm.

'Come inside and sit down. I'll make us a cup of tea and then we can talk about this properly.'

In the sitting room Isabella held the delicate cup and saucer on her lap, sipping at the tea to hide her distress. Louise, having sent Hannah to help Betsy in the kitchen, looked at Mercy over the rim of her own cup and then turned back to Isabella.

'Did Matt make you any promises, Isabella?'

She shook her head. 'No, but I wasn't expecting him to leave. He said he'll come back to me, but how do I know if he will? Besides, now I'm scared I might be...'

As her words trailed away Mercy cut in with brutal frankness. 'Bella's worried she could be in the family way.'

Louise whitened further, and in the midst of her own misery Isabella remembered that this very thing had happened to the other woman. It must be like a recurring nightmare to her.

'Oh, you poor girl! Drat that boy—how dare he take advantage of you! I had no idea this was happening.'

'None of us did,' Mercy said harshly. 'Though I'll admit I was worried. He has the look of a ladies' man, and Father has never kept a proper eye on Bella. But enough of that. Do you know where he is?'

Louise shook her head. 'We haven't heard from him, but he was talking of going to the goldfields at Clermont. I suppose Lloyd will have to search for him.'

'That would be a good idea.' Mercy set her cup in its saucer with a clang. 'You must have some responsibility in the matter, since it appears he's your son.'

There was a dead silence. Isabella blushed furiously, knowing she'd betrayed a confidence. 'I'm sorry, Mrs Kavanagh,' she stammered. 'Matt told me, but I only told Mercy this today.'

'Who else knows?' Louise looked from one to the other, her dismay and embarrassment obvious.

'Father guessed. I didn't tell him. As far as I know, no-one else.'

'I hope this will go no further. Ben has taken it hard, and it will cause so much talk if it becomes general knowledge.'

Mercy shrugged indifferently. 'People will put two and two together, Louise. I'm surprised I didn't see it before.'

'See what?' They'd all been so absorbed; no-one had heard Lloyd come in. He stood in the doorway, his moleskins saddle-stained, his rumpled hair still marked with the sweaty impression of his hatband. His eyes flicked quickly to Mercy and then back to rest on Isabella. 'How do you do, Mercy? G'day, Isabella.'

Isabella murmured a downcast greeting, but Mercy didn't bother with pleasantries. 'We were just talking about your son,' she informed him with a malicious air. 'Your eldest son.'

Lloyd's eyes narrowed. 'You'd better say which one you mean.'

'Why, Matt, of course.'

He just looked at her, his face expressionless. 'What's your problem, Mercy?'

His voice sounded unusually hard, and Isabella noticed how Louise quickly glanced at him.

Mercy carried on, undaunted. 'It's Matt who's the problem. He's done wrong by Isabella and taken off and left her. He should be made to marry her.'

Lloyd looked at Isabella, frowning. 'Is this true?'

She nodded, hanging her head.

Lloyd's face changed abruptly. 'The young lout! How dare he!' He swung about as if looking for something on which to vent his anger. 'If I'd known, I wouldn't have let him take off to those bloody goldfields!'

'Lloyd! Watch your language, please!' Louise looked more upset than ever. 'I think you'll have to go after him.' She hesitated, looking at the other two women. 'There's some concern about Isabella's condition.'

Her meaning, though cryptic, was clearly evident to Lloyd. His mouth tightened. 'I'll head out in the morning.' He looked at Isabella, his expression softening. There was something kind and unjudging in his face which instantly warmed her. 'I'm sorry, Isabella. Don't worry—I'll bring him back.'

Mercy put her cup down and rose to her feet. 'Well, if that's settled, we'll be on our way. Come on, Bella.' She gave Louise a brief nod. 'Thank you for the tea, Louise.'

As they walked past Lloyd, who still stood beside the doorway, Isabella heard Mercy say to him, 'Like father, like son, eh?'

She glanced quickly at Lloyd, noticing him start. His face coloured and he turned away. As they mounted their horses outside, Isabella saw that Mercy was smiling, a little, triumphant smile.

Lloyd and Louise watched from the front veranda as the two women rode away. Lloyd felt Louise's eyes on him and he turned to the door, avoiding her eyes. Anger and guilt churned in his gut, rising all the way up to thicken in his throat.

Louise's voice stopped him. 'Lloyd.'

He paused, his gaze flickering to hers.

'What was Mercy talking about?'

'What do you mean?' He was stalling her—he had a fair idea what she was referring to.

'I think you know.' Her voice was cold. '"Like father, like son.' Somehow I don't think she was talking about *our* pre-marital relationship. She was always inclined to blame me for that.'

Instead of continuing into the house, Lloyd walked over to the edge of the veranda and rested his hands on the railing. What on earth was he going to say? He stared across the paddock where a mob of kangaroos dotted the long grass, a big buck standing on his hind legs to watch the departure of the two horsewomen while the does grazed peacefully around him. He wished his life was as simple as that kangaroo's. Why couldn't Louise leave it alone? What was the point of digging it up now?

'Do you really want to know?' he said at last. He turned to face her, noting her white, grim face. His belly churned a bit more.

'You told me you'd never slept with Mercy.'

'When did I tell you that?'

'A long time ago. Before we were married.'

'That was true. I hadn't.' He looked down, unable to hold her gaze. 'Not then.'

He saw her body stiffen and her hands clench. Glancing up, he found her staring at him, her eyes wide and fixed. 'Was it her? That time you were caught by the river? I thought you'd been with someone, but I assumed it was some floosie in town...' Her voice trailed away.

'Louise, it was five years ago.'

'Does that make it all right?' Her voice was as sharp as the crack of a whip and he flinched as if he'd been struck. 'So it was Mercy?' The guilt on his face must have been all the confirmation she needed, for she let out a cry of pure anger and disgust. 'Lloyd, how *could* you? Our neighbour, your friend's daughter—how can you two look each other in the eye?'

Lloyd managed an ironic grin at that, though he'd never felt less amused. 'We *don't* look each other in the eye, generally.'

She drew a deep breath, her face hard with anger and disgust. 'How can you joke about it? Don't you have any shame?'

His own temper rising at the insult, he moved closer to loom over her. 'Yeah, I've got shame, all right! What do you think I am? I've tried to forget it, tried not to think of it when I was with you. But every time I see Mercy it's there, reminding me I used her. And now she hates me. I was always scared she'd tell you one day, just to spite me. And now she's managed to without even saying the words.'

Louise swung away, but not before he saw the tears starting in her eyes. She fumbled for her handkerchief and blew her nose. 'I could accept it if it was some faceless woman I didn't know,' she whispered unevenly. 'But Mercy—you say she hates you, but you know she's only angry with you. It's me she hates. She's always wanted you—you must be a fool if you don't know that.'

'Yeah, I'm a bloody fool!' Lloyd shouted. 'But if you'd let me near you it would never have happened. How do you think a man feels when his wife won't let him touch her?'

Louise's face was white. 'You know I wasn't myself after Rose died.'

'Do you think you were the only one suffering?'

Her lips trembled. 'I know I wasn't. It was hard on you, too, but how could an affair with Mercy solve anything?'

His face heated. 'It wasn't exactly planned. I didn't realize she was still carrying a torch for me.'

Louise made a derisive noise. 'You must have been blind. Why do you think she's always been so hostile to me?'

Something inside him shifted. 'I don't know—she's jealous of you, I suppose.'

'Exactly. Because she's in love with you.'

He moved closer to her and put a hand on her arm, withdrawing it quickly as he felt her flinch. 'Maybe, but I don't love her. Louise, you're the only woman I've ever loved. Don't let this spoil things for us now.'

She turned away and walked inside without a word. Lloyd drew an impatient breath and grabbed his hat from the hook on the wall. Jamming it on his head, he bounded down the steps and strode off in the direction of the shed.

Louise, remembering that Hannah was still in the kitchen with Betsy, found her there with her hands and apron covered in flour as she helped the maid roll pastry. The little girl appeared to be enjoying herself, her earlier chagrin at being sent away clearly forgotten. If either she or the maid had heard the raised voices coming from the veranda, they gave no sign.

The thought of settling Hannah back to lessons was more than Louise could deal with right now. 'You can have the rest of the day off school, Hannah. You may as well help Betsy finish the pudding.'

Hannah popped a piece of dough in her mouth and grinned at her mother. 'We're making jam roly-poly, Mother. I love roly-poly.'

'Don't eat the pastry, Hannah,' Louise admonished her, from habit. She left the room barely realising what she'd said.

In the sitting room she gathered the empty cups and placed them on the traymobile, her shaking hands rattling the cups in their saucers. Her mind whirled. God, why hadn't she realized it sooner? Mercy had always been a bit hostile, but she'd been positively strange the last few years. Ever since that time Lloyd had spent the night there… Yet she, Louise, hadn't even suspected he might have been involved with *her*.

Anger and jealousy consumed her as she imagined them together. Had they done it in Mercy's bed, she wondered, with her sleeping children in the next room? Had Lloyd …she broke off the thought, furious with herself for even thinking this way. It had happened five years ago, for God's sake, and it was stupid to be torturing herself with it now.

She couldn't let this distract her from the important issue at hand, which was Isabella. She remembered the girl's wan, shamed face with a pang of pity. So she must have looked herself once, when she'd arrived in England unwed and carrying Lloyd's child. But Lloyd hadn't treated her cavalierly, as Matt had treated Isabella—drat that boy! Was it the bad Ashford blood coming out in him? She hadn't thought he was much like Charles, even though the physical resemblance was strong, but this was exactly the sort of thing her brother would do.

Once away from the homestead, the two sisters parted company, Mercy returning to her home on the other side of the river while Isabella turned towards Kilbride. Before Mercy left, she drew her horse beside Isabella's and patted her sister's hand in a rare display of affection.

'Don't fret, dear. Lloyd will have the boy home in no time.'

'If he can find him.' There was a hard lump in Isabella's throat as she made an effort to swallow her tears. 'I've never felt so humiliated. If he's made to marry me, he'll hate me for it.'

'Oh no, he won't. If he didn't want to marry you, he shouldn't have done what he did.'

And that was that, as far as Mercy was concerned. Yet Isabella knew he hadn't forced her into anything she hadn't wanted to do, and it wasn't even as if Matt was older than her. Perhaps he was more experienced, but she hadn't forgotten he was actually a few months younger.

The next day, Louise came to visit. Isabella was glad her father was not at home, for as yet he knew nothing of her problem or of yesterday's excursion. He would have to be told soon, but she was dreading it.

'Oh, my dear girl.' Louise came to her and enfolded her in her arms. 'I wanted to let you know that Mr Kavanagh set off this morning. Let's hope he can find Matt quickly.'

Isabella hugged the older woman, and then she found herself crying, all the pent-up humiliation and misery of the past weeks overwhelming her. 'I feel so ashamed,' she sobbed. 'Matt never asked me to marry him. I was such a fool to let him have his way. It all seems so sordid and cheap now.'

'Hush.' Louise stoked her hair. 'Do you love him?'

Isabella nodded. 'I miss him so much. I can't stop thinking about him. All the things I used to enjoy—the horses and the cattle, my life here at Kilbride—mean nothing to me now.'

'That's what it's like when you're young and in love. When I was taken to England and I thought I'd never see Lloyd again, I just wanted to die.' She made a little, derisive noise. 'I'm not sure if men are worth the tears we cry over them.'

Isabella drew back, fumbling in her sleeve for a handkerchief to wipe her eyes as she was reminded that Louise had endured far worse than she. Her last, slightly caustic comment seemed surprising, though. Isabella had always thought the Kavanagh marriage to be a happy one. 'Had Mr Kavanagh asked you to marry him before you went to England?'

Louise nodded, smiling wistfully as if at some long ago memory. 'Yes, he had, and it was my own fault we weren't already married. I suppose in that way your situation is different. I'm truly ashamed of Matt for treating you so badly.'

Somehow it didn't seem fair to heap all the blame on Matt's head. 'I'm at fault, too, Mrs Kavanagh. I wanted to do what we did. I feel so...so...wanton.'

'Isabella.' Louise took her hands, squeezing them gently. 'Of course you wanted to be intimate with Matt. You love him, and he's such a handsome boy, enough to turn any girl's head.' She smiled gently into Isabella's tear-stained face. 'It's only natural, and it doesn't make you wanton. I hope Mercy hasn't been telling you that.'

'Oh, no.' Isabella found herself flying to the defence of her sister. Mercy had called her foolish, but really she'd been more inclined to heap the blame on Matt's head.

'Does your father know?'

'No, he doesn't.'

'Perhaps it's best not to say anything until you can be sure of your condition. You may be worrying him unnecessarily.'

That sounded sensible to Isabella. 'You're right, Mrs Kavanagh. I'm sorry—I'm forgetting my manners. Would you like a cup of tea?'

She showed her guest into the sitting room and left her there while she made the tea, putting cups and a plate of sliced brownie on a tray. The brownie was a recipe handed down from her mother, through Mercy, and used dried fruit and dripping which was more economical than butter.

Louise spent a comfortable hour with her, and although her cheerful, reassuring chatter did much to lift Isabella's spirits, she couldn't help noticing a strained look to Louise's mouth and eyes.

Louise related wryly how difficult it had been to slip away without Hannah, who was always eager to visit her favourite neighbour.

'I left her with Ben,' Louise said with a laugh. 'I coaxed him to take her riding, which didn't impress him much. He thought with his father away he had more important things to do.'

Isabella squirmed with embarrassment at the mention of Matt's younger brother. 'Does Ben know what's going on?'

Louise shook her head. 'We told him his father had to go to Rockhampton on business. I feel bad about the lie, but at this stage it's really no-one else's business. There's already bad blood between Ben and Matt.'

Isabella sipped her tea and nibbled on a piece of brownie. 'Matt told me that's why he left.'

Louise sighed. 'Unfortunately that's true. I feel we've mishandled the entire situation. Looking back, we should have told Ben and Tom long ago that they had an older brother. But I'd tried to put all that behind me.' She dabbed at her mouth with a serviette. 'I never expected Matt to come in search of us. I thought we'd lost him forever.'

'There's no point blaming yourself. You couldn't have foreseen the future.' Isabella took a deep breath. 'Oh, Mrs Kavanagh, this is so awful.' Tears welled again and she fought them back. 'I don't want Matt to be made to marry me if he doesn't want to. He'll resent me for it.'

Louise leaned close to pat her hand. 'Matt's sweet on you, I know he is. He's just very young and thinks he's not ready to settle down. That's what he told his father before he left. But he'll be happy to do the right thing, I'm sure of it.'

Isabella heaved a deep sigh. 'Oh, Mrs Kavanagh, I hope you're right.'

Chapter Thirteen

After Lloyd caught the Clermont train at Westwood, there was plenty of time for thinking. Curse it all, because the last thing he wanted to do right now was think.

What a mess it was. He was furious with Matt, and knowing he could hardly afford to criticize his son's actions only made him angrier. Was it the example he and Louise had set that had influenced Matt's irresponsible behaviour? The boy had dismissed him on those same grounds when he'd cautioned him about Isabella. That was when Jock was away on that droving trip, and Matt had spent a night over there, supposedly caught by the storm. Perhaps that's when the damage was first done.

Mercy had shaken him with that snide little remark yesterday. It was bad luck that Louise had overheard it. No doubt Isabella had, too, for she'd been closer. 'Like father, like son.' Hopefully, unlike Louise, Isabella wouldn't guess at its source.

He squirmed on the hard leather seat, reliving Louise's anger, wishing Mercy had kept her mouth shut. It was five years ago, but the guilt never eased. You'd think Mercy would want him to forget, but she seemed bound to punish him, as if she hadn't been equally responsible for what had happened.

Those times had been hard for them, for him and Louise. Nearly everyone lost children, sometimes more than one, but they hadn't been prepared for losing Rose, not like that. Sickness like the diphtheria which had claimed little Gertie Jamieson, Mercy's sister, was out of anyone's hands. Rose had just wandered away and he and Louise had never stopped blaming themselves for that. Why hadn't they watched her more closely? How could they have let it happen?

They'd floundered along until Hannah's birth lifted the shadows a little as far as he was concerned. Louise only sank deeper, pushing him away at every turn, denying him the comfort he needed and the physical gratification to which he was accustomed. Perhaps it was not surprising he had turned to Mercy.

Not that either of them had gone seeking it. He'd been to Banana, and had ridden home through a heavy storm. There'd been a fresh come down the river when he'd reached it, too high to cross safely, so he'd ridden back to Mercy's for shelter.

Of course, he should have guessed Forbes would be away; he wasn't often home. And he knew Mercy was lonely and unhappy. Somehow he'd always felt responsible for her marrying a cur like Forbes. She'd obviously done that on the rebound after he'd married Louise. But he hadn't realized she still cared for him, after all that time.

He remembered riding in that day, wet and cold, his trousers heavy and sticking to the sodden leather of his saddle. It was nearly dark, and Mercy came out to meet him with her kids clinging to her skirts.

'The river's up,' he told her, grinning, trying to act normal with her as if he'd never misled her and broken her heart. 'Is it all right if I sleep in the shed tonight?'

'Of course it is, Lloyd.' She gave him a forced, bright smile, in her turn trying to act as if she was happy and not flaming miserable like he knew she had to be, living with that bastard Forbes.

And so he turned his horse into the night paddock with the night horse and she found him a dry set of her husband's clothes. She shut the kitchen door behind him and he changed there beside the warm stove, where a fragrant stew bubbled along with the simmering vegetables. Over the tea table they made polite conversation about the weather and the gossip from town, and eventually he got her timid children to respond to his friendly attempts to draw them out.

Later, after the youngsters were in bed, he and Mercy sat and talked beside the stove while the rain dwindled to a gentle patter on the tin roof and eventually stopped. Mercy found him some bedding and insisted on accompanying him to the shed, leading the way with the lantern while he followed with his arms full of camphor-smelling blankets.

She'd softened as they talked beside the fire, her face glowing in the muted lamplight, her lips smiling as they hadn't smiled for years. The lines of strain and hard work had eased away, and she seemed young again. Pity and affection welled within him as he remembered the passionate kisses they'd indulged in years ago, when he'd thought it was all over with Louise.

The shed smelt familiarly of horse feed and saddle leather. Mercy laid his blankets on a pile of old bags in the corner and paused for a moment, as if reluctant to leave him. 'I hope you'll be warm enough,' she murmured.

'I'll be all right.' The unfulfilled longings which had been bothering him in the kitchen surged to the fore. He looked down into her eyes, smiling gently. 'I've slept rougher than this.'

'Of course you have. You were a teamster before I met you.'

'That was a long time ago.' He lifted his hand and touched her drab hair, remembering how it had once been thick and lustrous. 'You were only a girl, then.'

'Oh, Lloyd!' She stared at him, her lower lip trembling. 'Why do I still feel this way about you?'

He said nothing, just watched her gently while his fingers moved from her hair to her neck, stroking the curve of it. She drew in a sharp breath, her eyes widening and heating with desire. With a little moan she pressed up against his body, meeting his mouth in a fierce, hungry kiss. From there it was only a short step to the bed she'd made him on the shed floor, where they sank in a tangle of limbs and discarded clothing.

For Lloyd the pleasure was in feeling her response, after months of coldness and rejection. To stroke her body and hear her moan, to know she was ready and aching for him, was balm to his wounded soul. He loved her with all the pent-up passion of months, and she returned it with the fervour of a woman who has coveted for many years. But later, after the fire had burnt itself out, he began to realize what he'd done. Feeling sick with shame and regret, he succeeded in gently persuading her to return to the house in case one of the children woke.

Coward that he was, he hadn't waited to have breakfast the next morning. He sneaked into the house in the early hours to fetch his clothes which she'd hung to dry beside the stove, and took them back to the shed to change. He found his horse in the lifting darkness and saddled it, before returning to the house to say goodbye, his footsteps dragging with a mixture of embarrassment and dread.

She looked up from the porridge she was stirring at the stove, her face pale in the dim light. He hesitated in the doorway, twisting his hat in his hands.

'Aren't you staying for breakfast?'

He shook his head. 'I should be on me way. Louise will be worried.'

Her gaze dropped, telling him the mention of Louise hadn't been tactful. She turned stiffly away, but not before he saw the colour flare in her wan face. Guilt stirred, mingling with his compassion to make him feel like the lowest bastard on earth.

'Mercy,' he murmured. 'I'm sorry. I shouldn't have let this happen.'

She swung around abruptly, her face flaring. 'You're always sorry, damn you! If that's all you've got to say, why don't you just get out of here!'

There was nothing else he could do, so he left her and tried to pretend, when he finally got across the river and back to his wife, that nothing had happened. Mercy had seemed to grow bitter after that, and he knew she'd never forgiven him. As if she hadn't gone to him willingly. As if she'd needed to go anywhere near that shed.

One thing had come of it all. The knowledge that he'd jeopardised his marriage had made him realize how important it was to him, how much he still loved Louise. And if Louise had suspected anything back then, she'd never said a word, although she'd seemed to make an effort to take him back into her life. Gradually they'd rediscovered each other, and lately they'd been as happy as in the first years of their marriage, except that Lloyd had this nagging sense of guilt which seemed to hover at the edge of his consciousness, needing only a word or a look from Mercy to bring it to the fore. And Matt, damn him, had given Mercy the perfect opportunity to sink the hooks in, spurring him like a wayward horse.

Now in the space of a few minutes his marriage had turned cold and empty again, with Louise shunning him in bed last night, even this morning turning away from his goodbye kiss.

Lloyd hadn't been to Clermont before. He dozed fitfully on the hard seat throughout the night, wishing the journey was in daylight hours so he could watch the passing scenery. Dawn was breaking when they stopped in Capella and he was able to view the open country of the Peak Downs, where sheep grazed like little grey dots over the tussocky paddocks. When the train drew up in Clermont they were serving breakfast at the railway tearooms, where he tried to appease his depressed mood with a hearty meal of steak and eggs washed down with several cups of strong black tea.

He was directed to the livery stables where he arranged to hire a horse and saddle. He asked the wizened little man who ran the stables if he'd met anyone by the name of Matt Jones, but the fellow shook his head.

'Not that I can recall, but we get so many strangers here. What's he look like?'

'He's young, only twenty-one, tall with dark hair. A good-looking lad.'

The little man looked up at him with interest sparking his tired eyes. 'Your son?' He shook his head. 'Na, you said your name was Kavanagh, didn't you?'

Lloyd smiled briefly. 'It is, but he *is* my son. They say he looks a bit like me, but he's darker.'

'Ah.' The hostler gave an impudent grin. 'Well, I won't ask about the different names—that's your business. But I haven't seen him. Was he chasing gold?'

'Yeah, he was.'

'Go to the Gold Warden's office, see if he's registered a claim. If that fails, ask around the hotels. 'Course, the bars are the most likely place, but they're not open yet.'

Lloyd nodded. 'Thanks, mate. I'll be back later to pick up me horse.'

The gold warden wasn't too forthcoming at first. 'Have you any idea how many claims I've been registering each month?' he asked. 'Men have been flocking in.'

'It was probably about a month ago,' Lloyd persisted. 'A strong upstanding lad, tall and dark-haired.'

'Who's he to you?'

'He's me son and I need to find him. Family reasons.'

'Jones, you say?' The man rose and walked to the far end of his office, where a row of shelving was divided into a different pigeon-hole for each letter of the alphabet. He took a stack of papers from the 'J' file and resumed his seat before beginning to shuffle through them, reading aloud when he got to the Joneses. 'Jones, Albert Edgar. Jones, Frederick. Jones, Henry Arthur. Jones, Matthew Stephen.' He paused and looked up at Lloyd. 'Would this be him? He's filed a claim with a partner, one Seth Joshua Burrows, at the Black Ridge field. His age is indicated at twenty-one years, of no fixed address.'

'That'd be him.' Eagerness bubbled up inside him. 'Where's Black Ridge?'

'It's about twelve miles to the north, on the Miclere road.'

It had almost been too easy. I haven't found him yet, Lloyd reminded himself. He might be gone elsewhere by now. Men abandoned claims and moved on all the time. He reached over and shook the warden's hand. 'Thank you for your help, sir.'

It was desolate-looking country, Lloyd thought as he rode over hard stony hills towards Black Ridge. There were diggings everywhere, both abandoned and populated, the assortment of tents and tin shanties demonstrating the mercurial nature of the industry. The traffic on the road told its own story of desperation and hope, and he shook his head, wondering what it was that drove men to forsake jobs and families when so few of them ever saw their dreams realized. Grazing cattle wasn't the easiest or the most certain way to make a living, but as he thought of his comfortable homestead and settled lifestyle he felt no desire to exchange it for this.

Once he reached Black Ridge, he realized finding Matt wasn't going to be that simple. The field was much larger than he'd expected, with claims dotted over a square mile or more. When he began questioning people, he found many of them were unfamiliar with the names of their close neighbours, which was probably not surprising considering the itinerant nature of the population. His anger with Matt resurfaced. The little bugger was going to pay for putting him through this.

At last one of the hotelkeepers was able to help him. 'Matt Jones and Seth Burrows? Yeah, they've got a claim here somewhere, but I've no idea where.'

Lloyd decided the only way was to search claim by claim, asking questions and looking out for that familiar tall figure. Now that he was this close anticipation surged through him, making him realize how much he'd missed Matt in the last few weeks.

As he skirted a large claim where a horse worked a whim, trudging a staunch, well-worn circle to draw the earth and rock to the surface, he noticed a figure who seemed out of place amongst the rough-looking miners. The elegant clothes of the man contrasted even with those of his companion, who in his waistcoat and tie was possibly a mine foreman. But there was something else which attracted a second glance, something disturbingly familiar that made Lloyd pause. Then the man turned his face and there could be no doubt.

He had hated Charles Ashford for many years, at first with a passionate intensity for the beating Louise's brother had once given him, and for more than that later, when he discovered Ashford had lied to him and taken Louise and his child away. As the years passed his anger had dulled, and if he'd thought his brother-in-law felt one speck of remorse for his behaviour he could have forgiven him. But he knew Ashford would never admit to any wrongdoing; nor had he ever pardoned Lloyd for ruining his sister, as he saw it, and for reducing her to a life of comparative poverty.

Although it was possible Ashford would know where Matt was, Lloyd had no intention of asking him. The last thing he needed right now was a close look at that sneering face. Instead he questioned a man was who shovelling rock into a dray, presumably to be taken to the battery.

The fellow paused, wiping sweat from his brow with a dirty fist. 'Jones, you say? And Burrows? They're just a few claims away, over there.' He pointed in the direction of yet another shaft where a man was working a windlass.

'Thanks, mate.' Lloyd turned his horse with a sigh of relief. It was probably Seth Burrows at the windlass; a spindly-looking fellow in his thirties with a handlebar moustache. It was lucky he'd stopped to ask—if Matt was down the shaft he could so easily have missed him.

Dismounting, Lloyd stepped forward to introduce himself, holding out his hand. 'How do you do? Burrows, is it? I'm Lloyd Kavanagh.' When Burrows looked blank, he added, 'You're Matt Jones's partner, aren't you? I'm his father.'

'Oh.' Burrows looked surprised and Lloyd gathered Matt hadn't filled him in on the details of his pedigree. Then he seemed to gather himself and shook Lloyd's hand. 'How do you do? Matt's down the shaft. I'll call him up.'

Matt appeared in a few minutes, climbing the vertical ladder that clung to the timbered wall of the shaft, his hat, face and clothing covered in a fine layer of dust. He didn't spot his father until he'd scrambled out of the mine, complaining, 'What's going on, Seth? What'd you want me for?' Then he stopped abruptly. 'Pa!'

He coloured, looking confused, and Lloyd realized with a stab of pleasure it was the first time Matt had called him that. The quick surge of pleasure was quickly replaced by irritation as Lloyd remembered why he was here.

'I've got to talk to you, Matt.' He spoke harshly, feeling a twinge of satisfaction at Matt's suddenly worried expression. 'You sure left a tinful of worms at home.'

'What's going on?' Matt looked at him quickly, and then dropped his eyes in a tacit admission of guilt. Belatedly he seemed to remember Seth. 'This is Seth Burrows, me partner. Seth, I'd like you to meet Lloyd Kavanagh.'

'We've already met.' Seth glanced curiously at his partner, probably wondering why he hadn't introduced Lloyd as his father. 'I can carry on here for a while if you want to talk.'

'I'd be obliged, Seth. Come over to the camp, Guv'nor.' In front of the tent Matt pulled up a sawn-off block of wood for Lloyd before perching on another. 'Sorry, we haven't got any chairs, like.' He looked his father full in the face. 'Why'd you come? Is everyone all right at home?'

Lloyd stared hard at him, determined not to let him off too easily. 'Why don't you try and guess? Isn't your conscience bothering you at all?'

Matt coloured again and his eyes flickered uncertainly. 'Is it something to do with Bella?'

Lloyd took a deep breath, supposing he should at least be relieved she was in the boy's mind. 'She's fretting pretty bad, Matt. She didn't deserve to be treated the way you've treated her.' He scowled. 'Don't you plan on marrying her?'

Matt reddened further. 'I suppose I will, one day. But I haven't made enough money yet.'

As Lloyd remembered Isabella's distress, anger flared. 'You haven't made enough money?' he repeated. 'What about Isabella? Did you stop to think how she's feeling now you've run off and left her? If you couldn't afford to marry her, you shouldn't have bedded her!'

Matt's colour had ebbed, leaving him chalk-white under the dust and sunburn. 'Did she tell you that?'

'She told her sister Mercy, and Mercy brought her over to us, looking for justice! She's worried you've got her in the family way.'

Matt let the breath hiss out between his teeth and reached into his shirt pocket for tobacco and papers. With grim satisfaction, Lloyd noticed his son's fingers trembling as he opened the tobacco tin.

'Is she sure about that?' Matt's voice was tight and strained. 'I was careful, like—there shouldn't be no baby.'

'I think it's too soon to be sure.' Lloyd got to his feet and paced to the fire and back, needing some outlet for his anger and his keen sense of disappointment in his son, himself, and the whole bloody situation. 'But this is no way to treat a lovely girl like Bella! They're our neighbours and Jock Jamieson's been me good friend for many years. He trusted you with his daughter—we all did, more fools us.' He kicked angrily at a piece of wood that was protruding from the fire. 'I feel responsible for your behaviour—I should have realized what was going on.' He dropped onto the block again, leaning intently forward with his elbows on his knees. 'There's another thing. You must've told Isabella that you're our son. Now she's told Mercy. Soon the whole countryside'll know.'

'Shit!' Matt's fingers trembled as he rolled his cigarette, licked the paper and pressed it down, smoothing it longer than necessary. 'I didn't think Isabella would tell.'

'She probably wouldn't have if she hadn't been so upset. So what are you going to do about it?'

Matt looked miserable. 'What can I do? I can't wave a magic wand and turn back the clock.'

Lloyd gritted his teeth. 'No, but you can bloody come home and marry the girl! Or hadn't you thought of that?'

Matt jumped to his feet, the unlit cigarette pinched in his fingers. 'You've got no right to go crook at me! Your own track record isn't too good! I'm the living proof of that, aren't I?' He kicked at a nearby kerosene tin in frustration. 'So much for bloody gold mining.'

'Bugger the gold mining!! You can marry her and bring her back here if you're heart's set on it, but it's a rough place for a woman.'

Taking matches from his pocket, Matt paused, sneering. 'Look where you took me mother! Have you seen Banyandah?'

Heat flooded Lloyd's face. He *had* seen Banyandah, about twenty-five years ago. 'That's nothing to do with this. Besides, your mother never cared for the Ashford money.' Suddenly he remembered who he'd seen just before. 'Talking of the blasted Ashfords, did you know he's here?'

'Aye.' Matt lit his cigarette, his face grumpy. 'How could you miss him?'

How indeed, echoed Lloyd silently, knowing he'd probably vented some of his discomfort at Ashford's presence on Matt. 'Last place I expected to see that bastard.'

'There's money to be made here. Isn't that enough for him?' The ghost of a grin crossed Matt's face. 'I ran into him in the hotel dining-room the other night. Decided to join him for dinner.'

In spite of himself, Lloyd was diverted. 'You did *what*?'

Matt shrugged. 'He wasn't keen to acknowledge me, but I didn't give him a choice. Stuck-up bugger.'

'So what happened?'

Matt briefly described the encounter and Lloyd's anger eased as he silently applauded the lad's audacity. 'Trust bloody Ashford to be chasing gold,' he commented. 'The more they've got, the greedier they are.'

'That's all too true.' Matt surveyed their mine gloomily. 'Looks like I'll have to get Seth to buy me out. Just when we'd finally found a bit of decent gold.'

Lloyd looked at him keenly. As he'd hoped, Matt had decided to do the right thing, even if he sounded pretty grudging. 'Your share should be worth something, then. Do you think you can have it sorted out in time to head back tomorrow?'

'I suppose so.' Matt drew at his cigarette, trickling smoke out through his nostrils. 'But what about Ben? Nothing's changed there.'

Lloyd watched him closely. 'I meant what I said before you left. We'll help you find something of your own. Murdoch would sell if I made him an offer.'

Matt's eyes sharpened. 'That's Ironbark Plains, on the other side of the river?'

'Yeah. We could work the places together if you want. You and Ben wouldn't be under each other's feet, and he can still have Myvanwy when I'm gone.'

Matt was beginning to look a little less gloomy. 'Bella would like that, I think. It's still close to home—and Mercy. And I'll have the money from the mine to put into it.'

Lloyd nodded, wishing Mercy hadn't been mentioned. It was lucky Matt didn't know of his relationship with her, or he'd have even less credibility in his son's eyes.

He stood up, stretching his long body. All those hours in the train followed by the ride out here this morning had stiffened his muscles. He must be getting old. He glanced at Matt enviously, wishing he was still a lithe twenty-one years old. But no, when he was that age he was driving horse teams and battling to make something of his life. Middle age had its compensations. 'I'll leave you to break the news to Burrows. I'll get meself a room at one of the pubs.'

Matt gave him a sidelong look. 'We usually drink at the Royal. How about we meet there later?'

Lloyd huffed his disapproval. 'I hope you haven't been spending too much time in the pub.'

Matt shook his head. 'We usually keep it to a Saturday night. But it's not every day my father visits.'

Later, when Lloyd walked into the dining room to find Charles Ashford installed at one of the tables, a waiter hovering anxiously, he silently cursed his troublemaking son. If this was where Matt had eaten with Ashford, he'd have known jolly well his uncle was staying at the Royal.

Ashford stared at his brother-in-law in obvious surprise as Lloyd walked past his table. He didn't pretend not to see him, as he'd apparently done with Matt. But then, he'd once had the upper hand of Lloyd, and that gave him an air of superiority which still rankled.

'Kavanagh.' Ashford raised his eyebrows in an expression of sardonic amusement. 'This seems to have become a family meeting place.'

Lloyd paused, managing a smile. 'It's the first time you've recognized me as family, Ashford.'

Charles shrugged. 'Your son was in here last night. I take it your visit here is connected with him.'

'What's it to you?' Lloyd bristled. 'You've never made us your business before. I seem to remember you telling Louise she could go to hell for all you cared.'

Charles glanced quickly at the waiter. 'Not in those words, surely. How is Louise?'

'She's well. But don't let me keep you from your meal.' Lloyd turned away and crossed the room to an empty table. He could almost feel Charles's eyes boring coldly into his back. He'd been the one to walk away, and that wouldn't please Charles Ashford—particularly since Matt had provoked him earlier.

After he'd eaten, Lloyd made his way to the bar, where he had earlier arranged to meet Matt and Seth Burrows. They were both there already, drinking rum, and Lloyd paused in the doorway to covertly watch his son, hoping he hadn't been corrupted by the debauchery and lawlessness of a rough mining town. Burrows seemed a decent-enough chap, fending off the advances of one of the upstairs girls as Lloyd watched. The girls' open uninhibited presence came as a shock to him. It seemed the law was an infrequent visitor to Black Ridge.

As the night wore on the company became rowdier, but the barman quickly dealt with the few minor scuffles that broke out. Lloyd, Matt and Seth found themselves a table in a quiet corner where they were served by an eager-looking barmaid. Watching the way she contrived to lean over Matt each time she brought drinks to the table, Lloyd knew who was responsible for the prompt service.

'Watch her, Matt,' Seth cautioned with a grin. 'She's got her eye on you, lad.'

Matt smiled and shook his head. 'I'm not *that* hard up.'

Lloyd watched keenly, hoping Matt's discrimination was customary, and not assumed for his father's benefit. 'I think she has an admirer already.' He gestured towards a burly miner who was drinking nearby, monitoring the barmaid's every move with a possessive, angry glint to his eye. 'Watch out for him, Matt.'

Yet the girl seemed to be oblivious to the other man's scrutiny. The next time she came to their table, she scooped the empty glasses onto her tray, pausing at Matt's elbow. 'You gentlemen ready for more drinks?'

Lloyd declined, but Matt and Seth decided to have one more. 'My shout,' said Matt, pulling coins from his pocket. As he passed them to the barmaid she let her fingers trail against his, eyeing him flirtatiously. She turned away, deliberately brushing against his shoulder, and departed to fetch their drinks.

There was more of the same when she returned, leaning across Matt to place the glasses on the table. Lloyd heard an angry exclamation, and then the miner was looming over them, bloodshot eyes glaring at Matt. He grasped the girl by the arm and roughly pulled her away from the table. 'You leave my girl alone!'

Matt looked dispassionately up at him. 'I haven't touched her.'

Lloyd smelt the whiskey fumes on the man's breath, noted the way he lurched drunkenly and clutched a chair for support. His heart sank. The fellow was beyond reasoning with.

'I saw you! You've bin making eyes at her all night.'

'If anyone's been making eyes, it wasn't me.' Matt turned away from the man, picking up his glass to drink. The miner's fist shot out and the glass flew out of Matt's hand, smashing to pieces on the floor. The blow caught the edge of his mouth, and with an oath Matt jumped to his feet, hands balling into fists. He stepped to one side as the man followed through with another punch, his own fist connecting with his assailant's chin. The miner fell backwards to crash against a nearby table before sliding into a motionless heap on the floor.

It was all over so quickly, Lloyd scarcely had time to register what had happened. Men were beginning to crowd around, staring at the man on the floor. Apart from a bloodied lip, Matt was clearly unharmed, so Lloyd transferred his attention to his son's fallen opponent.

Crouching over the miner, he noted the blood seeping from a gash on the side of the man's head, trickling through his dirty matted hair to pool on the floorboards. Lloyd laid his hand on the burly chest, feeling for some sign of life. He put his cheek close to the man's mouth, praying for a whisper of breath, and then listened for a heartbeat. There was nothing. Everything about the man was alarmingly still, all the drunken rage and bluster extinguished in an instant of folly.

'Bloody hell.' He looked up at Matt, not wanting to believe it, not wanting to say the words. It was as if saying them would make them true.

'I think he's dead,' he said at last.

Chapter Fourteen

Matt's face turned white.

One of the onlookers made an angry exclamation, glaring at Matt. 'You bastard! You've killed him!'

Lloyd turned angrily on the speaker. 'It was an accident. You saw what happened—he hit his head on the table as he went down.'

By this time the publican had joined them. He bent over the prostrate man and gave him a quick examination before delivering his own verdict. 'He's dead, all right.' He looked up at Matt, his face cold. 'Don't you go anywhere, mate. I'll be sending for the traps in the morning, and they'll be wanting to talk to you.' He turned to face the crowd. 'There'll be no more fighting in here, you hear? You want to brawl, you take it outside.'

'Hey, wait a minute.' Seth, who'd joined Lloyd to make his own inspection of the body, grabbed the publican's arm. 'Didn't you see what happened? The lad didn't start the fight—look at the glass on the floor. This bugger punched him, and he only hit back in self-defence. The cove was drunk—that's why he fell.'

The publican shrugged. 'I didn't see what happened. Save your story for the traps. I'm not gonna sit by while blokes get killed in my hotel.'

Lloyd looked at the sea of faces that surrounded them, feeling the anger and frustration rise up in him. 'You blokes saw it. You'll be able to back our story. You don't want to see an innocent man go to goal.'

The men shuffled their feet and looked away, avoiding his eyes. One of them muttered something about not wanting to get involved, and only the one who'd accused Matt of killing the miner spoke up. 'He's guilty, all right, the bastard! A man's dead— someone's got to be responsible.'

Lloyd clenched his fists as the beginnings of an insidious fear prickled its way along his spine. He was about to say something abusive to the last speaker when Seth grabbed his arm. 'Steady on, Kavanagh. There's nothing we can do here. We might as well go and get some sleep, talk to the traps tomorrow.' Seth walked over to Matt, who still hadn't moved. It was as if he was rooted to the spot, held captive by shock. 'Let's go, mate.'

Matt dumbly followed his partner, Lloyd bringing up the rear. Matt still hadn't said a word, and only after they'd pushed through the batwing doors into the fresh cold air of the street did he finally speak. 'Flaming hell!' His voice trembled. 'I can't believe I killed him! I didn't even hit him hard.'

'I know, mate.' Seth's voice was soothing. 'The bloke was drunk, or else he wouldn't have fallen like that. It was his own stupid fault. But don't worry, we'll get you out of this.'

Lloyd was silent. Seth spoke with confidence, but he only wished he could share it. Many of the men in there probably had their own reasons for not wanting to be called as a police witness. To escape the scrutiny of the law, some of them would be long gone from Black Ridge by morning. Others, the friends of the dead man, were looking for a scapegoat and wanted Matt to pay for his death. But all Matt could do was stick it out and protest his innocence. Running would only make him look guilty.

'Looks like I won't be heading home in the morning after all,' Matt observed bitterly.

'We'll just sit tight, wait for the traps to come to us.' Lloyd tried not to let his apprehension show. 'If we tell the truth, surely they'll find someone to back our story. Go back to the camp, Matt. I'll be down there in the morning.'

As the two younger men walked off, Lloyd turned to the hotel's front entrance, feeling sick with reaction. Long gone were his teamster days, when he'd spent a lot of time in bars mixing with the roughest elements of humanity. He'd grown civilised in the intervening years. Now he found himself longing for his quiet home with his family around him, far from this raw, brawling place.

Charles Ashford was standing in the hotel lobby, casually leaning against the counter with the tip of his cigar glowing red in his fingers. Lloyd inhaled the pungent aroma of the cigar with a surge of revulsion, associating the smell as he did with the rich and ruthless. Ashford was the last person he needed to see right now.

Ashford made no move to step aside. 'I hear there's been some trouble tonight, Kavanagh.'

Lloyd stared at him, wondering what Charles's purpose was. 'Yeah, there was a fight and a bloke got killed.'

'Someone told me that boy of yours was involved in it.'

Lloyd gritted his teeth, wondering if Ashford was gloating. Surely his interest couldn't be genuine. 'Did they tell you it wasn't his fault? The other cove was drunk—he went for Matt first. Matt didn't even hit him hard, but he was so full he fell back and hit his head on a table.'

Charles looked at him as if considering something. For once that taunting smile was absent. 'Is there anyone else who'll corroborate his story?'

'His partner, Seth Burrows. The publican didn't see it and no-one else seems to want to get involved.'

'What a pity. They'll be looking for an independent witness.' Charles drew on his cigar and blew the smoke through his nostrils.

Then he stepped aside, waving Lloyd past with a nonchalant gesture. 'Sleep well, Kavanagh.'

A hot surge of anger made Lloyd clench his fists, but he looked away, determined not to let Ashford see it. He wouldn't give him that much satisfaction. Brushing past his brother-in-law, he mounted the stairs with a deliberate tread, his stomach churning. But what could he do? Ashford was a low bastard and nothing would ever change that. He was so different from Louise that it was incredible to believe they were brother and sister, raised in the same household.

Matt was sick with apprehension, his mind constantly replaying the skirmish at the hotel. He'd hadn't slept last night and this morning he'd tried to distract himself by keeping busy, packing his belongings and helping Seth work the mine, but the image of the dead man lying there on the floor seemed to be embedded in his memory, torturing him with guilt even as he told himself it hadn't been his fault. He hadn't wanted to fight, but the idiot hadn't given him much choice.

The mine was now officially Seth's. He'd agreed to buy Matt's share for twenty pounds, which was all the money he possessed, and his portion of the gold they'd already found. Lloyd had joined them by the time they'd finished breakfast, looking tired and grim. Like Matt, he seemed to need to busy himself with something, so he'd helped haul wash out of the mine and then they'd done a stint with the dry blower, working in the shade of a big ironbark which grew beside their camp.

It was noon when the police rode up to their camp.

'I'm Sergeant Gunning, and this is Constable Brown,' one of the men said, surveying them from his horse. The sergeant had a pockmarked face, a red handlebar moustache, and beetling eyebrows to match. 'Is there a man here by the name of Matthew

Jones?' He stared at each of them in turn, as if expecting them all to deny it.

'I am.' Matt stepped forward, taking a deep breath to calm his leaping nerves. Might as well get it over with, he thought.

Sergeant Gunning dismounted, handing his reins to the skinny little trooper beside him. 'Ah.' The officer gave him a hard look. 'I need to ask you some questions regarding the death of one Harold Martin at the Royal Hotel last night.'

A cold hard ball of dread settled in Matt stomach. 'I don't even know the man's name. If you say it was Harold Martin, I guess it was.'

'Do you admit to being involved in a fight with this man, Jones?'

'Aye, I do, but I didn't start it. The bugger reckoned I was sparking his girl, which I wasn't. She was the one doing the chasing.'

'So how did the fight start?'

'Martin came up, telling me to stay away from his woman. He was drunk. I told him I wasn't interested and tried to ignore him, but he knocked me drink to the floor and hit me in the mouth.' Matt pointed to the cut on his lower lip. 'Me lip was bleeding—I stood up and punched him on the chin. I didn't hit him very hard, but he was drunk and he fell back, banging his head on the table as he went.'

'I see.' The policeman had been writing in a notebook as Matt spoke, but now he looked Matt straight in the eye. 'That's not the story I was told this morning. They all reckon you started it.'

'Bloody hell!' It was Lloyd who cut in, his voice angry. 'Matt didn't want a bar of the woman, and he certainly didn't want to fight over her.'

'That's true.' Seth stepped forward, his voice firm and sure. 'I was there—I saw the whole thing. If anyone's telling you otherwise it's only because they want to blame someone for Martin's death.'

'Mmm.' The sergeant looked unimpressed. 'And who are you two men? How are you connected to Jones here?'

Seth spoke first. 'I'm Seth Burrows. I'm his partner in this mine. We've been working together for a couple of months now.'

'Did you know Jones previously?'

'No, but I can vouch for him. He's hard-working and decent, and I haven't seen him fight before.'

'And you?' The sergeant looked at Lloyd.

'Me name's Lloyd Kavanagh. I'm a grazier from the Banana district.'

'And what's your business here?'

Lloyd shuffled his feet and looked down for a moment. 'Matt's me son. I'm just visiting.'

The Sergeant raised his bushy eyebrows. 'Your son? I thought his name was Jones?'

Lloyd coloured. 'It's a long story, Sergeant, and it's got nothing to do with this.'

'Very well.' The policeman scribbled some more in his notebook. 'But now I'm going to ask you to come back to Clermont with me, Jones, while we investigate this matter further.'

The blood drained from Matt's face. 'Are you arresting me, Sergeant?'

'Not yet. I need to wait until we've had a doctor examine the body and give a verdict as to the cause of death.'

Events were spinning out of control, dragging Matt on an unplanned, frightening course. He glanced at his father, but Lloyd's grim, pale face offered no reassurance. Yesterday he'd been fretting about the restrictions of getting married, and now he could be facing a jail term for murder.

'You take me horse, Matt.' His father spoke quietly. 'It's still stabled at the Royal. I'll get hold of another one and follow you on to Clermont. I can bring your gear.'

'Aye, thanks, Guv'nor.' Matt briefly gripped his father's hand and turned to Seth. He tried to grin, though the muscles of his face were stiff. 'Come visit me in jail, won't you, mate?'

Seth shook his head, not smiling at the feeble attempt at levity. 'They haven't arrested you yet, and they won't if I have anything to do with it.' He shook Matt's hand, clapping him reassuringly on the shoulder. 'I'm going to Clermont with your father. We'll sort this mess out.'

Once he'd saddled his father's horse, Matt set off for Clermont in the company of the two policemen. The constable led a fourth horse, with the body of the dead man slung unceremoniously across the saddle. Matt averted his eyes from the blanket-wrapped body, trying not to think of how the man had died. He kept reminding himself it had been an accident—surely they couldn't charge him with murder?

In Clermont, the body was taken immediately to the Peak Downs Hospital and the doctor was fetched to do his examination. Relieved that he no longer had to look at the gruesome burden, Matt waited on the long, low veranda with the constable while the doctor carried out his duties in the presence of the sergeant.

When the sergeant re-emerged, his face gave no clue to the doctor's verdict. 'Come along, Jones.' The sergeant remounted his horse. 'We can talk some more at the police station.'

The police station was a couple of blocks away, in the next street. Matt found himself sitting opposite the sergeant in the front office, while the constable tended to their horses. Matt repeated the story he'd already told that morning, and was asked how long he'd been at the goldfields, where he'd lived prior to that, and why he'd emigrated from England.

'Do you have a criminal history, Jones?'

Matt shook his head. 'I've never been in trouble with the law before.'

'Is Jones your real name?'

'Yes, it is.'

'Do you care to tell me why it differs from your father's name?'

Matt sighed and briefly told the story of his parent's separation and his birth in England. 'I was raised from a baby by Edgar and Martha Jones at Fenham Manor, so they gave me their name.'

'Hmph.' The sergeant's eyebrows bristled disapprovingly. 'You sort are always the ones to end up in trouble.'

Matt's temper stirred. 'And what sort might that be?'

The constable, who'd rejoined them by this time, snickered but his superior refused to comment further. He shuffled papers on his desk and announced pompously, 'I must inform you that Dr Kent has pronounced the death to be caused by a blow to the back of the head, occasioned most probably by contact with a hard surface as the victim fell. Since the death was not caused by a direct blow by the accused, namely yourself, but by a fall resulting from the confrontation, I'm issuing you with the lesser charge of manslaughter.'

Matt stared disbelievingly at the two lawmen. He swallowed, his throat suddenly dry. He wanted to say something, to protest, but he seemed to have lost the power of speech. Numbly he thought, it's better than murder. But no... it was too unfair. He'd only acted in self-defence.

In a daze he let them lead him to the lockup, a tiny building next to the police barracks. Inside the single cell, the timber walls were stained almost black, the only furniture a narrow bed with a single folded blanket and a few old sacks in place of a mattress. A bucket stood in one corner and the room reeked of excrement, the only ventilation a tiny barred window high in the rear wall.

As the heavy door clanged shut, Matt stood there staring at it, feeling the walls close in around him. A grilled peephole in the door allowed the only contact with the outside world, but the flap that covered it from the far side hung unrelentingly motionless. He sank down on the bed, the wire base creaking and sagging under his weight, and buried his head in his hands. He fought to breathe, the stench and stale air threatening to suffocate him.

Eventually familiar voices roused him from that deep pit of despair and he straightened, staring at the door as if willing it to open. It didn't, but the constable's high-pitched voice announced, 'You've got visitors, Jones.'

The flap was lifted and he recognised his father's face, peering in. 'Matt! Hell, what a stinking hole! The traps said they'd charged you with manslaughter.'

Matt nodded, hardly trusting himself to speak.

'At least it's not murder, but you don't deserve this. We'll get you a lawyer, see what he can do.'

Seth looked in then. 'Keep your spirits up, lad. I know it's pretty rotten in there, but we'll try to get you out on bail.'

After they'd gone, Matt stretched full-length on the bed. The cell was stuffy and hot in the late afternoon sun, and he could only imagine how unbearable it must be in the height of summer. For the first time in his life he realized just what it meant to be imprisoned, confined in a tiny space with nothing to do and nothing constructive to occupy his thoughts. The walls seemed to be closing in on him, and afraid of losing his sanity, he concentrated on breathing deeply, deliberately emptying his mind.

He must have dozed off, for when he awoke the tiny cell was darker than ever. A constable whom he hadn't seen before brought him his supper—a slab of dry bread, a hunk of slimy corned beef and a pannikin of water. Matt was hungry, but his thirst was bothering him more, and after eating the salty beef, the meagre ration of water did little to quench it. When the constable returned to fetch his plate he asked for more water.

'You'd think this was some slap-up hotel,' the officer grumbled, but he did take the pannikin and return with it full of water. Matt drank it slowly, savouring it, knowing there'd be nothing more until morning.

Sleep was a long time coming that night. The wire base of the bed pressed through the sacks into his back and as it turned cold he shivered under the single blanket. He found himself longing for morning to bring the sun's warmth. When the constable at last arrived with his breakfast Matt was angry and miserable with fatigue, and the plain bread and water did nothing to improve his mood.

He was sitting on the edge of the bed, his head bowed into his hands, wondering how he was going to endure weeks, months, or even years of this, when he heard footsteps on the stair and the flap on his door flicked up.

The gruff tones of the sergeant came through the opening. 'Well, Jones, this must be your lucky day.' The key grated in the lock and the heavy door swung open. 'You're free to go.'

Matt jumped to his feet, blinking at the flood of morning sunshine that poured through the open door. 'What's going on? Have I got bail?'

'Better than that.' Underneath the moustache the yellowed teeth were bared in a wolfish smile. 'An important witness has come forward to back your story.'

Matt stumbled outside, following the sergeant to the police station. Inside the door he came to an abrupt halt, staring at the only occupant of the room. Charles Ashford lounged indolently on a chair, looking incongruously out of place in his elegant three-piece suit. Matt looked at him dumbly, not understanding, not knowing what to say.

'Mr Ashford has come forward on your behalf,' the sergeant explained. 'He saw the fight and he's verified that you acted in self-defence. As an independent witness, and such an important man at that, we must be swayed his testimony. He's also vouched for your good character. He says you worked as a stockman at his station for a time.'

'Aye, I did.' Fancy Charles Ashford coming to his aid! Matt looked gratefully at his uncle, even while a part of him cringed at the sergeant's fawning manner. 'I'm indebted to you, sir.'

Charles shrugged. 'I was travelling through town anyway. You'd better tell your father the good news.'

As Matt walked onto the street, he breathed deeply of the fresh air. Relief surged through him and he found himself reflecting how good it was to be alive and free. Compared to the awful prospect of a future behind bars, having to leave Black Ridge suddenly seemed insignificant.

He found Lloyd and Seth at the Post Office, waiting at the counter while the postmaster dealt with another customer. Lloyd looked as if he'd seen a ghost when Matt walked through the door.

'Matt! What's going on?'

'Mr Ashford got me out, like.' Matt saw his father's face change. 'He came forward as a witness, said the fight wasn't my fault.'

'But—' Lloyd broke off and grabbed Matt's arm. 'Come outside and you can tell us what happened.'

They found a quiet spot away from listening ears, where Matt described Charles's intervention. Lloyd shook his head, looking annoyed. 'But Ashford didn't see the fight. He was asking me about it afterwards. He can't have seen it.'

'Does it matter?' Seth shook Matt's hand, looking jubilant. 'He got you out, that's the important thing.'

Lloyd growled. 'So I'm supposed to be grateful to him now? The lying bastard!'

'Aye, and I'm bloody glad he did lie.' Matt glared at his father. 'If you'd spent half the day and a night in that stinking hell-hole, you'd be glad of it too!'

'So you think I haven't been doing me best?' Lloyd looked hurt. 'I was just sending telegraphs to a lawyer in Rockhampton, trying to get him to represent you.'

'You can tell him we don't need him, now.' Matt shook his head, wondering how his father could let his feud with Ashford influence him in a case like this. 'I don't care much for Charles Ashford, either, but I'm not too proud to accept his help. Not when it means getting off a manslaughter charge.'

Lloyd grunted. 'It just makes me sick that a silvertail like him can walk in and get you released, regardless of whether he's telling the truth. The three of us were protesting your innocence and no-one gave a damn.'

Seth gave a rueful grin. 'Yeah, it's crook, but that's the way of the world, and we've just got to be thankful it's worked in Matt's favour this time. Now, seeing the crisis is over, I'd better head back to me mine before someone jumps me claim.'

Lloyd took Seth's hand in a hard grip. 'Thanks for all your help, mate, and thanks for looking out for Matt here. If you ever find yourself down Banana way, be sure to look us up. There'll always be room for you to stay.'

'I appreciate that.' Seth turned to Matt. 'You look after yourself, young fella, and try an' stay out of trouble. Go home and marry that girl of yours.'

Matt grinned and shook Seth's hand. 'Come and see us sometime—I'd like you to meet her. I hope you find gold-—but not too much, or I'll be wishing I didn't have to sell out.'

At the railway station that evening, as Matt and Lloyd waited to board the train, Matt noticed the tall, elegant figure whistling up a porter to carry his luggage and spoke in a low voice. 'Looks like Ashford's going home, too.'

'Yeah, I see him.' Lloyd gave a humourless smile. 'I doubt he'll be sharing a carriage with us. He'll be travelling first class.'

As they hefted their luggage up the steps of their carriage, Ashford looked in their direction. Matt nodded and touched his hat, but Ashford looked away as if he hadn't seen him.

'Did you see that?' They found their compartment and Matt shoved his valise and his swag onto the rack above his seat. 'Me ever-loving uncle seems to have forgotten me already.'

'What'd I tell you?' Lloyd settled himself on his seat and drew his pipe from his pocket, looking sour. 'He'll never change. God knows why the bugger even did it. Perhaps it didn't suit him to have his kin in jail. Something to do with the family honour, I suppose.'

Chapter Fifteen

The journey to Westwood dragged endlessly. Lloyd seemed to have reverted to his former bad humour and Matt found his own mood of relief cracking under the strain. He'd had little sleep the night before, and now he alternately nodded off on the hard leather seat, and then jerked awake as his head lolled forward. The compartment was full, so there was no room to stretch out and nowhere to rest his head. His father's dour mood made him feel like a chastened little boy being dragged home to apologize for some misdemeanour. Lloyd obviously resented all the trouble Matt had caused him, and having Charles Ashford put one over him hadn't helped.

The two men reminded Matt of sparring dogs, each circling the other and growling threats, but neither willing to put it to the test in a physical fight. That was what happened to a bloke when he got old and respectable. He was sure the young Lloyd Kavanagh, the teamster, would have acted more decisively.

Unable to sleep, Matt found himself brooding over the mine. He'd sold his share of the claim to Seth at what was possibly only a fraction of its value, when it had only just begun to yield paying gold. As his father had pointed out, if the gold they'd found was only a flash in the pan, so to speak, he'd be proved to be well rid of it. But whatever the outcome, he'd wanted to stay and see it through. He hadn't wanted to return to Myvanwy yet, and he resented being forced into it.

According to his father, it no longer mattered what he wanted. He'd forfeited his rights by seducing Isabella. He knew it had been a low, selfish thing to do, though he hadn't guessed she felt quite so badly about it. He relived that last unpleasant scene with her, realising he hadn't taken it as seriously as he should have. Could she really be carrying his child? The thought of being a father was a frightening, if exciting, prospect, but there was no way he would knowingly have left her to the disgrace of bearing a child out of wedlock. Yet, if Charles Ashford hadn't got him out of jail, he might not have had a say in the matter.

At least Matt's mother seemed glad to see him, when they eventually reached Myvanwy. She gave him a big hug and made no recriminations. Probably a glance at her husband's stern face was sufficient to tell her he'd had enough of those. Louise only asked when he planned to see Isabella, and he said he thought he'd wait until the morning. It was late and he'd had enough of travel. One more day wouldn't make much difference.

He didn't say anything about the fight and his subsequent arrest. No doubt Lloyd would tell her later, but right now he didn't want to talk about it. The horrors of that tiny cell and the overwhelming feeling of claustrophobia were still too fresh in his mind.

Then there was Ben, who rode in at dark from checking fences, to be faced. Ben seemed surprised to see him and of course, none too pleased. Since it appeared his younger brother didn't know Matt was in disgrace—something to be thankful for—Matt mumbled something about being sick of goldmining. It stung his pride to have to say that, for it wasn't even true, and his resentment grew.

It was a cold winter's morning when he rode to Kilbride. It was good to be on a horse again. A magpie carolled from a nearby gum tree and a flock of pigeons flew up from the road, wings whirring, startling his skittish horse. The young mare was one he'd been working before he left and hadn't been ridden in his absence. She was fresh and tight, humping with the saddle when he girthed her and shying at logs and bushes along the roadside. He enjoyed the challenge the mare presented, all the more because it distracted him from his moody thoughts.

Jock was at home. Matt's heart sank. Now he was really in for it. But to his astonishment Jock welcomed him heartily onto the veranda, shaking his hand and inviting him inside. 'What brings ye back here, lad? I thought ye were goldmining somewhere. Come in and have a cup o' tea with us. I'll call Bella.'

Matt hesitated, hardly knowing how to react to this undeserved welcome. 'Thank you, Mr Jamieson, but I need to speak to you before I see Bella.' He took a deep breath and plunged headlong. 'I'd like to marry your daughter. Do I have your permission to ask her?'

Jock eyes widened in obvious surprise, but then his face broadened into a smile. 'Aye, of course ye do. Bella's been moping since ye went away. I wondered if she was fretting after ye. Perhaps this will cheer her up.' He called through the door, 'Bella! Someone to see ye!' before turning back to Matt. 'Did ye find any gold?'

Matt was describing his goldmining venture when Isabella appeared. She hesitated in the doorway as if reluctant to step out and greet him and Matt's heart lurched. If she'd been pining for him, he wouldn't have guessed it from her present demeanour. He'd almost forgotten how pretty she was. Her thick chestnut hair was piled in a loosely bouffant style, framing her fine features, and her white pintucked blouse added to the illusion of fragility. It *was* only an illusion, he knew, remembering her in the mustering camp and the cattle yards, pitching in with as much enthusiasm as any man.

'Isabella.' His resentment forgotten, he moved towards her, smiling to hide his uncertainty. How was he supposed to handle this? She wasn't returning his smile—far from it. Should he accept her father's invitation to come inside? He could hardly spurn Jock's hospitality and demand to talk to his daughter alone.

So at Jock's insistence he joined them for a cup of tea, which Isabella made and served in stony silence. Matt squirmed inwardly, noticing the puzzled glances Jock gave her. As soon as he'd drained his cup, he decided the agony couldn't be prolonged any further. 'Mr Jamieson, can I take Isabella for a walk? We have something to discuss.'

'Aye, Matt, of course.' Jock looked severely at his daughter, who seemed about to refuse. 'Off ye go, Bella.' He winked encouragingly at Matt. 'Whatever's troubling ye should be sorted out.'

She walked stiffly beside him, keeping a careful distance. The wide-brimmed hat she'd put on hid her face, but Matt could feel her animosity. What was wrong with her? Hadn't she been the one to demand he come home?

'Bella.' He let the word drop into the silence, testing it. 'Me father said you were upset, that I should come home.' He waited a moment but she made no response. 'Bella, I'm sorry. I behaved like a cad.' He stopped suddenly and took her arm, forcing her to face him. 'Are you—is there going to be a baby?'

'No!' The single word was emphatic, colour flaring in her cheeks. Her lips pinched together, but not before he saw them tremble. 'It was all a stupid mistake. I'm sorry—it wasn't my idea to drag you home.'

He took a step back, disappointment warring with relief. She wasn't forcing him into marriage after all. And yet, he'd kind of liked the idea of being a father. In a way. He liked kids, and there was something appealing about the idea of having one of his own.

'Well, you must be relieved about that.' She'd have been shamed, he knew, by a forced marriage and a baby's early arrival.

'No more than you, I expect. You can go back to your gold mining now.'

He stared at her. 'But that doesn't change things. I'm not going back. I should have asked you to marry me before.' He took her hands in his, feeling how cold they were, how unresponsive. 'I just spoke to your father. Will you marry me, Isabella?'

She pulled her hands away, hurt flooding her face. 'Why are you asking me? Because they said you must? No, thank you, Matt.'

He stared at her, dumbfounded. He hadn't expected this, and yet he should have. She was proud, he'd always known that. He made a valiant attempt to swallow his own dignity. 'I did wrong by you, Bella. Can't you see I'm trying to make it up to you?'

She stared up at him, her face white and pinched. 'But you don't love me, do you?'

Love? What was love? All he knew was, he'd never felt like this about any girl. The way he was right now, all tied up in knots, was new to him and confusing. Before he'd always been in control—always called the tune. He'd never been short of words, but now he didn't know what to say.

'I'm not going to lie to you, Bella. I think you're the loveliest girl I've ever known. You've been brought up decent, and I shouldn't have asked you to do what we did. I want to marry you to put that right.'

'And have you resent me for the rest of our lives? I'm sorry, Matt, but I'm not marrying you.' She turned and stalked off, back towards the house, her head held stiffly high under that bobbing hat. He stood there foolishly looking after her. He called to her but she didn't respond. Because he didn't know what else to do, he walked back to his horse and rode home.

When he walked into the kitchen, his mother looked up anxiously, her busy kneading hands coming to rest on the lump of bread dough. She glanced quickly at Betsy who was stoking up the firebox in the stove.

'Betsy, fetch me a load of wood, will you?' As the maid left the room Louise recommenced her kneading, asking quietly, 'How did it go?'

'Terrible.' Matt pulled out a chair and sank into it, resting his arms on the table. He ran a hand through his tousled hair. 'She knocked me back.'

'What?' Louise brushed away a persistent fly, leaving a smudge of flour on her cheek. 'But what about...'

'There's no baby.' Matt fingered the rough grain of the tabletop, not meeting his mother's eyes. 'She's gone all proud on me, asked me if I loved her. When I said I wouldn't lie to her, but that I cared about her, she got on her high horse, said she wouldn't marry me.' His fingers moved busily against the scrubbed timber, picking at a roughened piece with his fingernail. 'So that's that.'

'I beg your pardon.' Louise's steely tones made his gaze fly up, and he quailed at the anger in hers. 'That's *not* that! If you don't love her you had no business seducing her! She's a lovely girl and she deserves better than a scallywag like you. Naturally she's got her pride, but you'd better start trying to win her back.'

Matt stared at his mother, shocked. She'd never raised her voice against him before. She'd indulged him, probably favoured him, he realized, because he was the son she'd lost, and in the months he'd lived here he'd not borne the brunt of her anger. So this was something new. Something to think about.

Although he was surprised by his mother's displeasure, he was expecting an angry reaction from his father. He was not disappointed. He was in the shed greasing his saddle when Lloyd stalked in, his face tight.

'Your mother said Bella's knocked you back.'

Matt looked up at him, tossing the greasy rag from one hand to the other in an outward show of nonchalance. 'Aye, she did.'

Lloyd glowered. 'In case you've forgotten, her father's one of me oldest friends, and I'm not letting you seduce his daughter and just walk away. Jock doesn't know about it yet, but you can be sure Mercy'll tell him if you don't do the right thing.'

'What am I supposed to do?' Matt heard the truculent note in his own voice and squirmed inwardly. He felt like a thirteen-year-old kid, not a grown man approaching his twenty-second birthday.

'She wouldn't have given in to you if she wasn't in love with you. Win her back. The races are on in a couple of weeks and they'll be having a Race Ball.' Lloyd looked at him with measuring eyes. 'Don't tell me you don't know how to charm a woman.'

He walked away and Matt dipped his rag in the tin of rendered fat, rubbing the flaps of his saddle with unwarranted vigour. The rancid smell of the grease was suddenly overpowering. Bugger them all, he thought. He'd never pursued a reluctant female before and he didn't want to start now.

Louise had noticed Lloyd's bad humour since he'd returned from the goldfields, but as yet she hadn't probed for details. Whenever she looked at him the spectre of Mercy seemed to rise between them, and the hurt and betrayal was a stabbing pain in her chest. In her weaker moments she found herself wondering if that was the only time he'd been unfaithful. She remembered he'd been involved with a barmaid early in their acquaintance, and he'd made reference to some questionable behaviour in his adolescent years. At the time, she hadn't paid it too much mind, but now she found herself thinking of all these things and wondering if she'd been deluding herself about her husband all this time.

It was in this atmosphere of silent recrimination that they made ready for bed that night. Louise slipped into her nightgown and lay on the far side of the bed, listening to the rustling noises as Lloyd undressed. Then the springs creaked and the mattress sagged as he joined her, lying stiffly in the darkness without touching her.

'That bloody brother of yours was at Black Ridge,' he suddenly said.

'Charles?' Louise turned to stare at him, wishing she could see his face. Matt had briefly told her about the goldfield where he'd had his claim, though he'd seemed nearly as disinclined as his father to talk about his experiences. 'What was he doing there?'

Lloyd snorted. 'Mining gold, what do you think? He's got the biggest, richest mine on the field, with a heap of men working it for him, and he owns the battery where they all take their ore for crushing. As usual, the rich just keep getting richer.'

'Trust Charles. But he's not living there, surely?'

'No, he just happened to be up for a visit. I had the misfortune to run into him a couple of times.'

Lloyd's tone made it obvious there was a lot more to the story. Louise sat up in bed, wide awake now. 'What happened, Lloyd?'

He sighed. 'What didn't happen. Trouble seems to follow Matt wherever he goes.' He told her the full story, beginning with how he'd seen Charles in the hotel. Then he described the fight in the bar, and how Matt had been questioned by the police and eventually arrested. Louise listened in anguished silence, realising now why both men had been so uncommunicative. As Lloyd related how Charles had used his influence to free Matt, for the first time in over twenty years she felt a spark of warmth towards her brother. He must have been motivated by some family feeling—he could easily have walked away.

Wisely, she kept any gratitude to Charles to herself. Lloyd's obvious resentment exasperated her, even while she understood it had to do with his male pride. So she focussed on Matt's behaviour instead. 'Do you think it's our fault the boy's so wild, Lloyd? Is it something to do with being illegitimate, with being given up by his own mother?'

Lloyd shook his head. 'Blowed if I know. But what happened at Black Ridge wasn't really his fault. He just attracts the women like bees to a honey pot.'

Yes, as Mercy had said, 'Like father, like son.' While Lloyd was never as handsome as Matt, he'd possessed a similar allure to the opposite sex when he was young. And it seemed that middle age hadn't changed anything.

When Matt left, Isabella walked into the house without looking back. She strode past her father who sat in his chair with a newspaper, looking up at her with a perplexed expression on his face. If only you knew, she thought.

It was ironic that her monthlies had finally arrived only a day or so after Mercy had taken her to Myvanwy. She and her sister had decided there was no point in upsetting her father with the whole sordid, sorry business and so he remained in happy ignorance. But there was a part of her that wished he knew; the part of her that hated seeing him welcome Matt in that trusting way. Though she'd sensed Matt's discomfort, it was as if he was making a fool of her father.

She returned to the task Matt's arrival had interrupted; dusting the furniture with a homemade emu-feather duster. She found herself wielding it with more than usual vigour, pulling herself up short when a china vase fell to the floor and smashed into a hundred pieces.

'Damn it!' she wailed, shocking herself with her own language. That vase had belonged to her mother. She dropped to her knees, trying to salvage something from the shattered mess, but it was hopeless. Tears of anger and frustration welled up, threatening to engulf her.

Oh Matt, she cried silently. Why did he make her feel like this? It was nearly two months since she'd seen him and just the sight of him today had started her heart thudding, her pulse racing, all the defences she'd built crumbling down. It wasn't fair.

When he'd asked her to marry him it had hurt all the more, thinking he didn't love her, knowing he was only doing as he'd been told he must. If she'd been with child, she'd have had no option but to accept him. As it was, the thought of dragging a reluctant bridegroom to the altar was more than she could bear.

When she'd walked away a part of her had hoped he'd run after her, plead with her, tell her he loved her after all. But of course he hadn't and the pain had sliced at her heart, making her wish he'd stayed away. When he'd been out of the district she'd almost convinced herself she'd stopped pining for him. His return had made a mockery of that.

She glanced up as her father entered the room. 'What was that crash?' He stopped short, looking at the fragments Isabella was gathering together. 'Oh! Your mother's vase.'

'I'm sorry.' Isabella wiped at her tears with the back of her hand. 'I know it was a special one.'

'It's only a vase—don't cry over it.' He stared down at her, looking perplexed. 'What's the matter? I thought you'd be pleased to see Matt. Why are you so upset?'

She rose slowly to her feet, not meeting his eyes. 'Because he doesn't care for me the way I care for him.'

'Are you sure of that? He said he wants to marry you.'

'But I don't want to marry him, Father. It's over between us.' She went off to fetch the dustpan, leaving her father to his musings. He was better off not knowing the truth and besides, it was too humiliating to admit what a fool she'd been. She'd been through enough of that already. How was she ever going to hold her head up in front of the Kavanaghs? Did Ben know? If the story got around she'd be ruined, with no option but to marry Matt after all.

Jock had employed Alfred, Mercy's husband, to subdivide one of the paddocks with a new fence. Isabella would have preferred he engaged someone else, for she hated having Alfred on the property, but she knew her father had given him the work for Mercy's benefit. Alfred was camping on the job and only called at the homestead occasionally to stock up on provisions, wire and posts, but on the rare occasions that he'd encountered Isabella alone at the house, he'd made her skin crawl with his coarse manner. Isabella wouldn't trust him for a moment and she was tempted to tell her father so, but knowing Mercy's poor financial position she held her peace. It was doubtful Alfred's family would see much of the money he was earning, but a little was better than none at all.

One day she and her father were sitting at lunch when Alfred arrived. Of course Jock invited him to eat with them—he was after all his son-in-law. It was a Monday and Alfred had been to Banana over the weekend, only now arriving back at work. It appeared he'd spent the previous night with his family, excusing his late start by mumbling something about having jobs to do at home. Knowing how rarely he lifted a finger there, Isabella was inclined to think he'd been sleeping off a heavy weekend.

Alfred had barely started eating when he made a startling announcement. 'Have you heard the story 'bout Matt Jones and the Kavanaghs?' His red-rimmed eyes were avid as he glanced covertly at Isabella. 'Sorry, I probably shouldn't say anything in front of the girl.'

Jock gave him a long look. 'Since ye have mentioned it, ye may as well tell us the story.'

Alfred shrugged. 'It's just that he's apparently their son.'

Isabella's stomach flipped and she looked quickly at her father. Jock laid his knife and fork carefully on his plate and swallowed a mouthful of food before replying, his face expressionless. 'Where'd ye hear that?'

Alfred chuckled. 'It's all over town. Some scandal, eh? The Kavanaghs won't look so high an' mighty now. That Louise—thinks she's a bit above the rest o' us.'

Jock wiped his mouth with his serviette. 'I've known Mrs Kavanagh a long time. Whatever her faults, I don't find her snobbish.'

Alfred snorted. 'Don't ya? She looks down her bloody nose at me.' He glanced at Isabella. 'Sorry, Bella. Excuse the language.'

Isabella wished he wouldn't call her 'Bella'. Only people she was close to called her that, and she didn't count Alfred amongst them. If Mrs Kavanagh looked down her nose at him, who could blame her? Much as she hated to pander to Alfred's love of gossip, she couldn't resist asking, 'So what are people saying about the Kavanaghs?'

Alfred chuckled. 'It's not fit for a young lady's ears, Bella. All I can say is, it's obvious Lloyd and Louise Kavanagh would've wanted to keep this one quiet. Funny we didn't guess—Matt has the look of 'em, when you think about it.'

Jock cleared his throat. 'I was wondering if ye'll need more posts this week, Alfred. I was going to set Andrew to cutting some more for ye.'

Alfred mumbled something, obviously disappointed at the change of subject. Isabella hardly listened to them, her mind whirling. How had the story become known? Had Mercy talked? It was too coincidental that the news had been leaked now, so soon after her telling her sister. If Mercy had told Alfred, he would have taken great delight in spreading it through the hotels and subsequently the whole town. It was like him to then pretend innocence, as if the story had come from another source.

When Alfred had excused himself from the table with the comment that he'd better get to work, Jock looked at his daughter with a wry grimace. 'I feel sorry for the Kavanagh family if that story's got about. Even Matt—it can't be nice to know everyone's talking about ye.'

She said nothing, inwardly squirming with both the guilt that she was probably inadvertently responsible for the gossip, and the familiar agitation that seemed to strike her whenever Matt's name was mentioned. He would hold his head up and laugh at the gossips, she thought—he'd grown up with the slur of illegitimacy. No, Matt wouldn't be the one to suffer.

Ben would feel it more, she thought, remembering his resentment of Matt. He didn't share his brother's confidence or disregard for the opinions of others. She wondered if anything really touched Matt—if he thought of her at all. Of course his pride would have been hurt by her rejection the other day. But he was probably secretly relieved she'd refused to marry him.

The mid-year races were the first major social gathering Matt had attended in Banana, since the Christmas races had been cancelled due to the drought. He hadn't seen the town so busy before—all the station owners and their workers had come in for the occasion. The hotels were overflowing with guests and the campsite at the lagoon was more crowded than usual.

He and Ben joined the other single men with their swags at the lagoon, leaving Lloyd, Louise and Hannah to seek a hotel room. Ben had brought Duchess into town, leading her off his saddle horse. The filly was in fine shape, her chestnut coat gleaming, her trim flanks and muscled quarters hinting of fitness and power. Lloyd had lined up an old friend of his, who'd once been a professional jockey, to ride her. He'd also brought another horse for the grass-fed races, a gelding he'd raced in previous years and had taken out of the paddock with little preparation.

Around their camp fire that night, Matt and Ben shared a rum bottle with a group of young men from the surrounding runs. Matt sensed the curious glances the others were giving him, but he shrugged it off, thinking they must be wondering about his time at the goldfields. As the night wore on and tongues loosened, one of them let slip what was on their minds.

'There's a lot o' talk going round about you, Jones,' George Freeman slurred. George was a lanky twenty-two year-old with sandy hair and freckles, and Matt had already decided he couldn't hold his liquor. 'They're saying you're not really a Jones at all.'

Ben, sitting quietly on the opposite side of the group, looked up sharply. Matt's stomach flipped. Oh no, he thought. Ben'll hate this. 'People talk a lot of rubbish, like,' he said quietly. 'I wouldn't listen, George.'

'This isn't rubbish.' Another lad spoke up. 'I think it's true enough. You've only got to look at you, Matt. You're really a Kavanagh, aren't you?'

'You're telling the story.' Matt didn't look at Ben again, but he could feel the boy's tension from the other side of the fire. He passed the rum bottle to George. 'Have another swig, mate.'

Someone chuckled lewdly. 'Your Ma and Pa tried out the goods before they bought 'em, eh? A good two years before, seems like.'

'Shut your bloody mouth!' Matt glared at the youth who'd spoken. 'Any more comments like that, you'll get your face punched in, Brown. And anyone else who wants to be half-smart.' He looked quickly at Ben, who was sitting bolt upright, his face rigid in the flickering firelight. 'Just ignore them, Ben.'

Ben jumped to his feet. 'What do you care, you bastard? If you couldn't stay in England, why couldn't you stay at the bloody goldfields?'

The boy spun away, stumbling a little as the unaccustomed liquor caught up with him. They all stared after him as he disappeared into the darkness.

'Looks like you're not too popular with your little brother, Matt,' George muttered.

'That's nothing new. Shut up, all of you.'

Matt knew they'd seen him fight on one or two occasions, and he was bigger than all of them, so the subject was changed. This time he didn't join their banter, his mind whirling with the implications of their gossip. How had the story got around? Trust Ben to act like he was hard done by, but Matt wasn't overly concerned with his feelings. It wasn't him who was likely to be victimised.

He kept thinking of his mother, who would surely bear the brunt of it. People would snub her, and the races she'd been looking forward to for weeks would turn into an ordeal. All because he'd come looking for his family, not really caring what trouble he might cause. It made him squirm to admit the truth now, but hadn't a part of him wanted to cause a little trouble, to pay his mother back for dumping him all those years ago?

He wasn't in the mood for partying any more. He sat on the fringes of the group, hardly listening as he brooded over what his companions had said. Had Isabella let the cat out of the bag to spite him? Surely not. She wasn't the malicious sort and she was fond of his mother. She'd have to realize this would hurt her the most. Still, he'd ask her tomorrow.

In the morning, he made his way to the Banana Hotel where his parents and Hannah were staying. He found his mother and Hannah in their room, preparing for the races.

'Matt.' His mother looked pale when she answered his knock on the door. 'I didn't expect to see you. Lloyd's over with the horses.'

'It was you I wanted to see.' He looked at Hannah doubtfully, wondering how he could get rid of her. Then he remembered seeing a group of girls outside the hotel, bowling a hoop along the footpath. 'Hannah, do you want to play outside with the other kids?'

Obviously Hannah did, disappearing instantly in her frilly dress. Louise looked after her in dismay. 'Matt, she'll be filthy before we even arrive at the races.'

'It can't be helped.' Matt shut the door impatiently. 'I need to talk to you, Ma. There's talk around town, like.' He looked her full in the eyes, noticing her worried frown. 'Somehow they've found out who I am.'

Louise blanched. 'So that's it. I wondered why Mrs Barnes snubbed me last night in the dining room.' She drew in a deep, agitated breath. 'And people seemed to avoid us at breakfast, as if we had some horrible disease.'

'I'm sorry.' Matt's stomach clenched with guilt at his mother's distress. 'It's my fault. I should've stayed in England.'

Louise shook her head and touched his arm. 'No, it's mine and your father's—we were the ones who sinned twenty-two years ago. You're the innocent victim.' She turned away and took her hat from the bed, moving to the mirror to set it on her upswept hair. 'I'll endure this, Matt. When I first returned here after marrying your father, there was a lot of gossip. I learned to hold my head up and ignore it.'

She took hatpins from the dresser and deftly slid them in place. 'People have short memories. When something new comes along, they'll forget about this. It's time we acknowledged you openly as our son. We've nothing more to lose.'

Matt smiled at her reflection in the mirror as warmth tugged at him. 'I'd like to be a Kavanagh. Perhaps I'll change me name.'

'You may as well.' Louise smiled back. 'Matt Kavanagh has a better ring to it, anyway.' She glanced anxiously towards the door. 'Can you fetch Hannah now, please? Send her back here before she ruins her dress.'

The population of Banana seemed to have swollen threefold for the race meeting. The track had been carefully levelled and the roofs of the bough sheds replenished with new leafy branches to provide shade. One of the shelters housed long dining tables and another the Publican's Booth, where the less respectable of the men congregated to quench their thirst. Hawkers had congregated on the race track, setting up their wares on improvised benches beside their wagons.

Duchess ran in the first race of the day, the Trial Stakes for two and three-year-olds. Even for this opening race, dust flew from the horses' hooves, drifting over the spectators and settling on the ladies' fancy hats. But Duchess's blazed face was unmistakable as she won by a nose. Beside Matt, his mother cheered and clapped, obviously enjoying this special moment in what promised to be a trying day for her. Matt had already seen people shun her, only a few particular friends keeping her company. But she held her head high and smiled bravely while his father stayed at her side, forfeiting the company of his male friends.

It was easy for a male, Matt reflected. The men had given him curious looks and sly grins, and if a few hoity-toity ladies had looked the other way, he could live without them. His father seemed to be receiving similar treatment; but a lady was supposed to be chaste. In the eyes of some Louise was now a fallen woman and it hardly mattered that her indiscretion had happened so long ago.

Matt looked around for Isabella. He'd noticed her earlier with Mercy and her father, looking fashionable in a broad hat trimmed with feathers and a dark blue gown with those funny sleeves that ballooned out above the elbow and were tight below. He'd desperately wanted to take her away from the crowd where he could have her to himself. Knowing how she'd react to that, he'd suppressed the inclination, but he was determined to talk to her when he could.

When he finally spotted Isabella again, to his relief the older sister was nowhere in sight. Mercy seemed to be a bit of a dragon and he hadn't fancied approaching her, so now he seized his chance.

'Isabella.' She looked up at him quickly, her face whitening. 'Come for a walk with me, please. I need to talk to you.' Before she could refuse, he took her arm and propelled her away from the crowd. 'It's about me mother and father.'

'What about them?'

'The word's got out, like. About who I really am. Did you tell anyone?'

Isabella blushed, but then she stopped and faced him, angrily defiant. 'Yes, I told Mercy. I'm sorry. I think she's told Alfred, which would be like telling the world. I never meant to hurt your parents, but perhaps you shouldn't have confided in me in the first place.'

'I told you because you were special to me.'

'Ha! You told me so I'd feel sorry for you. So I'd let you have your way with me.'

'No, Isabella! It wasn't like that—' he stopped short, finding himself talking to thin air. Isabella had flounced off, skirts swishing and hat wobbling dangerously.

He stood there staring after her, wondering if what she'd said was true. Perhaps he *had* told her to soften her up a little. And it had worked. His throat went dry, remembering that night when she'd given him her warmth and passion along with her body. Possibly he hadn't appreciated the depth of her gift, and now he was paying for that.

He'd meant to ask if he could write his name on her dance card for tonight, but he was blowed if he was going to chase after her like a love-sick puppy. It was easy for his parents to say, but a man had his pride.

The Race Ball was held at the old public hall. The slab, shingle-roofed building still had the slits in the walls that were used in days gone by to shoot at marauding Aborigines. On this cold July night the gaps had been stuffed with newspaper to block the draughts, but despite this the ladies shivered in their low-necked evening frocks. Once the music began most people kept to the floor, not only for the pleasure of dancing but to keep warm.

Matt watched Isabella covertly while dancing with a variety of young ladies, including Isabella's young cousin Amelia, who was enjoying her first ball. Amelia eyed him warily, no doubt knowing there was some problem between him and Isabella, although Matt doubted very much if a girl of her age had been told the details. He joked with Amelia, making her laugh, and told her she looked pretty. When he led her back to her chair beside her mother she was flushed and smiling, and Mercy looked daggers at him. As he walked away he saw Mercy bend her head to her daughter and guessed she was being warned against him. Let her talk. He wasn't about to pursue a child like Amelia.

As he crossed the hall to join the men on the other side, he encountered Isabella on the arm of George Freeman, whom he'd been drinking with the night before. He stopped in front of them, forcing them to pause. 'Evening, George. Miss Jamieson.' He nodded formally to her, as if she was no more than a casual acquaintance. 'Will you keep a dance for me, Miss Jamieson?'

Isabella looked down at her card. For a moment Matt thought she would refuse, but that would be the worst of bad manners. It was probably George's presence that stopped her. She passed him her card and he used the attached pencil to scribble his name against a two-step. 'Thank you, Miss Jamieson.' He nodded to George and continued on his way without Isabella speaking a word.

The two-step was not a success. Isabella's body was rigid with tension and though her feet performed the steps correctly her stiffness spoilt the rhythm of the dance. She replied to his attempts at conversation in monosyllables. At last Matt gave up, conscious of a growing anger and frustration as the dance ended and he took her back to Mercy, again suffering her sister's hostile stare.

As the night progressed Matt noticed George Freeman partnering Isabella for several dances. She smiled at him as she no longer smiled at Matt. George made the most of it, obviously enjoying the way she hung on his arm and flirtatiously tossed her head, drawing attention to her exposed creamy throat. Matt watched them surreptitiously, unwillingly admitting Isabella looked prettier than he'd ever seen her in pale green, her chestnut hair piled high at the back and tumbling onto her forehead in a mass of curls.

Jealousy clawed at him. She should be dancing with him right now, not toying with that ginger-haired oaf who looked thoroughly smitten. After the intimacies Matt had shared with her, it was hardly proper of her to encourage George in that blatant way. Surely she couldn't have transferred her affections so quickly. The poor silly fool was taking it all in—next thing he'd be proposing marriage.

Matt swung away angrily. He wasn't engaged to anyone for this dance, but he needed something to distract him from the spectacle George and Isabella were making of themselves. Sitting out the dance on her chair against the wall, was a girl who worked behind the bar at the Bottom Hotel. He approached her recklessly, knowing her lack of popularity was due to her reputation. Some of the young men here might well have secretly enjoyed her company, but they wouldn't openly dance with her.

The girl eagerly accepted his invitation. As she moved into his arms she looked up at him slyly, pouting her red lips in a suggestive message which Matt understood only too well. Spotting Isabella out of the corner of his eye, smiling up at George, he determinedly looked down at his partner, focussing on the expanse of white bosom revealed by her low-cut gown. She pressed against him in obvious invitation and Matt wondered why he wasn't even tempted to accept it. Of course his reputation in this town would be shot to pieces if he left the dance with her. If respectable women thought he was in the habit of consorting with barmaids, they wouldn't allow him near their daughters, but right now he was too angry to care.

At last the dance ended and he saw Isabella get her cloak and leave the hall on the arm of George Freeman. He hustled his companion to her seat and followed them out, the anger which had been simmering in him all night building into a seething rage.

Chapter Sixteen

Isabella was furious. The day had been a disaster from the start, ever since Matt had pulled her aside to ask her if she was responsible for spreading the story about his ancestry. Not that he'd said that in so many words, of course, but that's what he'd meant. Guilt had flooded her, making her palms sweat despite the cold day. She hadn't wanted to hurt the Kavanaghs, but she'd done so by telling Mercy, who obviously hadn't kept it to herself. She'd heard the gossips twittering and bristled with indignation as she noticed some of the worthy citizens of Banana shunning her neighbours. *Let he who is without sin cast the first stone.*

But it wasn't only her concern for the Kavanaghs and her associated guilt which had spoilt her pleasure in the day. It was impossible to enjoy anything when she had only to look over her shoulder to see Matt...

Matt standing beside his mother, a supporting hand under her elbow. Matt drinking at the bar, laughing with some of his friends. Matt talking to some pretty young thing at a hawker's wagon, flashing those good strong teeth in a smile that was guaranteed to charm the most unsusceptible female.

If seeing him was enough to make the pain stab at her chest, talking to him, having him touch her as he had this morning, was worse by far. Then when she'd danced with him and he'd put his hand on the small of her back, his body disturbingly close while that brown, handsome face bent to hers, the ache had been as sharp and nagging as a rotten tooth.

She'd tried to distract herself with George, although she knew she was behaving badly. George's devoted, admiring eyes soothed her wounded spirit, but he didn't make her heart beat faster. Perhaps she needed to give him a chance—perhaps if he kissed her she'd recapture the magic she'd known with Matt.

Then Matt danced with that little tart from the hotel. The way she pressed against him, thrusting her near-naked chest under his gaze... Isabella suddenly needed fresh air. She picked up her cloak and tugged at George's hand.

'Let's go for a walk outside. I need a break from the crowd.'

George looked surprised and slightly shocked, but he didn't argue. They descended the veranda steps and walked down the street, into the shrouding darkness. George reached for her hand, linking his damp fingers with hers. At last they stopped to rest against a paling fence.

'Isabella,' he murmured. 'You're beautiful.' He put his hands on her waist, pulling her towards him, and then he bent his head and kissed her.

His mouth was wet, his lips tentative, inexperienced. It was nothing like kissing Matt. Isabella slid her arms around his neck, thinking, perhaps it'll get better. Once he learns how to do it properly...

'What the hell's going on here?' She knew that voice, knew it too well. The Devonshire accent was unmistakable even to George who pulled away quickly, guilt apparent in the stiffness of his body.

Matt loomed over them, his face furious in the meagre light, the whites of his eyes gleaming. 'Bella! What do you think you're doing? D' you want to be the talk of the town?'

'It's none of your business, Matt Jones!' Isabella's heart raced, her blood pounding.

'Aye, it bloody well is! Clear off, George. She's not for you.'

'Who are you to say? How dare you swear at George like that!' Isabella desperately grabbed George's hand. 'Stay, George!'

'Yeah.' George lifted his chin pugnaciously, meeting Matt's angry stare. 'What's it got to do with you?'

'It's got plenty to do with me. Bella's supposed to be marrying me.'

'That's not true!' Isabella heard the indignation in her own voice. 'I haven't said yes!'

But George, looking at Matt's angry face, apparently decided staying wasn't a prudent option. 'You better sort this out between yourselves, Isabella. I'll see you tomorrow.'

Isabella stared after his retreating back in sullen silence. She glanced up at Matt to find him glaring at her.

'What's wrong with you, Bella? You'll have everyone gossiping, the way you've been acting with George. It's not like you to behave like a hussy!'

'Isn't it?' Isabella met his gaze, her own anger rising. 'I thought that's just what I was, when you'd finished with me! Besides, who are you to talk? Dancing with that baggage from the hotel...'

'Bella.' He took her arms and pulled her to him, his voice softening. 'Don't let's fight about it. What we did doesn't make you a tart. I left the goldfields to marry you and put things right.'

The touch of his hands, the closeness of his body, awoke a flood of memories. Briefly she resisted, but his fingers at the small of her back, caressing her spine, made her knees go weak. Desire coursed through her, sapping her will. She leaned against him and he slid his arms about her waist, bending his head to take her upturned mouth. She went with the kiss, feeling a rush of emotion which compounded the physical response. The feelings were drowning her, drawing her under in a tide of sensation which she had no will to deny, until he moved in, pulling her close to the length of his body.

She wrenched away, swaying dizzily. Oh, she was a weak, stupid fool! 'Go away, Matt Jones!' she hissed. 'That's all you want, isn't it? Perhaps you *would* marry me, but only because you feel obliged to. I want something better than that.'

She swung away, ignoring his protest, hurrying back to the hall with angry, unladylike strides. As she mounted the steps she paused to steady herself, taking several deep breaths. Then she braved the crowd in the hall, wending her way through the dancers to find Mercy in her chair against the wall, sitting out yet another dance while Alfred drank rum outside.

'Where've you been?' Mercy spoke in an undertone, her face white and furious. 'Making a spectacle of yourself—don't you care for your reputation? I saw George come back, but where's Matt Jones?'

Isabella shrugged. 'Still outside—I don't know. You're not my mother, Mercy. We can talk later, but not now.'

Mercy bit her lip but was silent. Isabella hardly knew how she got through the rest of the night, but somehow she did, talking and laughing with her dance partners as if nothing was wrong. George didn't come near her again. Nor did Matt, though she saw him dancing with other girls, charming them with that engaging smile. Desperately she tried to ignore him, but somehow she never quite succeeded.

She was spared the lecture that night, for she was sharing a room with Amelia. Mercy came to her in the morning, sending Amelia to see to her younger siblings.

'Now you'd better tell me what was going on last night.'

Isabella sat on the edge of the bed, facing her sister who had taken the only chair. 'I was silly, I know. I went outside with George and Matt followed us.' Remembering Matt's righteous indignation, for the first time she was able to see the funny side of it, and managed a wan smile. 'He—Matt—gave me a lecture about ruining my reputation and chased George off. He's still saying he wants to marry me.'

Mercy snorted. 'Matt can talk—I shouldn't think he had much reputation left in this town and he's done his best to ruin yours. But it's time you forgot this playing hard to get nonsense. You've no choice but to marry him, Bella.'

Isabella squared her shoulders. 'As I see it, I do have a choice. No one knows we were intimate. If I marry him, I'll be miserable for the rest of my life.' Like you, she thought. I'll be another neglected wife, unloved, probably betrayed for other women. It wasn't fair to compare Matt to Alfred, who was scum of the worst order, but she wasn't convinced he'd make a good husband.

Mercy looked at her sternly. 'Men expect their wives to be pure, you know.'

'If I married someone like George, I'm sure he wouldn't know the difference.'

Mercy gave a sad little smile. 'But you don't really want to marry George, do you?'

Isabella bowed her head, looking down at her hands which were clasped in her lap. The knuckles were white. 'No, I don't suppose I do,' she whispered.

The next day Isabella made a point of spending time with Louise Kavanagh. Between her avoiding Matt and Louise avoiding Mercy, it wasn't surprising their paths hadn't crossed the previous day. The gossip was all of how Matt was their son, and she'd heard more than one woman comment on how scandalous it was. Today she'd heard them discussing Matt and his dance with the barmaid last night.

'Bad blood will out,' one matron declared. 'There's obviously a lack of morals in that family.'

'Louise Kavanagh was a rebel,' another said. 'She was an Ashford, remember, and she ran away from home. It's no wonder she ended up in trouble.'

'And Lloyd Kavanagh was a bit of a rough diamond,' the first one added. 'He set a few tongues wagging himself at one time.'

Isabella didn't stay to hear more. She stalked off angrily, knowing the Kavanaghs were better people than any of these gossiping old biddies. She found Louise sitting under one of the bough sheds with one of the few women who seemed to be supporting her. To her relief Matt was nowhere in sight.

They made small talk for a few minutes, until Louise's companion excused herself and moved away. Louise smiled wearily. 'I suppose you've heard the gossip.'

Isabella nodded. 'I'm so sorry. I feel terrible because I told Mercy, and I'm sure the story's spread from there.'

'Don't worry.' Louise patted her hand. 'There's been talk for some time—Ben came home from town with it months ago. The family resemblance is too strong to be ignored. It's just been confirmed now.' She sipped at her cup of tea. 'Matt's blaming himself for coming back here. As if he isn't more important to us than a few fair-weather friends we can well do without.'

Isabella smiled bracingly. 'They'll soon forget about this.'

'I know they will.' Louise looked at her earnestly. 'I'm more worried about you and Matt. What's the problem between you? I know he's proposed to you.'

'Only because he had to.' Isabella heard herself becoming defensive. 'He's not ready to be tied down—he told me so, only a few months ago.'

'Matt's grown up a lot lately. He's been so considerate to me over the last two days. I think you should give him another chance.' Louise took her hands in hers, squeezing gently. 'You know Mr Kavanagh and I would love to welcome you into our family.'

Emotion, lately never far from the surface, welled up, threatening to choke her. 'Thank you for that, Mrs Kavanagh. I'd like to be a member of your family, but I'm not convinced that marrying Matt would make me happy.'

'Just think on it.' Louise smiled warmly. 'I know he cares for you, probably more than he realizes himself just now.' She gathered her skirts and made to rise. 'They're calling the grass-fed race. We have a horse running in this—come with me to watch it, dear.'

The Myvanwy gelding, Sunlight, started well, but as the race progressed the galloping horses were enveloped by dust, making Sunlight indistinguishable from his competitors. The few ladies who remained trackside held handkerchiefs over their noses, while most retired to more comfortable surroundings. The finish was a blur of dust and flashing hooves, leaving Isabella and Louise in suspense until Lloyd joined them, confirming that their horse had run fifth in the field of eight.

'You can't win 'em all,' Lloyd remarked philosophically. 'Duchess did us proud.'

Isabella barely listened. She had noticed Matt approaching and for a brief moment he glanced at her, their eyes meeting. Then he looked away and seemed to change direction mid-stride. Instead of joining them he walked off towards the bar, mingling with a group of his drinking cronies.

The rejection cut her to the quick. Keeping him at arm's length while he was pursuing her was hard enough, but to be actively spurned by him was something new and hardly tolerable. She clenched her hands into fists, feeling her palms sweating and clammy beneath her gloves.

Ben, standing beside his father, scowled after Matt's retreating back. 'What's got into *him*?' He glanced down at Bella. 'I'm going to see the jockey. Want to come?'

Isabella turned to the lad, eager for any distraction. 'Certainly, Ben. Excuse me, Mr and Mrs Kavanagh.'

As they walked away Ben looked down at her, his thin face baffled. 'I take it things aren't working out with you and Matt.'

'I'd sooner not talk about it, Ben.'

He spread his hands in a conciliatory gesture. 'Whatever you like. I just wish he'd never come here.'

Isabella looked at him sharply. 'Do you think he deserves that? Surely he's just as entitled to a home and family as the rest of us.'

Ben coloured. 'He had one, over in England.'

'I don't imagine it's the same. He always knew he wasn't their son.'

'He's made things hard for all of us.'

'Nevertheless, your parents are obviously glad to have him.' Isabella wondered why she was sticking up for him when her own sentiments echoed Ben's. She wished, too, he had never come here. Perhaps her reasons had more substance than Ben's. She was the one with the broken heart, after all.

Chapter Seventeen

After the races, Jock and Andrew decided to muster at Kilbride to brand the late calves and wean the early ones. Jock spoke to Lloyd, who promised to send someone over to help them. Isabella hoped it wouldn't be Matt. She couldn't endure the torment of working beside him every day.

They planned to muster the far end of the property, where they would be camping for three nights, gathering the cattle into a holding paddock before driving them to the homestead stockyards. Isabella cooked in preparation, baking bread and boiling pieces of corned beef; packing flour, salt and soda for dampers; adding tea, sugar, treacle, potatoes and onions. She packed it all ready in the leather bags which hooked onto the packsaddles and rolled her swag with an extra blanket in anticipation of the cold winter nights.

They were all busy with preparations when Matt arrived at sundown. Isabella's heart skipped a beat and sank towards her boots when she saw him. He barely looked at her as the greetings were made, his face unusually grim, and Isabella suspected his presence wasn't his idea. And yet, she'd more or less expected it.

She knew the Kavanaghs were promoting this proposed marriage and would not miss an opportunity to thrust them together. Her father obviously favoured Matt, also. Perhaps she should tell him the truth, ask him to keep Matt away from her. But no, that wouldn't work. If her father knew how far their relationship had gone he'd be the first to push for marriage.

With the first mob of cattle secured in a holding paddock, they set up camp on the banks of the river that evening. A small tent had been carried on one of the two packhorses, to provide privacy for Isabella. After it had been pitched the men threw their swags around the campfire, stockpiling a huge stack of dead timber to keep the flames burning all night. Isabella was glad of the shelter her tent afforded, for it promised to be cold by morning, especially here by the river.

As she prepared their evening meal, boiling potatoes and onions in a billy over the open fire to go with the corned beef and bread, she tried to ignore Matt who worked close by. They'd hardly spoken all day. Matt hadn't attempted to seek her out, and although she told herself it was what she wanted, his apparent indifference stung. For once Isabella was glad of Andrew's protective attitude. As on that earlier occasion when Matt had worked with them, he'd kept Matt with him most of the day, leaving Isabella with her father.

In spite of herself she glanced at Matt, who was chopping wood for their fire. She quickly looked away, but it was too late. The picture of him swinging the axe was burnt indelibly into her mind; the corded muscles in his brown forearms, revealed by the rolled sleeves of his Crimean shirt; the long thighs in saddle-stained moleskin, braced against the swing of the axe. The physical work of the goldfields had hardened him, giving him a new air of maturity and self-assurance. His skin was baked as brown as any born-and-bred Colonial, and until he opened his mouth no-one would take him for an Englishman. Indeed, it was hard to think of him as an Englishman. His parents were Colonial-born and if not for the intervention of Charles Ashford, he would have grown up in Australia with his brothers and sister.

Isabella wondered if she would have fallen for him if he'd been her neighbour since childhood, the boy next door. She suspected part of Matt's allure lay in the very differences spawned by the foreign environment which had nurtured him.

After they'd eaten they sat close to the fire, toasting their hands and booted feet while the cold air nipped at their backs. The men talked, questioning Matt about his experiences at the goldfields. Listening to his soft voice as he described the harsh, wild conditions at Black Ridge, watching the firelight play over his hawkish profile, pain gnawed at her innards. If only he *were* her fiancé. If only she had the right to sit close to him and hold his hand in the knowledge they belonged together.

Yet she'd been right to refuse him. It was obvious he didn't care for her, or else he wouldn't be treating her so coldly now. Surely, if he loved her, he wouldn't have given up the pursuit so easily?

The next day found them mustering cattle in the far corner of the run, where the thick brigalow scrub provided a refuge for any half-wild cattle. These wayward animals had probably heard or sensed their presence the previous day and would be on their guard, ready for instant flight. Knowing every rider would be needed to control the cattle, they were together as a group when they came on a mob of thirty head or so grazing close to the protection of the heavy timber.

A big old cow spotted them first, thrusting her long-horned head high as she sniffed the breeze. Her agitation quickly communicated to the rest of the herd, which set off at a brisk trot. Matt spurred his gelding into an instant gallop. Andrew rode at his heels as they raced to wheel the cattle before they gained the refuge of the scrub.

Isabella was close behind the younger men, leaving her father, not an adventurous rider even in his youth, to follow at a steady canter. As the horsemen drew closer, the cattle quickened their pace. By the time they were able to overtake them the cattle were galloping and the brigalow loomed close. As Matt tried to turn the leaders away from the timber, the lead cow doubled back, ducking out behind him even as Andrew spurred his horse on, too late to block her.

A young cleanskin bull saw his opportunity and broke from the middle of the mob, streaking towards the scrub. Isabella strove vainly to overtake him, but as her horse gained his shoulder he stopped abruptly and shot out behind her. Her horse slammed to a halt and wheeled after him, but their advantage was lost and the micky gained the timber, crashing through the dense undergrowth where it was difficult to follow, let alone outstrip him.

Knowing further pursuit was useless, Isabella turned back. She was met by a mob in disarray, cattle splitting in all directions to gain the sanctuary of the scrub while the men were forced to abandon all hope of containing them.

'We'll follow 'em through to the fence!' Andrew yelled.

All they could do was ride through the brigalow on the heels of the herd, fanning out to ensure none of the animals stopped to hide in a thicket of bush. In no time Isabella lost sight of the others as she followed an old cow, slower than her fellows, who was inclined to sneak off on her own. At last she reached the fence-line and turned the cow down it. As she broke clear of the scrub she came on Matt, his horse lathered with sweat, holding a small mob against the fence.

'Where are the others?' she asked.

Matt shrugged. 'No idea. They've probably come out on the other side of the scrub.'

'Perhaps we should take these back to the holding paddock and hope we meet them on the way.'

Matt gave a twisted grin. 'You're the boss.'

Comparatively subdued now, the cattle made one or two half-hearted attempts to break before travelling off in the right direction. The old lead cow was there, head high as she trotted at the front of the mob, constantly veering towards the scrub. Matt stayed at her side, pushing her back into the mob. At last she seemed to yield and in an hour or so they had the cattle safely shut in the holding paddock, still with no sign of Andrew and her father.

Matt and Isabella rode over to the camp to drink. As they dismounted Isabella noticed Matt's face, seen at close quarters for the first time since they'd found the cattle. It was ashen, beaded with sweat, his mouth grimacing in pain. There were scratches on his face and bare forearms, and only then did she see the rent in the back of his shirt.

In her concern, she forgot to be guarded. 'Are you hurt?'

Matt glanced at her briefly, grimacing again. 'It's just a scrape. I went under a low branch, like.'

Isabella dropped her horse's reins and went to him, parting the torn edges of his shirt to inspect his back. The so-called scrape was raw and bleeding with bits of bark adhering to it. It looked nasty and extremely painful.

'Matt!' She took his arm and urged him to one of the logs they'd sat on last night, beside the campfire. 'Sit there while I get something to clean this up.'

First she poured him a drink before fetching a clean handkerchief and more water to bathe the wound. Matt glanced at her wryly as he drank, but he sat submissively as she knelt behind him, trying to pull the shirt away from the wound. 'It'd be easier if you took your shirt off. It's ruined, anyway.'

Obediently he unbuttoned it and shrugged out of it, wincing. Confronted with that expanse of bare back, the broad shoulders and muscled biceps, Isabella drew a deep breath. This was a mistake. The last time she'd seen him without a shirt, he'd loved her long and thoroughly. The scent of his body, the feel of his bare skin under her fingertips, sent memories rushing back.

Her hands trembled as she dribbled water onto the wound from the wet handkerchief. Matt winced again, his obvious discomfort diverting her from her unwelcome thoughts. Gently she bathed the dirt from the wound and patted it dry with a clean towel, knowing she was hurting him and hating it. 'It should be covered,' she muttered, 'but I don't see how. You'd need a great big bandage to go right around you. If only I had a sheet--'

'No, it'll be all right. A bandage'll only stick, like.' He gestured towards his swag. 'Can you get me another shirt?'

She unrolled his swag and found a clean shirt folded under the blankets. Again the familiar smell of him besieged her and she shuddered, wishing things were different, knowing if she'd married him she would be sharing these blankets with him tonight. Pain and longing pierced her, making her wonder if she was capable of refusing him if he turned to her now. She'd probably fall into his arms, weak, foolish woman that she was.

She returned to him with the shirt and watched as he pulled it on, gingerly easing it over his sore back. He didn't button it immediately, leaving it hanging open. As her gaze fell to his chest and the straggle of dark hair she knew so well, she drew in a sharp breath. His eyes met hers and suddenly, despite his pain, the response was there on his face, as stark and overwhelming as her own.

He stood up and moved towards her, his voice husky. 'Isabella.' He put out a hand in a tentative movement which she hadn't seen in him before.

If she'd kept looking at his face, perhaps she'd have succumbed to temptation. But in spite of herself her gaze dropped below his belt. Being hurt hadn't affected his physical response, and she knew wanting her wasn't the same as loving her. He'd never told her he loved her.

With a supreme effort she turned away, bending to retrieve the billycan of water and the handkerchief. She tossed the water away, aware of Matt still watching her. Her legs were like jelly and her breathing was shallow. She walked over to her horse, patiently standing with head hanging. She looked back over her shoulder. 'Don't you think we should find the others?'

A shadow crossed his face. For a moment she wondered if she'd really hurt him, but then she told herself it was just his pride. He was a man, wanting what men always seemed to want.

In his swag that night Matt lay on his side, listening to Jock and Andrew snoring, hearing a dingo howl mournfully and a cow bellow from the holding paddock. His back throbbed painfully, but it wasn't the only part of him that throbbed. He listened for sounds from the tent, only too aware of Isabella lying there in her swag. All was silent. Was she awake too, burning for him as he was for her? She'd almost had him convinced she didn't care for him anymore, until today. She wasn't the sort of girl to respond that strongly to a man she didn't love.

But what could he do about it now? He could hardly go to her with her father and brother sleeping only feet away. Images of her flitted through his mind as he remembered the times they'd been together, especially that last time beside the river in broad daylight …He stifled a moan, counting how many months ago that was. He hadn't been with anyone since, and the long abstinence was telling on him. It wasn't like him to be so choosey, but now it seemed the only girl he wanted was Isabella, and she was keeping him at arm's length.

They made another search of the scrubby corner the next day, hoping to find the animals which had eluded them. The same spear-horned micky who'd got past Isabella the previous day turned up in another mob of cattle, and Matt was determined not to let him escape. The micky stayed in the middle of the mob for a time, making Matt wonder if there would be an easy victory. But as they turned the cattle towards the holding paddock the animal displayed increasing uneasiness, holding his head high and watching both men and dogs for his opportunity.

When the micky left the mob, he did so at a gallop. Matt's mare leapt forward, responding to his subconscious command. He raced through a stand of box saplings, feeling the branches brush his face and body as he closed the distance between himself and the micky. He decided throwing the beast was the best option. After such rough treatment a wayward animal usually clung to the safety of the herd.

Matt spurred his mare on hard, riding her onto the micky and bending down to grab his tail. As his mare overtook the beast he pulled fiercely on the tail, tumbling the still-galloping animal off his feet to land with a thud on his side. Matt dropped his reins instantly and swung his leg over the cantle, leaving his fast-moving horse. He hit the ground running, but that was when things went wrong.

A log lay right in his path and he stumbled over it, landing flat on his face. By the time he was on his feet the partly winded micky was struggling to his own. Matt lunged forward, reaching for the tail again, but the micky swung around and came for him, head low and horns swinging. Matt reeled from the blow as he was caught in the chest and a sharp stinging pain lanced his cheek. He was thrown sideways, and then the micky was over him, grinding him into the dirt, snorting mucus over him and fanning him with his hot breath. Through a haze of dust and sweeping horns Matt saw the dogs come flying in and felt relief as the micky was diverted, turning away to do battle with the fierce blue heelers.

He tried to sit up, but the effort was beyond him. He lifted his head enough to look down at his chest, and recoiled in horror.

His shirt was in ribbons and there was blood pumping from a dozen gaping wounds. He sank back, feeling the weakness spiralling through him, keeping pace with the trees which seemed to be revolving in the sky above him. He thought of Isabella and all the living he hadn't done yet. He wanted to tell her he loved her, but darkness was closing in. Hang on, he told himself. She'll be here in a minute. Dimly he saw her face above him, white and horrified, and tried to speak. But the words eluded him as he sank into oblivion.

Isabella didn't even remember galloping to Matt's side and jumping off her horse. She bent over Matt, seeing only his ashen face, his right cheek bleeding from a deep gash. His eyes were open, looking at her, and for a moment she thought he was going to speak. Then his lids closed and he seemed to lose consciousness. For the first time she looked downwards, and the sight of his chest made her feel faint. Oh God! He was a mess, his shirt in shreds, blood pouring from horrific-looking wounds.

She knelt beside him, gathering his face against her breasts, cradling his dusty head, beseeching him. 'Matt! You're going to be all right! Don't die, please! I love you, Matt. Don't you dare die!' She broke off, sobbing, barely conscious of Andrew beside her and her father approaching.

'Bloody hell!' This was from Andrew who rarely swore. He knelt beside her, his face ashen as he stared at Matt. He put a comforting hand on Isabella's shoulder. 'Try and stop the bleeding and then cover him up to keep him warm. I'll ride home and get the wagon.'

Her father was there now, bending over Matt. All this time Matt didn't stir and Isabella felt the pulse at his throat. It beat rapidly beneath her fingers and she shuddered with a mixture of fear and relief. He was still alive, but for how long?

Whipping off her jacket, she removed her white linen blouse, ripping it into shreds with trembling hands. She tore away Matt's ruined shirt and folded the strips of cloth from her blouse, wadding them against the lacerations on Matt's chest and face, holding them in place with her hands to stop the flow of blood. Jock did what he could to help, tearing his own shirt into lengths to bandage the dressings in place. Then he unsaddled his horse and they covered Matt first with Isabella's bloodied jacket and then with the saddlecloth from Jock's horse, filthy as it was with in-ground dirt and the horse's sweat.

Jock put his arm about her and she sank weakly against him. 'Don't ye fret, lass. He's strong and healthy. It'll take more than this to finish him off.'

Isabella wanted to believe him, but she suspected her father was just trying to bolster her spirits. Even presuming there were no major internal injuries and he survived the long, rough journey back to the homestead, there would be a long road ahead of him. If infection set in...the closest doctor was in Rockhampton, too far away to call.

Time dragged on slothful feet as they waited for Andrew to return with the wagonette. Sitting with Matt's head pillowed in her lap, Isabella shivered in her camisole, her bare arms goose bumped by the cool morning breeze. Her father in his short-sleeved undershirt seemed to fare better—at least his shoulders and upper arms were covered.

After a time Matt stirred, moaning, and then his eyes flickered open. He tried to speak, but seemed unable to form the words. His face contorted with pain and Isabella's heart wrenched with helpless pity. Stroking his forehead, she murmured soothing, useless words.

'He should have some water, lass,' her father said. 'I'll ride to the river and bring some back.'

It was a good thirty minutes before Jock returned, riding with a quart pot full of water in one hand. Isabella gently lifted Matt's head, her father holding the quart pot to his dry lips while he thirstily swallowed a few mouthfuls of water. Then the effort seemed to be too much for him and he groaned, turning his head aside.

It was after midday when Andrew arrived in the wagon, the horses sweaty and blowing. 'I pushed 'em hard,' he said. 'I knew we'd have to take our time on the way home. How is he?'

'He's still alive,' Jock murmured in a grim undertone Isabella suspected she wasn't meant to hear. 'More than that, I can't say.'

Matt stirred enough to groan and cry out as the two men carefully lifted him, one at his shoulders, the other grasping his ankles. He muttered a couple of words Isabella was unfamiliar with, but she guessed from her father's face they weren't polite.

'He's probably got broken ribs,' Jock said. 'Thank God the bleeding's stopped. Did ye send a message to Myvanwy?'

Andrew nodded. 'I got my boys to ride over.'

They laid Matt gently on the mattress Andrew had placed on the bed of the wagon, discarding the filthy saddlecloth and covering him with blankets. Isabella sat in the wagon with him while her father drove, his horse tied behind. Andrew mounted her mare, setting off to their camp to release the confined cattle and spare horses. He returned with coats for his sparsely clad father and sister. Then he rode with the wagon, cantering ahead to open the gates as they came to them and stopping to close them behind the vehicle as it continued unchecked.

The trip seemed to take hours as Jock kept the horses to a plodding walk. Anything faster would have jolted Matt unbearably. As it was his face was bloodless and beaded with sweat, his mouth a thin, white line. Once they stopped long enough for Isabella to give him more water, but mostly she held his hat to shade his face from the sun and whispered encouraging words which she had no idea if he heard or understood.

Louise Kavanagh was already at the homestead when they arrived. She ran to the wagon as they drew up, her face drawn and anxious. 'How is he?' She peered down at the barely lucid Matt, whose head rested on Isabella's lap, touching his forehead and tenderly brushing back his dusty hair. Her face contorted. 'Oh God, why did this have to happen?'

'He's not good,' Isabella whispered, her voice breaking. 'He's in so much pain.'

'I've brought some laudanum.' Louise had the bottle in her hand. 'If we give him some now, perhaps it'll help when they carry him in.'

Matt barely responded as Louise held a measure of the laudanum to his mouth, but at last she was able to coax him to swallow it. Isabella ran inside to wash her hands and put clean sheets on a bed in one of the spare rooms. When she returned Jock and Andrew were preparing to carry Matt in, while Elsie hovered anxiously, making wailing noises, her black faced creased with distress.

'Oh, be quiet, Elsie,' Isabella snapped. 'Go make sure the kettle's boiling. And get me some clean towels.'

As Elsie trotted off, still moaning and wailing, Isabella silently berated herself. She knew such vocal demonstrations of grief were the Aboriginal way, but Matt wasn't dead yet and it only made things seem worse.

At last they had Matt settled in the spare room. Isabella found some Condy's crystals and made a solution with boiled water to wash the wounds. She and Louise cut him out of the ruined shirt—the second one in two days, Isabella reflected—and gently untied the makeshift bandages. First they washed his face, arms, neck and the uninjured areas of his chest before fetching fresh water to wash the wounds. Removing the blood-soaked wadding from each laceration was a delicate task, with the clotted wounds oozing fresh blood as the dressings were eased away. Matt was barely conscious, moaning and tossing his head from side to side in obvious pain.

'Where's Hannah?' Isabella finally thought to ask.

'I left her at home with Betsy. Lloyd and Ben were out working, so I wrote them a note.' Louise gently sponged dried blood from Matt's ribs, revealing an area of purple bruising. 'I asked Lloyd to come over as soon as he arrives home. Ben can stay with Hannah. It's no place for her here.'

'Father said he's probably got broken ribs.' Isabella gestured anxiously at the bruising.

'Probably.' Louise brushed a stray hair from her brow. 'But they'll heal. I'm more worried about infection or internal damage. His lungs may have been punctured.'

Louise bathed the wounds gently. The micky had raked Matt's upper body with his horns, making a deep gash in the muscle of his upper chest and a puncture wound below his breastbone, which still oozed blood. Another cut over his ribs, though shallower, exposed the bone. There were numerous other, lesser wounds, including the one on his face.

'We'll have to stitch these,' Louise said. 'Can you get me some needle and thread, Isabella? And matches.'

They managed to persuade Matt to take more laudanum before beginning the delicate operation with a needle sterilised in the flame of a match. Louise stitched the worst of the wounds closed and then Isabella took the needle.

'Here, let me have a go. You're getting tired.'

Matt had slipped into unconsciousness, which was a relief in one way, for Isabella suspected the pain must otherwise be beyond endurance, even with the help of the laudanum. It was a long, laborious task, but at last they were finished. They wrapped his chest in bandages torn from a clean cotton sheet.

As Isabella moved him to pass the bandages under his body, Louise noticed the abrasion and bruising on his back. 'Look, his back's hurt as well!'

Isabella had momentarily forgotten the earlier injury. 'That happened yesterday. He hit a branch galloping through the scrub.' She took a deep, shuddering breath as emotion threatened to overcome her. 'This just wasn't his week.'

Once Matt was settled back against the pillows, she began to remove his dirty moleskins.

Louise made a small, protesting sound. 'If you'd prefer, I can do that, Isabella.'

Isabella didn't pause. 'It's all right.' As she tugged at his buttons, she blinked back the tears. 'When something like this happens, it makes you realize what's really important. I wish I hadn't refused his proposal, now. Life's too short to waste.' She remembered Matt as he was the previous day, vital, active and ardent, and wondered if she would ever again feel his kisses and his arms around her.

'Oh, Bella.' Louise stared at her, her eyes moist with compassion. 'It's no use wasting time with regrets. Don't forget Matt treated you badly. If you'd fallen into his arms he'd have taken you for granted.'

She was right, Isabella realized. Keeping Matt at arm's length hadn't been a deliberate strategy, but perhaps it had been the right one in the circumstances. If only this hadn't happened...

Together they eased the moleskins over his hips, leaving him in his underwear, and covered him with a clean sheet and warm blankets. Then there was nothing left to do but sit at his bedside and wait. Jock and Andrew both looked in, but there was little to report as Matt hovered at the edges of consciousness. Occasionally they moistened his mouth with water and later, when he was fully awake and moaning with pain, Louise gave him more laudanum.

Lloyd rode in at dark, entering the bedroom with such a look of despair on his face that Isabella was momentarily distracted from her own anxiety. Louise seemed to hesitate, but then she went to him and they held each other wordlessly. He stood looking down at his son for a long moment before drawing Louise outside to confer with her in private. When they returned Lloyd put a comforting hand on Isabella's shoulder.

'Bella, go and rest a while. We'll sit with Matt. Have something to eat, get some sleep. We can take it in turns to sit with him.'

Isabella was reluctant to leave, but Lloyd's instructions made sense. She'd had nothing to eat since breakfast, and although she very much doubted if she'd sleep, there was nothing to be gained by having three of them hovering at his bedside. She could relieve them later.

She sent Elsie in with a tray of food for the Kavanaghs before sitting down to the evening meal with her father. Andrew had returned to his home and family. Isabella hoped Clara wouldn't come over. The last thing she needed now was that woman's overbearing manner.

Jock looked at her in concern as she toyed with the food on her plate. 'How is he, lass?'

Isabella shook her head. 'I don't know. I'm worried about infection. And heaven knows what's happened inside him. He's in so much pain when he's awake—I can hardly bare to watch him.' Her voice broke and she put her head in her hands, pressing her fingers to her eyes to hold back the tears.

But it was no use—they slid down her cheeks and dripped onto her meal, the last threads of control eventually snapping. She'd managed not to cry in front of Matt, for who could tell how much he might be absorbing? She'd also fought to put on a brave face for Louise's sake. But now the dam had burst and there was no holding back. She pushed her plate away and let the sobs consume her, her whole body shuddering with fear, grief and despair.

'Bella.' Her father got stiffly out of his chair and moved to her side, putting his arms around her. 'We'll pray for him. That's all we can do.'

Would prayers help someone like Matt, who'd expressed derision for all things religious? 'If we weren't so far from a doctor...' she whispered brokenly.

'Aye, lass, I know. I wished that when ye were born, too.'

Isabella looked sharply up at her father, realising through tear-blurred eyes how grey and worn he looked. At that moment he was a sad old man who'd experienced his share of grief, who still mourned the wife he'd lost in childbirth. Isabella clasped his hand in hers and reached up to kiss his wrinkled cheek. 'I'm sorry, Father. I've only been thinking of myself.'

He patted her shoulder. 'Ye are entitled to do that, lassie. I can see ye love the lad, though ye won't tell me what the trouble is between ye.'

She shook her head, ashamed at shutting her father out. 'I don't want to think about it now, Father. I'm too tired and too worried.'

'Aye, I can see that. Join me in prayer and then ye go off to bed. Have some sleep while ye can.'

They knelt together beside the table, hands tightly clasped and eyes closed as her father led the prayer. 'Dear Heavenly Father, we ask thee to care for your servant Matt, to heal him in body and comfort him in spirit...'

The ritual distracted her from her tortured thoughts and brought a little solace. Afterwards, to her surprise, Isabella did manage to sleep. When she woke and lit the lamp, the clock beside her bed showed half-past-twelve. Pulling on a dressing-gown and slippers, she tip-toed down the hall to Matt's room.

The Kavanaghs still sat by his bed, dozing against each other in the dark. They looked up sleepily as she came in. 'How is he?'

It was Louise who spoke. 'He's been sleeping. I gave him some more laudanum at eleven o'clock. Poor boy, he's in such pain.' Her voice broke and Lloyd slipped his arm around her, murmuring something soothing in her ear.

'I can sit with him now. Please, go and have some sleep, Mrs Kavanagh. I made up a bed for you both earlier.' She managed a wry smile. 'It's lucky there's only Father and me left here. We have plenty of room.'

Louise offered her own weary smile in return. 'When I was the governess here, the house was full of children. So much has happened since, but it seems like yesterday.' She and Lloyd looked at each other, and Isabella guessed they must be remembering those days when they'd been young and in love. Matt was the result of that love. How devastating it must be for them to have gained a son, only to face the possibility of losing him forever.

Isabella put her hand on Louise's arm. 'Go on, now. I'll call you if there's any change.'

Lloyd rose, pulling his wife with him. 'Bella's right, Louise. We should sleep while we can.'

In the spare bedroom, Louise changed into her nightgown and slid into bed next to her husband. When he reached for her she moved willingly into his arms, needing his comfort and closeness despite her exhaustion. There had been restraint between them for weeks, ever since she'd learned of his affair with Mercy. In all that time, in spite of the united front they'd presented at the races, she hadn't let him touch her. Yet, seeing Matt so near to death had made her reconsider her priorities.

Lloyd was just a man, with a man's failings. A moment's weakness... it was a pity his partner had been Mercy, but that couldn't be changed now. She'd be foolish to throw away the happy years they'd had for the sake of her pride. Especially now, when she needed him so much.

She slid her hand to the back of Lloyd's head, pulling his face close for her kiss. He murmured something and moved urgently against her, seeking his own consolation. They came together in fierce desperation, and afterwards they slept wrapped in each other's arms, Louise's tears drying on her flushed cheeks.

Chapter Eighteen

After the Kavanaghs had gone, Isabella sat close to the bed, watching Matt's sleeping face in the flickering lamplight. Her eyes moved apprehensively over every detail of his features, committing them to memory as if he might slip away from her at any moment, resisting all her efforts to draw him back. The cut on his face had been stitched, but it stretched angrily from his cheek bone nearly to his jaw. She pictured his face as she'd seen it last before the accident, unmarked by the slightest blemish. Her heart ached at the memory.

If he recovered he would have more than one scar to show for it, but that mattered little, if only he would survive. As she watched he moved restlessly, muttering in his sleep, and she laid her hand on his forehead. The skin felt hot and dry. Oh no, she thought. A fever was a bad sign.

She must do something. Quickly she went to the kitchen, stoking up the fire in the stove and filling a bowl with a mixture of hot water from the kettle and enough cold to make it lukewarm. Fetching washcloths from the linen cupboard, she hastened back to Matt's room. She sponged his face with the tepid water and, peeling back the bedclothes, started on his bare arms and upper chest, above the bandages.

Matt moaned and moved his head, his eyes flickering open. He peered up at her face in the dim light. 'Isabella?' he croaked. 'Flaming hell, it hurts.'

'I know, Matt,' she murmured in a soothing tone, fighting to stay calm. Time for more laudanum. She held the medicine glass to his lips. 'Drink this. It helps the pain.'

He swallowed the drug with a few mouthfuls of water and closed his eyes. Unsure if he was still awake, Isabella went back to sponging him. After a time his eyes opened again. 'I don't deserve this,' he murmured drowsily. 'You shouldn't be looking after me.'

'Shush, Matt. Save your strength.'

Weakly his hand moved on the sheet. 'Lucky you're not having a baby. If I die, there'd be another little bastard.'

'Matt,' she breathed. She bent down and kissed his dry lips to shut him up. 'You're not going to die.'

His hand flopped weakly as if he wanted to hold her to him, but lacked the strength. 'I love you, Bella.'

Isabella's tears rolled down her cheeks as she pressed her damp face against his. Oh, if only he'd told her that before! 'I love you too. Now rest, Matt. Please.'

The night passed and another day with the endless routine of watching, sponging when his fever rose, giving him water and dosing him with laudanum when he seemed most in pain. Isabella took the second shift again that night, almost reeling with exhaustion as she nodded in the chair beside his bed.

He slept for an hour or so, rousing her from her doze when he began muttering and tossing, his face fiery hot. Most of his words were incomprehensible, but as he thrashed in his sleep he said something that sounded like, 'I've killed him!'

Just a fever-induced nightmare, Isabella supposed. She fetched more water and began bathing him again, but this time it hardly seemed to help. She managed to get more liquid down his throat but he was burning up, his skin paper dry.

She decided to wake the Kavanaghs, loathe though she was to disturb them so soon. Lloyd's voice came in sleepy response to her knock and they soon joined her at Matt's side, Louise pulling a robe over her nightgown, Lloyd still buttoning his shirt and tucking it into his trousers.

Louise laid her palm on Matt's forehead, her face creased with anxiety. 'He's so hot.' She gestured at the basin and wet cloth, her voice crumbling. 'But you've been sponging him. There's not much else we can do.' Yet she wrung out a cloth and began the process all over again, wiping his face and neck while Isabella sat on the other side of the bed and bathed the length of his bare arm. Lloyd settled beside his wife, looking on helplessly, his face anguished. Until that moment Isabella hadn't guessed just how important his eldest son had become to him.

Matt seemed to be in the grip of another nightmare, brushing their hands away as they tried to bathe him. As he tossed and turned, he cried out, 'I didn't mean to do it. Don't lock me up!'

'What's he talking about?' Isabella asked, but though the Kavanaghs exchanged knowing glances they didn't reply.

Matt continued to mumble, mostly a meaningless jumble of words. Isabella thought he said, 'Charles Ashford', and something about a gold mine. And her name was in there too, plucked from the nonsense by her reluctant ears as she found herself fearing what he might say next.

By the time the first streaks of daylight peeped through the window pane, they were all exhausted. Matt's fever smouldered like living coals, consuming his body and burning the life from him in a relentless tide. His eyes were sunk into their sockets, his breath rasping. They kept moistening his mouth with water, but he seemed beyond swallowing. There was nothing they could do but bathe him, watch and pray.

Isabella left long enough to snatch a cup of tea and a piece of bread and honey, although the food seemed to stick in her throat.

She took cups of tea and buttered bread to the Kavanaghs as they sat in vigil, but they ate even less than she.

As the morning wore on, Matt's condition didn't change. The two women removed his dressings, finding the wounds red and inflamed. The most worrying was the puncture under his breastbone, which had an angry streak of red running from it. Louise looked at it and bit back a sob, her tight rein of control cracking for the first time. They bathed the wounds with Condy's crystals yet again and applied fresh dressings, soaked with Friar's Balsam, before re-bandaging.

Lloyd, who seemed to find the inactivity hard to bear, had gone to fetch fresh water. When he returned Louise voiced her worries about their family at home at Myvanwy. 'They'll be wondering what's going on,' she murmured distractedly, gathering the soiled cloths into a pile and walking to the window where she stared unseeingly across the paddocks. 'I wonder if Andrew would ride over with a message?'

Before Isabella could respond, Lloyd swung restlessly to his feet. 'I'll go. Anything's got to be better than sitting here.'

Sitting here watching Matt die, Isabella thought dully. But she didn't say it aloud. There was no need. They were all thinking it.

Louise went to her husband and slid her arms about his waist. 'Hurry back, won't you?'

'Of course.' He bent to kiss her gently. As he walked past the bed he put his hand on Isabella's shoulder. 'Keep your spirits up. He's tough. He'll beat this yet.'

Isabella didn't respond. She'd almost given up hope.

The day passed in a blur of dread and fear. By nightfall there was little change, but at least Matt was still alive. Isabella and Louise had taken it in turns to rest during the day, though they'd had precious little sleep. Lloyd returned, entering the bedroom as if he was afraid of the news that might await him there. When he saw there was no improvement, he slumped into a chair, putting his head in his hands.

'You know, I've hardly talked to him since he's been home,' he muttered. 'I was so wild with him. I wish...'

Louise looked at him compassionately and squeezed his hand, but she didn't speak. What comfort were words, Isabella wondered? They wouldn't keep Matt alive.

Clara arrived with a hot stew for their supper and fussed at Matt's bedside, offering advice, though she could suggest nothing they hadn't already tried. But she served up the meal for them and helped Elsie with the dishes afterwards, so Isabella was grateful to her.

At the Kavanagh's insistence she went to bed, succumbing to a fitful sleep in which her nightmares featured a distant, scornful Matt who always seemed to be walking away from her, deaf to her pleas to stay. After awakening in tears for the third time, she put on her robe and went to relieve his parents.

'His fever's broken.' Louise looked up at her, her voice conveying a spark of hope. 'He's starting to perspire.'

Louise refused to leave him and Lloyd wouldn't go without her, so the three of them watched as Matt sweated out the fever, drenching his bedding. Then he succumbed to chills, lying there shivering as they carefully moved him to change the soaked under-sheet and covered him with dry linen and blankets. He roused enough to drink a glassful of water, but Isabella didn't dare voice the hope that surged within her.

By morning he was sleeping peacefully for the first time. All colour was drained from his face and his eye sockets were deep and bruised, the skin stretched gauntly over unshaven jaw and cheekbones. The healthy, strapping young man was reduced to a shell, but, alone with him now that the Kavanaghs had at last retired to rest, Isabella pressed her lips to his stubbled cheek in a private prayer of thanks. It wasn't over yet, but after all they'd been through, surely God wouldn't take him now.

Matt slept all morning, awakening only briefly to drink a glassful of water. 'It's a healing sleep,' Louise said, her strained face easing. 'I'm sure he'll be all right, now.'

After lunch the Kavanaghs decided to return to Myvanwy to be with Hannah. Once Ben was freed from caring for his little sister, he arrived to visit, looking chastened. As he entered the bedroom and saw his brother lying there, his thin face stiffened with shock.

'Jees, he looks crook,' Ben whispered. He turned to Isabella. 'Father said they thought he was going to die, but I didn't expect—' he broke off, as if words failed him.

Matt's eyes flickered open, focussing briefly on his brother. He murmured something indistinguishable, then closed his lids again and appeared to drift back to sleep.

Ben stood there for a moment, just looking at him. Isabella touched his arm. 'You can sit with him if you like, but don't disturb him. He needs to rest.'

Ben shook his head. 'It's all right. I won't stay.' He handed her a parcel wrapped in brown paper. 'Mother sent over some clean things for him.' For the first time he looked directly at Isabella. 'Is he going to be all right?'

Isabella flinched, afraid to answer, afraid of being proved wrong. 'I hope so, Ben. He's much better than he was, that's all I can say.'

Ben looked down, flushing. 'I feel so bad. I didn't want him around, but I never wanted something like this to happen.'

Isabella reached out to touch his hand. 'Of course you didn't, Ben. It's not your fault.'

'Well...' he shifted awkwardly from one foot to the other. 'There's not much I can do here. When Matt wakes up, tell him I came, and that I hope he's feeling better soon.'

Ben stayed only to exchange a few words with her father, and then he rode off. Isabella wondered if this near-tragedy would help to heal the rift between the brothers. Ben's attitude today seemed promising.

Towards evening Matt was wide awake and fully lucid for the first time in days. He watched Isabella over the spoon as she fed him beef broth, the first nourishment he'd taken since the accident. 'I'm as weak as a kitten,' he murmured. 'I thought I was going to die.'

'We thought so, too. You had your mother and father pretty worried, that's for sure.'

He grimaced as if his ribs hurt him. 'Only me mother and father?'

Isabella's cheeks heated. How much had he absorbed and remembered? The declarations of love, easily given when he was insensible, came back to haunt her. What had come so readily then was suddenly as difficult as it had ever been.

'Of course we were all worried,' she told him briskly, dipping the spoon into the broth and holding it to his lips. She met his eyes briefly, noting the searching way they skimmed her face. He didn't look convinced.

'Thank you for nursing me.' He winced and swallowed a mouthful of soup. It obviously hurt him to talk. 'I think...you've spent a lot of time in here.'

'Along with your mother.' As she bent over him she wrinkled her nose at the sickly, fevered smell of him. But a bath could wait until he'd regained some strength—getting food inside him was the most important thing at this stage.

He drank half a bowl of broth and managed to swallow a few pieces of the bread she'd soaked in it. Then he closed his eyes, shaking his head when she asked him if he wanted more. In minutes he was asleep again, and Isabella sat silently watching him for a long time before she gathered up the unfinished food and took it to the kitchen.

'He's on the mend?' her father asked hopefully over the supper table.

She nodded. 'He drank some broth and ate a bit of bread. He's asleep again now.' She hesitated. 'I don't think he should be left alone all night. Will you help me make up a bed in there?'

Jock looked pained. 'That's hardly proper, Bella. I know you've had to spend a lot of time with him, but to sleep there... I'll stay with him if you like.'

Isabella pressed her lips together in annoyance. She knew how soundly her father slept—Matt could be burning up again and he'd never know. 'He's still very weak, Father. I haven't nursed him this far to risk a relapse now.'

Her father seldom denied her, and she knew she'd get her way this time. He helped her carry a mattress which she laid on the floor as far from the bed as the cramped confines of the room would allow, and typically left her to it while she made it up with sheets and blankets. Matt slept soundly, looking so innocuous with those dark lashes lying against the shadowed eye sockets that Isabella wondered what all the fuss was about. As she checked his temperature with her hand on his brow, she realized it was only the sweet ache of love and longing which pierced her that made this anything less than circumspect.

She slept in spite of her turbulent thoughts, too exhausted to not. She woke several times to tend him, giving him water and bringing him a bottle which he was thankfully able to manage himself. By morning he was wide awake, still in considerable pain but showing an interest in food.

'I'll get you some more broth.' She smiled at him, delighted with his recovery. 'We'll have you well again in no time.'

He managed a weak grin. 'I'll never get me strength back on broth.'

'It'll have to do for now.' She bustled out to heat it up, glad to keep busy. It wasn't fair that he only had to smile to have her wallowing in confusion.

As she spooned the broth into him, he nodded in the direction of the bed on the floor. 'You slept in here, Bella?'

'I didn't want to leave you alone, in case you had a relapse.' She sniffed. 'You need a bath. Once you've finished this, I'll give you one and change your bandages. That is, if you feel up to it.'

His grinned ruefully. 'I know I stink. But'—he winced—'do you think you should?'

She withdrew the proffered spoon, splashing soup on his chin as hot colour flooded her face. 'I'll call Clara over to do it if you'd prefer.'

He grimaced. 'Anyone but her.' He weakly gestured towards the withdrawn spoon. 'Just feed me'worry about the bath later.'

Suddenly Isabella found herself wishing his mother back to tend him. She gave him the rest of his meal in uncomfortable silence and reluctantly prepared his bath, telling herself it was only cowardice that was prompting her to wait for Louise.

Matt watched her with a wary expression as she brought in bowls of water and spread a waterproof sheet over the side of the bed. 'Be gentle, please,' he begged.

Isabella gave him a stern look. 'So long as you behave.' She tended to his wounds first, noting with satisfaction that they were healing, if still inflamed. As she eased off the old dressings, Matt's white face and gritted teeth distracted her from her own discomfort. She bathed the wounds tenderly, murmuring apologies whenever he flinched.

Once he was re-bandaged, it was time for the dreaded bath. The top half of him was comparatively easy—she'd been sponging that part of him for days now, though his present awareness made that task a little different. When she laid a concealing towel across his hips and made to pull down his drawers, a hand on her arm stayed her.

'Bella.' His eyes were serious, with none of the mockery of earlier. 'I can manage that bit.'

She nodded and finished pulling his drawers down the length of his long, hairy legs, then wrung the wash cloth out in the bowl of water and handed it to him. She turned her back and walked to the window, looking out over the paddock and trying not to think of what was happening behind her. The muttered curses told her just how much the effort was hurting him and her face flamed. She'd been his lover—it seemed as if she was failing him, that she couldn't spare him this much pain.

'You can look again now.' He lay against the pillows, the towel back in place. Weakly he handed her the washcloth and closed his eyes, as if even that small effort had exhausted him.

Isabella dipped the washcloth back in the bowl and attended to his legs and feet, drying gently between his toes and helping him into a clean pair of drawers. His mother had sent a nightshirt, but getting him into that would hurt him more.

His eyes were still closed, and she took advantage of the opportunity to study his face. The dark stubble on his jaw combined with the angry-looking gash to give him a devilish appearance. 'Would you like me to shave you?'

His eyes opened and he fingered the whiskers on his chin. 'It itches pretty bad. But the cut—' His fingers moved to it and he winced.

'I'll be careful. I can shave around it.'

His lips moved in a wan smile. 'Are you still mad at me, Bella? Can I trust you with a razor?'

It was impossible not to return his smile. 'Don't worry. If I slit your throat, there'd be a mess of blood to clean up.'

It was a delicate operation as she kept the soap and the sharp blade of her father's razor away from the wounded area. When she'd finished she gently wiped the soap off his skin and blotted it dry with a towel.

He reached up and caught her wrist in his fingers. 'Can you bring me a mirror?'

Isabella hesitated. At the moment his former good looks were but a memory, the disfiguring scar and the ravages of illness making him look like a battered scarecrow.

His fingers tightened on her wrist. 'I need to see—what that blasted micky did.'

She sighed in defeat and fetched the ivory-backed hand mirror from her bedroom, holding it up in front of his face.

Matt looked for a long moment. 'Aye, he made a mess of me. I won't be fighting the lasses off now.' Then he pushed the mirror away and turned his head on the pillow to stare at the wall.

Physically, Matt's condition continued to improve rapidly. By the next day, he was eating proper meals, although he was still too weak to sit without being propped by pillows. Since the episode with the mirror, however, he seemed withdrawn. Isabella wished she'd refused to bring it. As his health and strength returned and the scar healed, the disfigurement must surely improve. But for now, although his determination to get well hadn't diminished, it was as if he was trying to keep her at a distance.

Hoping to breech the wall of silence he'd erected, Isabella brought him a book to read. It was one she'd particularly enjoyed herself—Rolf Boldrewood's *Robbery Under Arms*.

Matt looked at it doubtfully. 'I've never read a book in me life.'

Isabella stared at him. 'Why not?'

He flushed. 'I don't read so well, like. I wasn't interested in the books they gave us at school. I always preferred to be running 'round the fields, or helping me father with the horses. He and Ma couldn't read at all.'

'You'd enjoy this book, I'm sure. It's about bushrangers.' Lifting the heavy volume, Isabella realized it would be beyond his strength to hold right now. 'I'll read it to you, and later on when you're better you can read some to me. I'll help you with the words you don't know.'

As she read, Matt's initial indifference disappeared as he quickly became enthralled by the adventures of Dick Marsden and

Captain Starlight. 'This is much better than the books they had at school.'

'I thought so, too.' A thrill of pleasure surged through her. Such a small thing, but it meant a lot that he shared her enjoyment of the story.

The next day Lloyd and Louise returned, driving the wagonette. Once they'd ascertained how much Matt had improved, Louise said, 'We brought the wagonette so we can take Matt home, if he's well enough.'

Isabella tried to hide her dismay. 'He's much better, but it's not necessary to move him. I'm managing perfectly well.'

'It's not proper,' Louise countered gently. 'Particularly now he's growing stronger. And in light of the way he's treated you in the past.'

Isabella's face heated as she glanced up at Lloyd. He had walked away a little and appeared to be showing an interest in the plants growing along the base of the veranda. She remembered how she'd wished for Louise when she had to bathe Matt, but decided not to mention that.

'It's perfectly all right, Mrs Kavanagh. He isn't giving me any trouble.' If only he wouldn't shut her out, like he'd been doing for the last couple of days. If the Kavanaghs took him away now, things might never be put right between them.

As she accompanied the Kavanaghs into Matt's room, Isabella observed her patient carefully, trying to see him with their eyes. In two days he'd improved dramatically. With her help he was sitting up in bed, supported by pillows. His eyes were not so sunken and his natural colour was coming back, although his face was still very thin. The edges of the gash were growing together, pulling the stitches tight. Soon they would have to be removed, before they became completely embedded.

His mother bent over him, kissing his cheek and ruffling his hair with her hand. 'You look so much better, Matt.' Her voice shook. 'It's amazing. I was sure we were going to lose you at one stage.' As she straightened Isabella noticed tears glistening in her eyes and her own blurred over in response.

'You couldn't get rid of me that easy.' Matt patted her hand awkwardly, and as she moved aside so Lloyd could greet him, clasped his father's outstretched palm. Lloyd swallowed, his weathered face closing up with emotion.

'Do you think you're strong enough to come home today?' Lloyd asked him. 'We've got the wagonette here with a mattress in the back. '

Matt looked quickly at Isabella. There was a flash of something in his eyes that she was sure—she hoped—was disappointment. 'Bella's been looking after me so well. But I suppose she could do with a spell, like.'

'I'm coping,' Isabella countered quickly. 'I really don't think you should be moved.'

'But it's not *right*,' Louise insisted. 'And you know why, Matt.'

Matt had the grace to flush.

Louise turned to Isabella. 'I take it your father's not at home. Is Andrew close by? Lloyd will need help to carry him out.'

'Andrew's ringbarking timber in the horse paddock, and Father's off checking cattle somewhere.'

Lloyd made a quick movement. 'If Andrew's not too far away, I'll go and find him. Just tell me where.'

While they waited, the two women sat beside Matt's bed and Louise told him of the doings at Myvanwy. During a break in the conversation, she picked up the book which lay on the chest-of-drawers, turning it over in her hand. '*Robbery Under Arms.* Are you reading this, Matt?'

Matt nodded at Isabella. 'Bella's been reading it to me, mostly. It's a good yarn.'

Isabella busied herself with tidying the bedside table. 'You'll have to finish it yourself, now.' She noticed his mother watching her. 'I've been helping him with some of the words.'

'Well then, I'll have to carry on in your place, Isabella.' A twinge of sadness crossed Louise's face. Perhaps she was thinking how she hadn't been there to teach Matt to read, as she'd taught her other children. In this case the illiterate foster parents would have been a poor substitute.

Much to Isabella's frustration, there was no opportunity for private speech with Matt before Lloyd returned with Andrew. Nothing of importance had been said between them and neither had repeated the declarations of love which had been made when Matt was seriously ill. Matt seemed to have erected a wall around himself, keeping her at a distance.

The men had found a camp stretcher. They placed an old mattress on it and prepared to transfer Matt from his bed. Isabella hovered anxiously. 'Remember he's got broken ribs. And we don't want his wounds tearing open.'

Lloyd smiled down at her. 'We'll be careful. We don't want to spoil all your good nursing.'

Yet, in spite of the men's efforts, Matt's white face and clenched teeth betrayed how much the moving process hurt him. Isabella wanted to shout at them, to tell them to leave him be. But she bit her lip and remained silent, following as they carried him down the hallway and out of the house, down the steps to the waiting horse and wagonette. Again, the business of shifting him from the stretcher to the mattress in the wagonette was a delicate one, but at last he was settled.

Wishing she was taller, Isabella stood on the footplate to speak to him, noticing the beads of sweat on his forehead and the white tinge about his mouth. 'Are you all right?'

He nodded. 'Aye. I'll be glad when this is over, but I'll survive.' He reached up weakly to grasp her hand. 'I owe you me life, Bella. If it hadn't been for you I reckon I would have died.'

'I don't need your thanks, Matt.' She stared down at his face, hoping for some encouragement, some sign that he loved her. But he dropped her hand and looked away. 'I'll come and see you soon. Just keep getting better, won't you?'

'Don't worry about me. I'll be all right now.'

As they drove away she stood watching them. The despair rose up in her, thickening her throat and threatening to choke her. Had Matt's previous declaration of love been inspired only by his fear of dying? Now that he was recovering, did he remember it and wish it unsaid? Surely it couldn't be merely the loss of his looks that was making him push her away. Did he think she was so fickle that she'd be bothered by a few scars?

Chapter Nineteen

The fear of further rebuff, together with the need to hide her own her vulnerability, made Isabella delay her visit to Myvanwy. For days she went about her work thinking of nothing but Matt, reliving every moment of his illness and convalescence, replaying their conversations word by word. Was there some clue to his true feelings amongst all that? Should she take the initiative and declare her love, hoping that would be enough to break down the barriers?

Almost losing him had made her realize just how much she loved him, in spite of everything, and how empty her life would be without him. Perhaps it would be foolish to let pride stand in her way. Even if his feelings weren't as strong as hers, surely it was better to have as much love as he could give her, than nothing at all.

By the time she finally saddled her horse to visit Myvanwy, she had worked herself into an agitated state, her stomach churning and hands sweating under her gloves. During the ride, when there was nothing else to do but think, she began to worry that he may have suffered a relapse while she was staying away. Perhaps she'd arrive to find him desperately ill again. Or worse, dead and buried.

But no, that was silly. If the worst had happened, the Kavanaghs would have let her and her father know.

When she arrived it was an anticlimax to find him sitting on a squatter's chair on the front veranda, reading a book which he put down at her approach. Though his tan had faded, his colour looked healthy, the scab beginning to lift from the cut on his cheek. He was dressed, his shirt unbuttoned over his bandaged chest, his long legs encased in white moleskins. Feeling at once relieved, defensive, and angry with herself for becoming so distressed over nothing, she hardly knew how to greet him. She stood there looking at him, and all she could think of to say was, 'Well, you look better than when I saw you last.'

He smiled at her, but it was a guarded smile, lacking in the old confidence and easy charm. 'That's not saying much. Forgive me if I don't get up.' He gestured to a nearby chair. 'Sit down, please.'

She arranged the folds of her divided skirt neatly as she sat. 'How do you feel?'

'Like I was run over by a bullock wagon. Me ribs hurt worse than the holes that flaming micky put in me, excuse the language. Once I get back on a horse I'm going after him, and this time I'm not coming off second best.'

For the first time she realized the accident had been a blow to his male pride—hardly something she'd considered when he hovered between life and death. 'You won't be going after that particular micky, Matt. Father took a rifle out there and shot him. Reckoned he wasn't worth anyone else getting hurt over.'

A mixture of disappointment and relief flickered across his face. 'Well, that's the end of that, then. I'm sorry I put a stop to the mustering. When are you planning to get back to it?'

'Ben's coming over to help us next week.'

He gave a rueful grin. 'I hope he has better luck than me, then. At least the little blighter's talking to me now.'

Pleasure warmed her. 'Oh, that's wonderful, Matt.' She picked up the book he'd been reading, turning it over in her hand. '*Robinson Crusoe.* So you're still reading. That's another good thing to come out of this.'

His mouth twisted. 'If I had to choose between all that and not nearly being killed, I know what I'd pick, Bella.'

She flinched, feeling as if he'd struck her. 'That wasn't what I meant, Matt. I know what you've been through, better than anyone.'

She looked up in relief as Hannah ran onto the veranda and threw herself into her arms. 'Isabella! I haven't seen you for ages!'

'I know, Hannah.' She hugged the little girl, drawing comfort from the small warm body. 'I've missed you. Your brother's had us all so worried.'

Suddenly she went still, appalled at her blunder, looking at Matt over the top of Hannah's dark hair. What had she said? Did Hannah know yet that Matt was her brother?

But Matt only looked amused at her discomfort. 'She knows.'

'Oh, thank goodness.' She turned away, devoting her attention to the doll the little girl carried under her arm. She was dressed in a frilly pinafore similar to Hannah's own, her china face painted with bright blue eyes and a red rosebud mouth. 'This is a lovely dolly. What's her name?'

'Jane.' Hannah held her up proudly. 'Isn't she pretty? Mother and Father gave her to me for my birthday.'

'Oh, dear.' Chagrin gripped her. 'I forgot your birthday. I'm sorry.'

'That's all right, Isabella.' The little girl looked grave, wise beyond her years. 'Mother said we've all had a lot on our minds lately.'

'Blaming me again.' Matt reached out to tweak Hannah's long hair. 'You're lucky Ma went shopping when we went to the races, or you wouldn't have got your dolly.'

'He calls Mother 'Ma',' Hannah explained earnestly. She moved closer to Matt's chair and slipped her arm through his. 'I'm glad he's my brother. I always knew he was someone special.'

Matt smiled indulgently at her, but then he looked up to find Isabella watching him and his expression changed. 'Go and find Ma, Hannah. Tell her we've got a visitor.'

Hannah ran off obediently and Isabella found herself floundering in apologies. 'Oh, I'm sorry. What a stupid thing to say. How long has she known?'

Matt shrugged. 'Since the races, I think. They decided it was for the best, since she was likely to find out anyway. Luckily she likes the idea better than Ben did—'

He broke off as Hannah reappeared with her mother in tow. After exchanging pleasantries, Louise suggested a cup of tea, but Isabella shook her head. 'I'd like to have one later, Mrs Kavanagh, but I need to talk to Matt. Can we have some time alone, please?'

'Why, of course.' Louise looked appraisingly from one to the other. 'Come on, Hannah. Time to get back to lessons.'

When they'd gone Matt struggled out of his chair. He stood there for a moment, breathing shallowly, holding one arm against his ribs. 'If you want to talk, Bella, we'll go for a walk. It's not private here.'

Isabella watched him uncertainly. 'Are you sure you can manage?'

'Aye, I'm sure.' He moved gingerly to the steps and descended them slowly, gripping the railing with one hand. 'I'm sick of sitting in this chair. Come on.'

There was nothing she could do but follow him. He led the way to the saddle shed, his face set with pain. Inside in the cool gloom he sank onto a bale of sweet-smelling lucerne hay. It was obvious the short walk had exhausted him and Isabella just stood there, waiting, uncertain how to proceed.

'Well.' He looked up at her. 'You wanted to talk.'

Isabella took a deep breath. It was now or never. 'When you were hurt you said some things—was that true? Or don't you remember?'

Matt gaze fell. 'I remember.' His voice was very quiet. 'But I don't want your pity, Bella.'

'My pity?' She stared at him. 'Did I say I felt sorry for you?'

He shook his head. 'No, but I can guess. I used to take it for granted that the girls all fancied me, like, but look at me now.'

'Oh, Matt!' Isabella stared at him in exasperation. Even now, scarred and gaunt from illness, he made her pulse beat faster. 'I don't feel sorry for you. I think you know I loved you before, and that hasn't changed. If anything, almost losing you has made me love you more.'

It was too dark to read his expression clearly, but his voice betrayed his disbelief. 'But I'm not the bloke you fell in love with, Bella.'

'No, you're not,' she agreed. 'I was captivated by the charming, handsome young man I met on the coach from Westwood, but I've realized now he was irresponsible and selfish. You've matured in the last year, Matt. And yes, you have scars, but you're still handsome in spite of them, and you'll be better looking yet when you're properly well again.'

He dropped his head, plucking a stalk of hay from the bale and twisting it in his fingers. 'I don't deserve you, Bella. There's something else I haven't told you. Something that happened when I was at the goldfields.'

Isabella frowned at him in surprise. 'What was that?'

He took a deep breath and looked her full in the eyes. 'I killed a man.'

He might have punched her in the chest. The breath whooshed out of her and the hope that had built up inside her came crashing down, like the proverbial house of sticks. 'What do you mean, you *killed* someone? Surely not deliberately?'

'No, I'm no murderer. It was an accident, but they charged me with manslaughter.'

He went on to tell her the full story, describing how the barmaid had been flirting with him that night. He must have sensed

Isabella's dismay, for he hastily added, 'I didn't want anything to do with her. I haven't touched another woman since I met you, Bella.'

As he detailed his arrest and the night spent in jail, with Charles Ashford's subsequent intervention, Isabella's mind whirled with shock and confusion. He seemed to be portraying another world, one far removed from her safe, sheltered existence. Suddenly she felt very naive, as if he was describing something not only beyond her experience but beyond her comprehension.

When he'd finished speaking there was a long moment of silence. At last she managed to say, 'I wish you'd told me this sooner.'

'When should I have told you? When I first came home? You wouldn't have a bar of me then.'

She was forced to admit the truth of that. 'I know, Matt. It's just a lot to take in.' She saw the misery on his face and her heart softened. Remembering the nightmares he'd had when he was ill, she realized the significance of them now. It was obvious he hadn't come through the experience unscathed. 'I can accept it was just an unlucky accident. But if it hadn't been for Mr Ashford, you'd probably still be in jail.'

'I know. I don't know why he saved me—he's not the do-gooder type. But I'm grateful to him.' He made a dismissive gesture. 'But if you'd sooner not marry someone who's got a man's death on his conscience, just say so. I've tried to put it behind me, but when I thought I was going to die, it felt like I was being punished for me sins.'

She studied him, noting his quick, agitated breathing, his obvious anxiety. 'I can forgive most things, Matt, as long as I know you love me.'

'Bella,' he breathed. Suddenly his face was alive with hope. 'After the accident I said I loved you, and that will always be the truth. But do you really still want me?'

Isabella's smile was a glow from deep within. 'Yes, I still want you, in spite of everything. If you won't believe me, I'll show you.' She knelt in front of him on the scratchy bed of hay, reaching up to cradle the back of his head in her hands. His hair was thick and springy under her fingers, just as she remembered. 'Kiss me, Matt, if you want to know how I feel.'

He put his hands on her shoulders and bent his head to hers. His lips moved softly over hers and then with a moan she deepened the kiss, opening her mouth to his. Tears of need and joy sprang to her eyes as she revelled in the taste and feel of him, so long denied. She dropped her hands to his knees, sliding them upwards, feeling the taut muscled length of his thighs through moleskin.

Matt groaned and brushed her hands away. 'You test a man's control, Bella. I'm no saint—you know that.'

'Nor am I.' She kissed him again. 'And if this is what I have to do to convince you...' She began to unbutton her jacket, watching his thin, intent face. Her eyes had adjusted to the gloom, enough to see his expression. It was all the reward she needed. 'I think we can do this without hurting you.'

But then he put his hands over hers, stilling her busy fingers. 'Oh, Christ. I wouldn't care if it did hurt.' His breathing was loud in the quiet shed, accompanied by a scuffle in the hay that was probably a burrowing mouse. 'But not here like this, with me mother up at the house wondering what we're up to, and me father and Ben likely to come home at any moment. Besides, I'm too feeble to do my share.' He bent to kiss her again. 'Will you marry me, Bella? As soon as we can find a minister to do it?'

Her tears welled up again as she kissed him back. Once she had dreamed of a white wedding with orange blossom and all her family and friends to see her walk down the aisle, but that hardly seemed important now.

'Yes, I'll marry you, Matt. As soon as you want.'

It was a long time before they returned to the house. Louise had grown anxious and was looking out for them, the pot of tea she'd made growing cold. Then she saw them walking slowly towards the front gate, hand in hand, their bodies brushing closely. As she looked on they stopped to kiss, carefully, Matt moving with a studied economy, Isabella avoiding contact with his battered body.

As the dark head bent to the chestnut one, Louise smiled to see them. At last they'd sorted out their differences.

Feeling Hannah press at her skirts behind her, she firmly turned the little girl away to the kitchen.

Thank you for reading Colonial Legacy. I hope you enjoyed it!

If you would like to know when my next book is available you can visit me at my website - www.heathergarside.com

You can friend me on Facebook at https://www.facebook.com/heather.garside1, visit my author page at https://www.facebook.com/Heather-Garside-733843639971164/ or contact me through my website.

If you enjoy my books, please consider leaving a review on Goodreads or the purchase site, if bought online. This helps other readers find my books.

Heather Garside grew up on a cattle property in Central Queensland and now lives with her husband on a beef and grain farm in the same area. She has two adult children and two beautiful granddaughters.

Along with her five novels, she has helped to write and produce several compilations of short stories and local histories. *The Cornstalk* was a finalist in the 2008 Booksellers' Best Award, Long Historical category, for romance books published in the USA. *Breakaway Creek* was a finalist in the QWC/Hachette Manuscript Development Program and was published by Clan Destine Press. It is a rural romance with a dual timeline.

Heather works at home on the farm and for many years helped produce a local monthly newsletter, amongst other voluntary activities. She enjoys patchwork and sewing and regularly attends a local craft group.

For more information about her books, please visit her website at www.heathergarside.com